L H.

Janet MacLeod Trotter was born in Newcastle and grew up in Durham. She has been editor of the Clan MacLeod magazine, a columnist on the *Newcastle Journal* and has had numerous short stories published in women's magazines, as well as a novel for teenagers. She received an award from the Arts Council towards writing a novel for young adults. This is Janet's twelfth saga. Her first saga, THE HUNGRY HILLS, gained her a place on the shortlist of *The Sunday Times*' Young Writers' Award. She lives in Northumberland with her husband and their two children. Find out more about Janet and her other popular novels at: www.janetmacleodtrotter.com

Praise for Janet MacLeod Trotter's previous novels:

'Trotter uses her experiences and imagination to bring strength and depth to her novels. Another thought-provoking book' *Lancashire Evening Post*

'Another action-packed, emotionally charged page-turner' *Newcastle Journal*

'Not only a good read but a vivid picture of the coalfield . . . You'll believe you're there' Denise Robertson

'A dramatic, powerful story of love and war' *Bournemouth Daily Echo*

'Another cracking tale' *Sunderland Echo*

'Well-researched, highly readable . . . compelling and utterly convincing' *Northern Review*

'A passionate and dramatic story that definitely warrants a box of tissues by the bedside' *Worcester Evening News*

By Janet MacLeod Trotter

The Hungry Hills
The Darkening Skies
The Suffragette
Never Stand Alone
Chasing The Dream
For Love And Glory
The Jarrow Lass
A Child of Jarrow
Return to Jarrow
A Crimson Dawn
A Handful of Stars
The Tea Planter's Lass

Janet MacLeod Trotter

THE TEA PLANTER'S LASS

headline

First published in 2007 by
HEADLINE PUBLISHING GROUP

First published in paperback in 2008 by
HEADLINE PUBLISHING GROUP

2

Cataloguing in Publication Data is available from the British Library

Paperback 978 0 7553 3093 5

Typeset in Bembo by Avon DataSet Ltd,
Bidford on Avon, Warwickshire

Printed in the UK by CPI Mackays, Chatham, ME5 8TD

Headline's policy is to use papers that are natural, renewable
and recyclable products and made from wood grown in sustainable
forests. The logging and manufacturing processes
are expected to conform to the environmental regulations
of the country of origin.

HEADLINE PUBLISHING GROUP
An Hachette Livre UK Company
338 Euston Road
London NW1 3BH

www.headline.co.uk
www.hachettelivre.co.uk

To Uncle Donald and in memory of
Uncle Duncan, who both began life in India –
humorous, kind, fun, generous, humane and with
that indomitable Gorrie spirit of optimism,
sense of justice and faith in the human race –
with admiration and love.

CHAPTER 1

Assam, India, 1904

'Gerrout!' bellowed Jock Belhaven from his study. 'And take that stinkin' food away!'

'But sahib, you must eat—'

There was a splintering crash of china hitting the teak door frame.

'Try to poison me, would yer?' Jock ranted drunkenly. 'Gerrout or I'll shoot you, by heck I will!'

In the next room Clarissa and Olive exchanged looks of alarm; they could hear every word through the thin bungalow walls. Olive, round-eyed with fear, dropped the bow of her violin at the sound of their father smashing more plates. Clarrie sprang up from her seat by the fire.

'Don't worry, I'll calm him.' She forced a smile at her petrified younger sister and dashed for the door, nearly colliding with Kamal, their Bengali

1

khansama, retreating hastily from her father's study, his bearded face in shock. A stream of foul abuse pursued him.

'Sahib is not well,' he said, quickly closing the door. 'He is snapping like a tiger.'

Clarrie put a hand on the old man's arm. Kamal had served her father since his army days, long before she was born, and knew the raging drunk beyond the door was a pathetic shadow of a once vigorous, warm-hearted man.

'He must have been to the village to buy liquor,' she whispered. 'He said he was going fishing.'

Kamal gave a regretful shake of his head. 'I'm sorry, Miss Clarissa.'

'It's not your fault,' she said hastily. They listened unhappily to the sound of Jock swearing as he threw things around the room.

'Your father is not to blame,' Kamal said. 'It is the ague. Whenever it is attacking him, he drinks to stop the pain. He will be right as rain in a few days.'

Clarrie was touched by the man's loyalty, but they both knew it was not just bouts of fever that bedevilled her father. His drinking had grown steadily worse since the terrible earthquake in which her mother had died – crushed by a toppling tree as she lay in bed, pregnant with their third child. Now Jock was banned from buying alcohol at the officers' mess in Shillong and treated warily at the tea planters' club at Tezpur on the rare occasions they travelled upcountry for a gymkhana or race meeting. No longer able to afford cases of whisky from Calcutta, he was dependent on cheap firewater from Khassia villagers or bowls of opium to numb his despair.

'Go and make some tea,' Clarrie suggested, 'and sit with Olive. She doesn't like to be on her own. I'll deal with Father.'

With a reassuring smile at Kamal, she took a deep breath and knocked firmly on the study door. Her father shouted back in a jumble of English and Bengali. Bravely, Clarrie opened the door a crack.

'Babu,' she called, using the affectionate name from her childhood, 'it's me, Clarrie. Can I come in?'

'Gan t' hell!' he snarled.

Clarrie pushed the door open and slipped inside. 'I've come to say goodnight, Babu,' she persisted. 'I wondered if you would like some tea before bed?'

In the yellow glow of the oil lamp she could see him swaying amid the wreckage like a survivor from a storm. Mildewed books torn from their shelves and shards of blue and white china – her mother's beloved willow pattern – were scattered across the wooden floor amid a splattered mess of rice and dhal. A fried fish lay stranded at his feet. The room stank of strong liquor and sweat, although the air was chilly.

Trying to hide her shock, Clarrie moved into the room, stepping over the mess without comment. To draw attention to it now would only madden him. In the morning her father would be full of remorse.

He watched her suspiciously, but his protests subsided.

'Come and sit by the fire, Babu,' she coaxed. 'I'll get it going again. You look tired. Did you catch any fish today? Ama says her sons caught some big mahseer in Um Shirpi yesterday. Perhaps you should try there tomorrow. I'll ride out and take a look, shall I?'

'No! Shouldn't be out on yer own,' he slurred. 'Leopards . . .'

'I'm always careful.'

'And those *men*.' He spat out the word.

'What men?' She steered him towards a threadbare armchair.

'Recruiters – sniffing around here – bloody Robsons,' he growled.

'Wesley Robson?' Clarrie asked, startled. 'From the Oxford Estates?'

'Aye,' Jock cried, growing agitated again. 'Trying to steal me workers!'

No wonder her father was in such a state. Some large tea estates like the Oxford were ruthless in their quest for new labour to work their vast gardens. She had met Wesley Robson at a polo match in Tezpur last year; one of those brash young men newly out from England, good-looking and arrogant, thinking they knew more about India after three months than those who had lived here all their lives. Her father had taken against him at once, because he was one of the Robsons of Tyneside, a

4

powerful family who had risen from being tenant farmers like the Belhavens, making their money in boilers and now investing in tea. Everything they touched seemed to spawn riches. The Robsons and the Belhavens had had a falling out years ago over something to do with farming equipment.

'Have you seen Mr Robson?' Clarrie asked in dismay.

'Camping over by Um Shirpi,' Jock snorted.

'Maybe it's just a fishing expedition,' she suggested, trying to soothe him. 'If he was recruiting for the tea gardens, he'd be round the villages dishing out money and opium as if he owned the place.'

'He's trying to ruin me.' Jock would not be mollified. 'Old man Robson was the same – put me grandfather out of business. Never forgive 'im. Now they're in India – *my* India. They're out to get me—'

'Don't upset yourself,' Clarrie said, guiding him quickly into the chair. 'Nobody's going to put us out of business. Tea prices are bound to go up again soon.'

He sat watching her, hunched and gaunt-faced, while she blew gently on the dying embers of the fire and added sticks. As it came alive again with a crackle, the room filled with the sweet scent of sandalwood. She gave her father a cautious glance. His chin was slumped on his chest, his hooded eyes drowsy. His face was emaciated, the skin as creased as old leather and his head almost bald. But for his European clothes, he looked more like a Hindu ascetic than a soldier turned tea-planter.

She sat back on her haunches, feeding the fire. In her mind's eye she could hear her mother's silvery voice gently chiding her: 'Don't squat like a common villager – sit like a lady, Clarissa!' It was sometimes hard to conjure up her mother's face these days – her cautious smile and watchful brown eyes, her dark hair pulled into tight coils at the nape of her neck. There was a photograph on her father's desk of them all taking afternoon tea on the veranda: baby Olive on her father's knee and an impatient five-year-old Clarissa pulling away from her mother's hand, her face blurred, bored with keeping still for the photographer. Yet her mother had remained composed, a slender, beautiful pre-Raphaelite figure with a wistful half-smile.

Ama, their old nurse, told her that she grew more like her mother the older she got. She had inherited Jane Cooper's dark complexion and large brown eyes, while Olive had the pale red hair and fairer skin of the Belhavens. The two sisters looked nothing like each other, and only Clarrie's appearance betrayed the Indian ancestry of their mixed-race mother. Sheltered from society as they were, growing up at Belgooree, she nevertheless knew that they were marked out in British circles as mildly shocking. Many men took Indian mistresses, but her father had broken ranks by marrying and settling down with one. Jane Cooper, daughter of a British clerk and an Assamese silk worker, had been abandoned at the Catholic orphanage and trained as a teacher at the mission school in Shillong.

As if that were not offence enough, Jock caused further embarrassment by expecting his daughters to be welcomed into Anglo-Indian society as if they were pure English roses. And to cap it all, this jumped-up soldier from the wilds of Northumberland thought he knew how to grow tea.

Oh, Clarrie had heard the hurtful comments at church and clubhouse, and felt the disapproval of the women from the cantonment in Shillong who stopped their conversations when she entered the shops of the bazaar. Olive hated these shopping trips, but Clarrie refused to let small-minded people upset her. She had more right to live here than any of them and she loved her home among the Assam hills with a passion.

Yet she shared her father's worry over the estate. The terrible earthquake of seven years ago had ripped up acres of hillside and they had had to replant at great expense. The tea trees were only now reaching maturity, while the market for their delicate leaves appeared to have vanished like morning mist. The insatiable British palate now demanded the strong, robust teas of the hot, humid valleys of Upper Assam. She wished there was someone she could turn to for advice, for her father seemed intent on self-destruction.

Clarrie glanced at him. He had dozed off. She got up and fetched a blanket from the camp bed in the corner. Her father had slept in here for the past seven years, unable to enter the bedroom in which his beloved Jane had died. Clarrie tucked it around him. He stirred, his eyes flickering open. His look fixed on her and his jaw slackened.

'Jane?' he said groggily. 'Where've you been, lass?'

Clarrie's breath froze in her throat. He often mistook her for her mother in his drunkenness, but it shook her every time.

'Go to sleep,' she said softly.

'The bairns.' He frowned. 'Are they in bed? Must say goodnight.'

As he struggled to sit up, she pushed him gently back. 'They're fine,' she crooned. 'They're asleep – don't wake them.'

He slumped under the blanket. 'Good,' he sighed.

She leaned over and kissed him on the forehead. Her eyes smarted with tears. She might be only eighteen, but she felt weighed down with a world of responsibilities. How long could they go on like this? Not only was the tea garden failing, but the house needed repairs and Olive's music teacher had just put up her fees. Clarrie swallowed down her panic. She would talk to her father when he was sober. Sooner or later he would have to face up to their problems.

Returning to the sitting room she found Olive crouched in a chair hugging her knees, rocking back and forth. Kamal stood by the carved table in the window guarding the silver teapot.

'He's sleeping,' she told them. Olive stopped her rocking. Kamal nodded in approval and poured Clarrie a cup of tea while she went to sit beside her sister. She put a hand to Olive's hair and stroked it away from her face. The girl flinched and pulled away, her body taut as piano wire. Clarrie could hear the telltale wheezing that preceded an attack of asthma.

'It's all right,' Clarrie said reassuringly. 'You can carry on playing now if you like.'

'No I can't,' Olive panted. 'I'm too upset. Why does he shout like that? And break things. He's always breaking things.'

'He doesn't mean to.'

'Why can't you stop him? Why can't you stop him drinking?'

Clarrie appealed silently to Kamal as he set her cup on the small inlaid table beside her.

'I will clear it all up, Miss Olive. In the morning all will be better,' he said.

'It'll never be better again! I want my mother!' Olive wailed. She broke off in a fit of coughing, that strange panting cough that bedevilled her during the cold season as if she were trying to expel bad air. Clarrie held her, rubbing her back.

'Where's your ointment? Is it in the bedroom? I'll fetch it. Kamal will boil up some water for a head-steam, won't you, Kamal?'

They rushed around attending to Olive's needs, until the girl had calmed down and her coughing had abated. Kamal brewed fresh tea infused with warming spices: cinnamon, cardamom, cloves and ginger. Clarrie breathed in the aroma as she sipped at the golden liquid, her frayed nerves calming with each mouthful. The colour, she noticed thankfully, was returning to Olive's wan face too.

'Where's Ama?' Clarrie asked, realising she had not seen the woman since lunchtime. She had been too busy in the tea garden supervising the weeding to notice.

Kamal gave a disapproving waggle of his head. 'Swanning off down to village doing as she pleases.'

'One of her sons is ill,' Olive said.

'Why didn't she say anything to me?' Clarrie wondered. 'I hope it's nothing serious.'

'Never serious,' Kamal declared, 'always toothache or wind. But Ama flies off like mother hen.' He made a squawking noise.

Clarrie snorted with laughter and Olive smiled. 'Don't mock,' Clarrie said. 'She fusses over you as much as any of us.'

Kamal grinned and shrugged as if the ways of Ama and her kind were beyond his comprehension.

Soon after, they all retired to bed. Olive snuggled up close to Clarrie between chilly damp sheets. On nights when their father was fuelled with alcohol, the thirteen year old always begged to share Clarrie's bed. It was not as if Jock ever barged in and woke

10

them, but any night noise – a hooting owl, the scream of a jackal or the screech of a monkey – set Olive trembling with unfathomable fear.

Clarrie lay awake long after Olive's noisy breathing had settled into a sleeping rhythm. She slept fitfully and awoke before dawn. There was no point lying there stewing over problems; she would go for an early morning ride. Creeping out of bed, Clarrie dressed swiftly and left the house, making for the stables where her white pony, Prince, snorted softly in greeting.

Her heart lifted as she nuzzled him and breathed in his warm smell. They had bought him from Bhutanese traders on a rare holiday in the foothills of the Himalayas, after her mother died. Her father had found Belgooree intolerable for a while and they had trekked for several months, Olive being transported in a basket slung between poles, her anxious face peering out from under a large raffia hat. Clarrie had fallen at once for the sturdy, nimble pony and her father had approved.

'Superior sort, Bhutan ponies. Of course you can have him.'

Clarrie had ridden him almost every day since. She was a familiar sight around the estate and the surrounding forest tracks. Hunters and villagers called to her in greeting and she often stopped to exchange news about the weather, information on animal tracks or predictions about the monsoon.

She saddled Prince, talking to him softly, and led

11

him out into the sharp air of pre-dawn and down the path that snaked away from the house through their overgrown garden. Once through the tangle of betel palms, bamboos, rattan and honeysuckle, she mounted, flung a thick, coarse blanket around her shoulders and set off down the track.

In the half-dark she could see the spiky rows of tea bushes cascading away down the steep slope. Columns of ghostly smoke rose from the first early fires of the villages hidden in the jungle below. Around her, the conical-shaped, densely wooded hills stood darkly against the lightening horizon. She continued through the forest of pines, sal and oaks, the night noises giving way to the scream of waking birds.

For almost an hour Clarrie rode until she reached the summit of her favourite hill, emerging out of the trees into a clearing just as dawn was breaking. Around her lay the toppled stones of an old temple, long reclaimed by jungle creepers. Beside it, under a sheltering tamarind tree, was the hut of a holy man built out of palm leaves and moss. The roof was overrun with jasmine and mimosa and he tended a beautiful garden of roses. A crystal-clear spring bubbled out of nearby rocks, filled a pool and then disappeared underground again. It was a magical place of pungent flowers with a heart-stopping view that stretched for miles. There was no smoke issuing from the swami's hut so Clarrie assumed he was travelling.

She dismounted and led Prince to drink at the pool. Sitting on a tumbledown pillar carved with tigers she gazed at the spreading dawn. Far to the east, the high dark green hills of Upper Assam came rippling out of the dark. The mighty Brahmaputra river that cut its way through the fertile valley was hidden in rolls of fog. Beyond it, looking north, Clarrie watched the light catch the distant peaks of the Himalayas. They thrust out of the mist, jagged and ethereal, their snow-capped slopes blushing crimson as the dawn awoke them.

Clarrie, wrapped in her blanket, sat motionless as if caught in a spell. Prince wandered off to graze as the sunlight gathered in strength and the remote mountains turned golden as temple roofs. At last, she sighed and stood up. This place always stilled her fractious thoughts. She left a pouch of tea and sugar at the swami's door and remounted Prince. A soft noise made her turn. At the pool a graceful fallow deer stooped to drink. Clarrie was entranced that the animal had crept so close to them without showing fear.

A moment later, a deafening shot exploded from the surrounding trees. The deer's head went up as if yanked on a harness. A second shot passed so close, Prince reared up in terror. Clarrie clutched frantically at the reins to calm him. A third shot hit the deer square on and its legs folded like collapsing cards.

Horrified at the brutality of the moment, Clarrie

slackened her hold. Prince danced in crazy, petrified circles, slipping on wet leaves. The next instant she was tossed from the saddle, thumping on to damp ground. Her head hit a stone and her vision turned red. She was aware of men's voices shouting and footsteps running towards her.

'You madman!' a deep voice thundered.

'Just a ruddy native,' another blustered. 'I fired a warning shot.'

'It's a woman, for God's sake!'

Clarrie wanted to carry on listening but their voices were fading. Who were they talking about? Before she could decide, she passed out.

CHAPTER 2

When Clarrie came round she was lying under a canvas awning. A man with a thick red moustache was squatting on a stool, peering at her.

'She's waking!' he cried, half standing.

Another man ground a cigarette under his boot and stepped forward. He towered over her, his dark brown hair cropped close to his scalp and his jutting chin clean-shaven. He surveyed her with keen green eyes. Clarrie knew this handsome man was familiar and that she should know him. But who was he and what was she doing here?

'Miss Belhaven?' he asked, with a quizzical arch of a thick eyebrow. 'We're thankful to see you open your eyes.'

'I'm most dreadfully sorry,' gushed the other man. 'I should never have shot that deer so close to you.

Would never have done it if I'd known you were – well – you were hidden in that blanket and wearing trousers like a man – I just thought . . . You see, I'd been tracking that fellow for twenty minutes – didn't want to waste the chance.'

The deer! Clarrie suddenly remembered the terrible sight of the beautiful doe shot in front of her eyes and Prince's terror at the flying bullets. She attempted to sit up but the movement made her head throb.

'Prince – where is he?' she gasped.

The taller man eyed her sardonically. 'I presume you're not addressing either of your rescuers?'

'Rescuers?' Clarrie gave him a withering look. 'You nearly killed my pony and me. And that poor deer . . .'

She sank back, touching her head where it hurt most. Someone had wrapped a bandage round it. She winced from the pain. 'Where is my pony, Prince?'

'He's tip-top,' said the man with the military moustache. 'The bearers are feeding him. I must say he's a fine fellow, Miss Belhaven. But I really don't think you should be riding out on your own at such an hour. I'm surprised your father allows it. These are wild and dangerous hills.'

Clarrie gave him a sharp look. 'The only danger seems to be from trigger-happy hunters.'

The man blushed and stepped back. 'I say, Robson, she's got her old man's fighting spirit, I see.'

His companion gave a low, rich laugh. 'I did warn you,' he said, never taking his eyes from Clarrie. 'The Belhavens are known for their fiery pride.' At once Clarrie recognised the deep voice with its hint of a north country accent like her father's.

'Wesley Robson!' she exclaimed. 'Now I remember.'

'I'm flattered,' he murmured, 'that out of all the young men seeking your attention at the planters' meeting, you should remember me.'

'Don't be,' Clarrie said indignantly. 'It was only because my father pointed you out as a troublesome Robson and told me to steer clear of you.'

Maddeningly, Wesley merely chuckled at this. 'And do you always follow your father's advice?'

She flushed. 'Of course.'

'So does he advise that his pretty young daughter should go riding this early on her own, a good hour from home?'

Clarrie struggled up, infuriated by his patronising tone. 'My father knows I am a good rider. I know these hills far better than either you or your friend will ever know them, for all you think you own the place.' Her head pounded as she got to her feet. 'Please bring Prince to me.' Then, to her shame, her knees buckled. Wesley caught her quickly.

'Steady,' he said, clutching her to him. He smelt of wood smoke and something earthier. She was close enough to notice a short scar puckering his left eyebrow that emphasised his sardonic look, and his sun-darkened face was creased with tiny lines around his eyes from squinting into the tropical sun. The vivid green of his irises was mesmerising.

'You're in no state to go riding off, Miss Belhaven.' His companion was adamant. 'Absolutely not.'

'You'll just have to let us look after you, I'm afraid,' Wesley said. Clarrie could hear the mockery in his voice. She felt acutely aware of his strong arms keeping her upright and his breath on her hair. Shakily, she sat down again.

Wesley ordered one of the bearers to bring her hot tea and scrambled eggs, ignoring her protests that she was not hungry. To her surprise she wolfed them down and accepted a second helping, while the men smoked and watched her as if she were some quaint new species they had discovered in the forest.

'Well done, carry on!' said the young subaltern, who told her he was Harry Wilson and at her service as long as he was stationed at the Shillong barracks. 'Wesley's a friend of mine – we met on the ship coming out – got on famously. Share a love of fishing and shooting. Wonderful country around here for bagging birds. I'm told it's good for wild pigs and bears too, but had no luck so far. Perhaps your father could advise?'

'His passion is for fishing,' Clarrie answered. 'He hates big game hunting.'

'Do you know that a leopard was found right in

the middle of town last week?' Harry continued as if she had not spoken. 'In broad daylight – wandered right through the native bazaar and into the cantonment cemetery. Sunning itself on a tombstone when they cornered him. Beautiful beast. Colonel's wife's having the skin made into a rug.'

Clarrie wondered if the garrulous soldier drove his comrades mad with his endless chatter. Perhaps silence embarrassed him or maybe he was missing home. She should not judge him harshly, for she had filled the empty hours of longing for her dead mother with all the songs she could remember. She had hated the silence of the house that had once been filled with her mother's singing. She closed her eyes against the memory.

'Harry, I think Miss Belhaven is tired,' Wesley intervened. 'Let's leave her to rest. One of us can ride over to let her father know she's safe.'

'Of course,' Harry said eagerly. 'I'll go. The least I can do.'

'There's no need,' Clarrie protested half-heartedly.

'You lie down,' Wesley ordered, ushering her further into the tent. 'Once you've rested we'll take you home.'

Clarrie capitulated, and lay down on the camp bed. Wesley covered her with her own blanket.

'It's a bit rough and ready,' he apologised, 'but comfortable enough.'

She suddenly realised that this was his tent and his bed. It smelled of camphor and a smoky male scent.

If her head had not been so sore she might have objected. But she just wanted to close her eyes and wait for the pain to go away.

She fell asleep at once. When she woke, her first sight was of Wesley sitting on a camp chair by the tent flap, long legs stretched out, reading. It surprised her. He gave the impression of a man of action, to whom reading would be a futile pursuit, yet his wide brow and strong features showed total absorption in the book. He sensed her watching and turned, and they regarded each other in silence. Clarrie reddened at the intimacy of lying in this strange man's bed while he guarded her close by.

'What are you reading?' she asked to hide her embarrassment.

He snapped the book shut. '*Sport in British Burma*,' he read out the title, 'by Captain Pollok. Borrowed it from Harry's mess. Very useful about the best places to fish in Assam – mind you, it's thirty years out of date. I could probably do better myself.' He cast it on to the floor, stood up and came across to peer at her. 'Feeling better, Clarissa?'

'Thank you, yes,' she said, dropping her gaze. It unnerved her that he was so close and using her first name as if they were friends. 'I would like to ride home now.'

'You're not riding anywhere yet. Let me take a look at you.' He reached out and took her hand. Clarrie jumped at the touch, her eyes widening in alarm. Swiftly Wesley let go.

'Why do you dislike me so?' he asked, frowning.

'I don't know you well enough to have any opinion of you,' she retorted.

He flashed a smile. 'I'd certainly like to get to know you better too.'

'That's not what I meant,' Clarrie said in irritation.

'So tell me,' Wesley challenged her, 'what *do* you think of me? Or are you just going to let your father's petty prejudice against my family prevent us from becoming friends?'

Clarrie was riled by his taunt about her father. He had no idea how much Jock had suffered and no right to dismiss him as petty. Her first impression of Wesley Robson as insufferable and arrogant was true. She had had quite enough of being confined in his spartan tent.

'I think you're swell-headed and too big for your boots,' she retaliated.

Wesley gawped in astonishment. He stood back and thrust his hands in his pockets. 'Well, a little more gratitude might have been nice.'

'Gratitude?' Clarrie cried. 'You've got a nerve! I was minding my own business, enjoying the dawn in my favourite spot, when I was shot at and – injured – and I've had a bad fright – and my head still hurts – and you made fun of me to your army friend as if I were still a child – and my father will be furious when he finds out – and I just want to go home!'

They glared at each other. A muscle twitched

21

furiously in his cheek. He was obviously not used to criticism, especially from a young woman. Well, she did not care if she had offended him. This was a mess of his making. He was the one who should be apologising to her.

Wesley turned and marched out of the tent. She heard him issuing orders to the bearers, and when she emerged they had organised a dooli, a makeshift bamboo carriage on poles.

'The servants will carry you,' he told her curtly.

'I'd rather ride Prince,' Clarrie said.

He swept her a mocking look. 'I'll lead your precious pony back. I'll not take the blame for you swooning and falling off. Can't have your father any more upset than he's going to be already.'

Clarrie gave him a furious look but climbed on to the dooli without another word. They set off at a running pace and it was not long before she regretted agreeing to be carried. With each jolt her body felt bruised and her head ached. She clung on, gritting her teeth. She should have insisted on riding back herself, but there was no sign of Wesley or Prince who were following on behind. The nearer they drew to Belgooree the more anxious she became. In what state would Harry Wilson have found her father? He might already have chased the young subaltern from the premises with curses and gunshot for putting his daughter in danger. Either that or still be sleeping off his hangover.

Finally the bearers staggered up the steep slope of

the estate and in through the walls of the compound. Kamal and Olive came rushing out to meet them.

'Miss Clarissa! Allah is merciful!' cried Kamal, helping her out of the carriage.

'Where have you been?' Olive accused her. 'I was frightened on my own. Are you very hurt?'

'No, just a bit sore,' Clarrie said, hugging her sister. 'I'm sorry for all the upset.'

Olive lowered her voice. 'We took ages waking Father this morning. I had to talk to Mr Wilson while Kamal got him shaved. His sister plays the viola, did you know?'

'No, but good for you.' Clarrie gave a strained smile. If it had not been for the wretched Wilson she could have returned from her ride with her father none the wiser.

Kamal sent the bearers to the kitchen for refreshments and fussed as he led the girls up the steps. There on the veranda, obscured by overgrown creepers, sat her father and Harry deep in conversation about fishing.

'There she is,' Jock called querulously, 'my Clarrie! Come, lass, and let me look at you.'

As he stood up, Clarrie was struck by how frail he was. His clothes hung off him and the arms he held out were shaking. His skin was the colour of yellowing parchment. The bouts of drinking were finally taking their toll. Today he looked worse than ever.

'I'm all right, Father,' she said quickly, 'just a graze on my head.'

He came towards her unsteadily and would have hugged her were Olive not still clutching on to her possessively. At once Clarrie smelled the alcohol on his breath. She glanced at the table and saw they were already drinking. He caught her look and went on the defensive.

'What possessed you to gan off gallivanting before sunrise? You should have woken me so I could have gone too. Really, Clarrie, what will this canny young officer think of us?'

Clarrie stared at him. She could hardly say he had still been sleeping off the excesses of last night when she left.

'I think very highly of you both,' Harry said quickly, standing up and offering her a seat. 'Please don't be hard on Miss Belhaven. The incident was entirely my fault.'

Jock sighed as if he had no appetite for an argument. 'Well, all that matters is that my lass is safely returned.' Clarrie saw the glitter of tears in his eyes and smiled in reassurance.

They sat back down and Kamal brought Clarrie a glass of rhododendron cordial and some of her favourite sweetmeats: honey snaps and coconut cakes. She shared them gratefully with Olive while Harry talked animatedly about fishing and Jock poured out more country spirit from a jug. Clarrie wondered when Wesley would arrive and thought it strange there had been no mention of him. Now that she was safely home, she was beginning to regret her hasty words to him. She had been in shock, but he had not deserved her contempt.

They were interrupted by shouts from the gatekeeper of another arrival.

'This will be your friend?' Jock asked.

'He's bringing Prince,' Clarrie said, getting to her feet and making for the steps.

'Yes, a fine chap,' Harry said, clearing his throat.

'A fellow officer, is he?'

'Not exactly . . .'

Clarrie stopped and glanced at Harry. She could tell by his expression that he had not told her father the identity of his friend. He had not wanted to be the bearer of more bad news.

'His friend is Wesley Robson,' she said, with a warning frown at her father. Jock looked disbelieving.

'*Robson?*' he spluttered. 'I'll not have him coming here—'

'Perhaps we should go.' Harry rose, red with embarrassment.

'Please sit,' Clarrie told him. She appealed to her father. 'I know this is difficult, but Mr Robson has been kind enough to look after me and bring back Prince. He is Mr Wilson's friend. So we must be civil.'

She walked down the steps before her father could stop her. Prince whinnied at the sight of her as he was led into the compound. Clarrie rushed forward and flung her arms round his warm neck. Behind came Wesley, still on his horse.

'Thank you, Mr Robson,' Clarrie said, looking up. 'Please come and have some refreshment.' He looked warily towards the house. 'My father wants to thank you too.'

He gave her a quizzical look, but nodded and dismounted. Kamal summoned a groom to lead the horses to the stables, while Clarrie led Wesley up past the brass flowerpots to the veranda. Jock nodded curtly and indicated a chair, but continued to glare at Wesley as he sat down. It was Clarrie who offered and poured the newcomer a drink. Harry filled the awkward silence by gabbling about fly fishing and relaying to his friend what Jock had told him about the local use of bark to poison fish to the surface.

Clarrie excused herself. All she wanted was to soak in a hot bath and change out of her grimy clothing. Olive followed her into the house.

'He's handsome, isn't he?' she said shyly, twirling her long red hair.

Clarrie glanced at her sister in the mirror as she removed her head bandage. 'I suppose so,' she said, gingerly touching the grazed bump on her temple. It looked clean. Whoever had treated it had done so efficiently, probably one of the servants.

'Well I think he's very handsome,' Olive said, turning pink. 'He's just the sort of man I'd like to marry one day.'

Clarrie turned and laughed in surprise. 'Really?'

'Yes, really.' Olive blushed deeper. 'Except it's obvious he's taken a fancy to you.'

'Don't be ridiculous,' Clarrie exclaimed. 'In fact I know he hasn't. He's the kind of man who only cares about himself.'

'Don't be so mean.' Olive frowned. 'Well, I like him what ever you say. And maybe one day when I'm grown up he'll care about me too.'

Clarrie snorted. 'Don't let Father hear you.'

'Why ever not? Father likes him. He was so enjoying their chat about fishing, he didn't even think to go out to meet you.'

As Clarrie realised her mistake, she felt the blood rush to her cheeks. 'Oh, you mean Harry Wilson!'

'Of course,' Olive said, giving her a sharp look. 'Who do you think I meant?'

Clarrie turned away and busied herself undressing. 'I was just being silly. I'm glad you like him. He's very friendly.'

Olive brightened. 'Can we ask him to stay for dinner?'

Clarrie's heart sank. 'If you want,' she agreed.

To her surprise, their visitors readily accepted the invitation to dinner, despite her half-hearted delivery and Jock's scowl of disapproval. While Harry and Wesley went off to fish below a nearby waterfall Clarrie reminded her father, 'You're always telling us how Northumbrians never send strangers from their hearth unfed. Besides, you and Mr Wilson were getting on like a house on fire.'

'It's not Mr Wilson I object to,' Jock blustered, and retreated bad-temperedly to his study. With a sigh of resignation Clarrie went to discuss the menu with Kamal.

'Has Ama returned?' she asked. Kamal shook his head. She scrutinised his face. 'Is there something you're not telling me?'

Kamal blew out his cheeks in a long sigh. 'The servants talk.' He shrugged.

'And?'

'They say her youngest son is very sick. She is nursing him.'

'What is wrong with him?' Clarrie asked in concern.

Kamal spoke very low. 'First it is malaria, now dysentery.'

'Malaria?' Clarrie was puzzled. 'But we don't get that in the hills.' The look on Kamal's face made her suspicious. 'Has he been working up the valley – for our rivals?'

Kamal nodded, looking round fearfully. 'This you must not say, Miss Clarissa.'

Clarrie's heart thumped. 'He's broken his contract, hasn't he? He's run away.' Kamal nodded again. She seized his arm. 'Which estate? Please don't tell me he's on the run from the Oxford?'

'Yes,' he mouthed.

'Heaven help us.' Clarrie shuddered. 'We have a fugitive from the Robsons' tea gardens in the village and their head recruiter coming for dinner!'

Kamal put his finger to his lips to silence her. Clarrie shook her head in disbelief. 'I must go to Ama – see if I can help.'

Kamal looked appalled. 'No, Miss Clarissa, you are making ten times worse. Your father will ask questions. He will be very upset at Ama's son going to work for big tea men. Then Robson sahib will find out and all hell is breaking loose.'

Clarrie hesitated. 'The last thing I want is to make trouble for Ama – or see Wesley Robson dragging her son away.'

Kamal nodded. 'You must rest. You are still with bad head.'

Clarrie gave in. 'Will you send some medicine down to Ama?'

Kamal agreed and Clarrie retreated to her bedroom to lie down. Olive came looking for her.

'Do you want me to read to you?' she asked.

Clarrie smiled. 'That would be nice.'

Olive chose a novel by Thomas Hardy from the bookcase their father had made for them and began to read. Her voice was clear and her reading fluent. Clarrie marvelled that her sister, largely self-taught, should be so accomplished in the arts. She was a talented painter too. Their mother had tutored them as small girls, but Olive had only been seven when their mother was killed. Clarrie had continued to teach her maths and both she and Ama had instructed her in sewing, dressmaking and cooking. But it was Jock who shared with her a love of reading and encouraged her musical and artistic ability. He had played the fiddle in his youth, and by the time she was ten Olive was playing his old violin as well as he. Jock's interest had waned in recent years, but Clarrie was determined that the housekeeping would stretch to pay for Olive's fortnightly lessons with a teacher from Shillong.

Clarrie fell asleep to her sister's rhythmic voice and only awoke when the sun had dipped behind the hill and the jungle was coming alive with evening noises. Feeling much better, she got up and swiftly dressed in her best dress, a hand-me-down of her mother's, of peach-coloured silk and creamy lace. She carefully brushed out her hair and arranged it in loose coils to cover her grazed temple. As she made ready, thoughts of Wesley kept coming to mind. Perhaps she had been too hasty in judging him. He was new to India and still finding his feet.

It began to dawn on her that Wesley might be useful to them. He was already making a name for himself in the tea trade and he had powerful backers. Why not turn his presence here to their advantage? She hurried to the kitchen, but Kamal chased her out.

'See to your guests, Miss Clarissa. All is in hand.'

From the sound of it, their visitors were on the veranda and Olive had been persuaded to play for them. Hovering for a moment in the shadows, Clarrie felt a swell of emotion at the soaring music and the sight of her sister's intense, impassioned face as she played. Olive was never happier than when consumed by music or absorbed in front of an easel. Clarrie felt a wave of protectiveness. She must ensure her sister's talents were nurtured. They must turn round the fortunes of the tea garden so her future could be assured. They needed an injection of capital to see them through the lean time before the new trees fully matured. A financial backer. She observed Wesley, relaxing in his chair, apparently deep in thought. They needed the sort of money that the Robsons and people like them could provide. Persuading Wesley might be difficult, and convincing her father to co-operate would be harder still, but she must try. She would start by being nicer to Wesley Robson.

As Olive finished playing and the men clapped, Clarrie took a deep breath and stepped into the lamplight. Harry sprang to his feet.

'Miss Belhaven, you look delightful. Feeling better, I hope?'

She smiled. 'Much better, thank you.'

Wesley was staring at her in surprise, as if he were seeing her for the first time. Belatedly he stood up and pulled out the chair next to his.

'Would you like to sit down?'

She nodded in acceptance and took the seat he offered.

'Were you successful at the fishing?' she asked.

Harry launched at once into a long story about the waterfall, the clarity of the river pools and the size of the fish. All the time, Clarrie was aware of Wesley watching her, the quizzical rise of his scarred eyebrow no indicator of what he was really thinking. He must be wary of her since their clash that morning when she had accused him of being arrogant and implied he was no friend of the Belhavens. Somehow she must put him at his ease if her plan to extract a loan were to succeed.

When Harry finally paused for breath, Clarrie turned to Wesley and smiled. 'Mr Robson, I hope you are as enamoured with our Khassia hills as your friend?'

He searched her face, his look suspicious, as if he thought she was trying to trick him.

'I like them very much,' he said. 'They have a wild beauty that I've not found elsewhere in Assam.'

She flicked him a look in return, but he seemed quite serious.

'Perhaps tomorrow you would like to see round our estate? The gardens are flourishing and we produce a very delicate superior tea. Isn't that right, Father?'

Jock frowned. 'Don't want the opposition learning all our secrets, eh?'

'Not the opposition,' Clarrie said quickly, 'a fellow tea planter.'

Wesley regarded her keenly, unable to hide his surprise at her defence of him.

'After all,' she continued, 'we need each other to prosper. There's room for us all in the marketplace, surely?'

Wesley finally smiled. 'You are quite right, Miss Belhaven; none of us can survive on our own. And I'd be delighted if you'd show me round.'

'No,' Jock snapped. 'I'll do the showing.'

There was an awkward pause. Clarrie changed tack, asking Wesley about life up the valley. Work hard, play hard, seemed to be his motto. He put in long hours learning the trade and took his enjoyment at the occasional race meetings in Tezpur or on hunting trips.

'Wesley's not the sort of man to while away his evenings playing cards at the club,' Harry interjected. 'Can't sit still long enough!'

Kamal announced that dinner was served and Clarrie led them into the seldom-used dining room. Its cold mustiness was kept at bay by a crackling fire and the damp stains on the wall were muted in the pretty candlelight. There was no shortage of conversation with the talkative Harry at table, and Clarrie made him laugh with anecdotes about the residents of Shillong. Olive became unusually animated too. Clarrie made sure her father was included as much as possible to keep him in good humour. So far, he was not drinking to excess and seemed stimulated by the rare company. To Clarrie's relief, Wesley was helping by deferring to her father's greater knowledge of Assam and asking him questions about everything from species of bamboo to variations in soil. Jock was flattered, and began to thaw towards the younger man.

The dinner was going so well that Clarrie decided to steer the conversation back towards tea growing again.

'What developments are there on the Oxford Estates?' she asked their guest.

Wesley waxed enthusiastic about mechanisation and the vast new machines they were installing for drying and rolling the leaves.

'It's the way forward,' he declared. 'Economies of scale and mass production.'

'But there will always be a demand for the more delicate flavour of tea,' Clarrie countered, 'that is grown at higher altitude and picked early in the season.'

Wesley shrugged. 'Maybe – if the estate is well run. But so many of the smaller ones have gone to the wall because they are just too costly and their practices are inefficient.'

'Such as?' Jock frowned.

'The system of labour,' Wesley said. 'You need workers on the spot, all year round, not coming and going with the seasons when it pleases them or when the harvest is bad.'

Clarrie tensed as her father bristled in reply, 'A happy worker is an efficient worker, I find. Our pickers live in the villages – go home every night to their families as they should.'

'So do ours,' Wesley pointed out. 'They just live on the estates where we can utilise their time better.'

'Like cogs in a machine.' Jock was scathing.

'It's hard work, but they are treated fairly. Many of them come from far worse places where they stand no chance of making a living.'

Clarrie, thinking suddenly of Ama's sick son, could not help asking, 'If life is so good for them, why do you have to force them into binding contracts to make them stay?'

Wesley gave her a sharp look. 'No one is forced to stay, but the system breaks down if you allow coolies to come and go as they wish. It doesn't happen in any other industry, so why should it in tea?'

'Even if they contract malaria and don't get treated?'

His eyes narrowed. 'You sound as if you are talking about someone in particular.'

'No.' Clarrie flushed. 'It was a general observation.'

'We have doctors who look after the health of the coolies and their families,' Wesley said. 'You must be ill-informed.'

Jock thumped the table. 'My daughter is very well informed. She knows more about tea than you ever will.' His indignation grew. 'And don't you dare blame the small gardens for the slump in tea prices. It's not our inefficiency – it's large estates like yours that got greedy and overplanted. You grow too much inferior tea. And using all these newfangled

35

machines and running gardens like factories will only make things worse. You might know all about boilers and farm ploughs, young Robson, but tea's a different matter. It can't be regimented.'

'But it can!' Wesley was equally animated. 'That's where you're wrong!'

'Perhaps there's room for both methods,' Clarrie suggested, trying to defuse the heated exchange and cursing herself for having challenged the young planter.

'No, there is not!' Jock and Wesley spoke at once.

Harry gave a false laugh, uncomfortable with the mounting disagreement. He blustered, 'I say, Miss Belhaven, you do seem to know a lot about the tea trade for a young girl. Best to leave these things to the men, don't you think? Perhaps while the chaps are looking round the estate tomorrow, you and your sister would like to watch me fishing instead?'

'Oh, yes!' Olive said at once. 'Wouldn't that be lovely, Clarrie? I could take my sketchbook.'

'You're an artist as well?' Harry cried, seizing on a change in topic.

'A very good one,' Clarrie said, smothering her annoyance at the soldier's belittling remarks to her. 'You could take your easel and paints, too.'

Olive's face lit up. 'Yes, please.'

'That's settled then.' Harry beamed.

Soon after, Clarrie and Olive withdrew to let the men smoke. Clarrie coaxed her sister to bed by promising that they would get up early to join Mr Wilson at the waterfall. She sat on the veranda listening to the muffled argument coming from the dining room. Her father and Wesley were still disagreeing about tea production. Clarrie felt utterly weary. It had been a foolish notion to think she could win either of the stubborn men round. They were too alike.

Half an hour later the guests emerged and took their leave.

'I think your father's a little tired,' Harry said. 'He's gone to his study.'

Clarrie nodded. Harry thanked her for dinner and bowed in farewell. Wesley gave her one of his bold assessing looks. Clarrie suspected he was as unsure of her as she was of him. She held out her hand and he took it as if to shake it, then changed his mind. He raised it to his lips and brushed her skin with a kiss. Her eyes widened and excitement surged through her at the contact. Wesley watched her, his dark brows rising quizzically as if he had felt the change in her. He held on to her hand for longer than was polite. Clarrie did not pull away.

Harry cleared his throat. 'Come on then, Robson, old man.'

'Thank you for such a pleasant evening,' Wesley murmured and let go of her hand.

Clarrie felt a ridiculous disappointment at his going. 'It was a pleasure,' she answered.

He gave her a sceptical smile, as if he thought she

was mocking him. 'I'll look forward to tomorrow with interest.' He turned to go.

'Mr Robson.' Clarrie stopped him. 'A word of warning about my father. He knows a great deal about India and tea. Please listen to him. He is a proud man, but if you gain his respect I know he will listen to you too.'

Wesley looked about to argue, then held himself in check. With a brief nod he turned away.

Then the two men were clattering down the steps and calling for their horses. She watched them mount and trot away through the gate behind the torchlight of their bearers. For several minutes she observed their progress through the trees by the glow of the flames. Then they rounded the hillside and were gone.

CHAPTER 3

Clarrie woke in the early hours, worried about Ama and her son. Her head throbbed again from the pain of the blow the previous day, but she ignored it and tiptoed out of the room. Ten minutes later, she was slipping into the compound of Ama's house and ducking beneath the low thatched roof, calling for her old nurse.

Ama came hobbling stiffly, wrapped in a shawl. She looked exhausted. Clarrie spoke to her in a mix of Khassia and English.

'How is Ramsha? Did Kamal send the medicine?'

Ama nodded with a weary smile. 'Thank you. He is sleeping better. The fever has left him. But he is so weak – just skin and bones. My fear is they will track him down before he is better.'

'Surely he is safe here?' Clarrie tried to be reassuring.

Ama's look was strained. 'Who knows? The coolie catchers don't care how far they run away. And there are always those who betray others for a few rupees.'

'You mustn't worry. We'll not let anyone touch him. A few weeks of good mountain air and your cooking will cure him.' Clarrie smiled in encouragement.

Ama put out her arms. 'You have a good soul, Clarissa memsahib. Just like your mother.'

They hugged. Clarrie was struck by how small Ama was now; like a fragile bird. When she had been a little girl, Ama's hugs had encircled her like a sheltering tree. The nurse had been far more demonstrative than her own mother and Clarrie had followed her like a shadow. Many a time Kamal was sent to fetch her from Ama's house and scold her for wandering into the servant's compound. But even as a child Clarrie sensed that Ama was an important person. She was the matriarch of her family and owner of their home, for among the Khassia property was passed on through the women. Clarrie had grown up taking it for granted that the women around her had status and were respected. Her father had encouraged her independence and never thought to confine her to the purely domestic. It always astonished her on visits to other Anglo-Indian homes how restricted and dull were the lives of the women.

Clarrie was still ruminating over such things as she trotted back up to Belgooree in the dawn light.

Suddenly, a rider emerged from the trees to her left. Startled, she reined in Prince. She recognised the chestnut stallion and the muscular frame of the horseman before she could make out the rider's face in the darkness. Wesley.

'What are you doing here?' she gasped.

'Looking for you,' he said bluntly. 'I thought you might be out for a dawn ride. Where have you been?'

Clarrie hesitated, feeling flustered. 'Just riding.'

He pulled closer, their horses nuzzling in curiosity. 'Would you like to ride a little further?' he asked. 'See the sunrise?'

She felt a jolt of excitement, and nodded. 'Very well. There's a good view from the top of Belgooree. Follow me and I'll show you.'

They rode uphill through the dense trees, skirting the compound and twisting up the steep pathway that Clarrie knew so well. Twenty minutes later, amid a cacophony of birdsong, they emerged into a clearing where the path petered out. Before them was a rocky outcrop. Clarrie dismounted and tied Prince's reins to a bush.

'If we climb up here we'll see the sun on the Himalayas. It's a bit of a scramble. Do you want to go further?'

His eyebrows shot up in surprise. 'Of course, if you can manage—' He stopped, seeing her derisory look.

Not waiting for him to dismount, Clarrie headed for the rocks and pulled herself up the first boulder.

'Hurry, if you want to catch the sunrise,' she called.

From there it was a hands and knees scramble up a series of rocks and slippery scree, dotted with scrub. In her haste to be at the top, Clarrie lost her footing and grabbed at a small bush. She cried out in shock as a large thorn pierced her riding glove and stuck into her palm. Letting go, she slithered backwards, skinning her knees through her jodhpurs. Wesley broke her fall by lunging forward and pinning her to the ground.

They lay panting, Wesley's athletic body pressed against hers. His breath was warm on her cheek. Her heart hammered like a horse at full gallop and she could feel the thud of his too. Neither of them moved.

'Are you hurt?' he finally asked.

She gulped. 'My hand – I grabbed a thorn bush.'

'Let me see.' He swivelled round, releasing her from his hold to inspect her hand. Gently, he removed the glove. The end of the thorn was still lodged in her palm. 'Hold still,' he ordered. With a swift movement he plucked out the remaining sliver.

Clarrie winced and smothered a yelp. Wesley reached into his jacket and produced a hip flask. He dabbed some whisky on to the wound.

'Ouch!' Clarrie cried. 'That feels worse than ever.'

He grinned. 'Just give it a minute.' He held on to her hand.

Clarrie struggled into a sitting position and he spotted her grazed knees.

'That looks sore,' he said, reaching for the hip flask again.

She pulled away. 'Don't you dare! I'm perfectly fine.'

Wesley's boom of laughter echoed around the rocks. 'I quite agree.' They regarded each other in the growing light.

'Why did you really come over so early?' Clarrie asked.

'As I said – I wanted to ride. I always wake before dawn. Harry's terrible for getting up at this hour. I thought you'd be up and I was right.'

'So you weren't out spying?'

Wesley snorted. 'Spying on who?'

'Seeing the lie of the land – the villages perhaps. You're the kind of man who is always thinking of work first.' She held his look. 'You must have half an eye out for recruits up here.'

'And if I had?'

Clarrie swallowed. 'Then I would tell you you're wasting your time. The Khassia aren't interested in working the big plantations. They are cattle people first and foremost – too attached to the land to wander beyond these hills, no matter how bad the harvest.'

He leaned closer, his green eyes narrowing. She was held by the intensity of his look, unable to glance away. She felt he could see right inside her and know that she was hiding something.

'You went to the village,' he said softly. 'I saw you.'

Clarrie gasped. 'You were following me!'

He did not deny it. 'Why didn't you want me to know where you'd been? You're keeping something from me. Not hiding one of our runaways, are you?'

Clarrie went hot with panic. 'Course not,' she lied. 'And you've no right to be sneaking round Belgooree or watching me!'

He smiled, not the least bit repentant. 'You intrigue me. I can't work you out, Clarissa. At first you seemed to loathe me, then last night you were different. Kind and attentive – and so beautiful. Gone was that wild girl riding about like a native and in her place was a grown woman. I must confess I was captivated.' He shifted closer still. 'Were you just being the dutiful hostess, or have your feelings towards me changed, as mine have to you?'

Clarrie stared at him, her cheeks on fire at his bold words. She should not be out here with him at all. What was she thinking of? She swallowed hard.

'I may have judged you too harshly – at first,' she admitted. 'We got off on the wrong foot. I don't want you to think badly of us Belhavens, no matter what's happened in the past. In fact, I was hoping we might be able to work together – that you and my father might do business.'

'Business?' Wesley threw back his head and laughed harshly. 'Oh, Clarissa! All this time you've been scheming about your father's tea garden and here I was hoping that you were being nice because you liked me.'

'I do,' Clarrie said hastily.

'But . . .?' Wesley prompted.

'But I also saw it as an opportunity for you and my father to bury your differences for the good of both our businesses. I thought if you saw our estate and its great potential you might be interested in – well – in finding some capital—'

For a moment, Wesley looked lost for words. 'You're looking for investors? Are things so bad for your father that he'd come begging to a Robson?'

Clarrie was offended. 'We'd never beg! And things are not bad – it's just a difficult patch. I'm sure there are plenty of others who would jump at the opportunity to go into business with my father. I was just giving you the first chance.'

Unexpectedly, Wesley took her hand and smiled. 'You are a truly remarkable young woman. Jock Belhaven doesn't know how lucky he is.'

He bent his head and kissed her wounded palm. Clarrie gasped at his touch. Their eyes met, and then he was pulling her to him. He planted a kiss firmly on her lips. Her eyes widened in shock, but she did not push him off. He hesitated, gave a half-smile and then took her face in his hands and kissed her again; a long, robust, hungry kiss that left her light-headed.

Her heart banged against her ribs as he broke off. She was half offended at his brazenness and half wanting him to kiss her again. The experience sent a judder right to her core.

Wesley surveyed her. 'You really would do anything for your father and Belgooree, wouldn't you?'

'What do you mean?' Clarrie asked hoarsely.

'Flirt with the enemy. Even allow a Robson to kiss you. How far would you go, sweet Clarrie?' He swept her with an insolent look.

In an instant, she raised her good hand and slapped him hard on the cheek. He grabbed it, his expression exultant.

'Now you're going to play the innocent little Clarissa, offended by a man's advances.' He laughed. 'But I've seen it in your eyes, Clarrie. I know you're a woman who responds to a man's kisses. You might be doing it to get money for your father's precious tea garden, but I think you enjoyed it none the less.'

If he had not been gripping her hand she would have struck him again for his outrageous words. The arrogance of the man!

'Don't flatter yourself,' she blazed. 'I took no enjoyment from it. But you're right about one thing – I'm only interested in you as far as you can help us at Belgooree. I don't suppose that will bother you, though; as a Robson I'm sure your main concern is whether we make a good business prospect.'

Wesley dropped her hand. 'Well, you don't mince your words, do you? Spoken like a true Belhaven.'

Clarrie turned from him and scrambled to her

feet. The rocks around them were glowing pink. Wesley caught her arm.

'Not so fast. You promised to show me the sunrise. Come on,' he ordered.

He went ahead, scrambling up the final ascent and reaching down to help her. She allowed him to haul her up past the thorn bush and the next minute they were standing on the hilltop in a ring of jagged rock, just as the sun burst over the eastern ridge. Clarrie pointed north to the snowy peaks of the Himalayas. Wesley gazed at them in awe.

'I've never seen them as clear as this,' he gasped. 'It's like the roof of heaven.'

Clarrie observed him. Most of the time he was either arrogant or mocking, but this was a glimpse of a different Wesley, one who could be humbled by the sight of such raw beauty. His rugged features looked almost boyish in wonderment. They stood in silence as the sun grew in strength. A parrot flew past screeching and broke the spell.

'I should be getting back,' Clarrie said. 'Olive will be fretting about being late for the fishing trip. She's quite taken with your friend Mr Wilson.'

Wesley grunted. 'You less so, I think. You should have seen your face when he told you to leave business to the men.'

Clarrie snorted. 'I'm used to that sort of attitude – come across it all the time in Shillong. But tell me, what's so shocking about daughters taking an interest in the family business when there are no sons?'

His mouth tugged into a half-smile. 'You have a point, I suppose.'

'Do any of the Robson women get involved in your family's affairs?' Clarrie asked.

'No,' Wesley admitted.

'Well, the day will come,' Clarrie declared. 'My generation will not be satisfied with playing second fiddle to men. I've read what's going on in England – things are changing already.'

Wesley scoffed. 'A few unnatural women demanding the vote, you mean? They won't get it – not in our lifetime.'

'Don't be so sure.'

Wesley laughed. 'I see Jock Belhaven's bred a radical in his tea garden. I'm not sure I want to do business with him after all.'

Clarrie gave him an anxious look. 'Please just keep an open mind, that's all I ask.'

As they prepared to climb down the outcrop, he asked, 'Why did your father not want you to show me round the estate?'

Clarrie blushed. 'I really don't know.'

'Nervous we might become friends?' Wesley suggested.

'I don't suppose,' Clarrie said drily, 'that he needs to worry about that.'

She heard Wesley chuckling as they descended.

Clarrie enjoyed the fishing trip more than she had expected. Harry allowed her to use Wesley's rod, a special one from Hardy's in Northumberland.

'Belhaven country,' Clarrie had declared. 'It'll bring me luck.'

It brought her a medium-sized mahseer that the bearers cooked with rice for their lunch. Afterwards, she dozed in the mellow sunshine while Olive painted and chattered to Harry. But as the shadows lengthened, she grew eager to return and find out whether Wesley and her father had struck up a rapport.

As she was packing up, Wesley cantered into the clearing, his face stormy. Clarrie tensed. 'Is everything all right?'

'Perfectly.' He did not dismount. 'Your pig-headed father has thrown me off his estate and told me I'm not to set foot here again.'

'What did you say to upset him?' Clarrie exclaimed.

'Hardly a word!' Wesley snapped. 'He didn't give me a chance. But perhaps you will.' He swung down from the saddle. 'Listen, Clarrie.' He took her by the arms. 'Your estate's in a worse mess than I thought.'

'Mess?' Clarrie echoed. 'Nonsense—'

'The trees you replanted – they're growing haphazardly all over the hillside – the way the Chinese grow them. You should have terracing and they should be much closer together – more bushes, more leaves, more profit. And the soil's all wrong up here – not sandy enough. Your father bought Belgooree with his heart, not his head – too interested in the fishing to worry about the tea, if you ask me.'

Clarrie listened to him, stunned. But before she could protest he had started off again.

'And as for the processing – it's archaic! You still have a shed full of men rolling leaves by hand. You'll never be cost-effective. The only way you can save your estate from ruin is to amalgamate with the big boys so you can use the modern machinery and change your practices. I tried to tell this to your father, but he sent me off with a flea in my ear!'

'I'm not surprised.' Clarrie found her voice. 'I can see you've done your best to insult and belittle him. He was making a good living at Belgooree when you were still in short britches.'

Wesley dropped his hold on her, his face grim. 'Times have changed. I thought you had more sense, but I can see you're just as blinkered as he is.'

Clarrie sparked back. 'Belgooree has a future – when we can find someone with the imagination to see how special it is and the drive to do more than just criticise. I thought you might be such a man,' she said with a look of contempt, 'but I can see I was mistaken. My father was right; you're as narrow-minded and full of your own self-importance as any other Robson!'

'And you Belhavens are all the same,' Wesley shot back. 'You just can't accept that we Robsons are better in business than you'll ever be.'

Clarrie turned from him in fury. 'Olive, pack up your things. We're going home.'

'But I haven't finished,' her sister protested.

'It's getting late,' Clarrie was sharp, 'and we've a half-hour ride.'

Harry waded out of the river, alerted by their raised voices. Clarrie could not be persuaded to stay any longer.

'Thank you for today's outing,' she said, helping Olive pack her saddlebag. 'I hope you'll call on us again, Mr Wilson.'

'Be delighted to,' Harry replied. 'And perhaps I could give you tea in Shillong when you next visit?'

'Oh, yes please!' Olive answered for them.

Clarrie pulled on her riding gloves and mounted, smiling at him in farewell. 'That would be very kind, thank you.'

Wesley stood fuming, his jaw clenched.

'Goodbye, Mr Robson,' she said curtly. 'I don't imagine we'll be seeing each other again in a hurry.'

He stared up at her, eyes blazing with anger. She felt a brief flicker of triumph that she had rendered him speechless. As she nudged Prince into a walk, he lunged forward and grabbed the reins.

'Let go!' she cried.

'Listen to me,' he said urgently. 'You're a fool to reject my advice. Belgooree is facing ruin. If you don't do something soon, you'll have nothing to offer anybody.' He held on to the snorting Prince.

'Quite frankly, the main asset your father has left to offer is *you*.'

Clarrie's eyes and mouth widened in astonishment. 'How dare you!' she hissed, wrenching the reins out of his grasp.

She kicked the pony into a trot, forcing Wesley to jump back or be trampled. She fled into the forest, glancing round only to make sure that Olive was following. She could not put distance between her and the hateful Wesley quickly enough.

CHAPTER 4

In the weeks that followed, Clarrie had time to reflect on Wesley's disastrous visit. Visanta, the season of spring, arrived unseasonably hot and without the early light rain that brought forth the delicate first tea buds. They picked what they could, but the agents from Calcutta frowned and grumbled over the pickings and offered them very little.

Early summer continued hot and dry. The leaves of the tea bushes grew sparsely and too small. They waited in vain for the rains to start.

'Monsoon will come soon,' Kamal predicted, 'if it is God's will.'

In the village they offered puja to the gods to send rain, for the hilly grasslands were scorched and the cattle growing lean. Clarrie heard the drums beating from dawn till after dusk.

But her greatest concern was for her father. Since

Wesley's disruptive appearance, he had sunk back into a deep depression as if he no longer believed in any future for Belgooree. Clarrie cursed the young planter for having sown such doubts in her father's already troubled mind. She tried to jolly him along, but he preferred to shut himself into his study and drink himself senseless.

It was at times like these that Clarrie wondered whether she had been wise to dismiss Wesley's help, however critical and begrudging. Perhaps the only chance of survival would be to submit to the demands of a larger estate and agree to what ever terms they cared to offer. For Wesley's prediction that they were facing ruin was becoming closer to reality with each passing day.

In desperation, she tried to raise the issue with Jock, but he was so horrified at her even contemplating doing a deal with the Robsons that Clarrie quickly backed down.

'Lass, you don't know what they're like,' he railed. 'They're ruthless, quite ruthless! They might win you round with promises, but they won't keep them. Robsons aren't happy until they've taken every last penny from you.' His glassy eyes stared at her in fear. 'Me grandfather and father were ruined by them and left without a business to pass on to me. The choice was go and work for Cousin Jared in his grim little public house in Newcastle or join the army.' He broke out in a sweat of agitation. 'I've done it all myself – a lifetime of hard work and saving.

Belgooree is mine. I'll be damned if I'll let them take everything away a second time!'

'They won't, Father,' Clarrie said, trying to calm him, 'of course they won't. We'll find another way to keep going.'

If Clarrie's feelings towards Wesley had been softening, things changed abruptly the following week. Ama came rushing to find her in the gardens, distraught and weeping.

'He's gone! They've taken him!' she wailed. 'They've stolen him back. My dearest boy!'

'Not Ramsha?' Clarrie gasped.

'Yes, my Ramsha.' Ama collapsed into Clarrie's arms.

Clarrie hurried back to the compound with her, trying to comfort the old nurse. Sitting on the veranda steps, reviving her with sips of lemon water, Clarrie heard how three thugs had come barging into her house and hauled her sickly son away.

'Are you sure they were from the Oxford?'

Ama nodded. 'They say they must make an example of him, or others will run away too. I tried to stop them. But they came when the men were out on the hill with the cattle. They pushed me over and kicked earth into the fire. All the time they are beating Ramsha with a big stick. Now I don't know if I will ever see my sweet boy again—' She broke off, sobbing.

Clarrie held her close. This was Wesley's doing. Impetuously, she had challenged him about his treatment of his workers and made him suspicious. He had followed her the next morning with the sole intention of discovering the runaway; she was sure of it. His talk about seeing the sunrise and riding with her had just been a cover. How foolish she had been not to realise. She felt a wave of shame and anger. She had led Wesley to Ramsha and was responsible for his capture. She would never forgive herself.

Clarrie took Ama inside, and she and Kamal tried to console her with tea and sweetmeats. But Ama would not stay and be comforted. She returned to the village and went into mourning for her lost son as if he had died.

As their situation worsened, Clarrie tried her best to protect Olive from the truth. For her sister's fourteenth birthday, she agreed to take her into Shillong and sent word to Harry of their trip. First, they visited the nuns at the mission where their mother had taught, and then Harry treated them to tea at the Pinewood Hotel and paid Olive compliments about the sketches that she showed him.

'You're terrific at birds,' he enthused. 'So much detail.'

Olive was thrilled and gave him several drawings to keep. As they were leaving, Harry took Clarrie by the elbow and asked her bashfully if she had heard from Wesley.

'No,' she answered shortly, 'nor do I wish to. Why do you ask?'

He blushed. 'Well, I know you had a disagreement over your father, but I rather had the impression that Robson was sweet on you.'

Clarrie snorted. 'I think you're mistaken. Mr Robson cares only for himself and his own advancement, as far as I can see.' She saw his embarrassment and quickly added, 'I'm sorry, I know he's your friend, but Mr Robson and I are incompatible.'

Harry brightened. 'Then you wouldn't mind if I – er – called on you when I next get a spot of leave?'

Clarrie gawped at him. She had only encouraged contact with the young officer to keep Olive happy. She felt no attraction towards him herself. Glancing over to her sister, she answered cautiously, 'Olive and I would be pleased to see you. You've been very kind to encourage her art and she values your friendship.'

He gave her a baffled look but nodded and shook her hand warmly. Rejoining Kamal, who was waiting for them outside, Olive pinched her sister on the arm.

'What was he saying to you?' she said petulantly. 'He's my friend. You're trying to take him off me. It's not fair!'

'Don't be silly,' Clarrie said. 'I've no interest in Mr Wilson. I only did this for your sake.'

'He wants to see you again, doesn't he?' Olive pouted. 'He's only pretending to like my pictures to please you.'

'He likes them because they're very good,' Clarrie reassured her. 'I promise you I have no intention of encouraging Mr Wilson in any way other than as a friend of yours.'

This seemed to mollify Olive, but over the next couple of weeks Clarrie received amorous letters from the subaltern that she quickly threw on the fire and did not answer. She assumed he was lonely stuck in a remote barracks and that she was probably the only eligible young woman he had met so far. His interest would wane as soon as he found someone more suitable or when he had heard enough derogatory remarks about the Belhavens to put him off.

Local speculation about when the monsoon would finally come grew to fever pitch. The second plucking of the tea bushes had been as fruitless as the first. Clarrie oversaw the process of withering, rolling and fermenting the tea with mounting alarm. Once the blackened leaves were dried and sorted, there was hardly enough to fill two chests.

When the agent came he took one look at their Orange Pekoe and declared it was greatly inferior to last season's. He left without buying any of it. Clarrie rode out to the remote hilltop where the hermit lived and wept bitterly. She could see no way out of their problems.

All at once, the swami appeared, leaning his wizened frame on his long staff as he gazed at her with rheumy eyes. She brushed at her tears and made a greeting with palms together and head bowed.

He smiled and spoke to her gently in Hindi. She understood little of what he said, but was comforted by the compassion in his voice. He squatted down beside her and began to sing: a thin high-pitched sound that filled the clearing like birdsong. When he finished, they sat in silence and a strange peace descended on her. She must not lose hope, the swami was telling her; she had a path to follow and she must take it and trust that all would be well.

As Clarrie stood up to go, the old man got nimbly to his feet and held up his hand in a blessing. She drew out of her pocket the pouch of tea and sugar that she always left on his doorstep and handed it to him. They smiled at each other in thanks and she went on her way fortified by the encounter.

A few days later, she saw the first black clouds amassing on the far horizon.

'The rains!' she cried out in sheer relief. 'The rains, the beautiful rains!'

Later that day, the sky grew as dark as dusk and the first heavy drops spattered the roof of the house. Soon the rain swept in like a heavy curtain of water, drenching everything in its path. Clarrie and Olive rushed out into the courtyard with Kamal and they danced around in the mud, shrieking and laughing like children. Jock appeared on the leaky veranda, pale as a ghost but smiling. He turned his face up to the rain and let it stream down his sunken cheeks.

Stretching his arms wide, he bellowed to the heavens, 'Belgooree!'

Afterwards, Clarrie wondered if there had been tears mingled with rain on his emaciated face.

The jungle blossomed in the following days, turning a luxuriant green. Trees and creepers flowered in a riot of colour: brilliant red and purple blooms shaped like parrots' beaks, yellow pendulous blossom and the fragrant white flowers of the bokul tree. The house almost disappeared under an abundance of honeysuckle and jasmine. Clarrie's favourite was the hibiscus that grew by the gateway, which bloomed white in the morning and turned a deep red by night.

For a week or two, the coming of the monsoon renewed her optimism and Jock's spirits rallied too. But the relief was short-lived. The rains had come too late for the delicate buds of the tea trees and anything they plucked now would be coarse and inferior in comparison. The leaves were so wet that drying them became more onerous, using up large quantities of charcoal. They would have little to offer their workers this season except pruning and weeding. Their finances could not improve until the following year at the earliest.

Rumours about their parlous situation must have started to spread, for letters began to arrive from creditors in Calcutta. A bank loan needed repaying, a tailor wanted a long-standing account settled and an exporter was owed money for tea chests. Jock refused to deal with them.

'Let them wait,' he said in irritation. 'I'll not be bullied.'

'They won't wait for ever,' Clarrie fretted. 'What are we ever going to pay them with?'

Jock had no answer. Clarrie took a deep breath and suggested, 'Perhaps it's time we thought about selling off part of the estate – or at least renting out the house? I'm sure shooting parties might be interested.'

He gave her a look of such desolation that Clarrie recoiled.

'This is our home,' he hissed, 'your mother's home. She's buried here. How could you suggest such a thing?'

Clarrie cried in desperation, 'Well it won't be our home much longer if we carry on as we are!'

After that, Jock locked himself into the study for three days and refused to come out. Her only escape was to go on long rides with Prince. Ranging in the hills was the only time she felt a degree of calm. She would gaze down on the tea garden far below and see it as small and insignificant among the majestic mountains and forests. These mountains would still be standing when the gardens and their inhabitants were long gone. It made her think of Wesley's comments about the Khassia hills being wild and beautiful. Had he ever returned here to hunt or fish without her knowing? If he had, he knew he was not welcome at Belgooree so would have given it a wide berth.

In such moments, she allowed herself to contemplate going to the Robsons to beg for help. Yet she knew she could not stoop that low. They were her father's enemies and Wesley was a callous recruiter who must have arranged for Ramsha to be dragged from his bed, beaten and hauled back to the miserable servitude of the Oxford Estates.

On one such ride, Clarrie observed a bank of cloud amassing to the north after a hot and humid day. Flashes of lightning illuminated its blackness. A north-wester, a violent storm, was on its way. She turned for home, gripped by a strange unease. The air was sticky and oppressive. As she urged Prince on, the clouds rolled closer. They rose in an arch whose summit was like the overhanging crest of a gigantic wave about to break. All about her the sounds of the forest quietened as if nature held its breath. The air stilled to a dead calm.

Clarrie knew then that she would not reach home before the storm broke. It must be less than a mile away and travelling fast. Eddies of wind began to whip up the leaves and dust around Prince's trotting hooves; the temperature dropped rapidly. Quickly, she turned into the forest to take shelter. Finding a mighty babul tree, she led Prince among its raised roots and tore down some bamboo branches for a makeshift roof.

Hunching down not a moment too soon, she gasped as a huge gust of wind burst around them in sudden fury. In minutes the bamboo shelter was ripped off and carried away, along with saplings torn from the soil. A loud clap of thunder came with vivid lightning. Prince whinnied in alarm. But the strong arms of the babul's roots protected them and Clarrie soothed the pony with soft words and caresses. Then the torrents of heavy rain descended. There they hid, listening to the rain crashing on the dense canopy of leaves above.

An hour later, the rain eased and Clarrie emerged, soaked but safe. Back out on the path, the air was cool and refreshing. The jungle shone an emerald green against the deep violet of the departing storm clouds. The forest floor steamed and dripped after the deluge. Clarrie breathed in its heady scent. The sense of foreboding she had felt so strongly before had passed with the storm. She picked her way home with care as Prince slipped and slithered on the pathway that was now a small stream. It was dusk by the time she reached the house.

There was consternation at her arrival.

'Where have you been?' Olive cried, rushing out to meet her. 'Why weren't you here when he came? Were you hiding till he went away? Father's in such a state.'

'What are you talking about? Who's been?'

'Miss Clarissa!' Kamal came hurrying out, holding a faded black umbrella over her head although she was already wet through. 'Come, come in the house and getting dry.'

He bustled her up the steps into the bungalow. Rainwater still ran off the roof into the water barrel and dripped from the creepers on to the faded outdoor furniture.

'I'm fine. Just tell me what's been happening.'

'Big fireworks,' Kamal said, his face creased in worry.

'Wesley Robson's been here,' Olive said, her look nervous. Clarrie's insides twisted at the name. 'He and Father had a terrible, terrible row. You should have been here to stop them.'

'I got caught in the downpour,' Clarrie explained. 'It wasn't safe to ride. Why on earth did Mr Robson come here?'

Kamal and Olive exchanged anxious looks, as if neither wanted to be the one to tell her. Kamal helped her discard her wet coat, pushed her into a chair by the fire and wrapped her in a blanket. Clarrie caught his hand.

'Tell me!'

Kamal let go a sigh and sat down. 'Robson sahib – he hears tittle-tattle that Belgooree for sale.'

'From who?'

Kamal shook his head. 'Maybe men in Calcutta have tongues wagging.'

'So what did Mr Robson want?'

'He come with offer. He say big Oxford tea gardens take Belgooree off Belhaven sahib's hands. They pay off all debts but run Belgooree like proper tea garden.'

'Proper tea garden?' Clarrie exclaimed. 'Of all the cheek—'

'Listen, Clarrie!' Olive begged.

Kamal's bearded face looked pained. 'He say

Robsons will do all running of gardens, not Belhaven sahib. And he is very much liking this place. Robson sahib wants to live here.'

'Live here?' Clarrie cried. 'And what about us? Packed off to some dingy boarding house in Shillong, no doubt. He must know Father would never agree to leave Belgooree. The arrogance of the man!'

'Mr Robson said we could stay,' Olive said, her face tense.

Clarrie saw her sister and Kamal exchange wary looks again, and frowned. 'I don't understand.'

'By marrying him,' Olive blurted out. 'If you agreed to marry Wesley Robson then we could all stay. He asked Father for your hand in marriage.'

Clarrie gawped at them. For once she was speechless.

'Robson sahib, he is saying it will save face for Belhavens,' Kamal added. 'He willing to save you all from gutter.'

'The gutter!' Clarrie spluttered. 'How dare he?'

'That's what Father said,' Olive answered. 'He shouted all these terrible things at Mr Robson. Said he would never allow him to marry you, even if he was the last man in India. Mr Robson got angry too. He said he wanted to speak to you and you should have a say in all this.' Olive began to pant as she gabbled out her words. 'But Father said if he went anywhere near you he'd shoot him with his own revolver. Father said you hated Mr Robson as much as he did and to never come back again. He said he'd starve before he let Mr Robson take everything he loved away from him—'

She broke off in a fit of coughing.

'Raise your arms,' Clarrie commanded, moving swiftly to rub her back and calm her. Kamal rushed to administer sips of chilled tea.

When Olive could speak again, she asked, 'Why does he hate Mr Robson so much?'

'He doesn't trust him,' Clarrie answered, 'and neither do I.'

'So you won't marry him?'

Clarrie gave her a sharp look. 'Of course not. It's unthinkable.' She grew hot at the thought. 'Besides, he doesn't even like me. He's only doing it to get his hands on Belgooree.'

'But why should he do that if it's worth nothing?' Olive asked.

'It is worth something,' Clarrie insisted. 'It's worth a very great deal, both as a tea garden and as a hunting ground. Oh, Mr Robson is very aware of its potential. Why do you think the Oxford Estates are so keen to get their hands on it? Robson is a ruthless businessman, first and foremost.'

Olive looked at her in disappointment. 'But if you married him, at least we could all stay here.'

'We will stay here,' Clarrie cried. 'But Father has made his decision and I support him. Marrying that man is out of the question.'

Shortly afterwards, Clarrie went to find her

father. He was staring out of the study window. She put a hand on his shoulder but he hardly stirred.

'Olive and Kamal told me about Mr Robson's visit.'

He looked at her with haunted eyes. 'He wanted to take you away from me. Not just my land, but my beloved daughter.'

Clarrie slipped an arm through his. 'He could never do that.'

'I told him he couldn't have you. Was I right to say what I did?' Jock searched her face for reassurance. Clarrie hesitated as she remembered how eagerly she had responded to Wesley's kisses. How disloyal she felt!

'Yes, of course. I could never be happy with such a man. And I know how much it would hurt you.'

Jock let go a long sigh that was almost a groan and closed his eyes. When he spoke again, his voice sounded lifeless and drained of emotion. 'Then never let us speak that man's name between us again.'

If Clarrie had hoped that her father's humour would improve once the threat of Wesley's proposal had been dismissed, she was sadly mistaken. He withdrew ever further into the cocoon of his study and a twilight world of intoxication and delusion where she could not reach him.

Sometimes, as summer turned to autumn, he would not emerge for days on end, and if he did, it was only to seek more spirit or opium. Shaking, and painfully thin, he would summon enough strength to ride into the village, bartering away knives, watch, fishing rod and saddle in return for alcohol or pellets of opium. Clarrie knew from the sickly-sweet smell leaking out from his den when her father was smoking the drug. It left him weak, trembling and melancholic, his joints and stomach aching. Neither she nor Kamal could get him to eat. He was wasting away before their very eyes and she was powerless to stop his self-destruction. Had she been wrong to dismiss Wesley's offer of marriage so quickly? Often his sensual, mocking face with its puckered eyebrow would come to mind unbidden and she would wonder what it would be like to be married to him. But she smothered such treacherous thoughts, for they did not help her father one iota.

With the arrival of winter and the cold season, Clarrie grew desperate, knowing that the slightest chill might see him off. They had a dismal Christmas with no money to spend on presents or treats in Shillong. One day in January, just after Clarrie's nineteenth birthday had come and gone without celebration, Olive's music teacher announced that her husband was being posted to Lahore and she would be leaving. Clarrie's initial relief that she would not have to scrape together any more fees was quickly followed by guilt, for Olive was distraught at her going. She moped around the house, refusing to practise.

'What's the point? There's no one left who appreciates my playing.'

'I do,' Clarrie tried to cajole her, 'and so does Kamal.'

'But you don't *understand* it,' Olive complained. 'Father's the only one who does, but he doesn't care the least bit any more!'

At her wits' end, Clarrie confronted Jock. She stormed into the study and yanked up the blinds, letting sharp light into the fusty, stinking room. Her father flinched and groaned.

'This has gone on long enough,' she berated him. 'I'll not let you give up on everything like this. You've got two daughters to support, or have you forgotten? When's the last time you bothered to listen to Olive playing her violin? Or the last time you went out to look at the tea garden – talk to your workers?' She advanced on the huddled figure on the camp bed and grabbed at the covers. 'Get up, Father. Get up at once!'

She tensed at what she saw. He was skeletal in his nightshirt, his pale wasted legs and arms half their former size. His head seemed too big for his body now and his eyes too big for his face. She steeled herself to bully him out of bed, panic gripping her that if she did not he would die there.

'I've got a good mind to ride over to the Oxford – tell the Robsons they might as well come and help themselves to Belgooree right now because Jock Belhaven's given up. Is that what I should do, Father?' she demanded angrily.

He stared at her as if she were a stranger. He did not move.

'Wesley Robson's right,' she taunted him. 'This place is in ruins. Who would want it in this state? I must have been mad not to accept his offer of marriage. Perhaps I will now.'

That struck home, for Jock's face clouded in pain and he struggled to raise himself.

'No – don't . . .' he whispered, his voice thin as a reed.

She leaned forward to help him. 'Then get up, Babu,' she urged, 'for my sake and Olive's – get up and *live*.'

But he sank back at once. 'I – can't,' he croaked. 'I'm too tired. You can manage things.'

'No!' Clarrie cried in alarm. 'Not without you.'

He looked at her with lifeless eyes. 'Write – to Cousin – Jared,' he gasped. 'He will – help you . . .'

'How can he help? He lives thousands of miles away in England. He runs a pub, not a bank. We need money, Father!'

He turned his face away and closed his eyes. 'I'm sorry. I just – want – to be – left alone.'

Clarrie stared at him in disbelief. All the months of anguish and fighting to keep Belgooree going had been for nothing. A rising tide of anger and fear threatened to overpower her. As she looked at her defeated father, something inside finally snapped.

'I hate you!' she cried. 'You're a coward! I'm glad Mother's dead and doesn't have to see how weak and useless you look lying there.' She shook with fury as she screamed at him. 'Where's my father?

Where's the brave soldier, the strong Northumbrian? You're not him. If you don't get up and try to help your own daughters, then I never want to speak to you again!'

He seemed impervious to her goading and lay still with his eyes closed as if she were not there. She might as well rant at the damp walls for all the difference it would make. Clarrie stormed from the room, slamming the door so violently that the whole house shook. She did not need to tell Olive or Kamal what had happened, for their shocked looks told her they had heard every furious word. She fled through the sitting room out to the veranda.

Gripping the balustrade, Clarrie heard Olive begin to cry in the room beyond, but for once she could not comfort her. She was so choked with anger that she did not trust herself to speak another word. She gritted her teeth, forcing back her own tears.

'Miss Clarissa.' Kamal stood at the door. 'Come inside and I will make you spicy tea.'

Unable to bear his kindness, she stumbled towards the steps.

'I'm going to Ama's,' she gulped and made her escape. As she mounted Prince, she heard Kamal calling her to stay. Olive came running out on to the veranda too.

'Let me come with you,' she wailed, 'don't leave me!'

'I want to go alone,' Clarrie called as she urged Prince through the gate. Kamal was trying to reason with Olive and coax her back inside. Clarrie swallowed down tears as she cantered towards the village.

Smoke from evening fires trailed into the starry sky as the last of the cattle were herded back home. She heard women singing through the twilight and calling to their children to come in. From somewhere a tune struck up on a bamboo pipe and filled the night sky with its haunting melody. All at once, Clarrie's pain was eased, as if a weight had been lifted off her chest.

She found Ama and her family sitting round the open fire chewing betel nut wrapped in pan leaves and spitting out the bittersweet red juice. At once Ama made her welcome, not questioning why she came at such an hour. One of her daughters brought Clarrie a bowl of rice and dhal and another some hot sweet tea.

Afterwards, the others withdrew, leaving Clarrie alone with her old nurse. She poured out her worries and told Ama of the row with her father.

'I said some terrible things – hateful things,' Clarrie confessed. 'But seeing him like that – I was so frightened and angry with him. I still am. I don't know what to do. Tell me, Ama!'

At first Ama said nothing, just continued to chew and stare into the fire, holding Clarrie's hand in her lap. Finally she spoke.

'Tonight you must put your anger to sleep. When

the sun comes up you will make your peace with Babu sahib.' She gazed at Clarrie with solemn eyes. 'He gave you life and you must respect him. He is a good man but his spirit is weary – it is lost and trying to find a way home. But he still loves you.'

Clarrie bowed her head as a wave of emotion surged up from inside. She let out a gasp and burst into tears at last. Ama drew her into her arms and rocked her while she sobbed out her heart, stroking her hair and whispering words of comfort.

Afterwards, Clarrie lay down with her head in Ama's lap, staring at the flames, her mind blissfully empty. Without having to ask, she knew Ama would let her stay the night under her roof, as sometimes she had done as a child. Later, she curled up on a rush mat under a heavy woollen blanket and went to sleep with the smell of wood smoke in her hair and the sound of cattle snuffling beyond the bamboo partition.

Clarrie awoke in the dawn light, strangely calm and released from all the fury of the previous evening. She stepped out into the bitterly cold morning, the blanket still wrapped around her.

She was helping stir the porridge when steps came pounding towards the compound. Kamal burst through the opening.

'Miss Clarissa!' he cried, his face creased in distress.

'What is it?' Clarrie jumped up in alarm, heart hammering.

'Your father . . .'

Suddenly his strong bearded face crumpled like a child's. He stopped in his tracks and let out a strange howl of pain. Clarrie froze.

'No,' she gasped. 'No!'

Rigid, she watched his tears brimming over and streaming down his cheeks. Kamal's grief told her everything. Her father was dead.

CHAPTER 5

Jock Belhaven was buried, as he had instructed, beside his wife Jane in the small plot behind the house, rather than in the cemetery in Shillong with the other British. He had been found by Kamal, not in his study, but in the marital bedroom, curled up in the musty bed where Clarrie's mother had died. The doctor from the cantonment said his weak heart had given out after years of recurring fever and ague. It was common for planters to die before the age of fifty-five.

Clarrie was haunted by the memory of her cruel words to her father – the last he would ever hear from her – and the image of him crawling away like a wounded animal to the sanctuary of his old room. Her guilt was compounded by Olive's bitter distress.

'You killed him!' she sobbed. 'How could you say those hurtful things to him?'

Clarrie did not try to argue, for part of her believed it to be true.

Few people outside the village attended the burial, conducted swiftly by a visiting missionary who was working at the mission hospital in Shillong. Two of the nuns from Loreto convent came, along with a tea planter from Gowhatty who had fished with Jock in better times. But he had been buried a fortnight before news spread to planters further afield and letters of condolence began to arrive. A brief note came from Harry Wilson but he made no attempt to visit. No word came from the Oxford Estates. Clarrie did not know if she felt bitterness or relief.

They continued in a state of limbo, dressed in mourning, waiting for something to happen. It was not long before the bank in Calcutta and other creditors were sending letters of condolence edged with steely insistence that the Belgooree estate must be sold. Clarrie was suddenly seized by the spectre of their being evicted and roaming the streets of Shillong – or worse, Calcutta – penniless. Perhaps they could beg the nuns to take them in. Yet the thought of such a restricted life filled her with gloom.

Olive's withdrawal from her was a cause of pain. The girl would hardly speak to her, punishing her for being left alone the night their father died. Olive had turned into a miserable, thumb-sucking child, refusing to do anything but lie on her bed and cry for long hours. Not even the long-suffering Kamal could comfort her.

Going through Jock's papers, Clarrie had found his cousin Jared's address and written to inform him of her father's death. She began to contemplate leaving India and venturing to this unknown north of England. Jock had spoken fondly of his upbringing on a hill farm in Northumberland, though the farm had long gone. The only relation left appeared to be his younger cousin, Jared, who had gone to Newcastle for work. Her father had been dismissive about his running a public house, but perhaps Jared had more business sense than her father ever had. If she could find work over there too, she would be able to support Olive until she was of age; then they could find a way of returning home to India. The more she worried over their situation, the more convinced she became that they would have to leave Assam to survive.

Even though Clarrie had heard nothing back from Jared, she wrote again, asking if he could help find her a position in Newcastle as a housekeeper or companion. She was good at cooking, sewing and bookkeeping, as well as dealing with servants and ordering supplies. She knew a great deal about tea, she told this unknown cousin.

Having sent the second letter, she fretted about what she had done, for she knew little about the man. Was he married? Did he have a family? Was he even alive? As Jock had not been good at keeping in touch and never wrote to anyone unless absolutely necessary, she had no way of knowing.

When a letter came back a month later in reply to her first, Clarrie felt a wave of relief that there was someone to whom they could turn. She rushed to tell Olive.

'Look, Cousin Jared has written! He says how sorry he is and how much he liked Father when they were boys. He signs it from Jared and Lily Belhaven. She must be his wife.' She sat down on the bed beside her sister. 'Isn't it grand to have family somewhere in this world?'

'What good are they so far away?' Olive moaned.

Clarrie tried to sound bright. 'They might find me work, that's what. I've asked them to.'

'What?' Olive sat up. 'You can't mean it? Go and live in England?'

'Why not?'

Olive looked appalled. 'We know nothing about it – except it's cold and rainy and full of smoky towns except where the King lives. And we don't know these cousins – they might be cruel and sell us into slavery.'

Clarrie laughed. 'Don't be daft. You've read too many fairy tales.'

'Don't laugh at me,' Olive said reproachfully. 'I'm serious. I don't want to leave here – not ever.'

Clarrie took her hands. 'Listen, I don't want to either. But it looks as if we have no choice. We have to sell Belgooree to pay off Father's debts. We can't run the place on our own, don't you see that?'

'There is a way,' Olive said, her look pleading. 'You could change your mind and marry Wesley Robson.'

Clarrie pulled away. 'How can you say that after what he did to Babu? Father gave up after Robson's visit – it knocked all the fight out of him.'

'No it didn't,' Olive hissed. 'You did that.'

Clarrie stood up, tired of Olive's complaints. 'I'm not going to argue.'

'It's your fault,' Olive shouted, 'your stupid pride. If you'd said yes to marrying Mr Robson then everything would have been all right. Father would have come round to the idea once he saw Belgooree thriving again.'

'You're in cloud cuckoo land,' Clarrie protested. 'It would never have happened like that. Robson would have taken the land and then broken his promise to us.'

'You're wrong,' Olive said, on the verge of tears again. 'It was our one chance. But you had to spoil it. If you'd married him, Babu would still be alive!'

Clarrie hurried from the room, the accusation ringing in her ears. It was nonsense! Even if she had submitted to such a hateful match, her father would never have given permission.

But she could not rid her mind of the invidious thought: had she hastened her father's death by her refusal to contemplate marriage to Wesley? It had been a dubious lifeline for Belgooree, but it had indeed been an offer to save them. Should she have tried to persuade her father to agree to it before it was too late? She would never know, but it only compounded her deep sense of guilt over her father's death.

The following week, the estate went up for sale. Olive continued to upset Clarrie with her constant refrain about her selfishness in rebuffing Wesley.

'What's done is done,' Clarrie snapped. 'It's too late to change anything now.'

'It might not be,' Olive urged. 'Why don't you write to Mr Robson and say you've changed your mind? Or better still, go and see him. I'd come with you.'

'No,' Clarrie cried, 'I couldn't. He hasn't even written about Father dying.'

'Then you don't love Belgooree as much as you say – as much as I do,' Olive accused her. 'If it was in my power, I'd do anything to stay here – even marry the likes of Wesley Robson.'

'Stop it,' Clarrie pleaded.

'I won't stop it,' Olive said, 'and I won't leave here. I'll never go to England or Newcastle and you can't make me!'

Clarrie tried to talk to Kamal about what they should do, but he would not be drawn.

'You must accept the will of Allah,' he told her and went about his work, sadness clinging to him like morning mist.

When a second letter came from Jared and Lily,

generously offering to take the girls into their home in Newcastle until they came of age, Clarrie felt a huge burden lift. But Olive made herself ill with crying. She had several violent coughing fits that left her weak and listless. She caught a chill that settled on her chest. Clarrie and Kamal nursed her with mounting concern. Olive said nothing, her eyes feverish and reproachful.

Clarrie began to contemplate the unthinkable: she would go and seek out Wesley Robson and beg for his help. She would speak the humiliating words of apology if that was what it would take to stimulate Olive's recovery. Calling in Ama to look after Olive, she set out with Kamal for Upper Assam.

All day, they rode downhill through forest and jungle, resting at night in a tea house, then onward the next day till they reached Gowhatty on the swirling Brahmaputra river. There they left their ponies at the resthouse and boarded a steamer that took them upriver for two days to Tezpur, where they disembarked and hired a tonga to take them into the hills around Nowgong.

At first, Clarrie had been so mesmerised by the temperate misty riverside that she had thought of little but the travelling itself. But as they journeyed into new territory and neared the Oxford Estates, her nervousness increased tenfold. What on earth was she going to say when she came face to face with Wesley Robson?

When they arrived at the estate gates, the sheer

scale of the tea gardens overawed both her and Kamal. They stretched for miles, covering the hillsides as far as the eye could see. Once they got permission to enter, it took them an hour to drive to the planters' compound, passing a collection of vast, well-built tea sheds. Scores of labourers were moving through the ranks of bushes, bent under their heavy loads. Clarrie was astonished to see this much activity so early in the season, but here the bushes were already in bloom and the air was mild and moist. At Belgooree they were still having night frosts.

At the heart of the estate, surrounded by beautiful ornamental gardens, were low bungalows and a clubhouse with a neat polo pitch in front.

The head mohurer came out of his accounts office to greet them and offer them refreshment. He was Bengali and chatted amiably with Kamal.

'He says he can take you to see the assistant manager,' Kamal told her. 'He is in the factory.'

Clarrie's insides clenched. 'What about Mr Robson?' she asked, dry-mouthed.

Kamal shook his head. 'I'm sorry, he is not here.'

Clarrie was dismayed. 'When will he be back?'

Kamal shook his head again. 'You must speak to assistant manager, Mr Bain.'

Inside the factory, the noise was deafening. Steam-powered machines cranked and hissed as gigantic rollers turned and fans whirred, drying out huge quantities of leaf. Clarrie thought of their small drying shed with its bamboo trays that took eight pounds of good timber to produce enough charcoal to dry just one pound of tea. She began to see what a gulf there was between the Oxford and Belgooree. No wonder Wesley had been so scathing.

Maybe this was why her father had been so reluctant to let her socialise with the planters of Upper Assam or visit their estates, for she would have seen how insignificant was their own. She blushed now to think how she had boasted to Wesley of their fine tea garden. Maybe there had been a place for such a small producer in former days, but one glance at this industrialised place showed her that Belgooree was now obsolete.

Mr Bain was cheerful and red-faced, and looked hardly older than she was. He steered her outside again. When she explained where she had come from, he did not hide his surprise.

'Belgooree? It's up for sale, isn't it? I heard the planter there has died.'

'My father,' Clarrie said.

'Oh Lord, I'm so sorry. What can I do to help?'

'I'm looking for Mr Wesley Robson,' Clarrie said, reddening. 'He expressed an interest in buying Belgooree last year.'

'Did he now?' The manager's fair eyebrows shot up.

'I was wondering when I could speak to him,' Clarrie asked.

'I'm sorry, Miss Belhaven, but he's not here any longer. Hasn't been since September.'

'September?' Clarrie gasped.

'Yes, I replaced him. He said he'd learned all he needed to. I must say he struck me as a man in a hurry.'

Yes, Clarrie thought, it sounded just like Wesley to believe he had learned all there was to know about tea growing in less than a year.

'Where has he gone?' she asked.

'Well,' Mr Bain blew out hot cheeks, 'I believe he was heading for Ceylon – compare the tea gardens there – see a bit of India on the way – hunt a few tigers, that sort of thing.'

'So he's not coming back here?' Clarrie said, feeling strangely deflated.

'Not that I know of,' said the manager, now eyeing her with open curiosity. 'I say, was there some sort of understanding between you and Robson?'

Clarrie flushed. 'No, nothing like that. It was purely a business call. We weren't ready to sell Belgooree before, but now, with my father's passing, we are.'

Bain nodded. 'I do understand, but I'm not sure it would have made any difference had he been here.'

'Why not?'

'Well, Robson's not the kind of man to let the grass grow under his feet. I suspect if his offer were turned down once, he wouldn't reconsider. He's the type of man to brush it off and go on to the next business idea.' He gave an apologetic smile. 'I'm sorry, this is not very helpful. Let me give you lunch.'

Clarrie declined. Suddenly she just wanted to be gone from this lush oppressive place. Instead she asked him to provide a tiffin basket with food for her return journey. He looked shocked that she had come this distance with only her father's khansama as chaperon. But she waved off his protests that she should at least stay the night and left him shaking his head in bafflement at her eccentric behaviour.

Clarrie had one other mission before leaving. Returning to the accounts office, she asked the Bengali overseer if she could take a look at 'the lines', the rows of labourers' huts. He seemed suspicious, but when she insisted she had the permission of Mr Bain, pointed her down to the workers' quarters. She was at once assailed by the stench of effluent. Small children played in the muck around the mud-built shacks. Ignoring the shouts of a chowkidar who was policing the lines, Clarrie stooped and entered one of the dwellings.

It was a tiny, windowless, airless single room and so dark that at first she could see nothing. The only light or ventilation was from a tear in the thatch. She imagined how the floor would turn to a sea of mud come the rains. Cooking pots and sleeping mats for half a dozen people were piled to one side, while from the smell of it the opposite corner was used as a latrine.

Clarrie emerged feeling nauseous. Once the humidity of summer returned, the mosquitoes would thrive here. She asked the agitated watchman in faltering Assamese whether he knew a Ramsha from Belgooree in the Khassia hills.

'A tribesman?' the man asked in disdain. 'They are too unreliable – always picking fights and running away.'

Clarrie described him, but the man shrugged, as if to say why waste time on such people? She grew angry.

'His mother is a family friend!'

Kamal tried to steer her away. 'He can tell us nothing.'

'I need to find Ramsha. I promised Ama.' She could not bear it if her whole trip ended in utter failure.

By the time they had walked back to the compound, word of her spying had spread and the assistant manager was there to confront her. Gone was his pleasant demeanour.

'You really shouldn't have been down to the coolies' lines,' he said in agitation. 'I never gave any such permission. If the manager finds out—'

'I'm looking for the son of a friend,' she said, standing her ground. 'I would like to tell her that I have seen him and that he is well.'

He gawped at her in disbelief. 'One of our coolies?'

'Please,' she asked. 'I promise I'll go after that. I'm not here to make trouble.'

With an impatient sigh, he strode to the mohurer's office and asked him to deal with her request.

'Then see that Miss Belhaven and her servant are escorted safely off the estate,' he said, and with a curt nod he left.

After a search through his records, the head mohurer shook his head in sorrow.

'I'm sorry. He died two months ago. Like many of the hill men, he was not suited to the climate here.'

'Or the conditions,' Clarrie muttered. Kamal steered her out of the office and back to their tonga before she caused another scene. Neither could bring themselves to speak until they were almost back to the Brahmaputra river.

The following weeks of clearing and packing up the house stopped Clarrie from dwelling too much on their approaching departure. With the house unsold, the bank was to take repossession and she was keen to leave before the humiliation of eviction. She had decided they must make the journey to England with what money they could scrape together from the sale of their personal possessions. An auction was held that brought curious visitors from the cantonment in Shillong; army wives and clerks keen to see the eccentric retreat of the Belhavens.

Clarrie sent Olive off with her sketchbook to avoid the gawping crowds and steeled herself to play hostess, serving out tea. At the end, there was hardly a chair left to sit on or book to read. She had drawn the line at Olive's violin, despite the pleadings of a policeman's wife who wanted it for her son. Olive's instrument was going with them to Newcastle, no matter what.

Tickets on the steamer from Calcutta to London were booked and Clarrie was anxious to leave before the monsoon started, when travel downriver became hazardous. Kamal had declined to go with them.

'I shall return to my village and run teashop,' he declared, 'maybe resthouse.'

Clarrie dreaded the moment she would have to say goodbye to Kamal and Ama. And Prince.

An army friend of Harry Wilson came up to buy Prince, offering a good price.

'No, he's not for sale!' she shouted, seeing the man giving her pony a good checking over.

Afterwards, Kamal tried to reason with her. 'You cannot take Prince to England. Your cousins have said so. Why not sell to soldier?'

Clarrie shook her head. 'I want to give him as a present to someone special who I know will look after him well.'

'You need rupees, Miss Clarissa,' Kamal sighed. 'Who is special someone? Not riff-raff in village?'

Clarrie laughed. 'Not riff-raff. You, Kamal. I want you to have Prince.'

His eyes widened in disbelief. He put his fist to his mouth and pretended to cough. 'I can't . . .' he spluttered.

'You can. I wish I could give you more for all you've done for us.'

'Thank you,' Kamal mumbled and turned from her to hide his tears.

On her final day at Belgooree, Clarrie got up before dawn and rode up to the swami's retreat. For the last time, she watched the sun rise and kiss the peaks of the Himalayas and listened to the stirrings in the forest. As she thought back to that fateful morning when Harry had shot the deer and Wesley had carried her unconscious to his tent, she wondered if things would be different now if she had never met them.

Wesley had stirred up the old bitter rivalry between Belhavens and Robsons and brought to a head the crisis over Belgooree's future. In the romantic solitude of this favourite place she could admit to having been attracted to him. Yet she despised herself for it. Wesley was driven and self-centred, and having seen the conditions in which Ramsha had lived and died at the Robsons' tea estate she would never forgive his heartlessness in tracking down Ama's favourite son. Her old nurse had been inconsolable at the news of Ramsha's death and the sound of her wailing and keening through the night had been almost unbearable.

The swami appeared and interrupted her thoughts. They greeted each other and the old man came forward and placed a garland of flowers around her neck as if he knew she was leaving. Into her hand he pressed a smooth pink stone, the colour of the mountains at sunrise. Touched, she thanked him and pulled a present for him from her pocket.

'They're seashells,' she explained, 'from a beach in Northumberland in England. My father kept them to remind himself of the sea – of his home. That's where I'm going. I've never seen this North Sea. My father said it's often the colour of storm clouds.' She put them into the hands of the holy man. 'I thought they would be nice in your garden.'

He nodded and smiled. As she left, he began to sing a high-pitched song of joy. She could hear it even after the jungle had closed about her again and he was long gone from sight.

Kamal cooked them scrambled eggs for breakfast that neither Olive nor she could eat. He was to accompany them as far as the steamer at Gowhatty and then go his separate way to West Bengal. The empty bungalow echoed to their footsteps as they took a last look round. On the veranda, Olive threw her arms about her and clung on.

'I don't want to go,' she wept. 'I'm sorry for all those things I said to you. I never meant them.'

Clarrie hugged her. 'I know you didn't.'

'Promise me you'll never leave me like Mother and Babu,' she pleaded.

'I promise,' Clarrie said, squeezing her tight. 'Now, come on. Kamal's waiting.'

With one last look at the closed and shuttered bungalow, she steered her weeping sister out of the compound and into the tonga that Kamal would drive while she rode Prince. They stopped in the village, and Ama came out with her daughters to tearfully hug them goodbye. Clarrie noticed Ama was wearing the brooch and necklace she had given her as a parting gift. They had belonged to her mother and now they were Ama's because she had been her substitute mother these past eight years.

'We will come back,' Clarrie promised, 'some day, you'll see.'

She was glad that she could ride behind the tonga for the next few hours through the jungle, where her weeping was drowned out by the screeching of birds and monkeys.

The following day they reached Gowhatty and the ghat where the steamer was moored. Here it was hot and humid and early rains had already swollen the river to twice the size it had been in April. Islands that had existed before were now submerged and the water was brown with silt carried down from the foothills.

In the garden of the resthouse, beside a defunct cannon, they said farewell to their beloved Kamal. Tears trickled into his beard as he allowed them to hug him goodbye and promised to let them know how he was doing from time to time.

'It is honour to know you and Belhaven sahib,' he croaked. 'May Allah protect you.'

'The honour was ours, Kamal.' Clarrie smiled and cried at the same time. 'You have been our greatest friend. Thank you.'

Then she stroked Prince and buried her face in his warm neck for one last time.

'Ride well, my Prince,' she whispered in his ear. The pony snorted and nuzzled her in disquiet as if he guessed at their parting.

Their last sight of Gowhatty, as the steamer pulled away from the busy ghat, was of Kamal astride Prince, saluting them. They waved and shouted to him until he was just a speck in the distance.

Numb, they sat on chairs on the foredeck and watched the wooded Garo hills to the east go by, far beyond which lay their home at Belgooree. As they progressed downriver, taking on passengers at Goalpara, the Brahmaputra widened almost into a sea. Crocodiles snoozed on sandbanks and the crew fished off the stern at night.

After two more days on board, they arrived at Rungpore, the railway junction from which they would journey onwards by train to Calcutta. Clarrie had only hazy memories of travelling this way with her parents in the days when they had gone to the big city for business, new outfits and a night at the theatre. Olive remembered none of it and grew more subdued and quieter the further from Assam they travelled. By the time they reached Calcutta and the mission house where they had booked two nights before leaving India, she had ceased to utter a word.

They sailed on the eighth of July, in a hot stifling wind, with the sun bouncing off the sea and dazzling the eyes. Clarrie had to squint and shade her eyes to catch the last glimpse of land as they juddered out into open sea. The teeming dockside with its chattering food sellers and cooking smells receded all too fast. India, the only home she had ever known, or ever wanted, vanished beyond her grasp.

Yet it was dark and the stars were littering the sky before either she or the silent Olive could bear to leave their post by the railings and retreat inside.

CHAPTER 6

Stepping off the train in the early morning into the echoing Central Station at Newcastle, Clarrie felt Olive's grip on her arm tighten like a vice. Everyone seemed to know where they were going in the cavernous building, summoning porters and rushing about with no time to spare for the strangely dressed young women in their bright woollen shawls and sola topis tied on with scarves.

'Don't worry,' Clarrie said. 'Cousin Jared promised he'd be here to meet us.'

They stood by their small trunk, arm in arm, waiting nervously for someone to claim them. They had sat up all night and were tired and hungry. As the platform cleared, Clarrie saw a man beckoning them from the barrier. She caught her breath. For an instant it could have been Jock, with the same bald head, long face and wiry frame. He stood with his hands on his hips too, in that impatient way of her father's. But the resemblance was fleeting. This man had enormous bushy sideburns that almost met in a beard and a potbelly that strained at the buttons of his brown waistcoat.

'Haway, lasses!' he bellowed. 'If it's Jared Belhaven you're after, then I'm your man.'

Clarrie saw that their cousin had no intention of paying to get on to the platform to help them. She bent to pick up one end of the trunk with one hand and Olive's violin with the other.

'Come on, Olive, grab the other end. It's not far.'

Her sister said nothing. But then she had hardly spoken during the whole of the long sea voyage, most of which she had spent confined to their cabin being seasick. As they struggled to the barrier with their luggage, a cheerful young porter hurried to help and tipped the trunk on to his trolley. He said something in a friendly fashion that Clarrie did not understand.

Jared greeted them with an awkward handshake. 'Jock's daughters, eh? Sorry 'bout yer father. Sad business.' He looked them over with undisguised curiosity. 'Well, which one's which?'

'I'm Clarissa – but Father always called me Clarrie. And this is Olive,' Clarrie said.

He smiled at Olive and pinched her cheek. 'You're a Belhaven all right – the spit of your father.' He added, less certainly, 'And Clarrie, you must look like your mother. I heard she was a bit Indian.'

'Yes,' Clarrie said, blushing. 'Half English, half Assamese.'

He gave her an odd look. 'Well, can't be helped.' Turning, he led them towards the entrance. 'Got the rolley waiting outside,' he told them mysteriously.

The rolley turned out to be a flat cart, pulled by a stout black pony. Jared ordered the porter to load the trunk on to the back. The boy stood whistling and waiting to be tipped. As Jared was ignoring him, Clarrie fished out one of her few remaining coins, a silver sixpence, and gave it to him. The boy's eyes widened in astonishment.

'Ta, miss,' he grinned, and pocketed it quickly.

As he disappeared, Jared rebuked her. 'A penny would've done. Doesn't do 'em any good to spoil 'em.' Before Clarrie could answer, he said, 'Where's the rest of yer luggage? Being sent on later, is it?'

'No, this is all we have,' Clarrie said.

He looked disbelieving, then shrugged. 'Well, no doubt you can buy some'at new to wear. My Lily won't mind takin' you to the shops.'

Clarrie nodded, though she wondered with what money they would buy new dresses. She would have to find work quickly, so as not to be a burden to her cousins.

Worries about money went quickly out of her mind as they clambered on to the cart and lurched out into the traffic. Jared whipped the pony into a trot, heading west. She and Olive gazed around open-mouthed at the vast, solid buildings on either side. Tall and bold, with elaborate stonework round doors and windows, their pitched roofs, cupolas and tall chimneypots thrust into the smoky grey sky.

Clarrie had seen grand buildings in Calcutta, but never such variety of styles, and all so blackened. The buildings in India had gleamed in the strong sunlight; here the stone was dark as soot.

Suddenly, Jared yanked them sideways to avoid an enormous, clanking vehicle. Olive squealed and clung to Clarrie as it towered above them, dinging its bell and rattling past.

'What was that?' Clarrie gasped.

Jared roared with laughter. 'Electric tram, lass. Do they not have 'em in India?'

'Not where we come from,' Clarrie said.

'Gets you into town in a jiffy,' he told them. 'But my Lily prefers to walk. God gave us legs to walk with, she says. And there's nowt you can't buy in the shops round Elswick, so what need is there to gan into the town?'

For the rest of the short journey, Jared chatted about his business. He ran a very respectable public house, or, as he preferred to call it, a hotel. There was a public bar and a sitting room where they charged a halfpenny more for waitress service. At the back, Lily had a very successful pie shop.

'We get them coming from all over for one of Lily's pies. Aye, even posh folk from Westgate Hill order regularly.' He glanced over at Clarrie. 'You said in yer letter you do cookin' and the like. You can give our Lily a hand in the kitchen while Olive helps me in the bar. Her young fresh face will cheer the customers no end.'

Olive gave Clarrie a horrified look.

'I'm happy to help out,' Clarrie answered, 'any spare time I have. But Olive's different — her health is delicate. And I was hoping she could go to school here.'

Jared jerked round in such surprise, he nearly fell off his seat.

'*School*? How old is she?'

'Just turned fifteen,' Clarrie said.

'Fifteen! Lasses round here start workin' at twelve or thirteen.' He barked with laughter as if she had told a great joke. 'No, no, you'll both have to earn yer keep.'

Clarrie's heart sank, but she gave her sister an encouraging smile. Olive's face grew more anxious the further they went. The grand buildings soon gave way to uniform rows of brick housing climbing up a steep bank, all belching smoke. Down to the left were factory sheds, cranes and hooting tugboats on a sludge-brown river. They trundled down a long street of shops, their windows shaded by faded awnings. It was already busy.

'This is Scotswood Road,' Jared told them proudly. 'You can buy owt under the sun along here.'

Clarrie stared at the shoppers on the dusty pavement, overdressed in heavy dark skirts and coats, even though it was promising to be a mild summer's day. As if to make up for the drabness of their clothing, they wore a wonderful variety of hats, wide-brimmed and adorned with ribbons, feathers and fake flowers.

A couple of barefoot boys, standing minding a carthorse, gawped up at them as they passed.

'Eeh, look at them lasses!' one exclaimed, pointing.

'Ganin' to a fancy dress ball, missus?' the other shouted.

Their exuberance reminded Clarrie of the village boys at home. She waved at them, which caused more shrieks of laughter.

'Take no notice,' Jared said. 'Couple of gutter-snipes.'

'I don't mind.' Clarrie smiled. 'We must look a bit funny in our sunhats.'

'Aye,' he grunted, 'you won't have much use for them round Elswick.' He swerved abruptly across the traffic and into a side street. 'This is Cherry Terrace,' he announced.

Clarrie hid her dismay. She had imagined a wide street of pretty cherry trees shading houses with railings and neat gardens. She had seen pictures of such English streets on the walls of the Pinewood Hotel in Shillong. But Cherry Terrace was narrow, cobbled and hemmed in by an unbroken chain of brick housing with not a blade of grass or tree in sight.

'Here we are!' Jared beamed, pulling up outside a row of dingy half-frosted windows. Above the doorway, faded gold lettering proclaimed it to be the Cherry Tree Hotel. 'You hop out here and I'll take Barny and the rolley round the back.'

Pushing open the front door, Clarrie was hit by a familiar nauseating smell of stale whisky and pipe smoke. Her father's study. She had to gulp down bile and banish the sudden image of Jock's emaciated body on the old camp bed. They were standing in a tiny hallway of dark varnished wood, with a door to the left marked 'Public Bar' and one to the right labelled 'Sitting Room'. The murmur of men's voices came from the bar. Surely no one was drinking this early in the day? Ahead was a third door, which Clarrie quickly opened.

'Cousin Lily?' she called.

They were immediately in a parlour-cum-kitchen and the smell of boiled meat was overpowering. Large pans steamed on a kitchen range and a sturdy table was covered in flour and rolled-out pastry. The wooden floor was bare and well scrubbed, the furniture spartan with only one upholstered chair by the fire. No pictures or ornaments hung on the walls, except for a gaudily illustrated religious tract about choosing the narrow gate. *Many will try but few will get in*, it warned.

Clarrie glanced at Olive, whose face was a sickly tinge of grey. Quickly, she steered her sister on to a kitchen stool. A small, burly woman with sleeves rolled up over thick arms and greying hair pulled into a tight bun bustled in from the scullery.

'Cousin Lily,' Clarrie said with a smile, holding out her hand.

'Mrs Belhaven to you,' the woman answered, ignoring the gesture.

'Of course,' Clarrie said, introducing herself and her sister.

'What's wrong with you?' Lily asked Olive. 'You look a bit green around the gills.'

'She's been very ill all the time at sea,' Clarrie explained. 'She could do with a few days in bed to recover and get her strength back.'

Lily snorted. 'No one in my household lies about in bed.' She approached Olive and put a hand to her forehead. Olive recoiled at the smell of onions on her rough fingers. 'Looks like you could do with a bit of feeding up, mind. You're a bag of bones. Do you like pork pie?'

'We don't eat pork,' Clarrie said.

Lily gave her an incredulous look. 'Why ever not?'

'Our khansama, Kamal, couldn't cook it. He's Muslim, you see. So we never did either.'

Lily blew out her cheeks as if scandalised by such talk. 'Well, you'll eat what you're given here and be grateful. I told Mr Belhaven he was asking for trouble having a couple of lasses under the roof. But he's as soft as putty. Says you're family and he couldn't do owt else. Though I don't know why he feels so beholden to that cousin of his. Jock was always a bad penny. Fancy wasting his army pension on a bit of jungle among them heathens. It was never going to come to any good.'

Without drawing breath, she continued to lecture

as she stirred the pots on the range. 'Now here you are, two orphans that we must take under our wing, as if we didn't have enough trouble trying to feed ourselves and keep a respectable business in this part of town. Still, the Lord sends these things to try us.'

Suddenly, Olive let out an anguished wail and burst into tears. Clarrie rushed to put her arms round her.

'What ever's the matter with her?' Lily cried.

'You've upset her with your talk of orphans, that's what,' Clarrie said. 'She's just a girl still and she's left behind the only home she's ever known thousands of miles away. Can't you see how frightening that is?'

Lily stared at her as if unused to anyone answering back. She huffed with disapproval, but came over and put a hand on Olive's bowed head.

'There's no need to cry, lass. I won't have tears in my kitchen. If you don't like pork you can have cheese and potato. Folk can't get enough of my cheese and potato pie. It's me most popular. Would you like that?'

Clarrie nodded. 'She'd like that very much, thank you.'

Lily stood back. 'Goodness me, can the lass not speak for herself or do you just like the sound of your own voice?'

Abruptly, Clarrie laughed. 'A bit of both, Mrs Belhaven.'

But Lily's stern face showed she had not meant to be humorous. Quickly Clarrie stood up. 'Can I help with anything?'

At that moment, Jared threw open the back door and entered.

'Ah, it's grand to see the pair of you getting on so well,' he said, beaming.

Lily snorted and gave her husband a withering glance. 'Get yourself out front. Those men want serving and I don't trust that lad Harrison not to undercharge.'

Jared went meekly, winking at Clarrie as if they were sharing a joke.

Exhausted from travelling though she was, Clarrie spent the rest of the day helping Lily to bake pies and listening attentively to her voluble criticisms of their customers, neighbours and rivals. She persuaded her to let Olive go to bed early, but by the time she was allowed to join her sister after the pub closed, Clarrie's head throbbed and her eyes ached with tiredness.

The attic room that was to be their bedroom was no bigger than the storeroom at Belgooree and almost as dark, with only one small filthy skylight for a window. They were to share a single bed, a table and one chair, and two tea chests balanced one on top of the other in which to store their few clothes. While there were gas lamps in the public rooms downstairs, they were given one candle to light their way from their bedroom down to the latrine in the back yard. 'Make it last the week,' Lily warned. They were to wash in the scullery.

Olive was petrified of the long descent past the Belhavens' bedroom and the spare room that was let out to travellers and allowed them to boast that their establishment was a hotel. Clarrie had to go with her. While she stood guard in the chilly yard, she leaned over the half-door of the adjacent shed to pet Barny. As she nuzzled the horse and breathed in his smell, she experienced a deep pang of loss for Prince and her past life.

What were Kamal and Prince doing now? How were Ama and her family? Was anyone living at Belgooree? She hated to think of strangers occupying her home, but hated more the thought that it might decay, unsold and unloved.

Back in the attic, the sisters lay sleepless and anxious about what lay ahead.

'I can't bear it here – this room's like a prison cell,' Olive whispered. 'And that woman's a bully. I'll not work in their horrible bar. They can't make me.'

'Don't worry,' Clarrie assured her, 'we won't stay here long. I'll find a good position.'

Olive clung to her. 'You won't leave me here, will you?'

'Of course I won't! How could you think such a thing? I'll always look after you, I promise.'

It seemed to Clarrie she had only just fallen asleep when a loud hammering on their door woke her.

'Time to get up, lasses,' Jared shouted, 'there are jobs to be done. No lying in bed today.'

As Clarrie groaned and struggled out of bed, Olive pulled the thin covers over her head and burst into tears.

CHAPTER 7

By the end of the week, Clarrie was near exhaustion. She had never worked as hard: up at five to stoke the fires, cooking and cleaning for Lily, serving customers and washing glasses for Jared until late at night. Her back ached constantly from heaving in buckets of coal from the coal shed and her hands were red raw from washing up.

But she was partly to blame for her workload. Right from the start, she stood firm over Olive. 'She's too young to be serving grown men in the bar,' Clarrie insisted, 'and the smoke from their pipes will set off her wheezing.'

'Well, I need someone to serve in the sitting room,' Jared grumbled, 'specially when it's busy of an evening.'

'How did you manage before?' Clarrie dared to ask.

'Had a lass – about Olive's age – workin' for us,' he said pointedly.

'She was useless,' Lily snapped. 'And once we knew you were coming, we got rid of her.'

Clarrie hid her dismay. 'I'll do it then,' she said. What ever her cousins thought, the situation would just be temporary.

'What about the young lass?' Lily retorted. 'Don't think she can sit around like royalty – we can't afford it. She'll have to do her bit to earn her keep.'

'She's very good with her hands,' Clarrie said, 'she can sew and mend. And she can help with the pie making if you teach her how to make pastry.'

'You've never made pastry?' Lily exclaimed.

'No, our khansama—' Clarrie broke off. She had quickly learned that her cousins hated any mention of their life in India or reference to their having had servants. She smiled. 'We'd be grateful if you taught us.'

Olive submitted to being confined to Lily's kitchen, though she hated letting Clarrie out of her sight. For her part, Clarrie found the evenings serving customers were preferable to being lectured and criticised by Lily. Having dreaded going into the smoky bar, she was surprised to find the men mainly congenial and friendly. Jared had boasted about her growing up on his cousin's tea plantation.

'By, it's the Empress of India!'

'How's the memsahib today?'

'Haway, hinny, fill it up.'

'See yer the morra, Clarrie pet. Gan canny!'

The one chore she baulked at was cleaning out the spittoon at the bar entrance. It made her gag.

'I'll not do it,' she told Jared.

He relented. 'That lad Harrison can manage, I suppose.'

'That lad Harrison' was a chubby-faced man in his thirties who needed everything explaining to him three times before he did it. Jared supervised him in the bar and he also delivered pies on the rolley. He got confused if his route was changed and upset if anyone shouted at him. But most of the time he was cheerful and eager to help. To Clarrie's relief Harrison found nothing repugnant in cleaning out the gobbets of spit in the brass spittoon.

In the sitting room, Clarrie was astonished to find herself serving women as well as men. Some came in with their husbands for half a pint of stout or a sweet sherry; others were unchaperoned. When she mentioned this to Lily, the woman sniffed in disapproval.

'Common as muck, of course. But long as they pay up and don't cause trouble among the men, we put up with them.'

Clarrie felt sorry for these women. Most of them looked undernourished and tired out. They would get merry on one or two drinks and start up a singsong. Sometimes they had children in tow whom Jared made stand outside.

One hot, late afternoon, when Clarrie took some

children cups of water on a tray, Jared lost his temper.

'What do you think you're doing? We're not a bloody charity!'

'But they're thirsty,' Clarrie said, shocked at his vehemence. She had never seen him this angry – she was almost frightened.

'And we'll have half the ragamuffins in the neighbourhood queuing up if they see how soft you are,' he shouted. 'Now get back to serving paying customers and don't ever do that again.'

After he had stalked off, the women in the sitting room consoled her.

'Don't listen to him, the miserable old bugger,' said one in a huge purple hat.

'Aye, he's just frightened of that dragon of a wife finding out,' a younger one sniggered. 'She hates bairns.'

'Ta, hinny, it was a canny thought,' a third said, draining her drink and getting stiffly to her feet. Clarrie noticed that she moved with a serious limp.

The women seemed decent enough, though there was a sour smell about them and their shoes were worn thin. She wanted to ask them why they came into such a dismal place where they could not take their children, but did not want to offend them.

'Well, it's a treat to be served by the likes of ye,' the limping one called Ina said, smiling. 'You've got a bonny face and a canny voice.'

'Aye, you're much too posh for this place,' grinned

Lexy, the youngest woman. 'Where'd old Mutton-chops find ye?'

'I'm family,' Clarrie answered. 'My parents are dead. Cousin Jared's taken me in – and my sister, Olive.'

The women commiserated with her. Their kindness nearly made her weep.

'You take care of yoursel', hinny. You're like a ray of sunshine after that battleaxe in there.' Maggie, the one in the purple hat, pulled a face and nodded towards the kitchen. 'Always looking down her nose at the likes of us.'

Ina lowered her voice. 'She's nee better. Me mam was the midwife brought her into the world and it wasn't into a palace, I can tell you. Lily-no-stockings, they used to call her.'

'Aye, that's why she's so mean,' Lexy added. 'Waters down the beer an' all. Bet she lords it over you. None of the other lasses could stick it for five minutes.'

'Other lasses?'

Lexy nodded. 'They've had more waitresses working here than I've had hot dinners.'

Clarrie smiled. 'Oh, I'll not be staying long either. Just as soon as I can find another position.'

The women hooted with laughter. 'Position, eh?'

'Well, good on yer, hinny,' said Ina.

'Haway, Maggie,' Lexy giggled to her friend. 'We must gan back to our "positions" at the washhouse!'

They clattered out of the pub with a cheerful

farewell. Despite their teasing, Clarrie laughed as she cleared up and hoped she would see them again.

To her relief, Sunday came and a promised late rising. But Clarrie was woken from a deep sleep by knocking at half past six. There were chores to be done and Sunday lunch to prepare before church at eleven. At ten thirty they assembled for the walk to church. Lily, dressed in a navy frock with black coat and black raffia hat, looked askance at Clarrie's peach dress and Olive's primrose yellow.

'Do you not have coats?' she asked.

'Just our shawls,' Clarrie said. 'We'll have to buy coats for winter.'

'You'll need them before then,' Lily was adamant. 'Can't have you ganin' to church looking like you're off to a dance. I'll look in the thrift shop tomorra. And you can't wear those hats!'

She bustled off to find something more suitable and came back with an old-fashioned lilac bonnet, which she plonked on Clarrie's head. Ignoring her protests, Lily tied it on with a huge black ribbon under her chin.

'That'll have to do,' she grunted. 'Olive's young enough to get away without a hat. We'll find her one for next week.'

Jared and Lily led the way up Cherry Terrace with the sisters trailing behind. So restricted by the bonnet was her view that Clarrie had to swivel her head left and right to see around her. Olive, subdued and quiet all week, got the giggles.

'You do look funny,' she whispered.

'I feel as if I'm in a tunnel,' Clarrie said. 'Let me know if I'm about to be run over by a tram, won't you?'

Olive slipped her arm through hers. 'You look like Little Bo Peep.'

'I feel like Old Mother Hubbard!'

They smothered their laughter as Lily glanced round with a glare of disapproval.

At the top of the hill, Lily and Jared stopped to catch their breath. Clarrie gazed about her. It was a sunny day and the first time since arriving that they had left the confines of the Cherry Tree Hotel. The hazy riverside snaked away into the distance, bounded on both sides by industrial sprawl and tightly packed housing. Beyond, though, were gently sloping green hills with clumps of woodland. Clarrie had a passionate urge to be free of the ridiculous bonnet and riding across those mysterious hills.

'Where is that?' she asked, pointing.

'That's County Durham to the south,' Jared answered. 'And west, and north,' he swung his arm in an expansive gesture, 'that's all Northumberland.'

Clarrie's heart missed a beat. Northumberland, the home of her father!

'Can you see Father's farm from here?' she asked in excitement.

'No, lass! That was miles to the north – and near the sea.'

'Will you take us there sometime?' Clarrie asked.

'Certainly not!' Lily interrupted. 'We haven't time for day trips. And there's nothing up there to see – just grass and water.'

At that moment Clarrie yearned for fresh grass and clear water. For an instant, she imagined herself back in the clearing by the swami's hut. The place where fate had thrown her together with Wesley Robson. Strange to think of him now. How he would enjoy seeing her brought so low after she had spurned him, Clarrie thought with annoyance. At least he was never likely to discover her in working-class Elswick.

She swallowed her disappointment at Lily's dismissive words, but was all the more determined that she would, one day, discover her father's old home.

The Belhavens worshipped at the John Knox Presbyterian Church on Elswick Road, an imposing building with a pillared frontage and a first floor gallery. Its pews were packed. Jared led them into one halfway down the aisle. The church was plain in comparison to the garrison church in Shillong or the nuns' chapel, with no candles or incense or priests in colourful robes. Jock, notionally Anglican, had seldom taken them to church.

Yet Clarrie remembered times when her Catholic-raised mother had held simple services in the garden at Belgooree on saints' days and the air had been noisy with birds. Sometimes her mother had taken her and Olive down to the village to observe the local festivals and to lay gifts of food on the temple steps. Clarrie had loved the exuberance of such occasions, when drums clashed and the people danced and sang, and they all got covered in red dye or garlands of flowers.

This service was far more sombre, with many prayers and a long sermon. Yet when it came to the hymn singing, the boom of organ and voices nearly took the roof off. Olive joined in, her pale face lighting up at the welcome music like a flower opening in sunshine. So far, Lily had forbidden Olive to practise her violin. 'Don't hold with fiddles – instruments of the devil. They lead to dancing and sinfulness.'

At the end of the long service, the smartly dressed and wealthiest members of the congregation filed out first from the front pews. A handsome middle-aged couple – the man tall, greying, clutching a top hat and walking with a stick, the woman florid with pretty blue eyes and noticeably pregnant – stopped by the Belhavens' pew.

'Good morning, Mrs Belhaven.' The man smiled. 'I hope you are well?'

Clarrie watched in astonishment as Lily blushed and simpered. 'Grand, thank you, Mr Stock. I hope the steak and kidney pie was to your liking?'

'Excellent,' he replied. 'Wasn't it, Louisa?' The man turned to the woman hanging on his arm.

'One of your best,' she assured Lily. 'Do send Harrison round for an order tomorrow. Mr Stock has clients to entertain later in the week and your pies are always popular at luncheon.'

Lily did a bob that was almost a curtsey. 'Yes, Mrs Stock, I'd be pleased to oblige.'

The Stocks exchanged pleasantries with Jared, Mr Stock giving Clarrie and Olive a curious glance. But when Jared made no attempt to introduce them, he and his wife moved on. Behind them came a tall young man not much older than Clarrie who so resembled Mr Stock that he was obviously a son, and a boy of about twelve with floppy fair hair and attractive blue eyes and an open smile like his mother's.

'Hello, Mrs Belhaven,' the younger boy grinned. 'Do you think you could take out the kidneys next time? Mama and I are not very partial to them.'

'Quiet, Will!' His father turned to reprimand him. 'Take no notice, Mrs Belhaven. Will speaks and then thinks afterwards. Don't change an ounce of your recipes, they're delicious.'

As they turned away, Clarrie caught Will's look and smiled. The boy blushed and hurried after his parents.

On the walk home, Clarrie asked about the Stocks. Jared puffed up his chest and said importantly, 'Mr Stock's a very respected solicitor. Lives in Summerhill off Westgate Road – very posh. I've used his services mesel'. Helped me buy them pair of flats in Benwell, didn't he, Lily?'

'Don't you go telling the lass our private business,' she scolded.

Jared looked apologetic. 'No, course not, dear.' He

cleared his throat. 'Anyways, Mr Stock's a real gentleman, and his missus – well, you can tell she's a cut above the rest.'

'Mind you,' Lily sniffed, 'it's not very ladylike to be expectin' at her age, if you ask me. Not right at all.'

'What's she expecting?' Olive piped up.

Lily went red. Clarrie said quickly, 'I think Mrs Belhaven means that Mrs Stock's going to have a baby soon.'

Olive gasped. 'Really? But isn't she too old? Her sons must be—'

'That's quite enough gossip about Mrs Stock and her family,' Jared interrupted, embarrassed by such frank talk. They continued the rest of the way in silence.

That afternoon, after a solid lunch of pork pie and vegetables, sponge pudding and custard, the sisters discovered just how dull a Sunday could be with their cousins. Before the Belhavens went off to lie down upstairs, Lily instructed them to wash up.

'Then you can rest,' she said with a magnanimous smile.

'I think we'll go out for a walk,' Clarrie answered. 'It's a lovely day, and I noticed a park on our way back—'

'*Walk*?' Lily cried. 'No, no, there's to be no ganin' out on a Sunday afternoon. If it's exercise you want, you can gan back to church for the evening service.'

Clarrie stared in disbelief. 'We've had hardly any

fresh air all week. What harm will a stroll round the park do?'

'Two lasses out on their own in the park?' Lily clucked. 'The place is full of undesirables! You'll stop in the house and read the Bible, that's what you'll do.'

'We're not children,' Clarrie replied, trying to keep her temper, 'and we're used to more freedom than this.' She would have said she used to ride on her own every day for hours at a time without coming to any harm, but knew that would antagonise the woman further.

'Well, for better or worse, you're living with us now,' Lily said, 'and you'll abide by our rules. Isn't that right, Mr Belhaven?' She gave her husband a stern look.

He nodded in embarrassment. 'Just put your feet up, eh, lasses? Sunday's a day of rest. Be glad of it.'

'Have the kettle boiling for tea at four o'clock,' Lily ordered. Jared smiled awkwardly and hurried after his wife.

The washing up done, Clarrie and Olive stared morosely at the large leather-bound Bible left on the fireside table. It was stiflingly hot in the kitchen. Clarrie thought she would go mad if she did not go out.

'We'll wait till they've fallen asleep,' she said quietly, 'then we'll go.'

'We can't!' Olive gasped.

'Yes we can.'

'But she'll find out,' Olive fretted. 'She's got eyes in the back of her head.'

'Even if she does, what can she do but shout?' Clarrie shrugged. 'And she does that anyway.'

'She'll throw us out and then we'll have nowhere – not even this hovel to call home. And they'll put us in the union workhouse and we'll be separated and—'

'That's not going to happen,' Clarrie insisted, putting her arms about her sister. 'Cousin Lily knows when she's on to a good thing – she's got us slaving for her like coolies. And it's not as if they're short of money; they're just mean. Cousin Jared let slip about their having property in Benwell as well as this place. I wondered where he was going yesterday in his suit and bowler hat. He must've been collecting rent, cos he came back and handed over money to Lily.' She squeezed Olive's shoulders. 'She'll not want to lose us, that Mrs Scrooge. For all she pretends that we're a burden, she's tickled pink at the idea of having her own servants. Thinks it puts her upsides with the likes of the Stocks.'

'She's not a bit like them,' Olive declared. 'She sounded ridiculous putting on that voice.'

Clarrie stood up and mimicked Lily, curtseying to her sister. 'Less kidney in your pies? Yes, Mrs Stock, I'd be pleased to oblige.'

Olive sniggered. Clarrie carried on.

'Mind you, a woman expecting at your age, it's

just not ladylike. You should've spent your Sunday afternoons indoors reading the Bible, not,' she took a dramatic breath, 'walking in the park and enjoying yourself!'

Olive smothered a giggle.

Clarrie grinned. 'Come on, let's go out and look for some undesirables.'

Olive got up and bobbed towards her. 'Yes, Mrs Stock, I'd be pleased to oblige!'

The park that Clarrie had glimpsed on their walk back from church was a sizeable one, neatly laid out with flower beds and benches, bowling greens and a brightly painted bandstand. To their delight, the park was full of people enjoying the sunshine, strolling in families or sitting listening to a brass band. They walked about, taking in the sights and observing the fashions. Their own dresses looked fussy and puffed up in comparison with the straighter cut of those around them. Yet many wore elaborately trimmed blouses and voluminous hats.

'I want one of those hats with huge pink roses and lime green ostrich feathers,' Clarrie declared.

'You'll look like the garden at Belgooree,' Olive teased.

Clarrie grinned. 'Exactly.'

'Then I want one with a parrot on,' Olive said, 'and bamboo leaves.'

'Well, I want one with two parrots and a monkey.'

'Two parrots, a monkey and a hibiscus bush,' Olive countered.

Clarrie snorted, 'Five parrots, a tiger, a betel tree and . . .'

'A Scots pine!' Olive cried.

Clarrie curtsied. 'Yes, Mrs Stock, I'd be happy to oblige.'

They both burst out laughing, light-headed at having escaped into the cheery sunlit park. People stopped and looked round, smiling sympathetically at the pretty, brightly dressed pair. They walked on, arm in arm, joking and giggling, drawing the admiring attention of young men who took their hands out of their pockets to tip their caps and grin as they passed.

Too soon, a clock on the pavilion told them it was already half past three. As they turned reluctantly to go, a steel hoop came hurtling down the path and caught Clarrie on the leg.

'Sorry!' a boy cried breathlessly, catching the hoop before it veered off into the road.

Startled, Clarrie turned to see the blushing face of Will Stock.

'That boy!' his father exclaimed, catching up. 'I'm terribly sorry. Are you hurt?'

'No, I'm not,' Clarrie assured him. 'I just got a shock.'

'Will! Apologise at once,' he said crossly, hauling the boy up by his jacket collar. The hoop fell from his grasp and clattered to the ground.

'Sorry,' Will said, puce-faced. 'I'm not very good with hoops – or any sports really. Except for riding.'

'The young lady doesn't need to know all that,' his father said impatiently. 'Just sorry would have done.'

Clarrie touched Will on the arm. 'Don't worry, I'll live. I'll walk bow-legged for the rest of my life but I'll live.'

The boy's eyes widened in alarm. Clarrie laughed. 'I was teasing. Of course I'm all right. The hoop was nothing. Where I come from you have to watch out for snakes and tigers on a Sunday walk.'

'Really?' Will gasped. 'You're not from Newcastle then?'

Clarrie smiled. 'No. We grew up in India. But we live here now.'

'Gosh, will you tell me about it?'

His father intervened. 'Not now, Will.' He scrutinised Clarrie with dark blue eyes. 'Haven't we met before?'

Clarrie nodded. 'After church this morning. We were with the Belhavens.'

'Ah, yes!' He nodded. Then he frowned again. 'But I don't quite see . . .'

'I'm Clarrie Belhaven, and this is my sister Olive. We're cousins of Mr Belhaven and – er – circumstances have brought us here.'

She was about to offer her hand when she saw how rough and reddened it looked and snatched it back. He nodded to her and the mute Olive. 'Herbert Stock,' he said.

She could see he was intrigued, but at that moment his older son appeared on the path with a slim, well-dressed young woman on his arm. Large hazel eyes dominated her sharp nose and small mouth, which she pursed in disapproval at this interruption to their promenade.

'Father, is Will causing mayhem as usual?' the older brother drawled. He had his father's even features and blue eyes, but his hair was prematurely receding and his chin was fleshy from too many rich dinners.

'On the contrary, he's found us two new friends, the Misses Belhaven,' Herbert answered. 'This is my elder son, Bertie, and a family friend, Verity Landsdowne.'

Bertie nodded at the sisters in a bored fashion, not attempting to shake hands. 'Are you related to the pie people?' he asked.

Clarrie flushed. 'Yes, but—'

'Jolly good,' Bertie interrupted. 'Plain but honest fare.' He turned away.

Verity sighed. 'It's so hot, Bertie. Do you think we could go back in the brougham now?'

'Of course,' Bertie agreed, and they moved off. Clarrie could see a pretty dappled grey mare and a carriage at the end of the pathway.

'Can we offer you a ride home?' Herbert asked.

'That's very kind,' Clarrie said, still smarting from Bertie's rudeness, 'but we like to walk. We don't have the chance—' She broke off, not wanting to have to describe her menial working week to this sophisticated professional man. In Indian society she would have been on a par with such as the Stocks, but here she was very much his social inferior. Still, that was no excuse for Bertie's offhandedness. She had found more common courtesy among the labourers of Elswick than he had in his little finger, she thought angrily.

Herbert doffed his hat in farewell, calling to Will to follow. Will, having retrieved his hoop, gave Clarrie a bashful smile.

'Watch out for the snakes and tigers,' he joked.

'We will,' Clarrie smiled. 'And keep practising the hoop.'

He waved at them and ran after his father.

By the time they got back to Cherry Terrace it was almost four and Lily was banging around in the kitchen making tea, her face thunderous.

'How dare you disobey me?' she upbraided them. 'You've broken the Sabbath day and brought disgrace on my house!'

Clarrie stood her ground. 'I'm sorry if we've upset you, but we were brought up to rejoice in God's fresh air and creation.'

'You were raised as little better than heathens,' Lily hissed. 'You've hardly darkened a church door – so don't you preach to me about God's creation. He made the seventh day as a day of rest and that means stopping in the house and reading the Bible.'

'A day of rest?' Clarrie exclaimed. 'I've been up since half past six doing chores! And Olive and I spent an hour washing up before we went out.

Sundays are supposed to be a rest from the working week and that means getting out and enjoying the sunshine as much as sleeping off Sunday dinner.'

Lily, crimson-faced, was momentarily speechless. Jared came in looking bleary-eyed.

'What's all the noise about, lasses?'

Lily stabbed a finger at Clarrie. 'That one – the wicked tongue on her—'

'We went for a walk, Cousin Jared,' Clarrie explained. 'I'm sorry for the upset.'

Jared gawped at her, taken aback by her boldness and unsure what to say.

'Tell her,' Lily ordered. 'Tell her she's never to do it again.'

Jared looked uncomfortable, pulling on his bushy sideburns. 'Well . . .'

'I don't see how it can be a sin,' Clarrie said quickly, 'when Mr Stock and his sons think it fine to walk in the park on a Sunday.'

'Mr Stock?' Jared queried. 'You saw him?'

Clarrie nodded and told them of the incident with the hoop. 'Bertie Stock mentioned how good your pies were again, Mrs Belhaven.'

'That's grand, isn't it?' Jared gave a cautious smile.

Confusion showed in Lily's face, but she would not be mollified. 'It's a matter for the Stocks and their conscience if they choose to flout the Sabbath. It won't happen in my house and as long as you live here, you'll do as we do.'

Clarrie was about to argue further, but caught

sight of Olive's anxious face. The girl was terrified of getting into trouble and Lily might take it out on her during the week when Clarrie was too busy in the pub to protect her. No use antagonising Lily when there were more important issues such as work and wages to be tackled.

Clarrie swallowed down her rebellious words and said, 'I'm sorry. I didn't realise how much it would upset you. We won't do it again.'

The tea that followed was subdued, with Jared the only one trying to jolly along the conversation. Soon afterwards, the sisters escaped to their stuffy attic room and lay with the skylight jammed open, listening to the evening chatter of starlings and the sound of children chasing each other down the back lane.

Clarrie could barely believe that they had only been there a week. It was hard to imagine they had led any other existence. India seemed impossibly remote, a dream she had made up or that had happened to someone else. She saw how easily they could be ground down by the day-to-day drudgery of life in Cherry Terrace and Lily's strict rule. It must be like this for countless thousands of workers, when just reaching the end of each gruelling day was triumph enough.

Clarrie knew then, in the confines of that dingy room, that she was going to have to fight to keep the memories of that other life alive, if she was not to lose hope. Pulling the swami's small pink stone on its leather cord from under her cotton shift, she fingered its smoothness and closed her eyes. She was once again riding through the coolness of the forest and trotting into the hermit's clearing just as the dawn broke over the mountains.

Clarrie let the tears come as she gripped the pebble and forced herself to remember. Nothing and no one, she vowed, would ever take away her precious memories, or blight the spirit of Jock Belhaven's daughter.

CHAPTER 8

Christmas Eve, 1905

'I'll go,' Clarrie volunteered, dashing back into the kitchen with a tray of dirty glasses. 'I'm used to horses and Barny knows me.'

'But it's very icy, lass.' Jared frowned. 'Perhaps I should go?'

'The bar's heaving,' Clarrie pointed out.

'Aye, you're needed here, Jared,' Lily snapped, giving Harrison, who was lying on the hard bench, a furious look, 'with that lad next to useless. There're twenty pies to deliver.'

Harrison lay crying quietly, his ankle bandaged after falling down the cellar steps to change a barrel of beer. It was their busiest day of the year and Lily was even more short-tempered than usual.

'Clarrie will have to go,' Lily sighed. 'Olive can

help in the sitting room – it's time she learned to pull her weight in the pub.'

Clarrie was about to object that Lily should be the one helping out now the pies were finished, but Olive quickly agreed.

'I'll do it,' she said, wiping her hands dry and smoothing back her red hair.

'Let me show you then,' Clarrie said.

'I know what to do,' Olive replied, though her look was anxious, 'I've watched you long enough.'

Clarrie threw her a look of surprise, but Lily was approving.

'See, you mollycoddle that lass too much. She's not a bairn. I'll see she does it proper – you get yoursel' off on the pie round.'

With a comforting word to Harrison, Clarrie loaded up the cart and led Barny out into the lane, patting his neck and whispering encouragement. The pony was nervous and skittish on the ice and Clarrie led him firmly by the reins, not attempting to climb on to the rolley. At the top of the bank, she breathed a sigh of relief. It was bitterly cold, the air sharp and the light nearly gone from the grey winter sky. Yet she felt a surge of excitement to be out in the dusk with the shops along Elswick Road decorated for Christmas with holly and colourful glass baubles.

She had bought Olive a sketchbook and pencils with the meagre wages she had extracted from the Belhavens. It had been one of several battles with Lily over the past few months. It had become clear early on that they had no intention of letting Clarrie find a job elsewhere.

'No one will employ the two of you together,' Jared had said, 'so there's no point lookin'.'

'That's all the thanks we get,' Lily had huffed, 'for takin' you in when no one else would? You'd be homeless if it weren't for our charity. The least you can do is help us out.'

'We are grateful for what you've done. But we've been working here very hard for a month with no wages. If we're staying we should get paid,' Clarrie had insisted.

'You get board and lodgings,' Lily retorted.

'But we've nothing to buy clothes with and we need boots for the winter. We need our own money. You could pay us what you paid the other lasses and then take off what's fair for our board and keep.'

Grudgingly, with Jared's encouragement, Lily had agreed to give them four shillings pocket money a week, a shilling of which they had to put in the collection plate every Sunday. The sisters had become adept at spotting bargains in the second-hand clothes shops around Scotswood Road and making their own underwear and nightclothes from cheap cuts of material from the draper's. But the paltry wages meant they could save nothing and were in no position to look for somewhere else to live. Besides, Clarrie would not know where to start. She had not been beyond Elswick and the west end of Newcastle since their arrival, nor seen the city's grand centre again. She had fought and lost the battle for an afternoon off a week.

'There's too much to do,' Lily had been dismissive, 'and we've never given ourselves an afternoon off in years.'

'It's not safe to gan into town on your own, lasses,' Jared had concurred. 'One day we'll take you for a look round, though there's nowt much to see.'

Clarrie did not believe him. Even from her limited view from the top of Elswick she could see the elegant spires of the city churches and cathedral, and the ornate sweep of Georgian rooftops beneath the pall of smoke.

She determined to enjoy her moment of freedom now and went about her deliveries with a light step, consulting the scrap of paper with the route and addresses. There were four houses in north Elswick to visit, plus a nursing home, a boarding house and cocoa rooms on Westgate Road. Peering inside the latter, Clarrie felt a stab of nostalgia at the sound of teacups clinking and groups of men warming themselves round a blazing fire playing cards and draughts. They had spent many a frosty winter's evening at Belgooree drinking tea and playing board games, with the scent of wood smoke filling the air. The smell here though was the acrid mineral smell of burning coal to which she was growing used.

She pressed on to her last delivery, the Stocks at Summerhill, as the street lamps lit up. Clarrie wondered what she would find at the tall elegant town house, nestling discreetly in a quiet square off busy Westgate Road. A month ago, Louisa Stock had abruptly stopped coming to church.

'She'll be confined to the house with the new bairn,' Jared had guessed.

'Aye, Mrs Stock won't be seen out the house till after the baptism,' Lily agreed. 'Wouldn't be proper.'

But no christening was announced and what puzzled Clarrie more were the long faces of the Stock men as they hurried from the Sunday service without stopping to chat. Only Will slowed at the Belhavens' pew end to give Clarrie a bashful smile, but he no longer stopped to chat about hoops or horses as he had done since their encounter in the park. Something was not right, and as Clarrie descended the steps to the basement kitchen, she hoped that no illness had befallen the friendly Louisa.

Will was the first person she saw, perched on top of the kitchen table, swinging his legs and eating a banana.

'Clarrie!' he cried. 'What are you doing here? Are those mince pies? They smell like mince pies – my favourite!'

A young girl in a kitchen maid's apron and cap shooed him off the table. 'Don't let Cook catch you up there. Ta,' she said to Clarrie, taking the tray of pies. 'You're new, aren't you?'

'She's a cousin of Mr Belhaven's from India, Dolly,' Will piped up.

'Don't tell stories,' the girl scolded.

Clarrie laughed. 'It's true.'

Dolly stared at her as if she had two heads. 'Fancy!' She backed away with the tray through a pantry door. 'Better hide these from Cook – she hates it that the master likes Belhaven's pies better than hers. She'll be handing these out to the Salvation Army if she finds them first.'

'Come and see my nativity figures,' Will said to Clarrie, taking her by the arm.

Clarrie hesitated, looking at her dirty boots and threadbare jacket. 'I can't go up like this.'

'Yes you can,' Will insisted, 'it's only in the hallway. You won't have to stand on the carpet.'

Dolly reappeared. 'I wouldn't worry. No one's ganin' to see you. The master and Mr Bertie are still at the office and the mistress is in bed.'

'I thought they'd be the type to have half the neighbourhood in for the celebrations,' Clarrie said.

'Not this year.'

'Has something happened?'

Dolly glanced cautiously at Will. 'Not for me to say.'

'Come on, Clarrie,' Will said impatiently, dragging her towards the kitchen door.

'Just for a minute then,' she relented. 'I can't leave Barny out there in the cold for too long.'

He led her up a flight of stone steps to the ground floor and through a green baize door. An open door across the darkened hallway showed a large drawing room also in darkness save for the eerie glow of a street lamp through the uncurtained windows. A broad staircase climbed away into the gloom, its banisters undecorated. As far as she could see, there were no decorations anywhere, or preparations for Christmas. Disappointingly, the house appeared empty, unlit and chilly.

Clarrie clutched on to Will, unsure of her way in the dark.

'It's just up on the landing,' Will said, guiding her towards the stairs.

'You said it was in the hallway,' Clarrie faltered. 'I'm not sure I should be here.'

'Please, Clarrie!'

She could hear the note of desperation in his voice. She allowed herself to be led upwards.

Soft light flickered at the end of the landing and Clarrie saw a nativity scene laid out on a low wooden chest. The house was so quiet that they crept towards it holding their breath. Up close, she saw that the neat figures were made out of stuffed material and dressed in bright clothing. There were tiny, delicate oxen and sheep, and a crib carved of wood cradled a baby swaddled in white cloth. The whole scene was lit by a row of miniature candles that bathed it in a cosy glow.

'It's beautiful,' Clarrie gasped. 'Who made it?'

'Mama,' Will whispered. 'She made it for me when I was five. I put it out every year, even though I'm too big to play with it now.'

Clarrie put out a finger and gently touched the baby. 'So small yet so neat. Olive would love to see this.'

'You can bring her if you like,' Will enthused.

'Thank you.' She touched his arm. 'You're a kind boy.'

His shook his head. 'No, I'm not. I'm a nuisance. That's what Papa says. Tells me to keep out of Mama's room and that I make too much noise.'

'Well, in my experience, you can be noisy and kind at the same time.'

He gave her a flash of a smile. 'I like you, Clarrie. Would you like to come for Christmas lunch?'

Clarrie laughed. 'I wish I could, but I have to be with Olive and help Mr and Mrs Belhaven with their dinner.'

'Did you have Christmas in India?'

Clarrie's insides jolted at the sudden mention. 'Yes,' she gulped, thinking of their last unhappy Christmas fretting over money and her father's drinking.

'Turkey and plum pudding?' Will asked.

'No, roast woodcock and ginger pudding.'

'I suppose Christmas doesn't always have to be the same,' he said, thoughtful. He fell silent as he stared at the crib. Clarrie was about to move away when he said, 'Mama had a dead baby.'

Her heart thumped. 'Oh, Will, how terrible. I am sorry. She must be very sad.'

Will shrugged. 'She doesn't talk about it. No one

does. They think I don't know because I'm only eleven. But I saw the doctor taking a box out of her room and he left it in the cloakroom while he went to talk to Papa.' Will hesitated. Clarrie could hear him swallowing hard. 'It was the kind of box I keep my toy soldiers in.' His voice sank to a whisper. 'I looked inside. It was all wrapped up like baby Jesus. But it was real. I touched it. It was warm.'

Clarrie stifled a groan.

'I know I shouldn't have,' Will said in agitation. 'Do – do you think I killed it? Maybe the doctor was taking it away to make it better.' He let out a sob.

She hugged him quickly to her. 'Oh, you poor lad! Of course you didn't kill the baby. The doctor would never have put her in a box if she was still alive.'

Will leaned into her hold and quietly cried. She stroked his hair in comfort.

'You won't tell though, will you?' Will said, pulling away.

'Of course not,' Clarrie reassured him, 'but you did nothing wrong. You mustn't blame yourself, do you promise?'

He nodded and wiped his eyes and nose on his sleeve.

'I must go now,' Clarrie said gently. 'Will you be all right?'

He nodded. As they moved down the corridor, he asked, 'Why did you call the baby a she?'

'I don't know,' Clarrie answered. 'I just had a feeling your mother was carrying a girl. Was the baby given a burial?'

'I don't know.' Will shrugged. 'Nobody told me.'

Clarrie descended the stairs holding his hand, her heart aching for his confusion and unhappiness. She felt sorry for them all and wondered how ill his mother was. As they reached the bottom, she sensed a movement above and turned. She thought she saw a figure in a pale gown go past the end of the banisters, but could not be sure.

Outside, it had begun to snow heavily. 'Look, Will,' Clarrie cried, 'isn't it beautiful?' She twirled around, turning her face to the falling snowflakes 'My first snow in England!'

Will was just as excited and ran about whooping with joy, kicking up snow. He scraped up a huge pile into a giant snowball and flung it at Clarrie. It caught her on the neck and she screamed in surprise. A moment later, she was chasing him around the quiet square, hurling snowballs back.

'Will!' a voice barked out of the dark. 'Is that you?'

As Will dashed forward Clarrie let fly a large snowball. The boy collided with the shadowy figure of a man just as the snowball hit its target. The pair were showered in wet snow. Will shrieked with laughter and shook it off, but the man shouted with indignation. 'Stop that, you little blighter!'

Too late, Clarrie realised it was Herbert Stock. She hurried over, skidding about in the fresh snow, hair dishevelled and clothing pockmarked with snowballs.

'I'm so sorry, Mr Stock,' she gasped. 'I just got carried away.'

In the dim gaslight, he peered at her through the falling snow. 'Who is it?'

'Clarrie Belhaven,' she panted. 'I was delivering the mince pies.'

'Clarrie! Goodness me, I thought it was a friend of Will's.'

'She is, Papa.' Will grinned. 'We've had a terrific snowball fight. Clarrie's as good as a boy.'

Clarrie laughed. 'I'll take that as a compliment.'

Herbert gave a rueful smile as he brushed snow from his shoulder. 'Indeed you should. I can see how accurate your aim is.'

'I'm sorry,' Clarrie repeated.

'Don't be,' he replied. 'I haven't heard Will so happy for weeks.'

Clarrie longed to give her sympathy for the loss of his baby, but did not want to get Will into trouble. Instead she said, 'I'm sorry to hear Mrs Stock has been unwell.'

He shot her a startled look.

'Dolly told me she was in bed,' Clarrie said quickly. 'Please let us know if there's anything we can do to help out – any extra baking or provisions.'

'That's kind,' he said stiffly, 'but we wouldn't want to burden you.'

'It wouldn't be a burden,' Clarrie assured him. 'I'm

used to running a household. I had to after my mother died. So I know how a little bit of help goes a long way.'

The sternness in his face softened. 'Thank you.'

'Can we have hot chocolate and mince pies now, Papa?' Will asked. 'And can Clarrie stay?'

Clarrie saw Herbert hesitate in embarrassment. 'I'm afraid I can't,' she said. 'I must get back to help at the hotel.'

'Do you live in a hotel?' Will gasped. 'Is it very grand?'

Clarrie stifled a bitter laugh. 'No, not very.'

As she hurried over to the patient pony, she heard Will telling his father about showing her the nativity scene. She flushed to think how she had gone brazenly upstairs as if she were their equal. Herbert Stock would probably be annoyed. In his eyes she was a lowly barmaid and maid-of-all-work. His son Bertie would not even deign to speak to her at church. In a year or so even Will would understand that he could not invite the likes of her into the house. She left quickly, banishing from her mind thoughts of the Stocks' genteel home. If she allowed herself to make comparisons with the grim surroundings of Cherry Terrace, from which there seemed no escape, she would go mad.

By the time Clarrie got back, the pub was crammed with drinkers and the atmosphere raucous. Some of the men had been there for hours. Olive was barely coping with the demand in the sitting room, rushing between the bar for drinks and the kitchen for clean glasses. Lily was washing up and making Harrison dry.

'Where the devil have you been?' she demanded, face flushed. 'Harrison could've done it quicker on one leg.'

'It's treacherous out there with snow on top of ice,' Clarrie panted, going to the fire to thaw out her numb hands.

'Don't think you can stop by the fire doing nowt,' Lily said sharply. 'Go and help that useless sister of yours; she's as slow as a carthorse.'

Clarrie exchanged looks of sympathy with Harrison and left the kitchen. She found Olive on the verge of tears.

'It's so noisy and they all keep shouting and I can't remember what they've ordered,' Olive whimpered in the passageway, clutching a full tray. 'And that witch Lily says I'm not quick enough.'

'Here, give that to me,' Clarrie said. 'Which table?'

'One to the right of the door, I think,' Olive sniffed.

'Go in the kitchen and offer to wash the glasses. Tell Cousin Lily she deserves to put her feet up.'

'She doesn't deserve any such thing,' Olive protested.

'If it gets you out of waitressing, then don't complain,' Clarrie replied, taking the tray in her frozen fingers.

She swung into the sitting room and weaved her way to the waiting table.

'Where's the red-headed lass gone?' one of the men asked. 'That bonny little elf.'

'Gone to help Father Christmas,' Clarrie answered, offloading the glasses.

'She was ganin' to sit on me knee,' he chuckled. 'She promised.'

'Our Clarrie will sit on yer knee, Billy,' his friend said, nudging him. He was a regular called Burton who sometimes played the mouth organ. 'She's the friendly type.'

'It'll cost you twice as much,' Clarrie joked. 'That's one and threepence.'

Billy paid up and Clarrie hurried to the next table calling for her.

She never stopped all evening, rushing between the two rooms, squeezing through crowds of drinkers with trays sloshing with beer. Some of them tried to grope her, others declared they were in love, a few grew abusive and Jared told them to temper their language or they could go elsewhere.

Clarrie began to feel faint for lack of food, but Lily would not let her stop to eat till they closed, telling her it was her own fault for missing tea. She knew with sickening dread that come closing time there would be drunken fighting in the street outside. The trick was to get them out before it started. There was a desperation to the men's drinking, as if they could blot out the drudgery of long hours at the yards and factories with beer and spirits. For a few hours, this dismal pub with its bare floors, dirty windows and rickety tables was a haven between the tyranny of the factory hooter and their cramped, smoky homes. Clarrie realised all this, yet it angered her. She had seen what drink did to a man; it began as a way of escape and ended up consuming him. If she had been Jared, she would have sent half of them home hours ago. The atmosphere was changing from jovial to loudly aggressive, with arguments breaking out and fizzing like striking matches.

When Jared finally called last orders there was a clamour for more drinks. Olive appeared with a tray of clean glasses and handed it to Jared behind the bar. She looked exhausted and her hands were red raw from hours of washing. Clarrie felt a pang of guilt at the sight of her once beautiful musician's fingers so swollen. But uncomplainingly, Olive helped Clarrie load up a full tray.

As they moved towards the bar door, a man stepped back unsteadily and barged into Olive, who knocked Clarrie's tray out of her hands. The next moment glasses were crashing to the floor and beer was spraying everywhere. There were cries of protest as men looked round or pushed out of the way.

'You stupid bitch!' the swaying man growled, his jacket drenched. It was Hobson, normally a quiet man and a foreman at Armstrong's armaments factory. He took hold of Olive and shook her hard. Olive half screamed.

Clarrie caught the man's arm. 'It was my fault. Please leave her.'

'Me new jacket – two weeks' bloody wages – ruined!' he ranted drunkenly, not letting go. Olive looked terrified.

'I'm sorry,' Clarrie said, trying to calm him. 'But it'll sponge down. I'll do it for you.'

She felt his hold on her sister loosen and she pushed him firmly away.

'What's ganin' on?' Jared called over the din, only now aware of the fracas. People were already crunching over the broken glass as if it did not matter.

'Just an accident,' Clarrie replied, trying to steer the foreman away from Olive.

'Are you all right, Mr Hobson?'

At once the man's indignation was reignited.

'Nah,' he slurred. 'Bloody lasses.'

For a moment, a glazed-eyed Hobson tried to focus on Clarrie. She could see he was very drunk. It was a look she had seen too often in Jock's eyes, one of aggression and menace when he seemed not to recognise her. She let go. Fear must have registered in her own eyes, for the next instant he bunched his fist and punched her full in the face.

Clarrie staggered against the bar in shock. Olive screamed out loud. Jared rushed forward. Someone next to Hobson punched him back. Fighting erupted in the bar. Excruciating pain had shot up Clarrie's nose. She doubled up in agony, clasping her

141

face, unable to open her eyes. All around she could hear men bawling and punching each other. She sank down and pressed against the bar, trying to get out of the way. A heavy boot caught her on the hip.

'Help me, help!' Olive shrieked from close by.

Clarrie flung out an arm, still unable to open her eyes. Her sister grabbed it. She pulled Olive into her hold and they clung on to each other as the fighting raged all around. Minutes later, she heard Lily's voice bellow over the brawling men.

'Gerroff home the lot of you!'

Clarrie squinted up to see Lily shoving people towards the door with a broomstick. Soon the place was empty and the noise moved into the street. She heard Jared bolt the outer door and return.

'Gerrup, the pair of you,' Lily ordered, prodding the sisters with her broom. 'What the devil happened in here?'

Clarrie staggered to her feet, her nose throbbing and pouring with blood. Before she could explain, Lily was berating them. 'Dropped a tray, didn't you? Look at all the broken glass. It'll come out yer wages.'

Olive stood up and clung to her sister.

'It wasn't all the lass's fault, my dear,' Jared said, steering Clarrie on to a chair and thrusting a dirty handkerchief at her nose. 'That Hobson was well out of order hitting her.'

The sight of her husband helping Clarrie seemed to madden Lily more. Her face was puce and her eyes glittered with anger. 'You stupid man – letting it get out of hand!' she snapped. 'I can't trust you with owt.' Then she brought her face close to Clarrie's and hissed, 'Bet you were givin' the man cheek. Were you?'

Clarrie flinched away. 'No, I was trying to calm him down. He was having a go at Olive.'

'You lasses!' Lily bawled. 'You're next to useless.' She kicked at an overturned chair. 'This was an orderly place till you came here, with your airs and graces, thinking yourselves better than the likes of the hard-working lads round here. They can tell when someone's got their nose too far up their face.' She glared at them with real loathing. 'Well, you can clear up this mess on yer own!' She shook the broom at them.

Clarrie had never seen her in such a state and feared she might hurt Olive. She stood up, swaying light-headedly, guarding her sister with an arm. 'All right, we'll do it.'

'And I don't care how long it takes,' Lily snarled, 'you'll still get up just as early to stoke the fire.'

Clarrie clutched Olive to stop herself fainting. 'Fire? But it's Christmas Day . . .'

'It's no different from any other in this house,' Lily declared. 'And I've pies to make for Boxing Day.'

She shoved the broom at Clarrie and stormed out. Sighing, Jared fetched a rag from behind the bar and helped to clean up Clarrie's nosebleed. It took them an hour to clear up the mess in the bar, tidy the sitting room, wash the glasses and put them away. Jared hovered about straightening tables and trying to help without his wife noticing. But she ordered him to take Harrison up the street to his lodgings and told the barman to be back at work in two days' time.

As he went, Jared mumbled, 'Best put a cold flannel on yer nose the night or you'll have a bruise like a prizefighter the morra.'

When they finally finished, Lily had gone to bed, locking the pantry as usual before she went. Clarrie was past wanting to eat but Olive clutched her stomach.

'I'm so hungry, Clarrie. She never gave me any tea.'

They searched the kitchen but could find nothing edible, except for some stale piecrust that was being saved for Barny. Olive munched on it unhappily.

'I hate her,' she said miserably. 'She was like a madwoman tonight. Why did Father never tell us how horrible his cousins were?'

Clarrie slumped on the bench beside her. 'Jared's not so bad and maybe Father never really knew Lily. He hadn't been back in years. Don't suppose he thought we'd ever meet them.'

'Well he should have thought of it,' Olive gulped, fighting back tears. 'He should've thought where all his drinking and debts would get us.'

Clarrie closed her eyes, utterly spent. 'It won't be for ever.'

'You always say that!' Olive accused her. 'But how is it going to change? We're like slaves here. That witch will never let us go!' She burst into tears.

Clarrie tried to put an arm about her, but Olive would not be comforted and shook her off.

'I'll run away,' she said. 'You can't stop me.'

Clarrie sighed. 'Where to?'

'I don't care. Anywhere! We should never have come to England. We should have gone with Kamal – anything but this. Now we'll never get back to India!'

Clarrie knew that it was useless to argue when Olive worked herself into a state; it only made things worse.

'Let's go to bed while we can,' she said, hauling herself up. The clock on the mantelpiece showed it was nearly midnight. 'It's almost Christmas Day. We're going to enjoy it what ever Lily-no-stockings says.'

Olive pulled a face but followed her up the dark staircase to the attic. They had got used to climbing up and down without light, saving their candle for reading in bed the handful of Jock's musty books that they had brought with them from Belgooree.

They put on extra clothing, gloves and woollen stockings against the icy cold and bedded down together. Olive allowed Clarrie to put her arms about her.

'Tomorrow, let's get out your violin and have some music,' Clarrie whispered. 'Brighten up the day.'

'She won't let us.'

'We'll get round Jared after he's had a Christmas drink. He likes it when customers play music in the bar.'

They fell silent, Clarrie slipping into a half-doze of exhaustion.

Suddenly Olive struggled to sit up. 'That's it!'

'What?' Clarrie murmured.

'She's a drinker,' Olive declared.

'Who?'

'Lily-no-stockings.'

Clarrie was startled awake. 'Don't be daft.'

'Yes, I'm sure of it,' Olive replied. 'She keeps something in a big pickle jar in the pantry. Saw her pouring it into a cup once and she gave me an earful for looking. Said it was white vinegar and it helped her digestion. Drinks it every day before her afternoon nap.'

'Why didn't you tell me before?' Clarrie asked, incredulous.

'Because I believed her about the vinegar.'

'Well, maybe it's true.'

Olive shook her head. 'That horrible man – Hobson – he was drinking the same stuff. It smelt the same – like sour flowers.'

'Gin,' Clarrie gasped. 'Hobson drinks neat gin; it's colourless.'

'Then that's what she puts in her pickle jar.' Olive was adamant.

'But I would've noticed.' Clarrie was puzzled. 'I can tell a drinker.'

'You're not with her as much as I am,' Olive pointed out. 'She's good at covering it up and she stinks that much of onions and cooking I only notice the other smell when she leans close and tells me off. She's always more bad-tempered in the mornings before she's had her vinegar.'

'Well I never!' Clarrie exclaimed.

'She was swigging away in the pantry tonight when I was washing up.'

'No wonder she came charging into the bar full of hell. That would explain her being so odd.'

'Do you think Cousin Jared knows?' Olive asked.

'I wonder,' Clarrie mused. 'Perhaps that's why he likes to employ young lasses in the bar – keeps her in the kitchen making pies.'

'Bet he doesn't know about the vinegar,' Olive said. 'She's just as bad as all those common women who come in.'

'They're not common, they're canny,' Clarrie said, thinking of Lexy and her friends. 'And at least they're not hypocrites like Lily, pretending to be holier than thou.'

Olive smirked. 'Gin-Lily, that's what we'll call her from now on. Gin-Lily-no-stockings.'

CHAPTER 9

Clarrie woke early on Christmas morning, frozen and aching. She no longer needed a hammer on the door, so used was she to getting up long before dawn. Her hip throbbed from where she had been kicked and her face pulsed with pain. Leaving Olive's present at the foot of their bed for her to find on waking, Clarrie limped downstairs. She placed two gifts on the table; handmade handkerchiefs for Jared and Lily that she had cajoled Olive into embroidering with birds.

It was only when stoking up the kitchen fire that she caught sight of her reflection in the steel fender. She gasped in horror. Rushing to the cracked mirror in the scullery, in the dim candlelight she saw that the bridge of her nose was swollen and her eyes puffed up into two purple bruises.

She covered her face in shock, tears of humiliation flooding her throat. What would people say when they saw her? She wanted to rush away and hide. Back in the kitchen she fought down the urge to weep, tears stinging her eyes and making her nose throb. She pulled her shawl over her head and flung it across her face like a veil. Nobody would see what that brute had done to her or she would die of shame. She crouched by the fire, her pulse racing. She felt small and vulnerable and utterly insignificant.

'Mornin', Clarrie.' Jared appeared yawning in the doorway. 'Happy Christmas!'

Clarrie gritted her teeth, stifling a howl of misery.

'Clarrie? What's the matter?'

Slowly she turned to face him and pulled the shawl away from her face. She saw him flinch with revulsion.

'I – I told you to put some'at on yer neb last night,' he stuttered. 'Let me have a proper look.'

She winced as he touched her face with awkward fingers.

'I'd say it's broken,' he tutted. 'You'll have to learn how to duck quicker next time.'

She stared at him in disbelief. She was in no mood for joking, but he seemed quite serious. He whistled through the gaps in his teeth.

'I've seen some beauties in my time, and this is one of them. Vinegar bandage, that's what you need. Cures most things. I'll get my Lily to fetch some when she comes with the keys.' He stepped round her, pouring himself a cup of tea from the pot Lily had measured out the night before and Clarrie had made and left to keep warm on the hearth.

She shrank into her shawl again, suppressing the urge to scream. Olive entered beaming and rushed over to thank her for the sketchbook and pencils. Her words died on her lips at sight of her sister's face.

'Oh, Clarrie!' she gasped, flinging her arms about her.

'What's all the fuss about?' Lily came in, looking bleary-eyed and foul-tempered. How had Clarrie never noticed before these tell-tale signs of her drinking? She pushed Olive out of the way and peered at Clarrie, her breath rank. 'Goodness me, lass, what a state you're in! You can't come to church looking like that.'

Clarrie shrank further back, trying not to gag.

'Fetch the vinegar, my dear,' Jared said. 'That's what she needs.'

Lily hesitated. Clarrie and Olive exchanged knowing looks.

'Vinegar be damned!' Lily blustered. 'I'm not wasting good preservative on a bit of bruising.'

Even Jared was open-mouthed at her callousness. 'But my dear—'

'Don't my dear me!' Lily shouted. 'It's the lass's fault for upsetting the customer in the first place. Mr Hobson's a respectable foreman. We can't afford to go offending the likes of him. Let it be a lesson to her.' She rubbed her forehead and turned bloodshot eyes on Clarrie. 'Now get up and stop lookin' so sorry for yourself. Olive, why isn't the table set?'

Olive's face looked anxious once again as she bent her head and hurried to obey. Clarrie pulled herself up, despair gripping her. Lily knew they would both do her bidding for they had no choice. Clarrie hated herself for being so cowed, but she no longer had the strength to resist.

The Belhavens left for church, leaving Clarrie to prepare the vegetables for dinner and carry on the pie making that Lily and Olive had started. When Olive asked to stay with Clarrie, Lily snapped, 'Certainly not! You'll say yer prayers for the both of ye.'

Left on her own, Clarrie quelled the desire to flee the house and escape to the park. How could she when she looked so unsightly? She somehow felt as guilty as if it were she who had been the drunken aggressor in a brawl. It made no sense, but the feeling of failure and having brought the attack on herself pressed down on her like a dead weight.

Listlessly, she carried out her chores. All she could think about was getting through the morning, then the rest of the day until she could fall into bed and take refuge in exhausted sleep. It was better to think of today as just like any other as Lily had declared, for to remember the thrill of Christmases of old in the crisp beauty of Belgooree with her parents and Kamal was to invite black despair.

Christmas dinner was a joyless affair: a reheated piece of mutton left over from pie making and boiled potatoes and turnip. The highlight was a small mince pie, of which the girls were served tiny slivers. Jared gulped back the one beer that Lily allowed him and tried to jolly the conversation along.

'Church was full. Singing was grand, wasn't it, my dear?'

Lily grunted. 'Not that you'd know a good note if yer heard it.'

'Still no sign of Mrs Stock,' Jared said. 'There's a rumour her bairn was stillborn and she's taken it badly.'

'She should be thankful for the two lads she's got,' Lily retorted. 'What I wouldn't have given for a pair of strong lads to run this place. Louisa Stock doesn't know she's born.'

Clarrie put down her spoon, her appetite gone. She had witnessed the deep sadness hanging over the Stocks' house like a funeral pall, yet Lily could not summon a kind word to say on the matter. All she thought about was herself and how hard a life she had been given. Clarrie saw clearly how Lily had allowed bitterness to eat into her and destroy any sympathy towards others. She did not know whether to despise or pity her.

'Don't waste that,' Lily cried, seeing Clarrie push away her hardly touched pie. 'I'll have it.' She shovelled the remains on to her own plate.

Olive hardly said a word all day. Only when they were alone upstairs did she pull a small package from her pocket.

'I'm sorry I haven't got you anything for Christmas,' she apologised, 'but Will Stock asked me to give this to you. He seemed really disappointed not to see you.'

In the candlelight, Clarrie unwrapped the tissue paper. Lying inside was one of the oxen from his nativity scene. It was made of corduroy with tiny black beads for eyes and pipe cleaners twisted into horns. The material was worn away where Will's small fingers had played with it over the years. A note was enclosed.

I know you like horses best, but Papa says they have oxen in India too. Hope you like it. Happy Christmas from William.

Clarrie gently curled her fingers round the stuffed figure. 'Dear Will,' she gulped. It was the simplest of gifts and yet the most generous, for she knew how much the nativity set meant to the boy. His kindness touched her heart.

Suddenly a sob broke from deep inside and the next minute tears were streaming uncontrollably down her cheeks. Olive threw her arms about her neck.

'Oh, Clarrie, don't. I hate it when you cry.' Then she was crying too. They clung to each other, grateful that they were not facing this ordeal alone.

'We will get out of here,' Clarrie whispered fiercely, 'we will!'

The bleak day ended like countless before it in their stark, freezing attic, but that night they drew comfort from Will's surprise gift. It was a sign of goodness in a frightening world. Deep down, Clarrie knew she would find the strength to fight on.

CHAPTER 10

1906

For nearly a month, Clarrie was confined to the house until there was no trace of the bruising to her face, though she was left with a permanent bump on the bridge of her delicate straight nose as a reminder of that terrible night. Lily made her work in the kitchen and forced Olive out to serve in the pub, which the girl feared and hated. Often the smoky bar would trigger her asthma, but Lily made no allowances. Harrison made Clarrie all too conscious of her appearance.

'Ye're a funny colour, Clarrie,' he kept saying, peering at her. 'Yer not feeling well?'

Clarrie grew to despise Lily all the more, confined with her in the hot, fetid kitchen being bullied and criticised. She noticed how much the woman drank in secret in the pantry and wondered again how she had never noticed before. Lily's temper after these furtive episodes was unpredictable; at best she grew drowsy and forgetful, at worst aggressive and abusive. Clarrie realised how much Olive must have put up with over the autumn months without telling her.

Though she dreaded it, the day came when Lily sent her back in the bar. Perversely, she chose Clarrie's twentieth birthday.

'We don't bother with birthdays in this house.' Lily was dismissive when Olive asked if they could bake her sister a cake. 'You can buy one out of yer wages but I haven't money to waste.'

Defiantly, on the birthday morning, Olive took out her violin from under the bed and played to Clarrie in the kitchen before breakfast. It was the first time she had touched the instrument in months and her fingers were stiff and out of practice. But Clarrie was overjoyed to see the light return to Olive's tired eyes as she played and the smile of satisfaction when she finished.

'That was the best present ever.' Clarrie kissed her sister. 'Thank you. Now put it away before Lily complains and chops it up for firewood.'

Olive looked aghast and rushed to hide it upstairs again, even though Clarrie had meant it as a joke.

Later, Clarrie braced herself to re-enter the bar, sweating and breathless at the thought of having to face Hobson again. It rankled that her cousins expected her to serve him as if nothing had happened. She was shaking so much that she nearly repeated the dropping of a trayload of beer. To her relief Hobson did not appear that day.

Unexpectedly, she was cheered by the appearance of Lexy, Maggie and Ina in the afternoon.

'Where've you been, hinny?' Maggie cried.

'We thought you'd run off with a lad from the brewery,' Lexy teased.

'Chance would be a fine thing,' Clarrie replied.

'By, you're thin as a stick, lass,' Ina commented. 'That dragon not been feeding you?'

'Aye, your sister's like a lat an' all,' said Maggie. 'Doesn't say much either, your Olive. Looked like she was about to burst into tears whenever I said owt to her.'

'You make me want to burst into tears whenever you open your gob, man Maggie,' Lexy joked. Maggie shoved her playfully.

'Never mind them,' Ina said, rolling her eyes at Clarrie, 'we've got some'at for you. Gan on, our Lexy.' She nudged her friend.

Lexy pulled out a bar of soap and popped it into Clarrie's apron. 'It's Pears not carbolic. Don't let the dragon get a whiff of it.'

'No, it's just for you,' Ina said.

Clarrie gawped at them. 'How did you know it was my birthday?'

They laughed in surprise. 'Eeh, we didn't,' said Ina, 'but isn't that grand?'

'That's ever so kind,' Clarrie blushed, 'but what have I done to deserve it?'

Maggie lowered her voice. 'We heard about that bother with Hobson. He's a nasty bugger in drink – uses his belt on his missus.'

'Aye,' Lexy nodded. 'She comes in the bathhouse all la-di-da – but we've seen the marks on her, poor woman.'

Tears sprang to Clarrie's eyes. She gulped, her throat too tight to utter her thanks. Ina put out a roughened hand and squeezed Clarrie's. 'Keep yer chin up, hinny. The likes of Hobson aren't good enough to lick yer boots. He's a coward for using his fists on you.'

'Aye,' Lexy said, 'and we'll pay him back, don't you worry. The next time his missus brings his clothes in the laundry, me and Maggie's ganin' to put pepper in his long johns.'

The women burst into raucous laughter. Clarrie smiled.

'That's better,' Ina said. 'You don't suit a sad face.'

'I couldn't be sad for two minutes with you lot around.' Clarrie pushed away Maggie's money. 'This one's on me. Keep your pennies for that pepper.'

Clarrie kept the soap hidden upstairs and she and Olive used it with the basin of water they carried up each night. Sometimes they had to prod through a thin layer of ice in the morning, so cold were the raw days of January and February.

Every time Clarrie used the soft soap and smelled its delicate perfume, she thought of the kind women and wondered at how they kept up their spirits day after day. She knew from chatting to them that Ina was widowed and had to sell second-hand clothes out of a wheelbarrow to feed her five children. Maggie had a drunk for a husband and Lexy's parents were dead and she was surrogate mother to her six younger siblings.

She did not begrudge them their snatched moments of camaraderie in the pub, but they deserved something better. The atmosphere could be volatile and fights broke out over a dropped halfpenny. Often the women were the butt of ribald jokes or abusive remarks, and at times Lily would barge in and chase them out for no apparent reason. Clarrie felt sorry for the gaggle of children who often came with them and had to huddle outside in the rain or sleet, waiting while their mother or elder sister warmed themselves with liquor. If only there was somewhere safer and more congenial for poor working-class women like them and their children to go. It seemed to Clarrie that nobody cared, neither brewer nor publican, as long as they kept paying for their drink.

One blustery spring day, when Clarrie had just finished hanging out washing in the back lane, she heard a delivery van clattering downhill.

'Watch yer washing, missus!' a young man yelled.

Clarrie dashed back out and grabbed at the flapping shirts and aprons. Too late, she saw that the van was careering towards her unattended. She jumped out of the way just in time. The pony came trotting by, gathering washing as it went. The washing line caught on the wooden canopy of the van and pulled the rest of the laundry with it. The youth ran behind, breathless, waving his cap.

'Catch him for us, missus!'

Clarrie shot after the pony and caught it at the end of the lane.

'Whoa, there!' She grabbed the reins and tugged it to a halt. The delivery man caught up. He had fair hair that stood up thick as a brush and lively hazel eyes. For a moment they stood catching their breath.

'Ta, miss,' he panted. 'Bella'd be off home given half a chance. She's too frisky by half.'

Clarrie patted the horse. 'She's a sturdy one. You have to be firm and show her who's boss.'

'Oh, aye?' He gave her a mocking look. 'Know about horses, do you?'

'Enough not to let one bolt and ruin other folks' washing.' She pulled off a shirt that had snagged on Bella's harness.

'Sorry, miss.' He blushed and began helping her gather up the strewn washing.

'The name's Clarrie,' she told him.

'Jack,' he replied, 'Jack Brewis. I'll put your line back up for you.'

Clarrie gave a half-laugh, half-sigh. 'Think I'll have to wash half of this again first.'

He hauled in the line of aprons from the van roof. 'Work at the Cherry, do you?'

Clarrie nodded.

'Bit rough in there sometimes,' Jack grunted.

Clarrie flushed. 'Can be. I've never seen you in, though.'

He glanced at her. 'Nah, I divvn't drink. Prefer to gan dancin' or to the Pavilion.'

'The Pavilion? What's that?'

He gave her an astonished look. 'The music hall on Westgate Road. Have you never been?'

Clarrie shook her head.

'By, you're missin' a treat.'

Clarrie smothered a pang of longing. How could she explain that she was a virtual prisoner, not even allowed an afternoon off, let alone an evening of theatre? She could just imagine Lily fulminating about devil's music and shameless harlots on the stage.

'What you selling?' she asked.

'Tea,' he replied, handing her a heap of laundry.

Clarrie looked at the van properly for the first time. Its bold lettering advertised the Tyneside Tea Company. Her eyes widened with interest.

'What kinds have you got?'

He scrutinised her tatty work dress and hobnail boots.

'The cheapest we do is Household tea.'

Clarrie put her hands on her hips. 'And what's that made of? Flowery, Orange Pekoe, Broken Pekoe, Souchong or Dust?'

He gawped at her. 'I divvn't knaw. It's good strong workers' tea. Me mam swears by it.'

Clarrie suppressed a smile. 'If you want me to buy some, you better try harder at selling than that.'

'All right, Clarrie,' he said in a teasing voice, 'we've got Assam Breakfast, Darjeeling and Ceylon. Ceylon's canny for afternoon tea – all the posh people are drinking that. Haway and have a look.'

He reached into the van and pulled out a basket with packets of tea, each type wrapped in different coloured rice paper. Clarrie picked out one and opened it.

'Hoy, what you doing?' he asked suspiciously.

'Smelling it.'

She breathed in the aroma of the dark leaves. It was strong and earthy, conjuring up humid heat. The next was more scented, a third smoky and the fourth a pungent mix of lesser grade leaves. She closed her eyes and could see the brown swirling Brahmaputra, and the hillsides of emerald green tea trees, steaming and dripping after the rain. She picked out the final tea and inhaled. At once its spicy delicate scent evoked a memory of sandalwood and oak, of spring water and dawn mist. Her stomach twisted with bittersweet longing. It smelled of Belgooree.

'This one,' she said, tears welling in her eyes. 'I want this one.'

He looked at her uncertainly. 'That's Darjeeling – it's canny pricey.'

'I know.' She smiled tearfully, pulling out the pouch of money she kept with her at all times.

As she handed over most of that week's wages, Jack eyed her. 'You're a funny one, Clarrie. How come you know so much about tea? Are you foreign or some'at?'

She hesitated. There was no use saying she was a tea planter's daughter; he would think she was telling tales.

'My father was a soldier in India – he learned a lot about tea and passed it on to me.'

He gave her a puzzled look. 'You talk different an' all. You're not from round here, are you?'

Clarrie shook her head.

Before he could ask any more, a voice bellowed from behind, 'What the devil's ganin' on here?'

Clarrie looked round, startled. It was a belligerent Lily at the yard gate. 'Come here, you little madam. What you done with me washing?'

Jack saw the tension on Clarrie's face and intervened. 'Sorry, missus,' he called up the lane, 'it was my fault. I'll fix it.'

'Be off with you!' Lily shouted back. 'And you get yerself back in here this minute, you shameless lass!'

'Bit of a charmer, is she?' Jack murmured to Clarrie.

'You better go,' Clarrie told him, 'before she boils you up and serves you in a pie.'

Jack snorted with laughter. 'Sorry for getting you into trouble. And ta very much for stopping Bella.'

'Thanks for the tea.' She smiled briefly, shoving the packet into her apron and turning to go.

'Hope I see you again, Clarrie,' he said as he

jammed his cap back on his head and pulled Bella forward.

'Aye, me too.' She waved and hurried up the lane with an armful of crumpled washing.

Clarrie weathered Lily's vitriolic words about her brazen behaviour, her uselessness at washing and her general idleness, for she knew that at the end of the day, when the Belhavens were in bed, she would treat Olive to a pot of real tea. For too long they had stomached Lily's cheap bitter Dust tea. She would infuse it with the ginger that Ina had bought for her to ease Olive's wheezing, as Kamal used to do.

Late that night, the sisters sat by the kitchen fire, sipping the steaming black tea, and talked quietly of their former life. Clarrie told Olive about the handsome delivery man and his runaway horse.

'He likes dancing and music,' Clarrie said approvingly, 'and he doesn't drink either.'

'I like the sound of this Jack,' Olive agreed. 'Do you think he'll call again?'

Clarrie sighed. 'If Gin-Lily hasn't scared him away.'

'Imagine going to a concert or a dance,' Olive said dreamily. 'When will we ever do that, Clarrie?'

Clarrie was about to promise that they would some day soon, but stopped herself. She had made too many promises to her sister that had come to nothing, and Olive was no longer a child to be comforted by easy words.

'I don't know,' she answered.

Olive bowed her head, her expression forlorn. Looking at Olive's wan face and her once glowing red hair now dulled and thinning, Clarrie felt a wave of tenderness towards her sensitive sister; she had endured their new life of hardship and displacement far more stoically than Clarrie could have imagined. Clarrie had always thought of herself as the strong one having to protect her younger sister, but in that quiet moment, as they sat drinking the special tea, she realised that she could not have borne the past months without Olive at her side.

Olive was the only one whom she could talk to about home and their past life, who understood how she felt. Olive reminded her so often of their mercurial father; she shared his passions, his mood swings and self-doubts. Olive was her one precious link with Belgooree and the parents they had loved and lost.

But it frightened Clarrie that her sister might lose hope. Her health had deteriorated rapidly over the winter in the damp and smoky house. Even Lily had grown so used to Olive's habitual cough that she no longer complained about it. She must do something to try to improve their lot.

Over the next few days, Clarrie thought a lot about the friendly Jack and his tea, looking out for his van in the hope that he would come again. It had been so refreshing to meet someone new and of her age who had nothing to do with the pub or its hard-drinking customers. But there was never any sign of Jack or his pony Bella.

One day, Lexy and Ina came into the bar without Maggie. Lexy was unusually subdued. When Clarrie asked where their friend was, Lexy shook her head.

'Her bastard husband!' she muttered angrily. 'He nearly killed her this time.'

Clarrie gasped. 'What do you mean?'

'Beat her black and blue,' Ina explained.

'What ever for?'

'Burning his bloody bacon probably,' Lexy hissed. 'He doesn't need a reason.'

Clarrie felt sick and sat down. 'That's terrible! Where is she?'

Ina glanced around fearfully and nodded at Lexy.

'She's at my house,' Lexy said.

'Shh, keep your voice down,' Ina whispered. 'His workmates drink in here.'

Lexy gave a defiant look round, but dropped her voice. 'I've got the bairns keeping an eye on her.'

'Won't he think to look there?' Clarrie asked.

'He's already been round, shouting his head off, but I kept the door locked.'

Ina sighed. 'It's only a matter of time before he finds her and drags her back.'

Clarrie felt anger rise in her throat. 'Can't anybody stop him? Why don't you tell the police what he's done?'

Lexy and Ina gave her pitying looks. 'They don't do owt,' Lexy snorted. 'What happens inside closed doors is a private matter. A man can do as he likes with his wife.'

Clarrie swallowed. 'Well, she mustn't go back. She must go somewhere else.'

'That's easier said than done.' Ina sighed. 'Her daughter lives nearby but she's as scared of the old man as her mam is.'

'And she'll lose her job at the washhouse if she doesn't gan back soon,' Lexy said bleakly. 'I cannot cover for her much longer.'

Clarrie could think of nothing to say that would comfort the women. All the rest of the day, she forced herself to carry on with the job she was beginning to hate with a passion. Although she had never served Maggie's brutal husband, she felt somehow complicit. How many alcoholic rages had she fuelled in other men? How many drinkers had Jared turned out at the end of the night to go home and beat their wives?

That night Clarrie could not sleep. She lay listening to Olive's wheezing breath and wrestled with her troubled thoughts. The next day was Sunday. On the walk to church, she plucked up the courage to ask what had been preying on her mind all night.

'Cousin Jared, I've been thinking of a new business idea.'

'Hark at her!' Lily snorted. 'Business idea indeed.'

'Let's hear what she has to say, my dear,' Jared said, glancing round at Clarrie. She knew anything to do with making money would gain his interest.

'I've heard that tea rooms are very popular these

days. So I was wondering if we could start serving tea in the sitting room? We could do it up nicely with cloths on the tables and curtains at the window,' Clarrie enthused. 'Sell Mrs Belhaven's pies and maybe cakes.'

Lily stopped in her tracks. 'Cakes?' she cried.

'Aye,' Clarrie said, 'like they do in Lockart's Cocoa Rooms. Olive and I could make them.'

Both Jared and Lily gawped at her, dumbfounded. He was the first to speak.

'Why ever would we want to do that? The men don't want to drink tea or eat cake,' he said dismissively.

'They might, if we made it homely,' Clarrie said, 'more welcoming.'

'If they want homely,' Lily snapped, 'they've got homes to gan to.'

'We'd get more women coming in,' Clarrie persisted. 'They don't have anywhere decent to have a sit down and a cuppa round here.'

Lily snorted with derision. 'Well we certainly don't want to encourage them. They should be at home where they belong, looking after their husbands and bairns. If Mr Belhaven wasn't so soft, I wouldn't let them common types in at all.'

Clarrie was crestfallen.

'And don't give me one of your looks,' Lily said. 'We haven't money to spend on fancy curtains or cloths – and the types round here wouldn't appreciate it if we did.'

Jared shook his head. 'No, Clarrie, the customers don't want that sort of thing. Tea rooms are for the middle classes and the city centre. We'd be out of business in a fortnight if we tried that round here. The men would just gan elsewhere.'

He and Lily turned their backs on the sisters and resumed their march uphill.

'Tea room!' Lily kept muttering. 'Never heard owt so daft.'

Clarrie gulped down her frustration. Changing their minds was a hopeless task. Olive slipped a comforting arm through hers.

'It's a grand idea,' she whispered. 'Not daft at all.'

Clarrie threw her sister a grateful look as they followed the Belhavens into church.

Louisa Stock had never been back at the John Knox Presbyterian since losing her baby. Word had spread among the congregation that she was an invalid and no one had seen her leave the house in Summerhill for months. There was never any mention of a dead baby; the most that was ever said was that Mrs Stock had 'women's troubles'. Herbert Stock's face was permanently drawn and anxious. He looked years older than he had the previous summer; his limp was more pronounced, and each Sunday he merely nodded at them as he left. Bertie still sang lustily and looked as bumptious as ever. Only Will hung back at the end of each service to speak to Clarrie, despite Bertie's command to him to hurry up. Will had been worried when Clarrie had missed church for a month.

'I thought you might have gone to bed and not got up, like Mama,' he had confided bashfully. 'I wanted to come and see you but Papa and Bertie said it was out of the question.'

During the service, Will kept glancing round and grinning at Clarrie, so much so that Lily pinched her and made her shift behind a pillar so the boy could not see her.

'Making a spectacle of yerself,' she hissed in disgust.

After the service, Lily marched her outside and was about to give her a lecture on seemly behaviour when Herbert Stock approached them. Lily quickly adopted her submissive bob and smile as he greeted them. Will came bounding up behind his father, grinning at Clarrie.

'I have come with a request from Mrs Stock,' Herbert said stiffly.

Lily looked astonished, but pleased. 'Of course, sir, we'd be happy to help. How is Mrs Stock?'

'Not well,' Herbert said tensely.

'Dear, dear, we're sorry to hear that,' Lily said. 'Aren't we, Mr Belhaven?'

Jared grunted in agreement.

'So what can we do for her, sir?' Lily asked.

'It's Clarrie I wish to speak to,' Herbert said, turning towards her and surprising them all. 'My wife would like to meet you. Perhaps you could be allowed to call at the house later this afternoon, say four o'clock?'

Clarrie darted a look at her cousins; they gaped with incredulity.

'Yes, Mr Stock,' Clarrie gulped, 'I'd be pleased to.'

Herbert gave a brief nod of approval. 'I hope that doesn't inconvenience you, Mrs Belhaven?'

Lily struggled to contain her outrage. 'N-no, I suppose not – but it seems a bit odd. Why the lass?'

Herbert replied awkwardly, 'My wife has heard a great deal about Clarrie from Will. She wishes to see her for herself. If it's not convenient, another time could be arranged.'

Clarrie saw Lily struggle to remain polite to one of her most prestigious customers. 'No, no, this afternoon will do.'

'Good,' Herbert said, touching his hat. He turned away.

'See you this afternoon, Clarrie,' Will called excitedly as they walked off.

Clarrie waved, ignoring Lily's furious look.

All the way home, Lily castigated her for fraternising with the Stock boy.

'Don't think you can start hobnobbing with the likes of them. It's not natural. Mrs Stock wants to warn you off being so familiar, more than likely. Mark my words, your airs and graces will get you into a heap o' trouble. Pride comes before a fall,' she sniffed. 'Isn't that right, Mr Belhaven?'

Jared walked with a frown. He gave a shake of his

head. 'It's a strange business. I wonder what she really wants?'

Only Olive was as excited as Clarrie. Later, when they were left to do the washing up, she said, 'I wish I was coming too. Do you think they'll give you afternoon tea? Bring me back a slice of cake, Clarrie. If they ask you again, say you'll take me next time!'

Hurrying over to Summerhill, Clarrie was caught in a spring squall and arrived wet through at the tradesman's entrance. No one answered her knock, so she went in to avoid further drenching. The kitchen was untidy and the range billowed smoke back into the room. She called out but no one replied. Clarrie took the back stairs that Will had shown her on Christmas Eve and emerged into the gloomy hallway. She stood for a moment waiting, but there was no sound of life from any of the rooms leading off the hall, only the heavy tick of the grandfather clock in the alcove. It was five past four.

'Hello? It's Clarrie Belhaven. Is anyone here?'

The front door opened and slammed. Will raced in.

'Clarrie! I've been waiting for you on the steps. How did you get past me?'

'I came in the back way,' she said, feeling awkward. 'Sorry.'

'Never mind, you're here now. Come on,' he said, 'Papa's in his study. He won't know you're here, cos you didn't ring the bell.'

Chastened, Clarrie followed him upstairs and

turned left along the landing. Will knocked on a door and went in without waiting for an answer. Herbert was dozing by a fire in a large room lined from floor to ceiling with books. A large mahogany desk stood in the elegant window, covered by a mass of papers spilling out of folders. Further documents stood in lopsided piles around the room.

'Papa, Clarrie's here!' Will cried, startling his father awake.

Herbert Stock looked up in confusion, his face creased in sleep and his eyes bleary. For a heart-stopping moment, Clarrie was reminded of her father waking in his study in Belgooree. Then Herbert struggled to his feet, smoothing a hand over his greying hair, and the fleeting similarity was gone.

'Miss Belhaven, thank you for coming. I didn't hear you arrive.' He held out a hand in formal greeting.

'She came in the servants' entrance,' Will said.

'Oh, of course.' Herbert shook her hand. 'You're cold and wet,' he said in concern. 'Come by the fire and warm up.' He pushed her gently towards the hearth. 'I'll go and see if Mrs Stock is awake.'

As he left, Will said, 'Can you play backgammon?'

Clarrie grinned. 'Very well.'

'Bet I can beat you!' Will fetched the set from behind a pile of books.

When Herbert returned ten minutes later, he found them in the middle of a lively game. Clarrie got up quickly. Herbert cut short his son's protest at being interrupted.

'Will, you can finish it later. Would you like to take Miss Belhaven to meet Mama?'

Will scrambled to his feet. 'Come on, Clarrie, this way.'

He led her back along the corridor, past the low chest on which the nativity scene had been displayed, and stopped outside the end door. He knocked gently and waited for an answer. A faint voice beyond said, 'Come.'

Clarrie was suddenly nervous of going into this stranger's bedroom, not knowing what she was going to find. It seemed intrusive. But then she thought of the state her father had been in when she had nursed him in his final months. It gave her the courage to step through the door. Illness and death no longer frightened her, for she had seen the face of both.

The room was curtained, dimly lit by one flickering gas lamp and unbearably stuffy from a roaring coal fire. There were dainty blue armchairs either side of the hearth and an elegant dressing table covered in glass jars, bottles and brushes gathering dust. A large four-poster bed dominated the far end of the room. Propped up against a mound of pillows was a tiny woman in a lacy cap. The table next to her was cluttered with medicine bottles.

'Mama,' Will said in a hushed voice, 'here she is!' He rushed towards the bed as if about to throw himself on top and then stopped.

Louisa raised a fragile hand and beckoned Clarrie forward. As she approached the bed she was hit by a sweet, sickly, bodily smell. Clarrie tried to hide her shock. This sallow-faced woman with hollowed eyes and straggly hair escaping her cap bore no resemblance to the pink-cheeked, bright-eyed woman she remembered.

'Hello, Clarrie,' she whispered in a papery thin voice. 'May I call you Clarrie?'

'Of course.' Clarrie smiled and stepped close, taking the hand that was offered. To her surprise the fingers were puffy, the thick gold wedding ring cutting into clammy flesh. 'I'm pleased to see you again, Mrs Stock. I'm sorry you've not been well. We miss you at church.'

Louisa's eyes gleamed with sorrow in the lamplight. 'Thank you.'

'Mama,' Will filled the pause, 'I'm beating Clarrie at backgammon.'

'You haven't won yet,' Clarrie laughed. 'Remember I've been playing it a lot longer than you.'

'How – are you – finding it – here?' Louisa asked in a slow, laboured voice. 'Have you settled?'

Clarrie hesitated. 'It doesn't feel like home yet,' she said frankly, 'but we manage, Olive and I. My Cousin Jared was kind to take us in.'

'Olive is your sister?' Louisa asked.

'Yes. She's the clever one – very artistic and musical – and she loves to read. Olive would love Mr Stock's library.'

'Perhaps – she could – borrow a book or two,' Louisa answered, her glassy-eyed gaze looking beyond Clarrie.

'Certainly, my dearest,' Herbert replied.

Clarrie glanced round in surprise, not realising he had followed them in. His face was full of tender concern.

'That's very kind, thank you. Olive would be so pleased.' Clarrie suddenly frowned. 'Except – Mrs Belhaven might not allow it. She only approves of reading the Bible.'

Will was incredulous. 'Doesn't that get a bit boring?'

'Will!' his father warned him. 'It's not for you to comment.'

'We could smuggle them in,' Will suggested, 'among the pie trays.'

'William, that's enough,' Herbert said. 'Why don't you and I go and rustle up some tea? Dolly said she'd leave it out ready.'

When they had left, Louisa indicated that Clarrie should sit on the chair by her bed.

'Clarrie, tell me – about – India. What – was it like?'

'It was the most beautiful place to live,' Clarrie said, sitting down. 'Our home was in the hills, surrounded by forests, among the Khassia people. I used to ride every day to see the sun rise over the mountains. I miss that greatly.'

'Go on,' Louisa said drowsily. 'I may – close my eyes – but I'm still listening.'

Once Clarrie began talking of her past life she found she could not stop. She told Will's mother all about Belgooree, her strong-willed Northumbrian father and her gentle half-Indian mother; about Kamal and Ama and Shillong, and the difficulty of growing tea in such a remote place; of Prince and the swami and the glory of the Himalayas. The only thing she did not speak of was the feud between her father and the Robsons, and Wesley's high-handed offer to save them. Thoughts of Wesley brought such a turmoil of resentment and guilt over her father's death that Clarrie could not even bring herself to mention his name. How he would gloat now to see her so humbled.

After telling Louisa briefly of her father's death and having to leave Belgooree for good, Clarrie fell silent in remembrance. In all the months of being in England, her cousins had never once asked her anything about Jock or the life she and Olive had led. She felt grateful to this invalid woman for allowing her to speak of it all at last.

Thinking Louisa had fallen asleep, Clarrie gently covered her swollen hand with her own and whispered, 'Thank you.'

Louisa's eyes opened and they stared at each other. 'I can see – why Will is – so fond of you,' she said.

Clarrie smiled. 'He's a very sweet lad.'

'Yes.'

They were silent for a moment. Clarrie thought

of the time when Will had shown her the nativity scene and she had been sure she had seen a woman in a nightgown crossing the landing as she left. Had Will's mother heard their conversation about the dead baby? She felt she had to say something, for the enormity of the loss pervaded everything – the room, the house, the family – like a miasma. She did not know how the birth had affected this woman's health, but she could see how sorrow was eating into her like a cancer.

'Mrs Stock,' Clarrie said gently, 'I'm very sorry that you lost your baby.'

Louisa withdrew her hand as if she had been scalded and let out a soft moan, turning her face away. Clarrie stood up. She had misjudged the situation. It was a private matter and now she had offended the kind woman who offered her friendship.

'I'm sorry if I've spoken out of turn,' she said. 'I didn't mean to upset you.'

As she stepped away, Louisa whispered, 'Stay.'

Clarrie stopped and waited. When Will's mother turned her face towards her, there were tears on her pallid cheeks.

'You – were – right,' she murmured. 'The baby – was a – girl. A beautiful girl.'

Clarrie moved quickly back and touched her arm.

'You heard me and Will on Christmas Eve, didn't you? You were there.'

'Yes.'

'He blamed himself,' Clarrie said quietly.

'Yes, poor boy. I haven't been able . . .' Her voice trailed away wearily.

Clarrie felt her throat tighten with tears. 'Did you give her a name?'

Louisa gave a shuddering sigh and shook her head.

'Perhaps you'd chosen one beforehand though?'

Louisa's eyes were pools of regret as she said, 'It was to be – Henry for a boy, Lucinda – for a – girl.'

'Lucinda, that's bonny.'

Louisa reached out her hand again and fumbled for Clarrie's. Clarrie held it gently in hers.

'I'll say a prayer for Lucinda,' she promised.

'I don't – even know where she's – buried,' Louisa groaned.

Clarrie searched for words of comfort. 'The Khassia believe that when a child dies, the soul takes the form of a bird and flies away, free from pain.'

'A bird?' Louisa repeated.

'Yes. The Khassia hills are full of beautiful, colourful birds.'

For the first and only time, Clarrie saw the trace of a smile flicker across Louisa's pained face.

'I like that,' she murmured. 'A beautiful bird.' She gazed on Clarrie with haunted eyes and whispered something so softly, Clarrie had to bend close to hear it.

'Thank you – for befriending – Will.'

After that, she closed her eyes and said nothing more. Clarrie tiptoed out and left her to rest. She met Herbert and Will coming up the stairs with a tray of tea and burnt toasted currant buns. Hearing that his wife was asleep, Herbert steered her back into his study.

'We're not very good at looking after ourselves without Dolly,' he apologised, offering her the plate of blackened teacakes.

'Is it her day off?' Clarrie asked, taking one anyway. Lily never baked sweet things, burnt or otherwise.

Herbert nodded, glancing at Will who was kneeling by the fire studying the backgammon game. He lowered his voice. 'Our cook had to leave unexpectedly last month to look after her sister's family. And, as you can see, my wife is bed-bound. She is used to doing all the household arrangements – takes pride in it – would never have a house-keeper.' He hesitated, looking uncomfortable. 'But domestically, well, things have slipped a bit, as you can probably tell.'

He paused to pour out the tea. It looked black as treacle. Herbert continued, giving her cautious glances.

'I've been trying to persuade Mrs Stock to agree to hiring some help while she convalesces. She's finally agreed that we need a housekeeper-cum-cook. Bertie's of the opinion we should advertise, but Mrs Stock doesn't want a stranger in the house.

She wants someone from the church.' He cleared his throat. 'That's why we thought – well, Mrs Stock wanted to see you first. It's important to her that it's someone who can put up with Will.'

'Put up with me?' Will piped up. 'What do you mean?'

'I'm talking to Clarrie,' Herbert said brusquely.

'Are you offering me the position of housekeeper?' Clarrie exclaimed.

'Umm, well, yes, I suppose I am. You did say you were used to running a household—'

'Yes,' Clarrie said at once. 'I'd like that very much. Of course I'll take it.'

Will jumped up and clapped in excitement. 'Oh, Papa, is Clarrie going to come and live here?'

'Yes.' Herbert smiled in relief. 'There's just one thing that concerns me. Are you quite sure the Belhavens can spare you? We don't wish to disrupt their business.'

Clarrie retorted, 'They managed fine before we came. I'm sure Mrs Belhaven will be glad to see the back of us; she makes no secret of how much she dislikes me and Olive.'

'Olive?' Herbert frowned. 'Oh dear, I wasn't thinking of offering a place to your sister too.'

Clarrie's face fell. She put down the over-strong cup of tea.

'I couldn't leave Olive in that place by herself, Mr Stock. You've no idea how hard it can be. She'd never manage on her own. Besides, she can bake and sew and play the violin – she could give Will lessons. She can paint too.'

'Oh, yes, Papa,' Will said eagerly, 'I'd like to learn the violin as well as the piano. Can I?'

Herbert scratched his chin in thought. 'It hadn't occurred to me. I'm sorry. I'll have to consult Mrs Stock. And Bertie, when he gets back from staying with the Landsdownes, will no doubt have an opinion on the matter.'

Clarrie nodded, her stomach clenching at the thought that the promise of escape might be snatched away again.

'And if we say no to hiring Olive as well,' Herbert asked, 'what would your answer be?'

Despite her longing to escape Cherry Terrace at any cost, Clarrie did not hesitate.

'I'd have to say no, Mr Stock. I've promised Olive I'll never leave her,' she said firmly, 'and it's a promise I will always keep.'

CHAPTER 11

'We're not a damned charity, Papa!' Bertie was indignant. 'It's bad enough you want to employ some half-caste Indian girl – a barmaid, for God's sake! – as housekeeper. Now we have to take in her wretched consumptive sister.'

Herbert was taken aback by his son's vehemence. 'She's not consumptive.'

'How do you know? She certainly looks as if a puff of wind would blow her over.' Bertie was contemptuous. 'We know nothing about these girls, except that they're related to those awful Belhavens. They run a spit and sawdust pub in the roughest part of Elswick and that pie woman stinks the church out on a Sunday.'

Herbert got up from behind his desk and started pacing in front of the window again. He was feeling browbeaten by his eldest son – had done for the past two days, since Bertie's return from the Landsdownes' country lodge near Rothbury. Bertie's criticism could be relentless, but he was an intelligent young man and far more in tune with what was socially acceptable than either of his parents. Perhaps that was the influence of Verity, whose brother Clive had been at prep school with Bertie. The Landsdownes were a step up the social ladder from the Stocks and Bertie was transparently in love with the demure daughter of the house. Pretty but vain and rather humourless was Herbert's opinion, but that was Bertie's affair.

'Papa,' Bertie threw up his hands, with a suddenly disarming smile that reminded Herbert of Louisa, 'you're a good man. I know you're trying to be kind to these unfortunate orphans, but what matters is whether they are capable at household affairs and suitable companions for Mama. I really don't see how the daughters of a second-rate major who made a mess of tea planting – and some Indian wife – can possibly be proper company for my dear, sick mother.'

Herbert looked at him in astonishment. 'How on earth do you know all that about the Misses Belhaven?'

Bertie suppressed a smug look. 'I've made it my business to find out, ever since you floated this madcap idea. The Landsdownes know something of the tea trade in India – some branch of the family are planters in Assam and tea brokers in London. Verity's very concerned about it all.'

Herbert felt niggled. 'Well, that's very good of her, but this is our decision, not the Landsdownes', for all their connections. I, for one, think Clarrie quite presentable; she's bright and industrious and always cheerful. Will adores her—'

Bertie gaffawed. 'You're going to make an appointment on the strength of what that scamp thinks? The boy's a dreamer – he thinks they're Indian princesses or some such nonsense. Lord above, Papa! You'll be employing a pixie for a gardener and a tooth fairy in the laundry next!'

'Don't be ridiculous,' Herbert sighed. 'And it's not just Will. Your mother seems set on taking them both in too. And quite frankly, I'm so concerned about her health that I'd employ anyone she wanted. Perhaps the Belhaven girls will be able to cheer her up.'

'But that's just it,' Bertie said angrily, sensing the battle being lost, 'she's in no condition to be making such decisions. We should be making them for her. And I believe we should be protecting her from these bizarre young women. They come without references, apart from Will's childish enthusiasm. We need to advertise the position in the normal way and take on someone competent for the job. Mama should have a properly trained nurse in attendance.'

Herbert felt stung by the implication that he was failing his wife. He had tried to bring in nursing help on several occasions, but Louisa had sent them away.

'I'm not ill,' she had said bleakly, 'I'm just tired.'

Herbert rubbed at his aching rheumatic leg and gazed out at the sheltered square. The first yellow trumpets of spring daffodils were opening.

'No, I've made up my mind,' he said, more firmly than he felt. 'I'm going to offer a place to both Belhaven sisters.'

He heard Bertie let go a contemptuous oath and march from the room, slamming the door behind him. Herbert let out a long sigh. He seemed incapable of making any of his family happy. Louisa always said that he was too lenient with Bertie yet too hard on Will. Well, he had stood up to Bertie now and no doubt his forceful son would take every opportunity to point out his foolishness in the weeks to come. Bertie's talent for being argument-ative was wasted as Herbert's articled clerk; he should have trained for the Bar. Herbert wished that his elder son would find contentment in something. Perhaps an engagement to Verity would help. He would try to encourage such a match. A happy marriage was a gift from heaven.

Herbert clenched his jaw to stop tears welling in his throat. His beloved Louisa was fading away in that fetid bedroom and nothing he said or did seemed to be able to stop her decline. It was as if she did not care if she lived or died. Since that terrible day . . . ! No, he would not dwell on it. She must get better. Life without her would be unthinkable. If only she would get well, he would never insist on sharing her bed again. It made him wretched to think his love and desire for her had caused her so much pain and heartbreak.

He strode to his desk and began to write out a letter of appointment to Clarrie and Olive. They would bring life and hope into this unhappy house. Between them, they would help his wife back to her former health.

'Get yersel' in here!' Lily ordered, holding out the thick, expensive envelope as if it scorched her fingers. 'Who's writin' you posh letters?'

Clarrie exchanged glances with her sister as she came in from the washhouse, wiping down her hands. Olive stood at the kitchen table, floury from pastry making, her look feverish with excitement and alarm. They knew their fate was sealed inside that letter.

'Well, open it!' Lily barked.

Clarrie took the letter and tore it open. She read the neatly written proposal, imagining Herbert Stock sitting at the mahogany desk as he penned it. Her heart thudded in shock. She read it again, just to make sure.

'It's from Mr Stock,' she gulped.

'What's he want?' Lily asked suspiciously.

Clarrie gave Olive a look of triumph. 'He's offering me a job as housekeeper – and Olive as housemaid.'

Olive clamped a hand over her mouth to stifle a gasp. Lily's jaw dropped open in disbelief.

'We're to start as soon as we can,' Clarrie said breathlessly. 'Next week if convenient.'

'Convenient?' Lily found her voice. 'I'll give him convenient!' she yelled. 'You plotted this, didn't you? First that daft boy and now his daft father – twisted him round yer little finger?' She marched on Clarrie. 'What else did you offer him, eh?'

Clarrie retorted, 'Nothing. He was the one offering me. Their cook's left and Mrs Stock can't cope. They wanted someone they knew from church.'

'From church?' Lily bawled. 'You're nowt but heathens, dirty little half-breeds! What they want you for?' She seized the letter from Clarrie's hand and grabbed at her hair, yanking it in her fury.

Clarrie cried out in pain.

'Leave her alone!' Olive shouted, dashing forward and digging her fingers into Lily's arm. 'You're hateful!'

Lily threw her off and shoved her backwards. Just at that moment, Jared rushed in and nearly fell over Olive sprawled on the floor.

'What's ganin' on?' He took one look at his wife gripping Clarrie's dark hair and cried, 'Lily, let the lass be! You can hear the carry-on halfway down Scotswood Road.'

Lily hurled Clarrie away from her with a scream of fury.

'Calm yersel', woman,' Jared said in alarm. 'What ever's happened?'

Lily shook the letter at him, her face purple. 'Treachery, that's what! That's all the gratitude I get for takin' in your cousin's little savages, and after showin' them the milk of human kindness. Thrown it back in me face. I knew they'd be nowt but trouble – didn't I warn you? But you wouldn't be told. Now they've wormed their way into the Stocks' house – my own customers! It's too much. I'll not let it happen. Tell them they can't go!'

She sank on to a hard chair and began a noisy sobbing. Clarrie helped Olive to her feet again, aghast at the sight of Lily in hysterics. The sisters held on to each other.

As Jared read the letter, Clarrie said firmly, 'We *are* going to work for the Stocks, Cousin Jared, and no one will stop us. It's why we came to England – to find employment and provide for ourselves so we wouldn't be a burden to anyone. We are grateful that you took us in and gave us work, but you should also be grateful that we've worked our fingers to the bone for you and Mrs Belhaven.'

Jared stared at her as his wife continued to sob. 'We're still responsible for you both,' he reminded her, 'until you come of age. That's not until next year, lass. We should've been consulted.' He gave her a stubborn look. 'I don't want to stand in the way of your advancement, Clarrie, but we'll expect to be compensated.'

'Compensated?' Clarrie echoed.

'Aye.' Jared nodded. 'You're family and you're wage earners. I'd expect Mr Stock to pay over half yer wages to us, yer guardians.'

Lily abruptly stopped crying and looked between them. 'That's right, you'll pay us. It's the least you can do. You'll not gan to the Stocks till it's sorted out.'

Clarrie held on to her temper. Family indeed! The Belhavens had a cheek to demand so much after the way they had treated Olive and herself. But it was a price worth paying to escape depressing Cherry Terrace and its endless drudgery.

'Half our wages then,' Clarrie agreed, 'until I turn twenty-one next year.'

Lily pointed at Olive and sniffed indignantly. 'Until that lass turns twenty-one.'

Clarrie faced her. 'No, Mrs Belhaven. Once I'm of age Olive shall be my responsibility and no one else's.'

She felt Olive's hand squeeze hers in support.

'We'll cross that bridge when we come to it,' Jared grunted, and retreated back to the bar.

CHAPTER 12

Lily did not speak to either sister again until they left the following week. She made them eat in the scullery and gave orders through Jared or Harrison. They were given heavy spring-cleaning chores, such as washing all the blankets, on top of their daily jobs.

But nothing could dampen Clarrie and Olive's excitement at leaving. Lexy and Ina were cock-a-hoop for their friend.

'Good on yer, hinny,' Ina cried, 'you deserve some'at better.'

'If it's high quality they're after,' Lexy laughed, 'put a word in for us, lass.'

Only when Clarrie asked after Maggie did their good humour vanish.

'Gone back to him, hasn't she?' Lexy sighed.

'Frightened not to,' Ina explained.

'Can't afford not to,' Lexy added indignantly.

Clarrie felt wretched for them all. She almost confided her idea of a tea room but thought that they might laugh at her too. Besides, she had failed to convince the Belhavens so it was never going to happen.

Clarrie and Olive had so little to pack that they left it to the Monday morning of their going. Jared had risked the wrath of his wife by offering them a lift on the rolley. When Olive looked under the bed, she gave a cry of distress.

'It's gone!'

'What has?' Clarrie asked.

'My violin – it's not there!'

Clarrie placed the candle on the floor and peered into the shadows. 'When's the last time you played it?'

Olive frowned. 'Weeks ago. You know how that woman hates it.'

'Lily!' Clarrie hissed. 'She'll have hidden it – just to spite us.'

At breakfast, Clarrie confronted her.

'Tell her, Mr Belhaven,' Lily replied via her husband, 'that I haven't hidden that instrument of the devil – wouldn't want it in my house.'

'Then where's it gone?' Clarrie persisted.

'Tell her,' Lily said with a satisfied look, 'that it's sold.'

'You've never sold it?' Olive gasped, her face crumpling.

'You had no right to!' Clarrie was furious. 'That belonged to our father.'

'Lily, dear—' Jared looked shocked.

'Don't Lily me,' she snapped. 'The money it fetched goes only a little way to paying for all the extra food this pair have cost me. So don't you gan feeling sorry for them.'

Olive was distraught. In the scullery, Clarrie tried to comfort her.

'We'll buy it back again,' she fumed, 'by heck we will! She might not tell us which pawnshop she went to, but we'll find it. I'll get word to Ina and Lexy to keep an eye out.'

Leaving the scullery for the last time, Clarrie got hold of the large pickle jar.

'What are you doing?' Olive gasped.

'Giving Gin-Lily a taste of her own medicine,' Clarrie said, and poured the gin down the drain.

It was a blustery April day when they left Cherry Terrace, perched up on the rolley with their trunk and waving a farewell to Harrison.

'Come and see us at Summerhill,' Clarrie encouraged him. 'We'll give you a cup of tea when you call with the pies.'

Clarrie had forced herself to say a civil goodbye to Lily, but the woman had ignored her and she had not lingered. Her spirits lifted higher with each yard that Barny pulled them further away from the pub. She sat with her arm round Olive, unable to keep a grin of delight from her face. Arriving at the back door of the Stocks' tall town house, Jared helped Clarrie carry the trunk down the basement steps.

Dolly came out to greet them in a billow of smoke. 'By, I'm glad to see you, miss. Range is smoking like a chimney.'

'Probably the flue,' Jared said. 'There's a sweep comes in the pub – I'll send him round if you like.'

'Thank you, Cousin Jared, that would be grand,' Clarrie said, climbing down. She gave Barny a final pat.

Jared hesitated. 'I know you haven't seen eye to eye with my Lily, but you will still order her pies, won't you?'

Clarrie quelled the resentment she felt inside; she knew how much they relied on that source of income. 'Yes,' she assured him. 'She makes good pies.'

Jared looked relieved.

Clarrie added, 'But you might want to keep an eye on what she keeps in her pickle jars.'

He coloured. 'Oh, the pickle jars.' He sighed heavily. 'I know all about them.'

Clarrie felt suddenly sorry for him. He had to deal with Lily's moods and sharp tongue every day of the year. 'We'll see you at church on Sunday,' she said, smiling. 'Thanks for the lift.'

'Ta-ra then, lasses. I'll miss you round the place.'

Clarrie gave him a look of surprise. 'Goodbye, Cousin Jared.'

Dolly showed them up to the servants' quarters

on the third floor. The room was plain but clean, with a washstand, a wardrobe and an iron-framed bed made up with fresh sheets. Light flooded in through a dormer window that gave a view high over the city's rooftops.

'Yours is next door,' Dolly told Olive, 'and mine's the room after that.'

'We have our own rooms?' Clarrie gasped.

'We've never had that,' Olive said, looking anxiously at her sister.

Dolly laughed at their astonished faces. 'Aye, it's grand, isn't it? I have to share with two sisters and a brother when I gan home. Can't wait to get back here after me day off.'

'What's it like working for the Stocks?' Olive asked.

'They're canny enough, the master and mistress,' said Dolly. 'Mind you, she's a proper worry – hardly eats and she's weak as a mouse. I have to help wash her cos she cannot get into the bath any longer. But you'll be doing that now. Master wants to see you in his study at ten – give you your orders. Mind you,' Dolly raised her eyebrows, 'it's more likely Mr Bertie will tell you what's what. He likes the sound of his own voice, that one. You would think it was him owned the place, not his da. Still, if you do what he says there shouldn't be any bother.'

Clarrie nodded, and Dolly turned to Olive.

'You stick with me and I'll show you what to do. There's a uniform in the wardrobe next door –

though you look a bit skinny for it. The Stocks like their servants to be smartly dressed.'

Olive gave Clarrie a worried look. 'Am I not to go with Clarrie to see Mr Stock?'

Dolly looked shocked. 'No, the housemaid only gans on the first floor when the master and Mr Bertie are out at the office – except if the mistress needs you. You're not to be seen – specially if they've got clients with them. Mr Bertie's very particular about that. But don't worry, the bells ring down in the kitchen if the mistress or Miss Clarrie need anything. Haway, then, Olive, let's get started.'

Olive gave Clarrie a look of panic tinged with resentment as she followed the chattering Dolly out of the room. Well, what did she expect? They were going to be treated like servants wherever they went and this house seemed better than most. Clarrie let out a nervous breath and made herself ready for her appointment with Herbert Stock.

'Do you have any questions, Miss Belhaven?' Herbert asked, standing in the window leaning on his stick. Bertie was lounging in an armchair watching her with undisguised contempt.

Clarrie's head reeled from all the information she had just been given about keys, supplies, ordering, mealtimes and menus. Olive would help Dolly in the kitchen and with general cleaning, while a woman called Marjorie came in twice a week to do the washing and ironing, and old Timothy gardened for the whole of the square and came in for his meals on a Tuesday.

As she searched for something to say, Bertie drawled, 'You do know about English food, I take it? It's just with you being Indian . . .'

Clarrie was needled by his condescending manner. 'My father was Northumbrian,' she reminded him, 'and I can recognise an English dish when I see one. I can cook most things.'

'You'll address me as sir,' Bertie reprimanded her, 'and my father too. I shall simply call you Belhaven.'

Clarrie flushed. 'Yes, sir.'

Herbert, looking uncomfortable, cleared his throat. 'Bertie, I thought you had a client to see at ten fifteen?'

'I cancelled the appointment so I could help with Belhaven.' He smiled thinly.

'Well, I think one of us should be at the office.' Herbert waved at him to go. 'I'll follow you over in twenty minutes.'

Reluctantly, Bertie stood up and stalked from the room.

Turning to Clarrie, Herbert explained. 'We've taken a small office on Westgate Road, so it's very convenient. Bertie's idea. He thinks it's more professional than having clients come to the house. I still like to entertain some of my commercial clients here, though – give them luncheon. Mrs Stock likes to arrange these things.' He stopped, his face tightening. 'She did like to,' he corrected. 'I suppose it depends on whether you can manage . . . ?'

'If that's what you want,' Clarrie said eagerly, 'then of course that's what I'll do.'

'Thank you, Clar— er, Miss Belhaven. What shall I call you?' He gave her a bashful look.

'Most people just call me Clarrie. I'm happy with that.'

'Clarrie it is then.' Herbert smiled and un-clenched his hands. 'Don't mind Bertie. He can be a bit particular about social conventions but he means well.'

Clarrie nodded, wondering how someone so pompous and full of himself could be son to Herbert, who appeared to have no airs or graces whatsoever.

'And what duties will I do for Mrs Stock?' she asked. 'Personally, I mean.'

'I'd like you to spend as much of your spare time with her as possible,' Herbert said. 'She's cut herself off from all social contact. Doctor says she's melancholic. Perhaps having a young woman for company might help and I know that she likes you.' His look was pleading. 'Do anything you can to raise her spirits, Clarrie.'

'I'll look in on her now, if I may?' Clarrie suggested. 'Just to say good morning.'

Herbert nodded, a look of relief lighting his face.

Clarrie found Louisa sleepy and uncommunica-tive, but returned later in the day with Olive and a tray of tea and pulled back one of the curtains.

'Daffodils are really coming on now we've had a

bit of spring sun,' she said cheerily, 'and the blossom's started. Just look at it, Mrs Stock.' She poured out tea into a thin china cup. The last time she had done that had been at Belgooree. Her hand shook as she placed it on the bedside table.

'This is my sister, Olive,' she said. 'Can we help you sit up?'

Louisa nodded, squinting in the bright afternoon light. Gently, the two sisters pulled her up against a pile of pillows.

'The musical one?' Louisa croaked. 'You play the violin.'

Olive nodded.

'Would you like Olive to play for you sometime?' Clarrie asked.

Louisa put her head back wearily and whispered, 'Perhaps.'

'The thing is,' Olive blurted out, 'Mrs Belhaven went and sold my violin without me knowing.'

Louisa's face clouded. 'Why?'

'For spite,' Olive said.

'Poor girl.'

Clarrie said quickly, 'Mrs Belhaven didn't understand what it meant to my sister. She needed the money. But we'll get it back.'

'Yes,' Louisa whispered, 'you must do that.'

Clarrie helped her take sips of tea until Louisa lost interest and sent the sisters away.

'Why were you sticking up for Gin-Lily?' Olive accused her as they hurried back downstairs.

'There's nothing to be gained by heaping our problems on to others,' Clarrie replied, 'especially a woman as ill as Mrs Stock.'

'She brought the subject up,' Olive pointed out. 'I thought I was going to give lessons to Will?'

'Just give it time,' Clarrie said. 'We need to gain their trust first – specially Mr Bertie.'

Olive pouted. 'I'm just a skivvy again like I was for the Belhavens. Nothing's changed.'

Clarrie rounded on her. 'Of course it's changed! You've got your own room, you can eat as much as you like and you don't have to go into that terrible pub every day not knowing if you're going to have to break up a drunken fight. And you haven't got Gin-Lily bullying you from morning to night!'

'Dolly's been bossing me about all day,' Olive said, close to tears.

Clarrie took her hands in hers. 'Listen, Olive, the day Father died our old life died with him. We have to look after ourselves now – no one else is going to do it for us – and that means we have to take what we're offered and work hard. You should be thankful to be a servant for a good family like the Stocks – there are scores of lasses out there who would give their right arm to be in your shoes, just remember that.'

She saw Olive blink back tears and knew how much more traumatic the upheaval of the past year had been for her delicate and sensitive sister. She squeezed Olive's hands.

'Things are going to get better from now on,' she said encouragingly. 'You just do your job and I'll deal with Dolly.'

The first month at Summerhill flew by. Clarrie worked as hard as ever, getting to grips with running the household, supervising the cooking, laying on luncheons for Herbert and his clients and helping with Louisa's daily care. She went to bed after midnight and was up again at four to draw up lists of duties for the day and do her paperwork in the quiet of the housekeeper's tiny sitting room off the kitchen.

She dealt with the tradesmen who came and questioned them about the neighbouring households and their staff. She made it her business to call on the other housekeepers around the square and introduce herself, asking their advice on suppliers and offering her help should they need it.

'We women can help each other out,' Clarrie said. 'You're welcome to call for a cup of tea on your half-day.'

Most were twice her age and rather taken aback by her forwardness.

'We tend to keep to ourselves,' one told her. 'The master and mistress like their privacy.'

But others were more welcoming, wanting news of Mrs Stock and glad of a friendly face. At the corner house belonging to a builders' merchant, Clarrie found a young widow called Rachel Garven who had only been in the job six months.

'It can be a lonely life,' Rachel confided. 'I'm from Cumberland and hardly know a soul in Newcastle. Any time off, I like to take the tram into town and just have a wander round the shops – be amongst people.'

Clarrie nodded in agreement. She knew about isolation at Belgooree when all the decisions had rested on her young shoulders and she saw it happening here; women weighed down with domestic burdens with nowhere to congregate and share their troubles.

'Perhaps we could go into town together one afternoon?' Clarrie offered. 'I've been here nine months and I've not been past Westgate Road.'

Rachel's eyes widened. 'I'd be happy to show you. I get Wednesday afternoons off and Sunday mornings.'

'I'll see what I can arrange.'

In the household, she divided duties between Dolly and Olive to minimise the friction between them. Dolly, being competent in the kitchen, was given most of the cooking to do, while Olive helped nurse Louisa and served at table after her morning chores. Clarrie helped out in all areas of the household, never asking the others to do something she was not prepared to do herself. As she had hoped, Olive's carping at having to get up early to lay fires and do endless polishing began to subside the more she grew to know Louisa. It was Olive, while helping wash her mistress and change the bed

201

linen, who remarked on her collection of Thomas Hardy and George Eliot novels.

'My favourite's *Mill on the Floss*,' Olive enthused. 'Father had a copy, but I read it so much it fell to bits.'

This sparked off the longest conversation Clarrie had ever heard Louisa have. From then on, Olive read to Louisa for half an hour every afternoon. Herbert was so delighted at this sign of his wife's taking an interest in something that he allowed Olive to borrow other books from his library for her own pleasure.

Distressingly, no one had been able to trace Jock's violin. Lexy had sent a message shortly after the sisters had left Cherry Terrace to say she and Ina had scoured all the neighbourhood pawnshops but Lily had not handed in a violin to any of them. But when Herbert got to hear of the violin's disappearance, he went out and bought Olive a new one.

'Now you can teach Will a tune or two, eh?' he said gruffly, embarrassed by Olive's tearful thanks.

So each evening, after supper, Will was to be heard in the old nursery on the second floor, scraping away on the new instrument, showing such promise that his father very soon bought him one of his own. Clarrie was amazed at Olive's patience with the boy, but she saw how playing again was reviving her sister's battered spirits. By summer, Olive was referring to herself as a lady's maid and music teacher when speaking to the other servants in the square.

She turned sixteen and began to blossom like a jungle flower after rain, her figure filling out and her face losing its pinched anxious look. Her reddish hair grew in thicker and more lustrous and when she smiled her pale brown eyes shone, making her whole face pretty.

Will, when he was not at school or practising his fiddle, followed Clarrie around like a faithful hound, chattering away and badgering her to play backgammon or cards. On wet days, he would take refuge from his critical brother or distracted father in Clarrie's sitting room and she would often find him curled up with a book on the lumpy sofa.

'Mama doesn't want to chat today,' he would tell her sadly, or, more mischievously, 'If Bertie comes looking for me I'm going to hide in the pantry.'

On the occasions Bertie found him down in the housekeeper's sitting room he would drag him out and reprimand Clarrie. He criticised her at every opportunity. Bertie had never revised his opinion that the Belhaven sisters were unsuitable and unqualified, and watched their growing popularity with his parents and brother with resentment. Clarrie observed that whenever Bertie returned from staying with the Landsdownes, or Verity called at Summerhill, his hostility towards her increased.

Verity herself treated Clarrie as if she were invisible. She neither acknowledged her nor responded to any of Clarrie's friendly comments about the weather or enquiries as to how her journey had been. Once, when Clarrie was arranging a vase of flowers in the drawing room, Verity called in with a friend after shopping. Olive took their armful of parcels while Verity swept uninvited into the drawing room.

'You!' She pointed at Clarrie. 'Bring us tea right away. We're utterly exhausted.'

Clarrie bit back a retort that no lady should be so rude to a servant and replied, 'Certainly, Miss Landsdowne.'

'Leave those flowers, Belhaven,' Verity commanded. 'You're doing it all wrong.' She flapped a glove at her.

As Clarrie crossed the room, Verity began rearranging the display.

'Can't expect a coolie to know how to do it,' she said to her friend.

Clarrie ground her teeth to stop herself answering back and hurried out.

When the school holidays came in August and Will had endless time on his hands, Clarrie found it impossible to keep the boy away from the kitchen quarters, even though she knew it would provoke censure.

One day, an infuriated Bertie rounded on Clarrie. 'You know he's not allowed down there, so stop encouraging him,' he barked. 'He'll never grow up to be a gentleman if he carries on mixing with the servants.' He gave her a particularly withering look. He was always rude to her out of his father's hearing, but on this occasion he seemed unusually maddened by her.

'My father may think it commendable that you're trying to ape your betters, but you're in danger of forgetting your position,' he went on. 'I don't know what society's coming to – maids teaching violin and borrowing books – housekeepers making social calls on the neighbours as if you're gentry! I blame all this nonsense on those unseemly women demanding votes and jobs as if they were men.' He wagged a plump finger at her. 'Well, don't think you can start any of that subversive behaviour in this household. We all know our place here – and you and that chambermaid sister of yours belong below stairs. Do you understand?'

Clarrie understood only too clearly. A couple of days later she was instructed that Verity Landsdowne and her parents were coming for dinner. It was a special visit and nothing was to go wrong. Herbert told her that the Landsdownes were shipping merchants, although Mr Landsdowne had handed over the day-to-day running of their business to Verity's brother Clive.

'Landsdowne likes to spend as much time as possible at his country lodge, Rokeham Towers, shooting and fishing. No doubt his daughter's had to drag him back to town now the shooting season's under way.'

'Well, I'm sure Miss Landsdowne's quite capable,' Clarrie murmured.

Herbert shot her a look. 'Capable of what? Dragging him back?'

Clarrie gave an innocent smile. 'Just capable.'

He gave her a bemused smile. 'Quite so. You'll discuss the menu with Mrs Stock.'

'Does she wish to join the dinner party?' Clarrie asked in astonishment.

'I don't suppose so.' Herbert sighed. 'But I want her to be a part of it. This is a significant occasion – something that will lift her spirits.'

'An engagement?' Clarrie blurted out.

Herbert gave her a look of consternation. 'I've said too much. Not for me to—'

'Don't worry, sir,' Clarrie smiled. 'I won't say a word.'

As she discussed the arrangements with a lacklustre Louisa, Clarrie could not help wondering how an engagement and marriage might alter things at Summerhill. Would Verity come to live with them, or would Bertie live elsewhere? Would Herbert take a lead from Mr Landsdowne and hand over more of his business to his son? If it gave him more time with Louisa and Will then perhaps he should. But Clarrie had seen enough of Herbert's dedication to his clients to know that his work was a vocation. He put in long hours and everyone Clarrie met remarked upon his reputation for reliability and trustworthiness. His work was his life.

Although Louisa refused to leave her bedroom when the Landsdownes came, Clarrie and Olive brought in extra chairs and made the room pretty with flowers so that she could receive her guests for a short while. The Stocks and the Landsdownes sat around the room with Louisa propped up in bed looking strained at all the attention. When Clarrie served out afternoon tea, ruddy-faced Mr Landsdowne astonished her.

'You must be the one whose father owned a tea garden in Assam?'

Clarrie gawped at him. 'Y-yes, sir.'

'We have connections in tea,' he said grandly, 'my wife's family. Young Bertie was interested in your background when you were offered your position. We were able to help.' He smiled as he said it, but his eyes were cold – like Verity's. Clarrie's insides clenched. What had been said about them? That her father had died of drink and in debt? That she and Olive had an Indian grandmother? Was that why Verity made disparaging remarks about coolies within earshot?

'Of course, my wife's relations are not just involved in tea,' Verity's father went on. He had the strange knack of addressing his comments to the Stocks but for Clarrie's benefit. 'Like all successful businessmen they have diversified over the years. Perhaps you know them – the Robsons?'

Clarrie banged down the teapot in shock, spilling drops on to the tray. Verity gave her a sharp look.

'Do be careful,' she snapped.

Clarrie went hot.

'Yes, I know of them,' Herbert answered. 'Made their money in farm equipment and boilermaking, didn't they?'

'Yes, and now they're doing tremendously well in tea,' Mr Landsdowne said with a satisfied nod, 'not just as growers but as importers and retailers. Making money hand over fist if James is to be believed.' He smiled at Louisa. 'James Robson is my wife's second cousin. Your housekeeper must have come across him in India.'

Louisa's face tensed further as if the effort to entertain them was all too much.

'No, sir, I didn't,' Clarrie answered quickly, watching her mistress with concern.

'Well, his nephew Wesley, perhaps?'

Clarrie's heart thumped. She swallowed hard, busying herself mopping up the spillage on the tray. All she wanted was to get out of the room and away from these people.

'He's done very well for such a young man,' Mr Landsdowne continued, turning to Herbert. 'At twenty-six he's been to plantations all over India and Ceylon, and now he's a tea broker in London. Knows everything there is to know about tea, so they say.'

'Is that so?' Herbert replied with a nod of admiration. 'A quick learner.'

Clarrie's annoyance flared. 'It takes many years to really know about tea,' she said. 'Year in year out – planting it, nurturing it through good seasons and bad – till it's in your blood.'

They all stared at her. She picked up the tea tray, blushing. How stupid of her to be provoked simply by hearing Wesley's hateful name.

Mr Landsdowne gave her a frosty glare as she hurried out, mumbling about making a fresh pot. Through the open door, she heard Verity say, 'It's a bit rich being lectured by the daughter of a failed tea planter, Papa.'

Clarrie froze beyond the door, unable to stop herself listening to more.

Her father snorted. 'Yes, my dear, it is. Especially when the Robsons are going from strength to strength.'

Bertie joined in. 'I'm sorry she was so outspoken. I'll have a word with her.'

'Come, come, gentlemen,' Herbert chided, 'the girl was merely speaking up for her father. She's to be pitied for her straitened circumstances.'

Verity's father grunted. 'Belhaven was always a failure in business from what I hear and always hankering to rise above his station. Had a grudge against the Robsons all his life because they were more successful. Keep an eye on his daughters, that's all I say.'

'Don't worry, Papa, Bertie knows how to handle servants,' Verity said sweetly, 'and so do I.'

Clarrie fled downstairs, furious at their contempt for her father and their condescension towards her and Olive. She felt like ripping off her starched apron and cuffs and marching out. No one spoke to a Belhaven like that! She banged around the kitchen, refilling the teapot, hot water jug and milk, muttering furiously.

A hinge squeaked behind her and she jumped round guiltily. The pantry door opened and Will peered out.

'Is it safe to come out?' he whispered.

Clarrie gasped. 'They've been looking for you! You've got to go and say hello to the Landsdownes.'

He rolled his eyes heavenwards. 'I don't want to. They're boring and Verity doesn't like me. She's always telling me to run along and leave her and Bertie alone.'

'Well, we all have to do things we don't want to.' Clarrie was short with him.

He eyed her more closely. 'You're all red in the face. Have you been crying?'

'No!'

Will plunged his hands into his pockets and sighed. 'You know Verity and Bertie are going to get married?'

Clarrie looked at his forlorn face and felt her heart melt.

'Does it matter, as long as it keeps Bertie happy?'

Will looked perplexed. 'But why her? She doesn't even play backgammon.'

Clarrie snorted with sudden laughter. She swung an arm round him. 'Oh, Will, you're a grand lad. Don't ever change.'

He put his arms round her waist and hugged her in return. 'I suppose if Bertie's happy, he might not bother telling us off quite so much.'

'That's right,' Clarrie agreed, 'either that or they'll both come after us.' She kissed the top of his head. 'Come on, we'll face them together – the Two Musketeers.'

With Will beside her, Clarrie returned upstairs with a proud lift of her Belhaven chin.

CHAPTER 13

'Miss Landsdowne wants a December wedding,' Clarrie told her friend Rachel when they met in the Empire Tea Rooms in town. It was their favourite haunt, a high-ceilinged café with stained glass windows, fresh flowers on crisp linen tablecloths and screens of potted palms giving privacy to customers who wanted it. Olive sat beside them doodling patterns in a notebook. 'She's forever coming round to talk about arrangements – Mrs Stock's worn out already.'

'Where are they going to live when they're married?' Rachel asked, pouring out a second cup for them both.

Clarrie grimaced. 'At Summerhill to start with. That's another thing – Miss Landsdowne wants to rearrange the whole of the second floor as an apartment for her and Mr Bertie. He says he has to be near the office and she likes being in town. The Landsdownes are giving them a house on their country estate for weekends.'

Rachel rolled her eyes. 'All right for some. Me and Bob had one room in a cottage and thought ourselves lucky.'

'I don't know where poor Will's supposed to go,' Clarrie said. 'Upstairs in the attic if that Verity gets her way.'

'He's a nice lad.' Rachel sighed. 'Bob wanted a son. Just as well we didn't, as it turned out. How would I have kept a lad with Bob gone?'

Clarrie saw the tears brimming in her friend's eyes and reached out a hand. 'Sorry. I shouldn't be chattering on about weddings.'

Rachel shook her head. 'I don't mind. I like you chattering on.' She blew her nose on a starched handkerchief. 'And I'm glad of the company. I'd never come in here on my own.'

Clarrie smiled. 'I'm glad too.' She turned to her sister. 'Let's see what you've done.'

'It's not any good,' Olive said, reluctantly handing over the notebook. It was a bold design of interwoven birds and flowers that seemed to jump off the page.

'It's very good,' Clarrie contradicted her, and showed it to Rachel.

Rachel nodded. 'You're such a clever lass. Where do you get your ideas from?'

Olive shrugged. 'They're just there in my head.'

The exuberant style reminded Clarrie of the lush natural beauty of Belgooree, but she did not say so. Olive became easily upset at any mention of their life in India; it was like opening up a raw wound.

'Well, it's better than most of the things hanging on the walls at Number Six,' Rachel said. 'The master likes maps and boats – dull as anything. You should paint this in bright colours, Olive.'

The girl blushed with pleasure.

'You're right,' Clarrie agreed. 'I just wish I had the money to buy her a proper set of paints.'

'I used to have paints and brushes and an easel,' Olive said reproachfully.

'And you will again,' Clarrie said, 'when we're not handing over most of our wages to the Belhavens. Just be patient.'

'Be patient?' Olive scowled, snatching back the notebook. 'That's all you ever say.'

Clarrie did not want to have an argument in front of her friend. She shared Olive's frustration, though she wished her sister could be less temperamental. Olive proceeded to sigh and drum her pencil on the notebook in a clear indication that she was bored and wanted to leave.

Clarrie tried to ignore her. These rare moments of luxury, of sitting down and being served by others, of talking to Rachel and eavesdropping on the middle classes of Newcastle, were what got her through the long week. There were a group of women having a meeting in an alcove discussing a local by-election. At the next table, four friends were working their way through three tiers of sandwiches and cakes while talking about their children. In the corner was a couple who had come in separately; Clarrie suspected it was a clandestine meeting.

Reluctantly, she finished her last drop of tea. 'Come on,' she said with an apologetic look at Rachel, 'we'll have a wander in the sunshine.'

The warm weather continued on into September. 'An Indian summer', Herbert called it. Thoughts of sitting on the veranda at Belgooree gave Clarrie the idea of encouraging Louisa out of bed to sit by the open balcony window and view the garden in the mild air. Her mistress was growing painfully thin. It was much easier for Olive and her to lift Louisa now her legs were wasted from lack of use.

Louisa sat sighing by the window, but seemed content enough to be left there. Her face would light up at the sight of a lanky Will racing home from school and waving to her from across the square. His legs were suddenly longer and more gangling since the summer holidays, and he would bound upstairs and plonk himself at his mother's feet to chatter.

One time, when Verity was trying to interest Louisa in the refurbishment of the second floor rooms, Will clattered in and knocked over a pile of material samples. Clarrie, who was serving tea, hurried to pick them up.

Verity tried to hide her exasperation with false laughter. 'What a clumsy boy you are!'

'Sorry,' Will said, rushing to kiss his mother, then proceeded to ignore his future sister-in-law. 'Look, Mama, my first conker!' He pulled out a shiny nut from the pocket of his shorts. 'Clarrie can help me string it.'

'Aren't you a little old for conker fights?' Verity asked. 'You're nearly thirteen. Clive was boxing by your age – doing men's sports.'

Louisa put a protective hand on her son's fair hair. 'He's still young,' she said fondly. 'Plenty of time for manly things later.'

It was shortly after this that Clarrie overheard Bertie suggesting to his father that Will be sent to boarding school.

'He needs toughening up, Papa. And he's spending far too much time with the servants. The boy's got no manners. He can be quite rude to Verity,' he complained.

Herbert let go an impatient breath. 'I'm the first to admit the boy can try one's patience, but I wouldn't want to send him away. Besides, your mother would never allow it. Verity will get used to him in time.'

The weather turned suddenly chill and autumnal, and Louisa retreated back to bed. No more mention was made of boarding school as Verity threw herself into elaborate preparations for the wedding. The couple were to be married in St Nicholas's Cathedral with a reception and ball at the Assembly Rooms the week before Christmas. Half of Newcastle seemed to be invited. Clarrie knew she was in for a hectic time, for Bertie wished to host a large reception the evening before the wedding and offer accommodation to relations travelling from Yorkshire.

It was Will who aroused her concern over Louisa.

'Mama's got a funny cough,' he told her, 'and she hasn't touched her supper again.'

Louisa ate so little that her abstinence had not struck Clarrie as odd, and anyway it was often Olive who went to and fro with her meals. Clarrie had been so busy of late with Verity's demands that she had spent little time with her mistress, other than to give her the regular bed bath. For the past two days, Louisa had refused to be washed or even touched, and whenever Clarrie had looked in she had been asleep. Why had she not taken more notice? Clarrie thought with a stab of guilt.

Bertie and Verity were out at the theatre, and Clarrie hurried to Louisa's room to find her mistress flushed and glassy-eyed, her breathing wheezy. When Clarrie put her hand to her forehead, she whimpered, 'Leave me alone! Please leave me.'

'You're burning hot, ma'am,' Clarrie said in concern.

Louisa began a painful coughing.

'I'm going to fetch the doctor,' Clarrie said at once.

'No,' Louisa gasped between coughs, 'no – more – doctors.'

Clarrie attempted to prop her up to ease her coughing, but she winced and shivered as if Clarrie had touched her with fingers of ice. In a panic, Clarrie went in search of Herbert and found him working in his study. The look of fear on her face brought him to his feet.

'What ever's wrong?'

'It's Mrs Stock – she's not at all well. I think she's got a fever.'

'Fever?' Herbert repeated. 'But I saw her this morning—'

Clarrie interrupted. 'She's hot as a fire and she hasn't been eating these past couple of days – just sleeping.'

'Why didn't you say anything?' he asked her sharply.

'I'm sorry.' Clarrie flushed. 'I think we should call out the doctor, sir.'

'I'll go myself,' Herbert snapped.

Clarrie shook her head. 'Let me, so you can go and sit with her.'

He nodded and went, leaving his work scattered across his desk.

When Clarrie returned with the doctor and showed him upstairs, Will was sitting anxiously on the bed while Herbert stood by the fire with his hands clasped behind his back. When the doctor entered Herbert chased his son from the room and Will took refuge with Clarrie downstairs.

'Perhaps Olive could read to her,' the boy

suggested, 'or I could play her a tune. Do you think that would help?'

'I'm sure it would, but maybe tomorrow when she's had a night's sleep. Why don't you go and find Olive – do some practising?'

Will seized on the chance to do something and ran off to look for Olive. Then the bell in the study rang for her and Clarrie hurried upstairs. The doctor was taking a quick nightcap with Herbert. Bertie had returned and was swigging back a large whisky.

'Mrs Stock has caught a chill,' the doctor told her.

'It's hardly surprising,' Bertie said loudly. 'Belhaven here has had my dear mother sitting for hours in front of a draughty window, as if we lived in the tropics.'

'Surely that's not the cause?' Clarrie said in consternation.

The doctor held up his hand as if it was fruitless to cast blame. 'I've prescribed medicine and a vapour rub. Her temperature is higher than it should be. You need to bathe her with a lukewarm cloth through the night to keep her cool. Try to get her to drink something if you can.'

'Yes, sir.'

'I'll return tomorrow,' he assured Herbert, with a pat on the shoulder. 'By then the worst may have passed.'

Clarrie was prepared to sit up through the night with Louisa, stung by Bertie's harsh accusation, but at midnight Herbert sent her to bed.

'I'll stay with her,' he said with a grim look. 'I can't sleep tonight.'

Clarrie stood up, exhausted but anxious, not wanting to leave. Louisa was fretful, her eyes closed. She moaned and turned her head as if in discomfort, yet did not respond to any of their questions.

As Clarrie left, she said, 'Ring for me if you need me, sir – what ever the time.'

Herbert nodded but his gaze never left his wife.

Clarrie made up a bed on the floor of the house-keeper's sitting room in case he should call, then lay down fully clothed. At three in the morning, as she was drifting off to sleep, she came wide awake at the sound of someone padding into the room.

'There you are!' Will whispered, clutching his violin case. 'I thought you were with Mama, but I went in and Papa told me to get out. He says I'll only make her worse. But I can't sleep. Can I stay here? *Please.*'

'Course you can.' Clarrie did not hesitate, even at the thought of what an irate Bertie might say. She got up and wrapped a blanket round Will's shaking shoulders. 'Curl up in the chair; I'll make us a hot drink.'

She boiled up some hot milk and stoked up the fire. Together they sipped and talked quietly about trivial everyday things. Eventually, Will yawned and grew drowsy. By the time Clarrie had taken their cups to the sink and rinsed them, the boy was fast asleep. She dowsed her face in cold water and went upstairs with a fresh pot of tea.

Herbert had gone to sleep with his arms splayed across the bed. As soon as Clarrie approached, she heard the change in Louisa's breathing. It rattled and rasped in her throat like pebbles in a fast-flowing stream. Clarrie gasped and banged down the tray. She had heard that sound before – in her dying father.

Herbert woke up with a start.

'What? What!' he said in confusion.

Clarrie took Louisa's hand; there was hardly a pulse. Suddenly, Louisa's eyes opened and fixed on Clarrie. She tried to speak. Clarrie turned to Herbert and put Louisa's hand into his.

'She's trying to tell you something,' she said with urgency.

As Clarrie stepped out of the way, Herbert clasped his wife's hand to his face.

'What is it, my love?' he asked, his voice cracking. 'Tell me!'

'W-Will,' Louisa murmured. 'Will . . .'

'Will what?' Herbert demanded. 'Shall I send for the doctor? Is that what you want?'

She shook her head and looked pleadingly past her husband to Clarrie. In that moment, Clarrie knew what she was trying to say.

'She wants Master Will,' Clarrie cried. 'I'll go for him.'

Without waiting for permission, Clarrie pressed

on the bell that rang in the quarters below and dashed out of the room.

A bedraggled Will met her halfway up the stairs, eyes wide in alarm.

'I heard the bell and you were gone—'

'Your mother wants to see you,' Clarrie said, her heart squeezing at the sight of his worried face. 'Go to her quickly.'

Will leaped up two steps at a time then turned. 'I forgot my violin – she'll want to hear it.'

Clarrie stopped him. 'You go ahead, I'll fetch it.' He hesitated. 'Go on!' she urged.

The boy ran on, calling out to his mother that he was coming. Clarrie rushed back for the instrument, heart pounding with dread. The violin lay under a tangle of blankets that Will had thrown off in his haste to answer the bell. She seized it quickly and hurried back upstairs.

Clarrie found Herbert still clutching his wife's hand, just as she had left him. Will hovered beside him. Louisa's eyes were half closed, her mouth half open. Her ragged breathing had eased a fraction.

The boy turned to Clarrie, his eyes full of tears. 'Mama's not saying anything,' he whispered. 'I don't think she knows who I am.'

Herbert said nothing. On impulse, Clarrie held out the violin.

'She wants you to play – that's what she said.'

Will hesitated, glancing at his father. 'Shall I, Papa?'

Herbert did not seem to hear him. All he could do was hang on to his wife's hand as if by doing so he could anchor her in this world.

Clarrie touched the boy's shoulder and nodded in encouragement. 'Do it for your mother,' she said gently.

Will clutched the violin under his chin and began a shaky rendition of 'Water of Tyne', which Olive had recently taught him. When he got to the end, he paused, then played it again, this time with more assurance, the notes soaring to fill the room.

At the last stroke of the bow, the sound reverberated around them as if reluctant to die away. The memory of the tune seemed to hang in the air, as silence settled once more. Total silence. Will stood with his violin suspended and Herbert gripped Louisa.

Clarrie stifled a gasp. Louisa's noisy breathing had stopped. She reached out to Will. 'She's gone,' she said softly.

But he flinched away, dropping his instrument, and leaped round the bed.

'Mama?' he cried. 'Mama!'

Herbert let out a terrible groan, as if a mighty blow had winded him. Clarrie picked up the violin and hurried to the door to leave them to their grief. Moments later, she heard Herbert roar, 'Get away! Don't touch her!'

Will screamed, 'She's not dead! She's not!'

Clarrie froze. She wanted to run back in and

throw her arms about the boy and comfort him, as his father should be doing.

'Get out!' Herbert howled like an animal in a trap. 'Leave me with her, for God's sake.'

Will came tearing out of the bedroom, sobbing and wild-eyed.

'Will—' She tried to stop him, but he pushed her out of the way and fled down the passageway, flinging himself down the stairs. She heard him rattling at the front door, trying to escape. Quickly, she ran along to Bertie's room and hammered on the door.

'Please, sir, come quickly!' she shouted and kept knocking until he answered.

'What is it?' he scowled, his usually slicked hair tousled.

'I'm sorry, Mr Bertie,' she gasped, 'it's your mother. Your father needs you.'

Seeing the state she was in, he went at once, asking no more. Clarrie clattered downstairs in pursuit of Will. He had unlocked the solid front door and left it wide open. She ran into the square, searching for him among the shadows in the dim gaslight. Please God, he had not run further into the town.

Clarrie heard weeping as she rounded the corner. Will was crouching down by the railings, shaking and wretched. She leaned down and touched him on the shoulder.

'I'm so sorry, Will,' she whispered.

'It's m-my fault,' the boy sobbed. 'I thought I could m-make her b-better with music. So b-babyish. I'm a stupid boy – a stupid, stupid boy!'

Clarrie knelt down beside him. These were Herbert's and Bertie's censorious words he repeated.

'Nothing is your fault,' she told him firmly. 'Your mother has been ill for a long time. She wasn't strong enough to fight off the chill she caught. Even the doctor couldn't save her.'

'He t-told m-me to g-go,' Will said, distraught. 'Papa h-hates me.'

'No, never,' Clarrie insisted. 'Your father is too upset to know what he's saying.' She pulled him into her arms. 'He'll need you, Will. You have to comfort each other, not run away. Promise me, you won't ever run away?'

He nodded and leaned into her hold. 'You won't go, will you? Now that Mama is—' He could not bring himself to say the word.

'Course not,' Clarrie promised. 'I'll stay as long as I'm needed.'

She held on to him in the chilly dark, wishing she could protect this loving, affectionate boy from the grief she knew was about to engulf him.

CHAPTER 14

That winter, No. 12 Summerhill was plunged into deep mourning. Herbert was inconsolable. Social engagements were abandoned and Bertie's wedding was postponed. Herbert shut himself away for long hours in his study, relentlessly increasing his caseload to blot out his grief. He was curt to Clarrie and no longer gave Olive free range of his books, punishing them for not bringing Louisa's deteriorating condition to his attention. For a time he was so cold towards them that Clarrie thought they might be dismissed and flung on to the street, but for some reason it did not happen.

Will moped around the house like a lost soul, subdued and unhappy. His thirteenth birthday came and went without celebration, save for Clarrie and Olive buying him sheet music and Dolly baking him a cake. Clarrie tried to comfort him as best she could, encouraging him to play his music. But Herbert could not bear to hear the violin.

'Stop that fearful noise, for pity's sake!' he would bawl along the landing. 'We're in mourning for your mother – have you no respect?' Then he would slam his study door closed again.

After several such reprimands, Will lost the appetite for playing and gave up his practising with Olive. Clarrie's heart ached for the boy and she wondered if she should intervene on his behalf. But Herbert seemed lost in a dark, lonely place and she was reminded of her father after her mother's death.

'Give it time,' she counselled Will. 'Your father must be allowed to mourn in peace, but he won't always want silence. As my old friend Kamal used to say, "Remember, the sun always comes back after the rain." '

Will stood with his hands plunged into his pockets and shook his head in disbelief. He came less and less to her sitting room downstairs and kept more to his own room or sneaked into his mother's and sat there alone among the dusty books and bottles of perfume; Herbert had forbidden anything to be touched or tidied. He was often late home after school and Clarrie knew that he wandered the town to delay his return to the unhappy house. But his father, if he noticed at all, seemed not to care.

Bertie was the most difficult of them all. His usual cajoling and bullying of his father into doing as he wished no longer worked. Herbert would not even talk about setting a new wedding date. Verity seldom called, shunning the desolate house, but Clarrie was sure that she was putting pressure on Bertie to act.

Bertie, who had shown little grief for a mother who paid him scant attention compared to Will, took out his frustration at the enforced mourning on the servants. He reduced Olive to tears by hurling shoes at her.

'Call these polished? They're a disgrace!'

He offended Dolly by sending back her food as inedible, and took every opportunity to humiliate Clarrie in front of clients.

'Belhaven, bring us tea – good English tea, none of that spicy native muck you drink.'

Once she overheard him explaining about her to a portly grocer who had eyed her frostily on the doorstep.

'Is she a half-breed?'

'Yes. Belhaven's one of my father's waifs and strays from church, I'm afraid.'

'He's a good man, yer father,' the grocer grunted. 'Just hope she's grateful.'

Clarrie inwardly seethed at their disparaging remarks, but forced herself to be outwardly impassive. She could not risk jeopardising her or Olive's employment at this stage, but one day she would be avenged of all the slights and petty cruelties.

At the end of January 1907, Clarrie turned

twenty-one. In triumph, she went back to visit her cousins at Cherry Terrace with the last wages she would hand over to them. She had seen Jared and Lily every week at church where she would hand over the payments, but she had never returned to the pub.

It looked as dreary and smoky as she remembered, the brick terraces grimy with soot and the lanes slippery with mud and stagnant puddles. She picked her way carefully to the back door and entered to the sound of Lily haranguing some poor waitress.

'Look what the cat dragged in,' Lily sneered on seeing Clarrie standing there in her housekeeper's uniform. At once, Clarrie could tell she was inebriated by the way she swayed and steadied herself against the table. Even so, the kitchen looked its usual hive of activity, pies cooling on the table and a coating of flour lying over the furniture. The young girl scurried away, sensing trouble.

'Hello, Mrs Belhaven. I've come with the last of our payments,' Clarrie told her without ceremony, holding out the package. 'I was twenty-one last week. Thought you'd want it now rather than wait for Sunday.'

Lily sniffed and took it. 'How thoughtful of you,' she said in a derisive tone, 'and happy birthday. Hope you weren't showing yersel' up by celebratin' when the Stocks are in full mournin'?'

'Course not. Where's Cousin Jared?'

'Off somewhere with the rolley,' Lily complained.

'Never here when he's needed. That useless lass and daft Harrison are all I've got to help me.' She flopped down on to a hard chair. 'Don't suppose you'd like to lend a hand for the afternoon?'

'Not on my afternoon off,' Clarrie said pointedly. 'I'm meeting a friend.'

Lily gave her a sour look. 'Ungrateful little madam,' she muttered.

Clarrie was stung by the accusation. 'Perhaps you should show a bit more gratitude for what Olive and I did for you, for a change – not to mention the money I've provided for nearly a year for nothing in return!'

Lily gawped in shock.

'Well, we've done enough,' Clarrie declared, 'and that's an end to it.'

Lily hauled herself up. 'That's what you think! You might be of age, but yer sister isn't. We're still her legal guardians and we want a share of her wages till she's twenty-one an' all.'

Clarrie advanced on her in fury, forcing Lily to take a step back. 'Just you try!' she cried. 'You'll not get a penny more of my sister's wages, and if you threaten her I'll get Mr Stock to take you to law. I'll not let you hold Olive back any longer – she's got more God-given talents than the rest of us put together and I'm going to see that she uses them.'

Lily was momentarily speechless; then, scowling, she said, 'You're full of hot air – wouldn't dare tak' us to law! I'll have what's rightfully mine.'

'You have no right over Olive's wages or over anything she does any more,' Clarrie declared. 'She's my sister and my responsibility. And if you want the Stocks to continue as your customers you'll drop any further demands.'

Lily swayed, her face betraying sudden doubt. 'You'd not harm me business?'

'You leave Olive alone and I'll leave your business alone,' Clarrie bargained. 'And while we're about it, you can tell me who you sold her violin to.'

'Can't remember,' Lily said with a dismissive wave. 'It was poor quality – hardly fetched enough for a sack of flour.'

'What would you know about the quality of a violin?' Clarrie protested.

'I wouldn't want to know,' Lily said, her lip curling with distaste. 'Playing them things leads to sin.'

'Well, when you remember, I want to know,' Clarrie said determinedly, 'so I can buy it back. It was my father's and belongs in our family.'

Suddenly Lily's face sagged like baking collapsing. She dropped on to a chair again.

'I knew you'd be bother, right from the start,' she grumbled. 'That fool of a husband of mine thought there'd be money left from India – couldn't believe that useless cousin of his could have lost it all!' She gave Clarrie a hate-filled glare. 'But I always thought the pair of you'd be trouble – what with that dirty foreign blood in yer veins.'

Clarrie gripped the back of a chair to control her

anger. 'My mother, who you despise so easily without ever having met her, had more kindness and goodness in her short life than you ever will should you live to be ninety. I'm proud to have her Indian blood running through my veins, so your insults don't hurt me.' Clarrie gave her a look of contempt. 'It's you I pity, cos it doesn't matter what's in your veins, you'll never be happy. As long as you carry on caring for no one but yourself, you'll stay a bitter and unhappy woman. I don't know how Cousin Jared stands it.'

Lily's face twisted in outrage. Hauling herself to her feet, she shouted belligerently, 'How dare you? Gerrout!' She picked up a wooden spoon and began hitting Clarrie with it. Clarrie raised her arm protectively and backed away as Lily screamed, 'I never want to see yer in me house again, do y'hear? Out! Out! Gerrout!'

Clarrie rushed for the back door with Lily stumbling behind, cursing. Quickly, Clarrie escaped across the yard and out into the back lane with Lily bawling after her. She hurried from the humiliating scene, shaken yet triumphant. She had finally given the bullying Lily a piece of her mind. Just let her try to take her threats about Olive any further. Under her blustering cruelty, Lily was nothing but a coward and a drunk; someone to be pitied more than feared.

Turning, breathless, into the street at the bottom of the lane, Clarrie collided with a man carrying a basketful of packages.

'Watch yer step!'

She grabbed at his tottering parcels. One fell to the ground and burst open, scattering black tea leaves over her shoes. 'Sorry!'

She looked up into the annoyed face of the delivery man as she tried to salvage the half-empty package.

'Jack Brewis?' she gasped.

'Aye, and who are—' he began, then stopped, peering closer. 'You're that lass who knaws all about tea. Clarrie, isn't it?'

She smiled and nodded.

'What you running away from so fast – the devil or the coppers?' he teased.

'Something worse.' She laughed in relief.

'That harridan at the Cherry Tree?' he guessed. 'That explains it.' He gave her a quizzical look. 'But I thought you'd left – haven't seen you about for months.'

'I was just visiting.'

'I kept an eye out for you,' he said.

'Did you?' Clarrie was pleased.

He grinned. 'Well, no one else round here spends money on Darjeeling.'

Clarrie laughed. 'Perhaps I'll buy some more then. At least let me pay for what I've spoilt.'

'Don't be daft,' Jack said at once, taking the half-empty package from her. 'One less packet won't make any difference. I might be out of a job shortly anyway.' He looked suddenly glum.

'Why's that?' Clarrie asked.

Jack sighed. 'Mr Milner's having a hard time of it. Some of the other tea companies are jealous like – don't want him to succeed – and are trying to spoil his business. You wouldn't believe the half of it.' He stopped and gave her an anxious look. 'I shouldn't be telling you this. What can a lass like you do about it, anyways?'

'Perhaps I can help more than you think. I work for a solicitor now – I'm a housekeeper,' she told him proudly.

His hazel eyes widened with interest. 'I thought you were looking canny smart. Who d'you work for?'

'The Stocks at Number Twelve Summerhill.'

'Summerhill, eh?' He whistled in admiration. 'By, you've come up in the world!'

'Aye,' Clarrie grinned, 'and I intend to go further.'

He gave her a mock bow. 'I'm honoured you're still speaking to the likes of me, Jack Brewis, tea delivery man, soon to be out of a job if Mr Milner can't see off the opposition.' Jack sighed heavily, unable to remain flippant. 'It's a crying shame, Clarrie, cos he's a canny boss. I was ill over Christmas and he paid me till I was back on me feet, though he couldn't afford it – not with his rivals ganging up against him. Thing is it's hard for him to prove anything, but he's sure they are.'

Clarrie put a hand on his arm. 'Tell him to speak to Mr Stock – if anyone can help it's him. He'd do anything for his clients. And he needs something like that just now – to feel he can help right a wrong – he's that grief-stricken about his wife dying. I worry he might never pull himself out of his despair.'

She saw Jack blushing and noticed she was still holding on to his arm. She flushed and quickly pulled away.

'Sorry,' she said.

'Don't be,' he smiled. 'I haven't enjoyed being knocked into and having me arm squeezed so much in ages.'

Clarrie spluttered with laughter. They stood for a moment considering each other. He was as handsome as she remembered and she was sure he was attracted to her too.

'Maybe I can help Mr Milner's business in another way,' she said.

'And how would that be?' Jack eyed her.

'By having a regular tea delivery to the Stocks,' Clarrie answered. 'After all, I'm in charge of ordering. The grocer we use has a very limited range of teas compared to yours.'

'I'd be happy to oblige,' Jack gave a cheeky grin, 'specially if you were there to take in the delivery.'

'Of course.' Clarrie smiled broadly.

They parted, Clarrie hurrying back to Summer-hill more light-hearted than she had been in all the long weeks since Louisa's death. She liked to think her decision to have tea delivered by the Tyneside Tea Company was an act of support for the fledgling business. But the way her heart skipped a beat when she thought of Jack's dimpled face and lively eyes, she knew there was a further motive – the hope that she would see a lot more of Milner's young delivery man.

CHAPTER 15

As Clarrie stood outside Herbert's study door, gathering the courage to knock, she felt her heart thud with nervousness as it used to do when dealing with her mercurial father. But she would not shirk this task; it was eight months since Louisa's death and Herbert must be coaxed from his grief if the household was to survive. Will was increasingly running wild, Bertie and Verity's engagement was under strain through lack of marriage plans and Herbert was becoming a bad-tempered recluse just as her father had, neglecting his clients and leaving more and more of his work to a resentful Bertie. He no longer took pride in his appearance, allowing his hair to grow too long and a ragged grey beard to cover his once smooth chin.

'Go away!' he growled beyond the closed door.

Clarrie disobeyed and went in with a tray of home-made lemonade and shortbread. Herbert was sitting in the gloom of the late evening, staring out of the window, a book lying unread in his lap. He looked like some wild-haired prophet silhouetted in the May dusk.

'I've brought you a drink, sir,' she said in a soothing voice that belied her hammering pulse.

'I said not to come in. Please take it away.'

'I'll leave it and you can help yourself, then,' Clarrie replied, advancing towards the table in the window and putting the tray down right next to him. He did not even glance at her. She took a deep breath. 'I was wondering if you'd heard from Mr Daniel Milner, sir, the tea merchant? We've started using his delivery service. I know he has a business problem and suggested you might be able to help.'

'Who?' he sighed impatiently, still not looking round.

'Mr Milner of the Tyneside Tea Company. Some of the other tea traders are trying to force him out of business – I'm not sure quite how—'

'You and your wretched tea!' he snapped, abruptly twisting round to glare at her. 'What is it to me?'

Clarrie flinched. 'I thought he sounded the sort of decent businessman you'd be pleased to help – he's building up an honest trade and other more powerful men are trying to put him out of business.'

Herbert sank back into his winged chair. 'Business, trade, honest or crooked, what does it matter? No matter how hard we work, we all go the same way in the end, to a cold grave.'

Clarrie was aghast at his bleak words. 'Of course it matters, sir! Everything matters – from the way we greet each other in the morning to the way the flowers close up for the night. Why would God give us life if none of it mattered?'

His hands tightened their grip on the chair arms. 'If life matters, why is it snatched away so easily, so randomly, so cruelly?' he hissed.

Clarrie stepped towards him and answered, 'I don't know. But doesn't that make it all the more important that we live each day to the full and don't waste time locked away in darkened rooms, cut off from what can comfort us?'

'Comfort?' he said bleakly. 'What is there of comfort in this world?'

'Your sons,' Clarrie dared to say, 'and your friends who want to see you happy again.'

Herbert thumped the chair in agitation and leaned forward to glare at her.

'I will never be happy again, never! How dare you even suggest it! You know nothing of love if you think I could ever get over such a loss.'

Clarrie wanted to shout at him that she and Olive knew all about loss. It was he who could not imagine what it had been like to lose everything – their beloved parents, their home, their childhood friends – and all before they had reached adulthood. But she swallowed her indignation.

'No one expects you to recover quickly from such a tragedy,' she said gently, 'but you aren't the only one suffering. By cutting yourself off from Mr Bertie and Master Will, you are making them suffer doubly. Mr Bertie is anxious to be wed and Master Will is a very unhappy lad—'

Herbert sprang to his feet. 'Don't you lecture me on my family! You of all people.'

'What do you mean, sir?' Clarrie stepped back, shocked by his vehemence.

'If you had done your job properly, my wife would be alive today,' he accused her, his look tortured. 'I trusted you to look after her and you failed me – just as Bertie said you would. If only I had listened to him, instead of letting Louisa's pity for your situation colour my judgement. I'll regret that to my dying day!'

Clarrie staggered back as if he had struck her. 'I will not take the blame for her death,' she gasped. 'I was her housekeeper, not her husband, and the poor lady was ill long before I came here. She was ill with grief for her baby daughter – the baby no one would talk about – that's what ate away at her health.' Clarrie could not stop herself as the anguish and frustration of the past months came pouring out.

'Did you know that Will blamed himself for his sister's death because he dared to touch her and no one took the trouble to explain to him what had happened?' she cried. 'Have you ever stopped to consider how miserable you're making him now by

240

refusing to comfort him? He's lost his mother – he adored her just as much as you in his own way – and he gave her comfort in her dying moments by playing to her. But you won't let him comfort you – so he thinks that his mother's death is somehow his fault too.' She shook as she spoke. 'Why are you so hard on him – hard on yourself – hard on everyone around you, who care for you most?'

He stood staring at her, his whole body rigid with rage. For a moment she thought he would strike her. She had gone too far. What had possessed her to say all she had? He would sack her on the spot.

'Go now,' he hissed between clenched teeth. 'Get out of my sight!'

Clarrie turned and fled. At the door she heard a loud crash of smashing glass and turned in fright. He had upended the tray of lemonade on the polished floor. Clarrie saw him pick up a paperweight and aim it in her direction. He let out a furious roar. She dashed through the door and yanked it shut as the missile thudded against the woodwork. It was just what her drunken father would have done, but to see such rage in teetotal Herbert was terrifying. She ran for the stairs, gulping back a sob in her throat. Her good intentions had rebounded and made things ten times worse, all because of her outspokenness.

Up in her room, she burst into tears. What a useless housekeeper she was! She would never get used to having to curb her opinions in deference to others. In a few moments of madness she had undone all her hard work of the past year and more. How could she face her employer again?

Clarrie covered her mouth to stifle her crying. She had left herself no option but to hand in her resignation. Herbert would expect it; Bertie would rejoice in it. And Will? He hardly spoke to her these days, so perhaps he would no longer care.

Clarrie forced herself to stop weeping and dried her face. She must put in a good word for Olive – she at least should not lose her job. The recklessness was hers and hers alone. Even Herbert would see that.

She lay awake all night, and early the next morning she went downstairs with her letter of apology and offer of resignation. She slid it under Herbert's bedroom door and went below to stoke up the range and make tea and porridge.

Twenty minutes later, an imperious ring from the study bell startled her. Her insides clenched as she made her way upstairs, preparing for Herbert's wrath.

'Come in,' he ordered when she knocked.

She found him standing in the window, the dawn light illuminating the grey streaks in his unruly hair. He held up her letter, turned to her and shook it accusingly.

'I'm sorry, sir,' she gulped. 'I had no right to say all those things.'

'No, you did not,' he said, his look severe. He

stepped away from the window and limped round the desk. He regarded her for a long moment. His face was drawn, deeply lined with pain and fatigue. He looked as if he had aged ten years in less than one. 'But you spoke the truth. I have been selfish in my grief – I have felt so guilty—' He broke off, swallowing hard. There were tears in his eyes. 'And it took the frank words of a young woman to make me see it.'

To Clarrie's astonishment he handed back her letter. 'I'd like you to reconsider.'

'You – you don't want me to go?' Clarrie stammered in confusion.

'No, I don't,' he replied. 'Please stay, Clarrie – for my sake as well as Will's.'

She could see how hard it was for him to humble himself to her. At once she said, 'Of course I'll stay. I don't want to leave at all. Thank you, sir.'

'No, Clarrie, it's me who should be thanking you.' He gave the ghost of a smile.

She quickly shoved the letter into her apron and turned to go.

'And Clarrie,' Herbert stopped her, 'tell Will I'd like to have breakfast with him before he goes to school.'

'Yes, sir,' Clarrie said, her heart lifting in joy as she closed the door behind her.

CHAPTER 16

Summer 1907

That summer was the happiest Clarrie had experienced since the death of her father. She often met Rachel for tea or walks in the park on fine afternoons. With the extra wages she now had to spend, she treated Olive to an easel and paints, and twice they borrowed the Stocks' bicycles and cycled to the edge of the city to picnic while Olive painted. Most of all, Clarrie looked forward impatiently to Thursday afternoons when Jack would call with their tea delivery and she would find some excuse for him to stay – a dripping tap to fix or a kitchen implement to mend – and then reward him with a cup of tea and Dolly's home-made seed cake.

'What you scribbling?' Jack once asked of Olive, sitting across the table from him.

Olive blushed. 'Just sketching.'

'Show him,' Clarrie encouraged her.

Olive shook her head vigorously but Jack reached over and snatched it.

'No, don't!' Olive squealed.

Jack barked with laughter. 'It's me and you, lass,' he said, showing it to Clarrie, 'with Cupid sitting on the teapot!'

Clarrie put her hands to her face and spluttered. 'Really, Olive!'

Red-faced, Olive grabbed it back. 'It's just a bit of fun. Jack wasn't supposed to see it.'

Jack found their consternation amusing. 'How many other drawings have you done of me, eh? Got a rogues' gallery in yer bedroom?'

'Hark at him!' Clarrie joked. 'Won't be able to get back out the door with the size of his head.'

'Yes,' Olive pouted and snapped shut the sketchpad, 'you're not that good-looking.'

Jack snorted with amusement. 'By, you Belhaven lasses know how to keep a lad in his place. I'm the envy of all the delivery men this side of the Tyne – little do they knaw how badly I'm tret.'

Clarrie gave him a playful shove as he pulled on his cap and stood to go. At the door he asked her, 'Would you like to gan to the Pavilion tomorra night?'

Her eyes widened in delight, but she hesitated. 'I don't know if I can get away in time. Miss Landsdowne's coming for supper.'

'I'll serve them,' Olive offered.

Clarrie shot her a grateful look. 'Are you sure?'

'Course I am,' her sister replied. 'I've done more dishing out than you ever have.'

Jack grinned. 'That's settled then. I'll call for you at quarter to eight.' He blew Olive a mocking kiss. 'Ta very much, me little cupid.'

Olive rolled her eyes. 'I'm doing it for Clarrie, not you,' she retorted.

Jack went, chuckling with laughter.

Through the summer months, Clarrie and Jack went several times to the music hall and cinema. He would buy her chocolates and afterwards walk her home, give her bashful kisses at the kitchen door and tell her she was bonny. For all his banter about lasses and being a ladies' man, his embraces were inexperienced and fumbling. It made Clarrie blush to think that her only comparison was with the passionate and assured touch of Wesley Robson. She should not even be comparing them! Jack was kind and funny and ten times more the gentleman than the brazen Robson would ever be, despite Wesley's social advantage. Yet it irked Clarrie that she could not quite banish Wesley from her mind whenever Jack put his arms round her and gave her a goodnight kiss.

The household at Summerhill saw changes that summer too. Herbert gradually came out of the depths of his depression, making an effort to spend mealtimes with Will and throwing himself back into his work. Bertie and Verity's wedding was set for September and Verity returned with enthusiasm to refurbishing rooms on the second floor. Will was moved to a smaller bedroom but seemed not to mind.

He spent most of his spare time with his school friend Johnny Watson or performing with the church choir. Olive still gave him occasional violin lessons, but during the long summer evenings he preferred to be playing tennis or helping out at stables belonging to Johnny's father. He finished his final term at prep school and once the school holidays came went away for three weeks to Scotland with Johnny's family, returning ruddy-cheeked and more diffident with the servants.

Talk of sending him to boarding school resurfaced. Bertie was keen.

'It'll make a man of him,' he told his father. 'He's been tied to Belhaven's apron strings for too long. I'd have given anything to have such an opportunity. Look at Verity's brother – so accomplished in sport as well as business – a true leader. That's what boarding school did for Clive.'

'I'm not so sure,' Herbert prevaricated. 'He seems happy enough at home.'

'That's hardly the point,' Bertie replied. 'He'll never have the gumption to leave home if you don't make him.'

Herbert sighed. 'We'll see what the boy wants.'

To Clarrie's surprise and dismay, Will elected to start the next term at the school in Yorkshire that Clive Landsdowne had attended.

'Won't you miss it here?' she asked him when he came downstairs looking for food. The boy was constantly hungry and growing like a runner bean.

Will shrugged. 'Of course I'll miss you and Olive and Dolly – and Papa,' he added quickly. 'But it's not the same without Mama.'

Clarrie put an arm about him. 'No, it's not.'

Gently he wriggled from her hold. 'And Clive says it's great fun at this school and I can do riding at weekends. I'll have proper music lessons too.' He blushed and stammered, 'Not – not that Olive isn't a good teacher.'

'And what about your friend Johnny,' Clarrie asked, thinking of reasons to make him stay, 'won't you miss him?'

'That's babyish talk.' Will was scornful. 'Anyhow, Johnny's going to school in Edinburgh next term.'

Clarrie could see he was determined to go. 'Well, I'll miss you very much,' she admitted, patting his wavy hair.

He patted her back playfully on the head and smiled. 'No you won't, you'll be too busy going about with Jack the tea boy.'

Clarrie laughed and prodded him. 'Don't be so cheeky!'

He swung himself off the table, snatching one of Lily's pork pies as he went, and ran out of the kitchen giggling.

It was during August that Clarrie met Daniel

Milner, the tea merchant, for the first time. He came for a meeting at the house – the first time a client had been seen at Summerhill since Louisa's death – and she laid on a light luncheon. He was a small wiry man with dark hair, a bushy moustache that lifted when he smiled and a forthright manner.

'Miss Belhaven? I believe it's you I have to thank for introducing me to Mr Stock. My lad Brewis has told me all about you.' Clarrie blushed as he added, 'All of it good, of course.'

Clarrie smiled. 'I hope you're going to stay in business, sir, cos we all like your tea very much.'

'Good.' Milner looked pleased. 'I'm glad it's not just our Jack that takes your fancy.'

At this point, Herbert appeared. 'Who's Jack?' he asked.

'My delivery man,' the merchant said. 'Did you not know he's courting your bonny housekeeper?'

Herbert gave Clarrie a startled look. 'Are you, Clarrie?'

'No – not really, sir,' Clarrie stammered, her cheeks burning. 'We're friendly, that's all.'

He gave her a quizzical little smile. 'Well, it's none of my business. I just hate the thought of losing such a good housekeeper so soon.'

'You won't, sir,' Clarrie answered and hurried to pour out a glass of sherry for his visitor.

As she came in and out during luncheon, she could not help overhearing some of their conversation. She was fascinated by their talk; she had always taken more interest in business and commerce than in music and literature.

She gathered that other tea merchants were trying to force Milner out of business by cheating him on prices. Clarrie knew that nearly all tea was sold at auction on Mincing Lane in London.

'. . . tipped me off that the broker was doing me on the price of Assam,' Daniel Milner was saying as Clarrie cleared the plates of cold meats and pickles. 'Broker was quoting me false prices and getting me to bid more for my tea than I needed to.'

'It's very distressing to hear of agents acting in such an unscrupulous manner,' Herbert tutted. 'They're supposed to be acting in the best interests of their clients, not against them.'

'Aye, well there are those in the tea business who will trample on the little man if they think it'll harm them just one penny,' Milner said, 'and they'll try all the tricks in the trade to do it. Course the broker denied it when I challenged him, and I can't find out exactly who's behind the plot. They've closed ranks against me, the outsider.'

'But there's absolutely no need for such behaviour. There's plenty of business to go round,' Herbert said. 'Tea is booming.'

Milner grunted. 'It annoys them to see a working man like me coming in and doing things better than them – undercutting their prices by delivering door to door. They want it all – shops, tea rooms, house-to-house. See me as an upstart.'

Clarrie had to restrain herself from joining in. It was precisely that attitude that had squeezed her father out of tea growing – powerful families like the Robsons wanting to control everything, buying out the small gardens and consolidating their power. She wanted to shout out that she knew precisely which family would be behind such a plot; nobody would want the Tyneside Tea Company to fail more than the Robsons. Hadn't the Landsdownes boasted about Wesley's being the sharpest tea broker in London? She had no doubt he would be behind this attempt to price Daniel Milner out of the market. He was quite ruthless when it came to business; Ama's luckless son, Ramsha, was testament to how far Wesley would go on behalf of Robson interests.

Suddenly, Clarrie was aware that the two men were staring at her.

'Is there something wrong, Clarrie?' Herbert asked. 'You wish to say something?'

She hesitated, torn between warning them about Wesley and not being seen as interfering. The fact that the Robsons were related to the Landsdownes complicated the decision. How could she make accusations about Verity's relations when all the proof she had was her instincts? It would put Herbert in a very awkward position. Clarrie swallowed.

'Would Sir like coffee here or brought up to the study?'

He gave her a puzzled look. He never drank

coffee after midday. 'No coffee, thank you. Just bring us up a jug of water.'

Clarrie nodded and left, feeling frustrated at having to keep quiet. As she went, she heard them continue their talk of Milner's lack of ready cash and Herbert's offer to invest in his company. She would just have to trust to Herbert's good sense. Somehow, she was sure that the Tyneside Tea Company would survive with his good guidance.

CHAPTER 17

'Out of the question, you silly boy!' Verity cried. 'Whoever heard of servants being invited to one's wedding?'

'But I'll hardly see them if they don't come,' Will said in disappointment. 'I only get the one day off school – I'll have to go back on the four o'clock train.'

Verity, who did not care if Will attended her wedding or not, said sniffily, 'You're supposed to be interested in seeing your brother and me being married, not gossiping with those wretched Belhaven girls.'

Clarrie overheard this exchange shortly before Will went away to boarding school for the first time. She was in his room packing his new leather trunk and felt a rush of affection for the kind boy. When he came in looking dejected, she gave him a brief hug.

'Olive and I will come to the cathedral to watch,' she promised. 'Miss Landsdowne can't keep us away from there.'

'But you won't be at the reception,' Will complained. 'There'll be no one interesting to talk to – just lots of boring grown-ups.'

Clarrie smiled. 'I think out of two hundred guests, you'll find someone to chat to, don't you? By then you'll be able to talk to Clive about your new school.'

'Suppose so,' Will agreed.

The next day, he left, dressed in his new uniform, looking young and scared. In the privacy of his bedroom he threw his arms about Clarrie, buried his face in her apron and cried. She held on to him fiercely for a long moment while she gulped down her own tears, then gently pushed him away.

'I'll see you on the wedding day,' she reminded him, 'and it'll be the Christmas holidays before you know it.'

After he had gone, the house seemed echoingly empty without the clatter of his boots on the stairs or snatches of song ringing along the corridor. Clarrie kept glancing at the kitchen door, half expecting him to come charging in and swipe food off the cooling racks, but knew that it would be months before he would. Olive missed him too. She spent the mild September evenings playing the violin at the open window in Will's room, on the pretext of airing it out and dusting his things.

'Poor little mite,' Dolly would say. 'Fancy sending him away like he's done some'at wrong. The bosses' classes have some strange ways.'

Late at night, when Clarrie was locking up and going to bed, she would hear Herbert moving around in his study, restless. Sometimes the study light would still be on when she came down in the early morning. She was sure he missed his younger son more than he cared to admit, but his way of coping with this new parting was to immerse himself in yet more work. It was his lifeline and Clarrie was just thankful that he had grasped it rather than drown in despair and grief. With his hair clipped short and his chin nicked with careless shaving, his exposed face was often haggard and careworn. But the occasional smile crept to his pale lips and Clarrie was encouraged to hope that in time he might find peace of mind.

Then the time of the wedding drew near and they were all thankful to be kept busy.

One morning, Herbert called Clarrie to the study.

'I hope you are looking forward to having a new mistress in the house,' he said, clasping his hands and looking at her warily. 'It will be more lively, I'm sure. Bertie and Verity are far more keen on entertaining than I ever was.'

'Sir.' Clarrie nodded, wondering where the conversation was leading.

He cleared his throat. 'Verity has pointed out to me that you can't possibly be expected to manage everything in the new household – that you must have help. I'm afraid I've been selfish not thinking of this before.'

'I'm quite happy with my job, sir,' Clarrie said quickly, 'and I'm sure with Olive's help I can easily manage the new situation.'

'Well, yes,' Herbert said, dropping his gaze and moving papers around on his desk. 'Nevertheless, Verity comes from a large household and has been used to having her own lady's maid. She will be bringing the woman with her. Er – it means you and Olive will have to share a bedroom. Will that cause any problems?'

Clarrie felt dismay, but was not surprised. She had been waiting to hear what Verity's demands on the staff would be. Of course she would want her own hand-picked maid.

'Not at all, sir,' she assured him.

'Good,' he said, looking relieved. 'I'll leave it to you to sort out the details with Verity's maid.'

Two days before the wedding, a large van drew up to deliver four trunkfuls of Verity's trousseau and her lady's maid, called Lavender, to unpack it all in the lavishly decorated new bedroom suite.

Lavender was a stout woman with pinned-back frizzy hair and a large birthmark on her cheek whom the Landsdownes had employed as Verity's nurse since babyhood.

'Real name's Mary,' she told Clarrie as the latter helped her hang up Verity's dresses in the walnut wardrobes, 'but Miss Verity chose Lavender cos it was her favourite plant in the garden.' She gave Clarrie a look of satisfaction as if she should be envious of such an honour. 'She's always been such a sweet lass. My little sugar lump; that's what I've always called her. I told her it would break me old heart if she even thought of going without me. So you've no need to concern yourself with Miss Verity's personal arrangements – I'll be supervising the laundering of her clothes and how her meals are prepared.'

'If that's what she wants,' Clarrie said, secretly thankful she would not have to be at Verity's beck and call.

'Oh, yes, that's what she wants.' Lavender was adamant.

Clarrie left her fussing over an arrangement of handkerchiefs and hurried off to tell Olive and Dolly gleefully that the haughty Verity had been known for years as 'my little sugar lump'.

The evening before the wedding day, the Stocks hosted a reception at a club in town of which Bertie was a member. Herbert had refused to let him hold it at the house as originally planned the previous year.

'It's not appropriate,' his father had decreed. 'The year of mourning for your dear mother has not yet passed and this house will not be used for celebration.'

When Bertie had told him he was being unreasonable, Herbert had shouted, 'Isn't it enough that I have agreed to your marriage at this time? Showy receptions are not a necessity in my book. Your mother and I were content with a simple service at the Presbyterian church and a family tea. You young people are far too demanding!'

Herbert put in the briefest of appearances at the club, just long enough to be civil to Bertie's guests, and soon retreated from the merriment and drinking, of which he did not approve. Clarrie took a jug of iced mint tea to his study. She sensed that he was brooding about the day to come, seeing it as an ordeal to be got through without showing his emotions.

'It'll be good to see Will tomorrow,' she said cheerfully.

'Yes,' he said, without looking up from his book.

'And Mr Bertie seems very happy,' she added, pouring him a glass of the sweet-smelling tea.

He glanced at her. 'Are you trying to tell me something?'

Clarrie bit her lip. 'No – well, yes. I think Mrs Stock would have been happy that you've allowed Mr Bertie to go ahead and marry before the year's up. I think it was brave and kind. That's all.'

His wiry eyebrows knitted in a frown and she thought he would reprimand her for her impertinence. Then abruptly he snorted with a mix of impatience and amusement.

'Clarrie, you are the most strange and unusual girl. Whenever I think I should be telling you off, I end up wanting to thank you instead. Why is that?'

Clarrie smothered a smile. 'Perhaps because I'm a Belhaven and we can't help speaking our minds. I'm sorry.'

'Don't be,' he said. 'It's refreshing in a servant.'

She nodded and went out, hiding her irritation at being reminded of her subordinate position. As Clarrie went to bed late that night, hearing the sound of Bertie returning with his best man, an old school friend called Tubby Blake, she thought restlessly of life beyond Summerhill. One day she would work for herself and not be anyone's servant; she would be a successful businesswoman running her own tea house. Lying in bed, she thought of Jack and what marriage to him might be like. She was very fond of him, yet he did not stir her in the way Wesley had. No one had since. But such strong emotions were not the basis for a sound marriage. To make a success of a shared life together a couple needed stability and common sense – qualities that Jack possessed.

Also, Jack had ambition to match hers and was level-headed too, despite his pretence at being carefree. If Milner's company grew and was successful, he would gain quick promotion and perhaps one day have a share in the business. Together they could open their own teashop or café. But there again, Milner might be driven out of business and Jack might never be more than just a delivery man. Perhaps thoughts of marrying him were futile?

What mattered most was that she continued to provide security for herself and Olive. She had promised her sister always to take care of her and that's what she would do. If Jack could not provide such security, then she would not wed him, however much she cared for him. For Clarrie's greatest fear would always be the thought of being cast into the world once again, homeless and penniless.

CHAPTER 18

Clarrie was up extra early to supervise breakfast and help Olive with carrying hot water to the guests. Three of Bertie's friends were staying in the house, including the best man, and they expected a hearty breakfast to start the special day. Tubby Blake had brought his valet, who had slept in Clarrie's sitting room and flirted with Dolly when he wasn't upstairs polishing shoes and helping the men dress.

Clarrie enjoyed the sound of their male laughter reverberating in the dining room, and the air of expectation. For too long the house had been a place of sadness and tiptoeing. Their good humour was infectious and even Bertie greeted her with a smile.

'Good morning, Belhaven! Kedgeree smells good. Tuck in, chaps – got to line the stomach for Landsdowne's champagne!'

Herbert, who since Will's departure had reverted to eating a meagre breakfast in his study, joined them downstairs. He looked tired and strained, but Clarrie noticed how pleased his sudden appearance made his elder son.

'Papa! Come quickly; Tubby's eaten most of the bacon already.'

'Good morning, gentlemen. Please don't get up,' Herbert said. 'I'm sure Clarrie can arrange more if we need it.'

'Certainly, sir.' Clarrie hurried off to replenish the dishes.

There was so much to get done that morning that Clarrie doubted they would reach the cathedral in time to see the bride arrive. But she had promised Will that she, Olive and Dolly would be there. They ended up running down Westgate Road and Collingwood Street, holding on to their hats in the breeze, as the clocks were striking eleven.

It was too late to see the wedding guests going into St Nicholas's Cathedral, but they arrived as the bridal party was drawing up outside in two gleaming carriages.

'Doesn't she look a picture?' Dolly cried, as they pressed closer to the cathedral entrance to watch. The coachman was helping Verity, in a profusion of silk and lace, her rather narrow face hidden behind an elaborate long veil, down from the landau. Her maid of honour and three young bridesmaids dressed in lilac satin disembarked from the other carriage to help arrange and lift the long beaded train. Proudly, Mr Landsdowne took his daughter's arm.

As they processed into the cavernous cathedral, a blast of organ music announced their arrival. Clarrie felt Olive grip her hand, stirred by the sound.

'Imagine getting wed like that,' Olive gasped. 'That beautiful dress – and the organ playing!'

Clarrie glanced at her sister, whose face was full of longing under the second-hand straw hat. They both had on their best coats and Olive had added fancy trims to their hats, but neither of them would ever be able to afford Verity's silk wedding dress no matter how hard they worked. Clarrie quelled her resentment at life's unfairness.

'When your time comes,' she whispered to Olive, 'you'll look twice as pretty as Miss Landsdowne what ever dress you wear.'

Olive rolled her eyes in disbelief, but did not withdraw her hand from Clarrie's until the heavy doors shut and they could hear no more. They stood around waiting and chatting to people in the crowd, some of whom knew the families while others had just gathered out of curiosity.

Just as they were growing bored and beginning to get chilled in the gusting wind, the doors were thrown open once more and the cathedral bells began to peal in celebration. Bertie and Verity were husband and wife. They came out proudly smiling, raising hands to the waiting crowd and giving each other coy looks of satisfaction. Soon their guests were pouring out behind them, laughing and greeting one another.

Olive and Clarrie gazed at the well-dressed gathering, the men in top hats and tailed coats and the women in beautiful costumes and enormous hats bedecked with ribbons and feathers. They had never seen such opulence and glamour. Bertie was marrying into wealth and he looked particularly pleased with himself, Clarrie thought.

'Master Will!' Dolly suddenly shouted. 'Over here!'

Clarrie caught sight of the boy, standing awkwardly with hands thrust in pockets. He looked round and for an instant Clarrie saw embarrassment flick across his face. Then he grinned at them from under a shaggy fringe of hair and came loping across, allowing himself to be briefly hugged by all three. They bombarded him with questions.

'How's school? Are they treating you well?'

'I swear you've grown another three inches!'

'Are you eating enough?'

'Tell me about your music teacher. What's he teaching you?'

'Have you made any friends yet?'

Will rolled his eyes and told them to stop fussing. Yes, he had settled in fine. He was learning the cello as well as the violin, there was plenty to eat and he had a friend called Spencer-Banks.

'Spencer-Banks?' Dolly queried. 'That's a daft name for a lad.'

Will laughed. 'It's his surname. We all get called by our surnames.'

Just then, Herbert waved him over. A carriage was waiting to take them the short journey to the Assembly Rooms on Westgate Road. Clarrie's heart squeezed to think how brief was their reunion with Will. Despite his cheerful greeting, he still looked so young and lost in his tight collar and too-large hat. The absence of Louisa seemed to hang over them, reminding them that she should have been there beside Herbert and Will on such a day.

Dolly pressed a tin into his hands. 'Here, I've baked you an orange cake. I'm not carrying it all the way home again.'

'Thank you . . .' Will began, his voice suddenly croaky.

Clarrie put a hand on Will's shoulder and gave it a quick squeeze. 'Take care of yourself. We'll write if you like.'

He nodded, his eyes filling up with tears.

'Gan on and enjoy yourself at the party.' Dolly pushed him away. As he went, she added teasingly, 'Ta-ra, Stock!'

He grinned. 'Bye-bye, Dawson!'

They watched him re-join his father and climb into the carriage. Other guests were still streaming out of the cathedral.

'Have you ever seen so many folk at one wedding?' Dolly cried.

Suddenly, Olive seized Clarrie's arm and gave a

stifled gasp. Clarrie followed her gaze. There, in the middle of a group of younger guests, escorting a tall young woman in a stylish red hat, was Wesley Robson. Clarrie's insides somersaulted. He looked as handsome as ever, tall, debonair and immaculately dressed from his gleaming spats to his white bow tie. His dark brown hair, once close-cropped, now curled around his ears and thin sideburns framed his prominent cheekbones. His dimpled chin was still clean-shaven. She saw him lean towards his companion, lips twitching in amusement, and say something that made her laugh.

The woman had pale blonde hair and translucent skin. She was dressed in a shimmering grey dress with long gloves that hinted at delicate hands beneath. Hands that would never cook or scrub or polish, Clarrie thought with a surge of resentment that quite took her by surprise. Why should she care whom Wesley chose as his companion? She despised him and his kind. Yet she could not stop staring. Her heart thumped and her palms felt suddenly clammy. He must not see her.

'What's wrong?' Dolly asked. 'Looks like you've seen a ghost, Clarrie.'

In shock, Clarrie pressed her hands to her mouth; she could not speak.

'That man,' Olive nodded at Wesley, 'we used to know him.'

Dolly looked impressed. 'Used to work for him, did you?'

'No!' Olive said, offended. 'We knew him in India before we lost everything. He wanted to marry Clarrie.'

'Don't!' Clarrie hissed.

Dolly let out a snort of disbelief. 'Aye, and I'm the next Queen of England!'

'It's true,' Olive protested. 'Tell her, Clarrie. Tell her we used to mix with the likes of Wesley Robson.'

Clarrie shook her head. She knew there was no point in harking back to their old life for it only caused resentment when they did. Dolly might think they were trying to belittle her. They belonged to the servant class now, and it did no good to boast about a time when they did not.

'I'll call him over if you don't believe me,' Olive said indignantly.

'Stop it!' Clarrie ordered, taking hold of Olive. 'I'll not have us humiliated by Robson in front of all these people. Just imagine how he would crow over us.'

Olive saw the fury in her eyes and fell silent. At that moment, Wesley looked around as if sensing he was being talked about. He scanned the onlookers with mild interest. For an instant, his gaze rested on Clarrie. Her breath froze in her chest. Then the woman in the red hat said something to draw his attention back and he turned away.

Clarrie took a gulp of air, heart hammering. She felt a strange mix of relief and pique. He had not recognised her. With stupid pride she had imagined that he would pick her out immediately from a crowd, the way she had so easily seen him. But to his eyes she was just a bystander, a dowdy working woman in a serge coat and an unfashionable hat come to gawp at her superiors. At that moment, she felt a wave of humiliation far stronger than if he had stridden across the flagstones and ridiculed her for her diminution in status.

Soon after, Wesley and his group of friends moved off, strolling along Collingwood Street towards the Assembly Rooms, laughing and bantering among themselves. Clarrie felt dizzy with the shock of seeing him, her emotions all churned up. With the excitement abruptly over, Dolly was keen to get back to the house.

'See if Mr Blake's valet wants feeding,' she smirked.

Clarrie was reluctant and saw from her sister's expression that the same deflated feeling gripped her too. There would be a lull in their duties during the afternoon while Herbert and the guests were out.

'Let's treat ourselves to tea and cake at the Empire,' Clarrie suggested. 'It's the least we deserve.'

The sisters set off through the Bigg Market towards Grainger Street, arm in arm. In the luxurious calm of the tea room, with its tinkle of crockery and murmur of voices, the sisters' spirits revived.

Out of the blue, Olive asked, 'Are you going to marry Jack Brewis?'

Startled, Clarrie said, 'What ever made you think of that?'

Olive gave her an impatient look. 'Don't pretend

it hasn't crossed your mind. Jack's nice and kind and it's obvious how much he cares for you.'

Clarrie put down her cup a little shakily. 'Yes, Jack's canny, but . . .'

She could not put into words the strange yearning, a longing for something else, that gripped her chest. It was ridiculous to think that one glimpse of Wesley should leave her with this feeling of dissatisfaction. It had nothing to do with him, yet she could not empty her mind of the sight of him or stop herself wondering what he was doing now. Was he sitting at a long dining table, raising his voice over the clatter of silver and china to converse with Newcastle's high society? Would he be dancing later with the sophisticated woman in the red hat who had the languidness of the rich and leisured? Was she his wife?

Then Clarrie realised how ridiculous were such thoughts. What did it matter? She would never be a part of the Robsons' world – would never want to be. Jack, though, was a different matter. He was nice-looking, good company and a suitable match for a young woman with nothing but a respectable job to her name. Jack was attainable.

'But what?' Olive prompted.

Clarrie took a deep breath. 'But nothing.' She smiled at her sister. 'If Jack asks me, I'll say yes.'

Olive's eyes opened wide in excitement. 'Will you really?'

Clarrie laughed. 'Yes, really!'

Olive suddenly frowned. 'But if you marry Jack,

you won't leave me behind at Summerhill, will you? Being bossed around by Miss Landsdowne without you there would be unbearable.'

Clarrie reached over and covered Olive's roughened hand with hers.

'No, of course I won't,' she assured her. 'What ever happens, I want us always to be together.'

She saw the relief on her sister's face and felt a surge of fondness and loyalty. Looking after Olive was the one thing that gave her life purpose. They would always have each other.

Much later in the day, Herbert returned to Summerhill looking exhausted. He ordered tea to be brought up to the study. Bertie and Verity had left for a week on the south coast, waved off at the station by a raucous crowd of friends who had then gone on to dine in the city. Herbert had thankfully called it a day.

'I'm afraid Tubby and the others might be rather late,' he apologised, knowing Clarrie would have to stay up until they came in.

'I don't mind, sir,' she told him. 'Plenty time to rest when they've all gone tomorrow. It was grand to see Will looking so well. Did he get away on the four o'clock?'

Herbert nodded and yawned. Clarrie left him, sensing he wished to be alone. When she came back to collect the tray he was sound asleep in his arm-chair by the hearth. She put some coal on the fire, covered him with a blanket and tiptoed out.

The commotion in the square later that evening did not stir him. Clarrie rushed down to find a group of Bertie's friends tripping in the front door. Tubby was at the centre of about a dozen young men smelling of drink and cigars and laughing loudly at each other's jokes. He led them towards the drawing room in search of more whisky.

'Just a nightcap before bed, eh?' He waved at Clarrie, forgetting her name.

'You'll find the decanters in the dining room,' she told him. 'I've laid out chicken and ham sandwiches too, Mr Blake. If you'd like a hot drink . . .'

'No, no, whisky's what we want. Good girl,' he said, weaving his way back across the hallway.

'Sir, you'll remember that Mr Stock doesn't like noise after midnight on a Saturday,' Clarrie said forthrightly.

Tubby did an exaggerated shooshing noise with a finger pressed to his lips. 'We'll be ever so quiet,' he mocked, 'long as you come and tuck us up in bed.'

Clarrie answered with composure. 'Goodnight, Mr Blake.' She left them to it and retreated downstairs, annoyed that she would have to wait up to lock the front door when the revellers who were not staying left. She had let Olive and Dolly go to bed before her. Blake's valet was snoring in her sitting room, so Clarrie decided to go outside for a breath of night air to help her stay awake. On her way out, she wrapped herself in a shawl, pulling it over her head.

The wind had dropped. The night was still and chilly, with a smattering of stars between the clouds. Hidden from view by the tall buildings was a bright harvest moon throwing light into the square like a gas lamp. A servant from the house opposite was putting out a crate of empty milk bottles. She waved across at Clarrie.

Waving back, Clarrie walked over to the central garden and let herself in through the wrought-iron gate. It smelt of damp leaves. She breathed in deeply and closed her eyes. For an instant she conjured up the earthy, dank smell of the jungle. She was back in Belgooree among tall trees, listening to night sounds and smelling the wood smoke. How she yearned to stretch out her hand and feel Prince's warm, muscled flanks, to open her eyes and see spirals of smoke drifting above the trees from village fires. A wave of longing engulfed Clarrie. So acute was her desire for her old home that she was left trembling and weak-kneed. She let out a low moan.

'Are you all right?' a deep voice asked out of the dark.

Startled, Clarrie opened her eyes. There was no one there. Then she saw the glow of a cheroot in the darkness. There was someone sitting on the bench under the beech tree. That was how she had smelt wood smoke. A tall man stood up and moved towards her, swaying slightly, as if inebriated. She could just make out that he was wearing a tailed coat. It was probably one of Bertie's friends who had not made it into the house.

Only when he stepped into the moonlight did the outline of his strong-featured face become clearer. With horror, Clarrie saw that it was Wesley.

'You're upset?' he queried.

'No,' Clarrie said, quickly pulling the shawl across her face. She wanted to turn and run but that might make him more curious. He discarded his cheroot and ground it under his shoe.

'Come 'n' sit down.' He gestured at the bench. Clarrie shook her head. 'What y'doing here?' he asked, peering closer. 'Girl like you – shouldn't be out alone.'

He was staring right into her eyes, the only part of her face showing. Her heart thumped hard in her chest. He leaned so close she could smell the wine on his breath, see the gleam of interest in his green eyes.

'Strange,' he murmured, 'seeing you hidden in that shawl – it reminded me of someone. Moonlight – playing tricks.' He reached out and tugged at the shawl, trying to see her face. Clarrie gripped it hard.

'Don't – sir!' she hissed.

'Those eyes,' he said. 'My God, it's uncanny. Who are you? Where've you come from?'

Clarrie swallowed. 'I – I'm – me name's Dolly, sir,' she stammered, putting on Dolly's accent. 'I work round here.'

'Why come in the garden?' he asked.

'No reason,' Clarrie said, glancing away. She felt breathless under his scrutiny.

Wesley laughed abruptly. 'Meeting someone, were you? A secret liaison?'

'No,' Clarrie said, 'just out for a bit fresh air – same as you.'

He leaned close. 'There's something about you, Dolly . . .'

Clarrie held her breath. She felt caught in his gaze. Any moment he would discover who she really was and her humiliation would be complete.

'I must gan,' she whispered, stepping away.

'Wait,' he said, catching her by the arm. 'Stay a bit and talk.'

Clarrie tried to wriggle from his hold. 'Why talk to the likes of me when you've all them fancy friends?'

'What friends? Do you know me?'

'N-no,' Clarrie stuttered. 'You just – look like you've been at the big weddin'. Everyone round here's been talking of nowt else.'

'The big wedding,' Wesley grunted. 'It certainly was that. My fancy friends, as you call them, are still celebrating – polishing off Bertie Stock's whisky most likely. I've had enough. Not much of a drinker. Can't keep up with them.' He smiled flirtatiously and pulled her to him. 'Give me the company of a pretty young woman any day.'

Clarrie's heartbeat drummed in her ears at their

proximity. How had this happened? She felt sick with both fear and a treacherous flare of desire.

'Please, sir,' she said tensely, 'let me go.'

Wesley's voice was a low rumble like distant thunder. 'Let me see your face first,' he commanded.

Clarrie was suddenly indignant. How dare he behave like that towards her, just because he thought her a lowly servant girl! She threw off his hold and with lightning speed raised her right hand and slapped him hard on the cheek. As she did so, her shawl slipped from her face.

Wesley staggered back and steadied himself. 'Sorry – too much drink—'

She turned and fled. Then she was out of the garden and running for the basement steps as fast as she could. All she could hear was the noise of blood rushing in her ears as she flung herself down the steps and back through the kitchen door. Had he followed her? She leaned against the door, shaking and gasping for breath. No footsteps sounded behind her.

Relief washed over her. But what if he decided to join the men in the dining room? Clarrie closed her eyes and tried to calm her thudding heart. She would wait down here until they had all left or gone to bed and hope that no one summoned her for more food or coal for the fire. Only then would it be safe to go upstairs and lock up.

She sat and dozed on a kitchen chair, jerking awake each time her head nodded forward. Shortly after one o'clock she heard the front door slam and voices laughing drunkenly in the street outside. She waited another quarter of an hour, then went upstairs to the empty dining room to clear the clutter of dirty plates and glasses.

It was after two o'clock before she hauled herself up the attic stairs to bed. She lay utterly exhausted by the emotions of the day. Seeing Wesley had shaken her badly. Just when she thought she had control of her life and had smothered her feelings of loss for Belgooree, he had appeared like a summer storm and stirred up her deeply buried longing. How strange that he had been there in the garden when she had been thinking so vividly of her old home. It was as if he had the power to conjure up her most profound emotions, her strongest desires. She curled up, hugging herself to stem the physical ache she felt inside.

Clarrie hated him for destroying her peace of mind, for making her dissatisfied with the new life she had forged for herself and Olive. She felt tears of anger sting her eyes, but she refused to cry. She was stronger than that. She would feed off this new rage that he had provoked in her. Every time she thought of Wesley from now on, she would remind herself how she must advance her position, carve out a good life for Olive and herself, until she could look him in the eye as an equal once more.

'I promise you,' she whispered in determination, 'that day will come.'

CHAPTER 19

Once Bertie and Verity returned from honeymoon, Clarrie had little time to dwell on the events of the wedding day. She was kept busier than ever running the new household. Verity quickly assumed the role of mistress of the house and the Stock men happily deferred to her wishes in anything to do with the domestic arrangements.

She would summon Clarrie daily to her second floor sitting room with its charming view over the square and dictate her list of chores. She was particular about which grocers they used, how the servants were dressed and at what times of day they could be allowed into the bedrooms to clean. She quickly cancelled the order for Lily's pies, despite Clarrie's protest.

'They are stodgy and quite unhygienic.' Verity was

dismissive. 'I really can't serve up food that's been cooked in a public house.'

'But they rely on orders from the likes of the Stocks,' Clarrie pointed out.

'We're not a charity, Belhaven,' she snapped. 'I'm sure Dolly can manage to produce such pies – and if she can't we'll soon find someone who can.'

'Dolly can manage very well,' Clarrie said, 'but an extra pair of hands in the kitchen wouldn't go amiss.'

Verity agreed. 'I suppose with all our entertaining that might be a good idea.'

Within a week, Verity had persuaded Bertie of the need for a kitchen girl. Clarrie sent word to Lexy at the washhouse in Elswick and she lost no time in sending round one of her sisters to apply for the job. A week later, fifteen-year-old Sarah was taken on to the staff and came in daily. Lexy sent Clarrie a bar of Pears soap in gratitude.

Verity took every opportunity to remind Clarrie and Olive that they were there to serve and not to fraternise with their employers. An elaborate code of uniforms was introduced. Clarrie and Lavender were put into mauve dresses for morning, beige for serving afternoon tea and black for evening wear. Olive and Dolly wore navy during the day and black dresses with lacy white aprons after four in the afternoon. Sarah wore grey and was not to be seen above stairs while the Stocks were up and about.

There was much entertaining during the week and Verity had regular 'at homes' and afternoon teas for the steady stream of friends who called. Lavender fussed over her mistress, delighting in telling Clarrie how many changes of outfit Verity needed – sometimes five or six a day if there were evening engagements.

Marjorie, the Stock's arthritic laundry woman, was swiftly retired in favour of two brawny young women who could cope with all the extra washing and ironing of clothing, bedding and table linen.

Herbert and Bertie spent long hours at the office, returning only after six in the evening. Often Herbert would order a light supper in his study, shying away from the formal meals that Verity demanded in the grand dining room. This seemed to suit his new daughter-in-law, who found his uninterest in lavish dinners perplexing and his manner austere. Clarrie suspected his diffidence was his armour against the outside world, which he avoided unless it was a matter of business. She knew his feelings of loss for his Louisa were still raw and he had long outlived his appetite for society.

He seemed happiest on the weekly outing to church, sitting up at the front alone in the Stocks' pew, singing lustily or deep in thought. As Bertie and Verity spent most Sundays at their country cottage, they seldom attended with him. When in town, Verity preferred to go to the cathedral.

Clarrie did her best to keep Verity happy and reserved any mutinous thoughts to herself. She would bide her time until Jack's career progressed and he proposed and then she would have great pleasure in telling Verity and Bertie that she was leaving. Only on one matter did she clash strongly with Verity – over Jack's delivery.

'I don't see why we have to have a separate tea delivery,' Verity complained. 'It would be much better if we ordered everything through Clayton's Emporium. I happen to know the tea they import is first class.'

Clarrie's jaw clenched. She knew exactly which family sold their tea through Clayton's. The Robsons. Most of the houses in the square got their tea there and Jack was finding it hard to convince housekeepers to change their habits and order from him. He was having to travel much further afield to outlying areas where no one bothered to deliver.

'The Tyneside Tea Company specialises in tea,' Clarrie said, 'and they give very good value for money.'

Verity arched her brows. 'I was forgetting you think of yourself as a tea expert. Nevertheless, the Landsdownes have always patronised Clayton's for their grocery needs and that's whom I wish to use here.'

Clarrie hid her annoyance. 'Perhaps you should consult Mr Herbert first. The Tyneside Tea Company is one of his clients.'

Verity shot her a look of irritation. 'Really, Belhaven, I'll not be dictated to by my housekeeper. And I wouldn't dream of bothering Mr Stock with such petty domestic detail.'

Clarrie, though, would not let the matter rest. She made an excuse to go into Herbert's study the following evening with a plate of fresh shortbread. He regarded her over his spectacles.

'You have something on your mind, Clarrie?'

She nodded and told him of her concern.

'Certainly, Mr Milner needs all the help he can get,' Herbert sighed, putting down his pen. 'But I've told Bertie I won't interfere in the way his wife runs the house and it seems to me—'

'But sir, it just takes one or two well-to-do customers to cancel their delivery and then word gets around and others follow. Surely you don't want your client to go out of business after all the hard work you've put into saving him?'

Herbert stared at her in surprise. 'I'm impressed by your loyalty,' he said. 'But something tells me your worry has more to do with the fate of the delivery man — what's his name? Jack? — than Mr Milner's business.'

Clarrie blushed. 'Sir, Jack Brewis and Mr Milner's business depend on each other.'

Herbert surveyed her for a long moment and then nodded. 'Leave it with me, Clarrie — and thank you for the shortbread.' Then he bent once more to his work and she left him alone.

Jack's tea delivery stayed. Verity, furious at being overruled, took her pique out on Clarrie by making sure she was occupied upstairs whenever Jack called. Somehow, probably through Lavender, she had learned of Clarrie's fondness for the delivery man. Every Thursday afternoon Verity detained Clarrie in the drawing room, serving tea to her friends, or sent her out on some errand to the milliner's or tailor's that she would entrust to no other. Under Verity's regime, Clarrie was needed most evenings until late and it proved almost impossible to arrange a night at the cinema or the music hall with Jack.

Frustrated though she was, Clarrie could do nothing about it save pass on messages through Olive. Once, when Verity and Bertie were leaving on Saturday for the country instead of Sunday, she told Olive eagerly, 'Tell Jack I can get away Saturday evening if he wants to go to the Pavilion.'

But back came the disappointing answer that Jack would not return in time from his round.

'Says he's up to the pit villages round Stanley and won't be back until nine.'

It began to dawn on Clarrie that Jack was making little attempt to see her and she began to fret.

'Do you think he's found another lass?' she asked Olive. 'He must meet dozens on his travels.'

'Don't be daft,' Olive said. 'He always asks after you when he calls.'

'But he never tries to call back at other times of day to see me.'

'Cos he's working that hard,' Olive pointed out. 'He can't keep calling on the off chance you've got five minutes to spare.'

'But he won't meet me on a Sunday afternoon either,' Clarrie said.

'You know his mam's religious and they have to stop in after church,' Olive replied. 'It'll be different once he's put enough by for his own place.'

'That's true,' Clarrie admitted. 'But that might not be for ages.'

'You'll just have to be patient,' Olive shrugged, 'like you're always telling me.'

Apart from waving to him from the upstairs window, Clarrie only managed two outings with Jack that whole autumn, once to the pictures and once for a walk in Elswick Park. Jack was subdued, almost wary of her.

'Tell me what's the matter,' Clarrie insisted.

But he shrugged and told her it was nothing. Clarrie put it down to his worrying over his job. She was encouraging. 'Mr Stock has great faith in Mr Milner – thinks he's going to build a great tea business given time.'

Winter came, and Verity's demands for lavish entertaining grew in the lead up to Christmas. By then, Clarrie was seeing so little of Jack that even Olive was growing alarmed.

'He's talking about Mr Milner changing his rounds – giving him south of the river.'

'Why would he do that?' Clarrie asked in dismay.

'Milner's expanding and Jack's his best salesman, I suppose. He's good at talking folk into becoming regular customers.'

Spurred on by Olive's warning, Clarrie managed to arrange a rare evening at the Pavilion with Jack, and then Verity sprang an unexpected dinner party at which she had to preside.

She sent Olive along in her place so as not to disappoint Jack. Afterwards Olive was critical.

'You can't keep on like this.' Olive was blunt. 'He thinks you don't care for him.'

'But I do,' Clarrie insisted.

'Well, not enough. You're going to do it again.'

'Do what again?'

'Miss your chance at marriage,' Olive declared.

'Don't bring that up!' Clarrie said crossly.

But Olive was working herself into a state of indignation. 'Well, it's true. If you married Jack now we could get out of this place.'

'And do what?'

'Set up our own café the way you've always wanted to do,' Olive said. 'Work for ourselves instead of that stuck-up Verity.'

Clarrie gave a huff of impatience. 'I'd like nothing more. But we can't afford it yet – not on the sort of wages Jack makes. We'd still have to work for others.' She saw Olive's face crumple and rushed to console her. 'One day we will have our own tea room, just you and me.'

But Olive pushed her away. 'Don't treat me like a baby. You're happy here – more than me. You'll just stay here being loyal to Mr Stock till you're an old maid.'

'No I won't,' Clarrie protested.

'If I were you I'd be marching Jack up the aisle double quick before he finds someone else,' Olive said.

'You've changed your tune,' Clarrie retorted. 'A few weeks ago you were telling me to be patient and wait.'

'Aye,' Olive cried, 'and a few weeks is a long time. If you don't marry him now I worry that we'll never get away from here.'

Clarrie lost patience. 'You're not being practical! Jack still lives at home with his mam. He's hardly got enough to support me, let alone you as well. And I'm not about to give up this place just to be at the beck and call of Jack's mam. Maybe in a couple of years me and Jack will have put enough by to afford our own place.'

The look of disbelief on Olive's face made Clarrie's heart sink. She determined that she would waylay Jack on his next visit, no matter what Verity had planned for her.

The following Thursday, Olive took her place upstairs, so she could do so.

'Come and have a cuppa in my sitting room,' she said, pushing Jack through the kitchen before Dolly or Sarah could delay him. He perched on the edge of the sofa looking nervous, clutching his cap.

'I can't stay long,' he said.

Clarrie nodded, dismayed at how ill at ease he looked. She poured him some tea and handed it over. He slurped his drink, avoiding her look.

'Olive says you're expanding south of the river,' she began.

'Aye, business is picking up,' he said, looking more comfortable. 'We've doubled our customers in the past month. Folk are getting used to the idea – specially when they see us coming back regular. They know we won't let them down.'

Clarrie let him talk about business, but feared a bell would jangle overhead and summon her away before she had a chance to bring up what was on her mind. Eventually, she blurted out, 'Jack, I need to know if we're still courting.'

He flushed and put down his cup. 'I'm not sure.'

Clarrie's throat dried. Only now did she realise just how much she was relying on Jack for her future plans. Escape and security were bound up in Jack's advancement – in forwarding that advancement.

'Is there someone else?' she forced herself to ask.

His brow furrowed. 'I could ask you the same question.'

Clarrie looked at him, nonplussed. He sounded accusing.

'You're the one I care for, Jack.'

Abruptly he stood up. 'I thought you did,' he said, 'but I've heard otherwise.'

She stood up too. 'Heard what? From who?'

'Talk. Round the square,' he said. He was scarlet with embarrassment.

'What talk?' Clarrie was indignant.

'You were seen late at night with another lad,' he accused her, 'cuddling and that.'

Clarrie laughed at such nonsense. 'That's not true! I hardly ever get to meet you, let alone other lads. I don't *know* any others – and I wouldn't want to.'

He eyed her, his look more hopeful. 'So you never met another man in the garden?'

'No, Jack, I promise!'

He looked relieved. 'Knew I shouldn't listen to gossip. That lass across the square was just trying to cause trouble. Said you were covered in a shawl so as not to be seen, but you still waved at her bold as brass before ganin' to meet some posh lad. Must've been someone else she saw. I thought maybe's you'd been seeing him and that's why you've been avoiding me. Mind you it was ages ago – the night of the Stock weddin'.'

Clarrie gave a small gasp, her hand flying to her mouth. Jack gave her a sharp look.

'Oh, that.' Clarrie reddened. 'She did see me – but it wasn't what she thought. I was just getting a breath of air – had no idea he was in the garden.'

'Who?' Jack's expression tensed.

'Mr Robson.'

'So you did know him?'

Clarrie hesitated. 'Well, me and Olive knew him before – before coming here. But there was nothing—'

'Did he court you before me?' Jack demanded.

Again Clarrie hesitated too long before denying

it. 'No, not courting – it was complicated. But he means nothing to me – quite the opposite.'

'That's not how the lass tells it,' Jack said stonily.

'Don't be ridiculous,' Clarrie said in panic. 'He was just one of Mr Bertie's guests – I had no idea he would be there. It was just a chance meeting.'

'Maybe it was,' Jack said, 'but you didn't rush off as soon as you saw him, did you?'

Clarrie felt her cheeks burning. 'Nothing happened – never could happen.'

'Cos he's too posh?' Jack said scathingly. 'But you would if you could. I can see it all over your face. You still fancy him, don't you, Clarrie? I'm just a delivery boy, not good enough for the likes of you.'

He jammed on his cap and strode to the door. Clarrie went after him, grabbing his arm.

'Stop, Jack, please! You couldn't be more wrong about him. It's you I want to wed.'

He shrugged her off. 'I'll not be second best to anyone,' he said, 'least of all some posh bugger who thinks he can have any lass he wants.'

'Don't say that,' Clarrie gasped, 'it's not true. Why won't you believe me?'

As he wrenched open the door, he said, 'I'll never be good enough for you, Clarrie. Deep down, that's what you think. And after what I've heard today from your own gob – you're not good enough for me neither.'

He stormed through the door, past a gaping Dolly and Sarah, who had been hovering to listen. When

Olive returned downstairs, she found the women consoling a weeping Clarrie. Only later, when they were alone, could Clarrie confess to her sister what the argument had been about.

'You never told me you'd spoken to Wesley,' Olive said, astounded. 'What did he say once he knew we were working here?'

'He doesn't – I pretended to be Dolly and in the dark he never guessed.' Clarrie's upset turned to anger. 'That wicked man!' she hissed. 'Is there no end to the trouble he causes us? Now I've lost Jack—'

Olive hugged her in comfort. For once she did not chide Clarrie or say 'I told you so'. She just held her sister until her weeping subsided, as so often Clarrie had done for her.

CHAPTER 20

Christmas came and Will returned for the holidays. His arrival was a blessed distraction for Clarrie. When he came down to the kitchen, she flew at him and hugged him in delight.

'I can't tell you how good it is to see you!' she cried.

He laughed good-naturedly and hugged her back. 'Can I help stir the pudding?' he asked, shovelling a newly baked scone into his mouth.

Sarah eyed him in wonder, never having seen any of the Stock men venturing so far below stairs.

'You'll get used to him,' Dolly said. 'Right little scavenger.'

But after that, Will spent most of his time visiting his former school friends or being taken shopping by Verity and fitted out for bigger clothes. Snow fell just before Christmas and he disappeared for a day's sledging with Johnny. On Boxing Day, Bertie and Verity took him off to the Landsdownes' country estate to hunt and shoot rabbits. All too soon it was time for him to go back to school.

Clarrie worried that Herbert had hardly paid him any attention and suggested they go for a walk together on Will's final day. Herbert grew irritable.

'Can't you see I've too much work, Clarrie? I'll thank you not to interfere.'

Will hid his disappointment. 'It doesn't matter – I was planning to go riding with Johnny anyway.'

The following day he was gone and they did not see him again until the Easter holidays. By then, Verity was being unusually difficult and demanding, staying in bed until late and craving sweet biscuits and sarsaparilla in large quantities.

By high summer she was announcing to close family that she was expecting a baby. Bertie was thrilled and fussed over her more than ever. But the excitement in the household was soon marred by a battle between Verity and her father-in-law over converting Louisa's old bedroom into a nursery.

Verity railed tearfully at Bertie, not caring that Clarrie was in the room. 'But the room's been standing empty for nearly two years. It's such a waste! It's the ideal size for a nursery. You must tell him.'

'Dearest,' Bertie tried to calm her, 'you know how difficult it is – Papa's very sensitive about that room.'

'It's creepy – he treats it like a mausoleum.' Verity

shuddered. 'It's time he came to terms with his loss.'

'I quite agree,' Bertie said, 'but it is his house, after all.'

'Well, it's my baby!' Verity wailed. 'I'm making myself ill with worry over where it will go. Can't you see that?'

But Herbert was equally stubborn.

'There's plenty of room on the second floor,' he told Bertie. 'She has a dressing room the size of my study. Besides, I don't want to be disturbed by a baby crying when I'm trying to work. Babies and children should be kept upstairs out of earshot.'

Clarrie agonised over whether to intervene. She understood Verity's frustration over a large room going to waste, but to Herbert it was more than just a bedroom, it was a shrine to his dead wife. Everything remained untouched, as if he feared that changing anything would somehow be a betrayal of her memory. She also wondered if Herbert was privately dreading the arrival of a baby in the house. It would be a reminder of the stillborn daughter he had lost three years ago that had precipitated Louisa's ill health and death.

To her surprise, it was Bertie who came to her for help.

'Belhaven, you seem to have some influence over my pig-headed father,' he said bluntly. 'Do you think you could make him see sense over this nursery business?'

'It's not my place,' Clarrie demurred.

'That's never stopped you before,' he retorted. Clarrie said nothing. 'Listen,' he said, trying to be conciliatory, 'I know we haven't always seen eye to eye, but I can see that you've done a competent job here – and Verity thinks you're a good housekeeper for someone so young.' He reddened at the effort to be complimentary. 'I'd be grateful if you could do anything to persuade my father to change his position – Clarrie.'

It was the first time he had ever called her by that name. Clarrie felt a small flicker of triumph. Bertie was acknowledging how indispensable she had become to the Stocks.

'I'll try,' she agreed.

She waylaid Herbert on his return from his early evening walk. He had got into the habit since Verity's arrival, so as to avoid pre-dinner drinks and inconsequential chatter. On the watch, Clarrie saw him turn into the square and went out to snip some roses in the central garden.

'Sir.' She beckoned him. 'Do you think you could reach those ones higher up, please?'

He stopped to help, leaning his stick against the railings. The day was still warm and he was flushed and perspiring in his dark clothes.

'I've lemonade in the bottle. Would you like some?'

Herbert nodded and sat on a nearby seat, swigging thirstily. Clarrie carried on snipping roses and dropping them into her basket, glancing at him each time she did so.

'Go on,' Herbert said, eyeing her. 'You've something to tell me.'

Clarrie gave him a guilty look, and then laughed. 'How do you know?'

Herbert grunted. 'You have that determined look in your eye, as if you're taking a deep breath before tackling something unpleasant.'

Clarrie smiled and put down her secateurs. 'You don't miss much, do you, sir?'

'Come and sit beside me, Clarrie,' he ordered. 'Is it Bertie who's sent you?'

Clarrie sat down carefully, her hands clasped in her lap, and nodded.

'I won't be swayed,' Herbert said firmly.

'I didn't think so.'

'But you think I'm wrong about this nursery business?'

'No,' Clarrie said gently, 'there's no right or wrong to it.' He waited for her to go on. 'I just wonder what – what Mrs Stock would have wanted for her first grandchild.'

Herbert said nothing. When she slid him a look, she saw that his jaw was clenched and his eyes were glistening.

'I just can't,' he whispered, his voice cracking. 'It's too soon.'

Instinctively, Clarrie put out a hand to touch his. 'I understand – my father was the same about my mother. He couldn't bear to sleep in the same room ever again after she died.'

Herbert let go a small groan and a tear rolled down one cheek. Clarrie said, 'If you can't bear the thought of a baby in the house, why don't you make it possible for Mr Bertie and Miss Verity to have a place of their own?'

He turned to look at her, frowning. Swiftly she withdrew her hand. As usual she had been too forthright.

'I'm sorry. I spoke out of turn.'

'No, Clarrie, I'm glad you did. I never thought of it. But you're right — now that they are embarking on a family it's high time they had their own home.' He regarded her. 'Where does such wisdom come from in one so young?' he mused.

Clarrie gave a rueful smile. 'Not always so wise, I'm afraid.'

'And what of your future, Clarrie?' he asked unexpectedly. 'Are you still being courted by Mr Milner's lad?'

She flushed. 'No, sir. We had a misunderstanding.' She stood up.

'I'm sorry,' he said, watching her as she collected her basket. Clarrie nodded and hurried inside, before he asked any more. She had not seen Jack to talk to since the previous year. He came fortnightly rather than weekly now and sometimes she watched him approach. He had grown a moustache. Recently he had traded up to a larger van and wore a new suit. Business was certainly blossoming. But she never asked Olive about him and her sister never mentioned his visits for fear of upsetting her.

To Clarrie's delight, news that Bertie and Verity were house-hunting spread below stairs in a matter of days. Lavender thought she was the first to hear about it and break it to the others.

'Madam has expressed a preference for living in Jesmond.' She aped her mistress's words. 'Such a pleasant area yet still handy for the town.'

Clarrie and Olive shrieked with joy once the woman was out of earshot.

'I can't believe we'll be rid of her so soon!' Clarrie cried.

Soon Olive was worrying. 'But what if Mr Stock doesn't need us once they've gone? He might manage with just Dolly and Sarah.'

Clarrie smothered her sudden doubt. 'I'm sure he'll take care of us.'

A large, double-fronted house in Tankerville Terrace was chosen and quickly purchased. Verity spent the following month being driven to and fro to oversee its decoration. They were to move in November, the month before the baby was due, in time for her confinement. Two weeks before their removal, she summoned Clarrie to her sitting room. She was propped up in an armchair against a wall of cushions, looking large-bellied and uncomfortable. The room was stuffy from the blazing fire.

'Belhaven, I'm drawing up a list of staff that I'll need at Tankerville,' she said, waving a sheaf of notepaper. 'I want you to help me.'

Clarrie looked at her in confusion. 'Me, ma'am?'

'Yes, you,' Verity said irritably, fanning her flushed face. 'As my housekeeper it's important that you have some say in the servants I choose.'

Clarrie's heart sank. 'Y-your housekeeper?' she stammered.

'Yes,' Verity said loudly, as if she were stupid. 'You'll be coming with me as my housekeeper.'

'But I work for Mr Stock,' she protested.

'It's all arranged with Mr Stock,' Verity said, waving the papers impatiently. 'Now come on, help me.'

Clarrie stood rooted in disbelief. She had not even been consulted! She would not be passed around like a piece of furniture. And what would happen to Olive?

'I'm sorry, ma'am,' she said defiantly, 'but I'm not leaving Summerhill. Not unless Mr Stock sacks me.' With that she turned and left Verity open-mouthed with incredulity.

It turned out that it was Bertie who had high-handedly tried to appropriate Clarrie as housekeeper without his father's say-so. When Herbert discovered what was going on, he took Bertie to task.

'You can't treat the Belhaven girls like that – they should have been consulted and so should I.'

Bertie tried to brush it off as a misunderstanding. 'You're right, of course, Papa. It's just that our needs are greater than yours as regards servants. Verity thought you wouldn't mind.'

'But I do mind.' Herbert was indignant. 'If Clarrie and Olive wish to stay here, then they shall.'

The sisters were greatly relieved, but it marred the final days of Verity's rule. She made spiteful comments within their hearing and had both of them running after her with all kinds of demands right up until the day of departure. Sarah, the kitchen maid, went to the new household to train as a parlour-maid.

'I don't mind,' she said brightly. 'Working for Miss Verity's a picnic compared to running after me family.'

A week before Christmas, Will came home and Verity gave birth to twins – Vernon and Josephine. All the Stocks and Landsdownes gathered for Christmas at Tankerville, Verity and Bertie keen to show off their new house and babies. Dolly went home to her family for three days, and after church Clarrie and Olive were left to themselves.

They decided to take a picnic and cycle out west until the armaments factories and terraced ranks of Benwell and Scotswood petered out into fields. It was sunny and mild and Olive sketched the bare trees and vivid outlines of brown hills against pale blue sky.

Clarrie gazed north. 'Some day soon, we're going to go and look for Father's farm,' she said. 'I won't feel a part of this place until we do.'

Olive was absorbed in her drawing and Clarrie did not think she heard. But when they packed up to go, Olive said, 'It'll just be a farm.'

Clarrie looked at her in surprise. 'Aren't you the least bit curious to see where he came from?'

Olive shrugged. 'Not really. It'll be smelly and clarty and a long way from shops.'

Clarrie laughed, a little shocked by her sister's indifference. It also struck her for the first time how Olive was picking up a local accent, using words that Dolly and Sarah would. 'You have turned into a town lass, haven't you?'

Olive gave it some thought. 'Aye.' She smiled. 'I have – long as it's the posh end.'

It was dark when they arrived home. They had just stoked up the fires when Herbert and Will came in. Clarrie offered to bring them up a light supper, but Will groaned. 'Couldn't eat another thing.'

'That must be a first!' Clarrie teased.

'There was enough to feed the whole of Tyneside,' Herbert grunted. 'Just a cup of tea would be fine.' As Clarrie and Olive took their coats, he added, 'Why don't the pair of you join us in the study? Unless you have other plans,' he added bashfully.

'We could play backgammon,' Will enthused. 'You'll never beat me now, Clarrie, I play all the time at school.'

'Good to see your expensive education is being put to good use,' Herbert said drily.

Clarrie laughed. 'I accept the challenge.'

'Olive, please bring your violin,' Will urged. 'Then we can play together.'

The four of them spent the evening by the study fire, Clarrie and Will playing board games while Herbert and Olive read, then Herbert and Clarrie listening while Olive and Will played their instruments.

It was the nearest thing to winter evenings at Belgooree with her parents and Kamal that Clarrie could remember. She felt deeply grateful to the liberal-minded Herbert and his affectionate younger son for allowing them a taste of family life.

The next day, Herbert was back working at his desk and Will went off to visit Johnny.

'Why don't you invite him here?' Clarrie suggested. 'We'd be happy to cook what ever he likes.'

Will was enthusiastic and Clarrie realised no one had ever suggested such a thing before. It would never have occurred to his father, and Verity would have been against having an extra tiresome youth under her feet.

Johnny Watson was a lively dark-haired boy who giggled as much as Will and spoke with a trace of a Scottish accent. At Will's request, Clarrie and Olive made them Indian dishes of curried lamb and chickpeas with rice, with flat unleavened bread that the boys helped them fire on the stove hotplate. Johnny was agog at such daring and Will's familiarity with the servants, but joined in with enthusiasm. Clarrie showed them how to scoop up their food with the bread.

Herbert found them sitting at the kitchen table eating and Clarrie jumped up guiltily.

'I'm sorry, sir. I thought you were at the office.'

He hesitated, frowning at the boys.

'It's very good, Papa,' Will said, mouth crammed with food.

'Smells it,' Herbert agreed, pulling out a chair. 'May I have some?'

Clarrie grinned in relief. 'Certainly, sir.'

All too soon, Will and Johnny were returning to school and the house seemed forlornly empty again. As 1909 progressed, Clarrie even looked forward to duty visits from Verity. She would come on Thursday afternoons – 'she doesn't realise Jack's broken off our courtship,' Clarrie said drily to Olive – and bring the twins to see their grandfather. Herbert would return early from the office to see them and to everyone's amazement appeared to dote on the babies. He would tickle their chins and pull faces, and carry them about the room jiggling them vigorously until they cried. Often Clarrie would be handed a squalling baby to pacify and she would swaddle it to her front and carry it until it was lulled asleep, as she had seen Ama do in her childhood.

One summer's afternoon, when the study door was left open to allow a breeze, Clarrie heard Bertie's raised voice.

'. . . too many! You don't need all three.'

'I don't interfere in your household so don't interfere in mine,' Herbert growled.

Clarrie, bringing up a jug of fresh water, realised they were talking about her, Olive and Dolly. She stopped on the stairs, uncertain.

'We on the other hand could do with more servants – Lavender can't cope on her own with the twins. She's too old. Perhaps Belhaven could come to us for a while until they settle, Papa.'

Herbert snorted. 'Until they're off to boarding school, you mean. Once Verity's got her, she'll not hand her back.'

'What difference does it make?' Bertie asked. 'You can keep the musical one. You don't need both.'

Clarrie stood on the stairs, indignant. If Herbert gave in, she would hand in her notice there and then.

'Please, Papa, at least consider it. Verity's really quite insistent that it should be Belhaven senior. She has a knack with the twins, it seems – a born nursemaid.'

'Very well,' Herbert sighed, beginning to give way, 'I'll give it some thought.'

'We'll pay her well, if that's what's worrying you,' Bertie assured him.

Clarrie could not face them. Furious at being discussed in such a way, she turned and stalked back to the kitchen. Olive was alarmed when later that evening Clarrie blurted out what she had overheard.

'They can't split us up,' she cried, 'they just can't.'

'They won't.' Clarrie was adamant.

'And I don't want to go and work for that awful Verity,' Olive fretted.

'Neither do I. We'll go somewhere else. We're very employable now,' Clarrie said proudly. 'There are agencies we can go to who'll find us work. I didn't know such things existed when we first came over, or I'd've got us out of the pub a lot sooner.'

Clarrie steeled herself for a summons to Herbert's study. It was the end of the week before he plucked up the courage to confront her, by which time she was in such a state of anxiety that she could hardly speak two words to him for fear of being rude.

He was standing in his customary defensive position by the window behind his desk, his hands clutched tightly on his walking stick.

'Clarrie,' he began, 'please sit down.'

'I prefer to stand, sir,' she said, tight-voiced.

He shot her a wary look. She stared back at him defiantly. He glanced away and looked out of the window, his fingers clenching. She felt a sudden stab of pity. This was as difficult for him as it was for her. Then she hardened her heart. He was about to get rid of her because he was too weak to stand up to his demanding son and selfish daughter-in-law.

'I know what you're going to ask,' she said sharply, 'and the answer's no.'

He swung round and gaped at her. 'How could you possibly?'

'I happened to hear you and Mr Bertie talking

about it.' Clarrie blushed. 'I wasn't eavesdropping – I was on my way upstairs and the door was open.'

Herbert stepped quickly round the desk towards her. 'I'm sorry—' he began.

'Well, we won't go. Me and Olive. And we won't be separated. If you don't want us here, we'll find somewhere else – somewhere we're appreciated.' Clarrie glared at him, the indignation she had kept at bay suddenly spilling out. 'It may be a petty matter of domestic economics to you and Mr Bertie, but for me and Olive this has been our home for over three years. And we've grown to care for it – for Master Will—'

Dropping the stick, he reached forward and grabbed her hands. 'Clarrie, stop!'

She broke off, trying to control herself. He had never touched her before. She could see how agitated he was by her outburst, but she would not go without telling him how she felt. 'All I ask is that you give us a good reference,' she said stiffly, pulling her hands away.

He stared at her with troubled eyes, his gaunt face strained.

'No, Clarrie,' he said, his jaw clenching.

'No?' she repeated, anger curdling inside again. 'Why not? It's the least you could do, sir.'

'Because I don't want you to go!' he cried.

She stared back, unsure. 'You don't?'

'No! I want you to stay. I want your sister to stay,' he said impatiently.

'But sir, you said to Mr Bertie—'

'Forget what I said,' he snapped, 'and just listen to me for a minute.'

Clarrie gulped. He seemed furious with her now. She had spoiled things between them by speaking her mind and she need not have said anything. He was not going to send her to Verity's after all.

She saw a pulse throbbing in his temple as he struggled to master his temper.

'I did consider giving you the chance to work for my son. You are young. It would be a livelier household. A more prestigious position. All this I considered with your welfare in mind.'

'Thank you, sir, but—'

He held up a hand to silence her. 'But I had another reason for sending you away.' He gave her a stern, penetrating look. Clarrie went cold inside. She had a sudden wild thought that Herbert had somehow learned of the incident in the garden with Wesley, that he had heard damaging gossip about her.

'The thing is,' he said, 'I've grown to care too much for you – more than a man should for his housekeeper.'

She stared at him, wondering if she had heard correctly.

'You're shocked, aren't you?' he said grimly. 'I know I'm old enough to be your father and that my feelings are not reciprocated. But I can't help it. My admiration for you has grown into something far warmer. I could not have got through these past terrible years without your help. Just to hear your footstep on the stair or your voice calling from below has been a comfort, Clarrie. I cannot imagine what this house would be like without you in it.'

'Sir?' Clarrie said in bewilderment. 'How can I stay here now you've told me this?'

His look grew urgent. 'Clarrie, I don't want you to go. I want you to stay and . . .' He struggled with his words. 'The question I wanted to ask you before . . .' He took her hands in his again. 'Will you marry me?'

Clarrie jolted in shock. 'Marry?' she gasped.

He nodded, his expression anguished. 'I know it wouldn't be for love on your part, but I can offer you much. This house and a secure future for you and your sister. Olive could take up her music again, and her painting. I could help you finance the tea room that Will says you've always wanted.'

Her heart hammered. As Mrs Herbert Stock, both she and Olive would never be homeless. They would have social standing. They would never have to scrub another hearth again, or do another's bidding. Olive could resume her music lessons. And her own tea room! That would make the Veritys and Wesleys of this world sit up and take note. Instantly her excitement deflated. Herbert's family would be furious; they would stop it. Her anxiety showed.

Abruptly he let go. 'I can see the suggestion is distasteful to you,' he said bleakly. 'I'm sorry, I didn't mean to cause you embarrassment. I'm an old fool.'

As he stepped back, Clarrie clutched at his hand and held on. 'Not a fool, sir,' she whispered. She was amazed by his confession, for she would not have guessed his feelings in a hundred years. He looked so unsure of himself, almost boyish in his vulnerability. For such a diffident, cautious man, it must have taken some courage to risk his pride by telling her of his secret regard. She realised that the flood of warmth she suddenly felt towards him meant that she cared for him too. It was not love, but it was respect and affection. Herbert was offering her the kind of stable marriage to which she aspired, and she was certain she could make it work.

'Yes, I will,' she said. 'I will marry you.'

He frowned at her, uncertain. 'You will?'

Clarrie smiled in reassurance. 'I'd be honoured to be your wife, sir.'

Herbert grabbed her to him and let out an exultant bark. 'Dearest Clarrie!' He pressed her to his chest. 'Thank the Lord!' He released her, but held her hands between his, smiling with relief.

Clarrie laughed. 'So what do we do now, sir?'

Herbert snorted. 'From this moment onwards, you stop calling me sir.'

Clarrie blushed. 'That will take some getting used to. It wouldn't feel right calling you by your first name – not until we are . . .'

'Married? Go on, Clarrie, say it! Married, married, *married*.'

She gazed at him in astonishment. She had never seen him so gleeful.

'What will your family say?' she asked nervously.

His face clouded for an instant. 'We won't care what they say. Besides, Will will be overjoyed. He adores you.'

'It wasn't Will I was worrying about,' Clarrie said drily.

'We'll face them together.' He raised her hands and gently kissed them. 'With you beside me, Clarrie, I can face the world again.'

CHAPTER 21

Autumn 1909

Word of Herbert's proposal caused a storm among his family and acquaintances. Bertie was furious, Verity hysterical, the Landsdownes coldly disapproving. Only Will sent them a warm letter of congratulations. Fellow churchgoers glanced askance at Herbert and muttered when he insisted on Clarrie and Olive's sitting in the forward pew with him instead of behind with the other servants. Even Dolly revolted and handed in her notice.

'It wouldn't be right,' she told Clarrie frostily. 'One minute you're one of us, the next I'm bobbin' and curtseying like you're some'at special.'

'It won't be like that,' Clarrie insisted. 'I won't ask any more of you than I do as housekeeper.'

'It won't be the same.' Dolly sniffed in offence, as if Clarrie had done it as a deliberate slight.

She left a month later. On Clarrie's advice, Herbert did not replace her immediately.

'Olive and I will manage the cooking in the meantime. Best wait till we're wed, so a new cook won't know me as the housekeeper first.'

Olive, who had been thrilled by her sister's unexpected news, took Dolly's leaving badly.

'She's the only friend I've got,' she said tearfully. 'Now I've no one to natter with.'

'You've got me,' Clarrie reminded her. 'Soon you'll be leading a different sort of life – a lady of leisure. You can go back to your music and drawing. Won't that be wonderful?'

Olive appeared to cheer up at her words. But if Clarrie's attention had not been so taken up with hostility from other quarters, she might have noticed her sister's growing ambivalence towards her forthcoming marriage.

But Bertie and Verity's opposition was vocal and relentless. Clarrie knew by the strain on Herbert's face that his son was making life difficult at the office and Herbert increasingly stayed at home to do his work in the study. Verity refused to bring the grandchildren round to see him and no more invitations came to visit the house in Tankerville.

One day, when Herbert was out, Bertie marched into the house to confront Clarrie. He cornered her alone in the kitchen.

'I know your game, Belhaven,' he said with a contemptuous jut of his fleshy chin, 'you're after my father's money. You're trying to take what's rightfully mine!'

'I most certainly am not.' Clarrie was indignant.

'Trying to step into my dear mother's shoes. It disgusts me. Don't pretend for one minute you love him.'

'It's none of your business,' Clarrie gasped.

'Oh, but it is.' In fury he pushed her up against the table and grabbed her chin in a vice-like grip. 'Don't play the prim little madam with me,' he snarled.

Clarrie felt suffocating panic. His hatred of her was palpable.

'I don't want what's yours,' she cried. 'I just want to live in peace and dignity with your father.'

He gave a savage laugh. 'I don't believe you. How did you wheedle your way into his affections? With some native witchcraft? A love potion?'

Suddenly with his other hand he grabbed her hair and jerked her towards him. Fixing wet lips on hers, he gave her a smothering kiss. Clarrie fought him off in revulsion. Pushing him back, she grabbed a kitchen knife and brandished it.

'Keep away from me,' she hissed.

'Or what?' he said coldly.

'Or your father will get to hear of this,' she said.

They glared at each other in loathing. Bertie looked away first.

'What will it cost for you to go — to leave my father alone?' he demanded. 'I can pay you enough to rent somewhere — you and your needy little sister

– set you up in a boarding house so you can be your own boss. I know that's what you want.'

Clarrie wanted to spit at his offer. First he threatened her and then humiliated her with a disgusting kiss; now he was trying to bribe her. He was beneath contempt.

'I don't want your money,' she replied hotly, 'and I don't want your inheritance. If that's all that's bothering you and your wife, then I suggest you speak to your father about money matters. It's none of my concern.'

Bertie's look was still suspicious.

'Now I think you should go,' she said.

'Upstart little bitch!' he cursed. 'If you go ahead with this marriage, I'll make sure you're blackballed from society. No one who's anyone in this city will invite you to anything.'

Clarrie said in derision, 'Well, that's a relief.'

He spun on his heels and stalked out at her effrontery. Minutes later, when Olive came clattering in at the back door, Clarrie was still shaking.

'I've just seen Mr Bertie leaving – looked like the devil was chasing his tail. What did he want?' she asked anxiously.

'Trying to bully me not to marry his father,' Clarrie said, trying to hide her distress.

Olive came closer and saw how upset her sister was. 'Oh, Clarrie, do you think it's wise getting wed after all? Everyone seems to be against it.'

Clarrie set her face firmly. 'They'll get used to it in time. It's hardly the first time a man's taken his housekeeper for a wife.'

'Aye, but some folk are more set against us for being part Indian than for being servants,' Olive said unhappily.

'Don't you listen to such talk.' Clarrie's anger ignited. 'I'm proud of who we are. And it makes no difference to people who really care about us – to Herbert and Will.'

Olive sighed, her look still troubled. Clarrie put out her arms to her. After a moment's hesitation, Olive allowed herself to be hugged.

Despite Clarrie's defiant words, the engagement dragged on into the autumn, the date for their wedding never quite being finalised. She began to worry that Herbert was regretting his rash proposal, buckling under the weight of family censure. She lived in dread of Bertie's forcing his unwanted attentions on her again. He was not to be trusted. As long as she remained a servant and not Herbert's wife, she was vulnerable to the younger man's bullying.

'Perhaps if we give them a little more time, they'll come round to the idea,' Herbert said with a pleading look.

'They won't.' Clarrie was blunt. 'They probably won't ever speak to us again – at least not to me. Are you prepared for that?'

'Surely not,' Herbert sighed.

As winter approached, Clarrie came to the painful conclusion that the marriage was doomed before it had even begun. Her dreams of being Herbert's wife and companion, of opening a business with Olive, were just that: dreams. One evening, she steeled herself for the ordeal of making Herbert see the impossibility of their union. It was pie in the sky.

'I'm sorry,' she told him sadly, 'but I'll not be the cause of your estrangement from your family.'

He looked at her in consternation. 'Don't say that. It won't happen.'

'It already has. You can't keep ignoring it.' Clarrie laid a hand on his arm. 'Bertie has made it quite plain I will never be accepted by him and Verity.'

'Bertie.' Herbert scowled. 'What has he said to you?'

She held his look. 'That I can never step into his mother's shoes. Not that I would ever try, but Bertie hates the very idea of someone taking his mother's place.'

Herbert reddened and looked away. 'He doesn't realise how happy you make me, but that will come in time.'

Clarrie shook her head. 'If only that were true. Like you, I thought he would come round to the idea, but he's never going to. It makes life impossible for you. You two have to carry on working together.'

Herbert clutched at her hand. Fiercely he said, 'I don't care how difficult Bertie makes my life, I just want us to be married. I've delayed too long and now you're having second thoughts. The idea of losing you frightens me far more than anything Bertie might do.'

They gazed at each other, Clarrie's heart lifting to see the love in his eyes. She knew she could make Herbert happy after his deep grief over Louisa. Why should she not take this chance at happiness for herself too? She was tired of struggling, of fretting about the future, of working her fingers to the bone. If others were offended, so be it.

'Then,' Clarrie said quietly, 'you have to face up to what is really worrying your son.'

'What is that?' Herbert asked, still gripping her hand.

'Money. He's terrified I'm going to steal his inheritance.'

'That's nonsense,' Herbert protested.

'I know it is, but that's what he thinks.'

'I'm sure you're mistaken—'

'He came to see me,' Clarrie interrupted. 'He made it quite plain he thinks I'm only after one thing – your money.'

Herbert gave her a sharp look.

'It will poison our marriage,' Clarrie said quietly. 'How long before you think it too?'

'I don't care why you're marrying me,' Herbert said, 'I'm just thankful that you are.'

'Maybe now,' Clarrie smiled wistfully, 'but in time it might come between us – if your family carry on shunning us.'

Herbert looked stubborn. 'I won't give you up, Clarrie. Tell me what I should do.'

Clarrie was heartened by his vehemence. 'The only way to set Bertie's mind at rest is to sign things over to him now – the business – before we marry,' Clarrie urged. 'So no one can make accusations after.'

'But it's my own legal practice,' Herbert protested.

'And one day it will be his,' Clarrie pointed out. 'You need to settle things with him, so he doesn't see me as a threat. We don't need much to live on – you're not nearly as extravagant as Bertie and Verity. And you could set something aside for Will. But why not hand over to Bertie now what he'll get in time anyway?'

Herbert looked at her long and hard. 'If you think that will speed us towards our wedding day, then I'll gladly do it.'

Her spirits soared at the warmth she saw in his eyes. He raised her hand to his lips and kissed it.

'I love you, Clarrie,' he murmured.

She smiled. 'Yes, sir.'

The wedding was finally set for the New Year, just before Will was due to return to school. It was to be a quiet affair: a simple ceremony at the John Knox Presbyterian Church followed by a tea dance at the Empire for a couple of dozen guests. These were mainly church friends and a handful of clients, including Daniel Milner, who Herbert trusted

would wish them well. Clarrie invited her friend
Rachel Garven and the women who had first shown
her friendship at the pub: Ina, Lexy and Maggie. The
women were amazed and thrilled to be asked, taking
delight in putting together outfits grand enough for
the Empire Tea Rooms. Against Olive's wishes, an
invitation was also sent to Jared and Lily, but back
came a curt reply from Lily that Friday was a strange
day to have a wedding and they would be far too
busy at work to attend.

Herbert, urged on by Clarrie, made his peace
with Bertie by transferring the ownership of the
practice. It was not enough, however, to mollify the
affronted Verity. Both she and Bertie refused to
attend the wedding, and Bertie asked his father not
to embarrass the Landsdownes by sending them an
invitation either.

Verity wrote: . . . *regretfully, we shall be away for New
Year, staying with friends in Perthshire. We hope the day
goes to your satisfaction.*

'Can't be too rude,' Clarrie said drily to Olive,
'just in case Herbert changes his mind and cuts them
out of his will.'

But she was silently relieved that they would not
be there to spoil the day. She could no longer look
at Bertie with equanimity since he had forced his
kisses on her in the kitchen. She was revolted by the
memory. The less she saw of him the better.

Will, in contrast, brightened up the holidays and
increased her excitement at the thought of the

wedding day. Clarrie hugged him fiercely when he agreed to give her away. He seemed quite overcome by the request.

'Me?' He blushed. 'Are you sure you want *me*?'

'Of course.' Clarrie smiled. 'You're more like family to me than anyone I can think of.'

'Then yes,' he said, eyes shimmering with emotion, 'I'd be honoured to.'

Clarrie and Olive took him shopping for a new suit. At almost sixteen, he now towered over them and spoke to them in a deep voice at odds with his fresh-faced looks. Like a young colt, he dashed about energetically on gangly limbs, shaking his mop of fair hair out of his eyes. But when he boomed with loud laughter, Clarrie was reminded that he was halfway to being a man.

'Would Johnny like to come to the wedding?' Clarrie asked him, shortly beforehand. 'There'll be plenty to eat.'

Will agreed with enthusiasm and she felt deeply grateful for his affectionate nature and lack of snobbery. He had refused to go to Bertie's for Christmas without his father or Clarrie and Olive, although he went with Bertie and Clive for a day's shooting at Rokeham Towers. Maybe in time, Clarrie thought in hope, Will would be the one to mend the severed ties between Herbert and Verity's family.

1910 arrived and the week of the wedding. Everything was ready. Clarrie's dress of white velvet with a simple veil hung in the wardrobe, as did Olive's bridesmaid's dress of powder blue that complemented her coils of red-gold hair. On Herbert's insistence, Louisa's room had been emptied of its dusty bottles and musty furnishings and refitted with new curtains, bedding and floor rugs of Clarrie's choosing. It would be their bedroom.

With Will's help, the sisters rearranged the furniture so that the bed faced on to the large window and the view of rooftops and city spires. Clarrie, who wanted the room to look as different as it possibly could from Louisa's sickroom and private domain, chose fabrics in emerald, turquoise and tangerine. At the windows she hung white muslin instead of heavy brocade so as to let as much light into the room as possible.

She surveyed the sweep of counterpane with its vivid green birds of paradise nervously. She did not like to think too long about what it would be like sharing the marital bed with Herbert. He was not unattractive – must have been good-looking in a severe sort of way when he was young – but he was sixty, as old as her father would have been had he lived. She was still rather in awe of him, and the thought of intimacy with her former master made her insides lurch about like seasickness.

To stop such unwelcome thoughts Clarrie kept busy with needless tasks and errands. Two days before the wedding she called into the Empire Tea Rooms. Although the tea menu and quartet of

319

musicians had been chosen weeks before, and Clarrie had been into the tea room twice since then to double-check the arrangements, she could not resist one more visit just to be sure.

'Any excuse to go into that place,' Olive said, rolling her eyes and declining to accompany her. 'You would think you owned it.'

Clarrie laughed. 'Maybe one day . . .'

As she walked into the lofty-ceilinged tea house, she had to admit that Olive was right. She loved its smell of polish and baking, and the cheerful lamplight at each table contrasting with the gloomy raw January day outside. She felt at home here, the tensions of a busy day falling from her shoulders the moment she walked through the swing doors with their leaded panes of coloured glass.

She noticed at once that extra potted plants – ferns – had been placed on the windowsills and two bold brass lamps in the shapes of wood nymphs stood either side of the dais where the band would play. A series of Chinese prints had been hung against the dark panelling, adding to the Oriental feel.

The manageress, Miss Simpson, came forward to greet her and show her to the alcove table that was Clarrie and Rachel's favourite.

'I haven't come to eat,' Clarrie confessed. 'Just wanted to make sure everything was in hand for Friday.'

'Please.' Miss Simpson ushered her into a seat.

'Have a pot of tea on the house.'

'It must be nerves,' Clarrie confessed, 'but I can't settle to anything.'

'That's to be expected.' The matronly woman smiled. 'But don't you worry, we're all prepared.'

'I knew you would be.' Clarrie relaxed and sat down.

'As I said, we're setting up extra tables round the corner for the regulars,' Miss Simpson went on. 'We've got new Chinese screens we can pull across, so it'll be more private for you.'

'I like the new paintings and plants – and those bonny lamps.' Clarrie nodded towards the dais. 'Where did they come from?'

'New owner sent them in,' Miss Simpson said, lowering her voice. 'Call me old-fashioned, but I think they're a bit vulgar. Not nearly enough clothing on.'

Clarrie said in amusement, 'Perhaps you could drape them in napkins? Don't want the customers swooning.'

Miss Simpson went away chuckling. 'Betty,' she instructed one of her waitresses, 'get Miss Belhaven a pot of Darjeeling.'

Clarrie unpinned her broad hat, sat back and sighed in contentment. There were less than a dozen people in the café and the low-level murmuring was restful. She closed her eyes and thought how lucky she was to have found Herbert. Soon she would be Mrs Stock and the past few years of struggle would

Her tea came. Clarrie savoured the small rituals of pouring the golden liquid from pot into cup, dropping in two sugar lumps with the delicate metal tongs, and stirring with a silver teaspoon.

The outer doors opened and closed, sending eddies of cold air rippling around her ankles. Clarrie shivered and put her hands round the teacup for warmth, lifting it to her lips and savouring the delicate aroma before sipping. As she did so, a man in a cape and top hat strode into the room, directly towards her. Catching sight of Clarrie, he checked his step. Even before he removed his hat, she knew from his tall stature and vigorous walk that it was Wesley.

His dark brows with their familiar scar knitted in a frown of bewilderment, as if he could not believe his own eyes. He came to a halt at her table, staring hard.

'Clarissa?' he demanded. 'Can it be you?'

She felt a jolt at his use of her full name. No one had called her that since Belgooree. With shaking hands she put down her cup. It rattled against the saucer.

'Mr Robson,' she said, standing up.

He was quick to say, 'Please don't get up.'

She was too used to being the servant, she thought in annoyance, sitting down again. But it was he who seemed wrong-footed by the sudden encounter.

'How are you? What brings you here? I can't believe . . . May I sit down?'

Despite the uncomfortable pounding in her

chest, she nodded in assent. He pulled out the chair opposite, unfastening his cape, scrutinising her all the while. A waitress appeared quickly and took his coat, hat and gloves with a bob of respect. Miss Simpson bustled over.

'Mr Robson, what an honour. What can I get you?'

'Tea, thank you,' he smiled at her distractedly, 'and gingerbread.'

The manageress beamed. 'Certainly, sir.'

Clarrie's insides twisted in envy at the way Wesley inspired deference without seeming to notice. It should not surprise her that he would make it his business to be known in the city's tea houses, however infrequently he came back to Newcastle. She was thankful she had not come across him here before now. He leaned towards her, eyeing her intently.

'You look well,' he said, 'very well indeed.' When she said nothing he continued, 'I'm sorry about your father's death. Tell me what happened – to you and Olive. I heard you went away to relations. But no one seemed to know where. I assumed you were still in India somewhere. Thought I might come across you, but never did. I want to know everything, Clarissa!'

Clarrie gripped her chair, quite taken aback by his urgent questioning. What did he care what had happened to her?

'Things were very difficult after Father died,' she

said tensely. 'We had to leave Belgooree. We came here to Newcastle – to my cousin and his wife.' She was not going to tell him that they had been reduced to virtual slavery in one of the west end's rougher public houses.

'You've been in Newcastle all this time?' he asked, astounded.

'Yes. We had no choice. We would rather have stayed in India, but we had nothing.'

Wesley's jaw tensed as he nodded. 'I heard Belgooree was sold.' He looked at her with a glint of impatience. 'But you did have a choice. I was willing to help.'

Clarrie felt anger flare. 'Yes, you made no secret of how you coveted my father's estate. A good business proposition. No doubt the Robsons picked it up for a song.'

He leaned closer, eyes narrowing. 'We didn't buy it, though we should have. Some speculators thought they could make easy money, but they made no better job of it than your father. The last time I was up that way two years ago it was all overgrown – practically gone back to jungle.'

Clarrie's heart squeezed in pain. She could not bear to think of her old home derelict and the tea bushes grown wild. Had her parents' graves disappeared under tangled undergrowth, or been dug up by leopards? She clutched at the table, stifling a groan.

Wesley quickly covered her hand with his. 'I'm sorry to upset you. I didn't know about your father's death until long after you'd gone, please believe me. If I had, I would have tried to help.'

Clarrie snatched her hand away, alarmed at his touch. 'What good would knowing have done?'

He leaned away. They studied each other in tense silence.

When he spoke again his tone was mocking. 'No, you're right. The proud Belhaven girls would not have allowed a mere Robson to come to their aid. Isn't that so?'

Clarrie remained silent. She did not want to think about how things might have turned out if Wesley had still been in Assam when the catastrophe happened.

Suddenly he leaned forward again and said in a low voice, 'But you did come looking for me, didn't you? You came to the Oxford. Bain, the assistant manager, told me when I came back from Ceylon the following year. Why did you make that journey? What did you want to ask me, Clarissa?'

His green eyes glittered knowingly. He was enjoying her discomfort. The last thing she was going to admit was that she had gone to say she would marry him after all.

'It was Olive's idea,' she said, flushing. 'It was desperation.'

Wesley gave a short laugh. 'Blunt as ever, Clarissa.'

'No one calls me Clarissa any more,' she said in agitation. 'I'm known as Clarrie here.'

They were interrupted by the arrival of his tea

and gingerbread. As he helped himself, Wesley gave her a sardonic smile. 'Perhaps I should just call you Miss Belhaven so as to avoid any offence?'

Clarrie eyed him. 'You could – but not for much longer. I'm to be married the day after tomorrow.' She felt a rush of triumph at his dumbfounded expression. 'That's why I'm here, finalising arrangements. We're having a small tea dance at the Empire. It's my favourite tea room in Newcastle.'

Wesley swiftly regained his composure. 'Mine too.' He fixed her with his penetrating look. 'And who is the lucky gentleman?'

Clarrie smiled with satisfaction. 'I believe you know him. Mr Herbert Stock, the solicitor.'

'Bertie's father?' he almost bellowed. Heads turned to glance in their direction.

'Yes.' Clarrie blushed, infuriated by his look of amused disbelief.

'But he's an old man!'

'He's a good man,' Clarrie said defensively, 'which is the best kind.'

'Good and dull,' Wesley declared. 'From what I know of you, Clarrie, you'll be bored to tears with him.'

His arrogance enraged her. 'Well you don't know me,' she said, almost choking with anger, 'and you've no idea what my life has been like these past six years – for me and Olive. You'll never know what it's like to skivvy for a pittance, not knowing if you'll have a roof over your head next day or whether

Olive will die from an asthma attack because we can't afford the doctor! You and your kind think you rule the world and that no one should stand in your way. Well, that's not what I want. I just want a marriage to a good man who will treat me and Olive with respect. And you can laugh at me all you want, Wesley Robson, but I'd rather be marrying Herbert, however old he is, than share my life with the likes of you!'

She jumped out of her seat, seized her hat and barged her way past him. He tried to grab her arm as she went.

'I'm sorry – don't go – tell me more—'

'I have nothing to say to you,' she hissed, shaking free, mortified that people at nearby tables had stopped to listen to their argument.

In humiliation, she fled from the café without looking back. She ran aimlessly along the city's streets, and then, terrified he would come after her, she jumped on a tram and found herself going in the wrong direction. Getting off in Sandyford, she walked westwards as sleety rain began to fall. By the time she reached Summerhill, she was drenched and chilled to the core.

Olive fussed over her, removing her wet clothes and wrapping her in a rug.

'Where've you been? I thought some'at terrible had happened.'

Clarrie saw the anxiety etched on her sister's face and decided not to tell her about the encounter with Wesley. She would not burden Olive with the knowledge that Belgooree had gone to rack and ruin.

'Got on the wrong tram,' she shivered. 'Stupid of me. Head in the clouds at the moment.'

'Dafty!' Olive said with relief, as she rubbed her hair dry. She made her a hot drink. Handing it over, she said, 'You really do care for Mr Herbert, don't you?'

Clarrie gave her a guilty glance. Her mind had been full of the encounter with Wesley and how disturbed it had left her. She took the cup and nodded.

'I'm glad.' Olive gave a rueful smile. 'I can't believe how different your life is going to be in less than two days' time.'

'And yours,' Clarrie said quickly.

Olive's look was thoughtful. 'I suppose so. But it won't be the same.'

She went off to hang the wet clothes in the drying room before Clarrie could ask her what she meant.

CHAPTER 22

On the day of the wedding, Clarrie woke feeling shivery and apprehensive. She had probably caught a chill. Olive helped her dress, chattering in excitement as she unbound the rags from Clarrie's hair and arranged the long black strands into elaborate coils with ringlets framing her oval face.

'How bonny you look,' she declared. 'Like that photograph of Mother.'

Clarrie surveyed her image in the small mirror above the washstand. Tonight she would look into the full-length looking glass in the marital bedroom. Her large dark eyes shone with a feverish light. Her head pounded. She must shake off this lethargy.

'You're so clever with your hands,' she told Olive, trying to sound bright. 'No hairdresser could have done a better job.'

She turned round and saw Olive's pleased expression. Tonight Olive would move into Bertie and Verity's old bedroom. Ina's daughter Sally would come from tomorrow to be maid to the household and lodge in the attic bedroom that the sisters had continued to share even after the other servants had left. No longer would they hear each other's breathing in the night, or whisper in the dark when they could not sleep. Only for a brief spell when they had first come to Summerhill had the sisters ever slept apart.

Clarrie felt a sudden pang of loss at the thought. She held out her arms.

'Oh, Olive, I'm going to miss you!'

'Me too!'

Olive ran into her hold and the pair of them burst into tears. They clung together crying.

'Aren't we daft?' Clarrie sniffled. 'It's not as if I'm going away. We'll still be together every day.'

'I know,' Olive sobbed, 'but it f-feels like the end of s-something.'

It was Clarrie who pulled away first. 'Well, it's not the end of us two being together. I promised you, remember?' She smoothed Olive's red hair away from her tear-stained face. At nineteen, she was a pretty young woman, and it suddenly struck Clarrie that Olive would soon be of marriageable age too. Not that her sister had expressed an interest in anyone romantically since her girlish crush on the soldier Harry Wilson. Clarrie would advise her when the time came, for she still felt as protective towards Olive as if she were her own daughter. Nothing would change that.

'Come on, let's get you ready now.' Clarrie smiled. 'Don't let Sir hear us wailing as if we're off to a funeral.'

'You know what the hardest thing will be?' Olive sniffed. 'Calling Mr Stock by his Christian name.'

Clarrie nodded in agreement. 'Herbert,' she said tentatively. 'Herbert. Herbert. You try it.'

'No.' Olive sniggered.

'Go on.'

'Herbert.' Olive giggled. 'Herbert, Herbert.'

'That's it,' Clarrie encouraged her. 'Together!'

'Herbert, Herbert, Herbert, *Herbert*!' they shouted, falling on to the bed and convulsing in laughter.

It broke the spell of anxiety. The unease that had gripped Clarrie since long before dawn vanished in their shared hilarity.

A carriage was laid on to take the sisters to the church but Herbert insisted on walking up the hill with Will, despite Clarrie's worry that the cold would set off his rheumatism. Low clouds threatened snow and they hurried into the church as the first flurry arrived.

Clarrie, fuzzy-headed from her brewing cold, was aware of Will taking her cold hands in his and trying to warm them up and then the next moment she was walking towards Herbert on Will's arm, seeing everything through a blur of gauzy veil. Yet Herbert's admiring look as her veil was pulled back and the way his sombre face creased into a broad smile lifted her heart.

The ceremony was short and dignified, and she emerged on Herbert's arm into swirling snow. Quickly, they clambered into the carriage with Will and Olive, and rode precariously downhill into town. The Empire seemed even more welcoming than usual as they escaped out of the blizzard into its cosy gentility.

The band struck up the bridal march as Clarrie and Herbert appeared arm in arm, brushing snow from each other's clothing. Miss Simpson guided them to a long table at the top of the room next to the musicians and her waitresses began to bring out platefuls of dainty sandwiches, buttered scones and slices of cake.

Soon all the guests were gathered and tucking into the tea, faces glowing in the lamplight as they warmed up. Before the dancing, Herbert gave a short, bashful speech, thanking their friends for attending.

'After my first wife died,' he said, clearing his throat, 'I never thought to find such happiness again with any woman. Was certainly not looking for it.' His eyes glittered as he gazed at Clarrie. 'But there she was, in my own household, being brave and kind and looking after us all, when sometimes getting through the day seemed an impossibility.'

He rested a hand on her shoulder. 'Clarrie has

given me a new lease of life. She is a gift from God. I still have to pinch myself to be sure I haven't dreamed that this beautiful young woman has agreed to be my wife. But she has and I'm profoundly grateful. So is my son Will, to whom Clarrie has been a caring mother since his own passed away.'

He smiled. 'So please, enjoy the tea and dance if you wish. And thank you for coming to share in our happiness on such an inhospitable day.'

The guests clapped and Will jumped to his feet to propose a toast to his father and Clarrie. They raised their teacups. 'To Herbert and Clarrie!'

Clarrie was amused to see Lexy and her friends winking and pulling faces at having to drink just tea. Herbert had wanted no liquor to spoil the day. 'Tea's the best fillip anyone could want,' he had declared.

As the guests clapped and sat down again, and the musicians struck up, a man moving out of the shadows by the Chinese screens caught Clarrie's attention. She froze in shock. It was Wesley, arms folded, observing them with mild amusement. He saw her looking at him and arched his brows, his look insolent. How dare he come here and spoil her day! Clarrie's heart thumped in agitation. She felt sweat breaking out on her brow. A moment later Wesley was summoning one of the waitresses and then he disappeared behind the screen.

'Clarrie dearest,' Herbert said, 'are you feeling well?'

She realised she was breathing hard, her palms

sweating. She was turning hot and cold. She tried to focus on what he was saying.

'I was hoping you would dance with Will. Save my embarrassment.' His look was apologetic. 'The walk to church was as much as I could manage.'

Clarrie had hoped to persuade Herbert on to the dance floor, if only for a sedate waltz, but he was self-conscious about his limp and adamant in his refusal. At that moment, Clarrie was not sure she was capable either. Her head swam in the heat of the room. Will, though, was eager. She tried to summon some enthusiasm as the boy led her on to the polished floor. Others swiftly followed their lead.

'You've been practising,' Clarrie said, impressed by his handling.

Will grinned. 'With Johnny's sisters.'

While he chattered on about them, Clarrie could not help glancing round to see if Wesley would dare to show his face again. Why had she been foolish enough to tell him of her marriage plans? She might have known he would use the knowledge to make her feel awkward. He had come to mock her for marrying an old man, for having a simple wedding with ordinary guests more at home in the terraces of Elswick than the mansions of Jesmond. Well, whatever his reasons, Clarrie determined, she would not be belittled by his sneering from the sidelines.

As she and Will made their way back to the table, a waitress was coming towards it bearing a huge basket tied up with silver ribbon.

'Compliments of the Empire,' she said, grinning.

'How kind!' Herbert exclaimed as he rose to take the hamper.

'Very,' Clarrie gasped. 'We must thank Miss Simpson.'

'Oh, it's from the owner, miss,' the waitress replied.

'Goodness me.' Herbert beamed. 'Then we must thank him or her.'

'Shall I fetch 'em, sir?' the waitress asked.

'If they're here, please do,' Herbert said.

She bobbed and left them. Clarrie undid the ribbon, curious. It was full of delicacies: cheeses, cakes, nuts, crystallised fruits, teas and coffee beans.

'So generous!' she cried.

From behind a deep voice said, 'It's well deserved.'

She whipped round to see Wesley. He gave her a short bow and shook Herbert by the hand.

'I know you, don't I?' Herbert asked.

'Wesley Robson, a cousin of Verity's.' He smiled. 'I was at your son's wedding.'

'Of course,' Herbert said, shaking him by the hand. 'This is most generous of you, and quite unexpected.'

'I was a friend of Clarrie's father in India,' Wesley answered. 'It's a small token of my esteem for the Belhavens and for yourself.'

'We're most grateful,' Herbert said, looking in astonishment at Clarrie, 'aren't we, my dear?'

They were both looking at her. She was finding it difficult to breathe and her pulse raced alarmingly.

Esteem for the Belhavens? Friend of her father's? What barefaced lies! But worse than his impudence was the revelation that he owned this café – her special place. Only two days ago she had boasted to him about holding her wedding party here. Then she cringed to think how she had upbraided him in his own tea room and stormed out. She felt engulfed in a hot wave of embarrassment.

'Clarrie?' Herbert prompted.

'Yes,' she said faintly, avoiding Wesley's look, 'very grateful.'

'Perhaps I might be permitted to dance with the bride?' Wesley asked.

'I'd be happy if you would.' Herbert smiled. 'I'm afraid I can't.'

Clarrie looked at her husband in alarm. The last thing she wanted to do was dance with Wesley, but how could she refuse? Herbert nodded at her in encouragement.

'Go on, my dear. I want you to enjoy this day as much as I am.'

Wesley held out his hand to Clarrie, his look challenging. She swallowed hard and forced a smile. When she offered her own hand it was shaking and clammy. Wesley led her on to the dance floor and took her in his arms. Clarrie's heart thudded erratically and her head swam. She thought she might pass out in the heat.

'Clarrie, are you all right?' he asked, tightening his grip.

'Yes,' she gulped.

He swung them across the floor. Her head began to spin.

'Look at me, Clarrie,' he murmured.

Reluctantly, she did. They were so close she could see the vivid green of his eyes between dark lashes, the dimpled cut of his chin. She felt a kick of longing, as potent as when he had first kissed her years ago. Appalled, she tried to summon her previous anger.

'Why didn't you tell me you owned the Empire?' she accused him.

He held her look. 'You never gave me the chance. Ran off like a spring hare.'

Clarrie flushed. 'I'm sorry. It was rude of me.'

'You were upset and that was my fault,' he said. 'But it was very unsettling to suddenly come across you like that. And to think you'd been living at the Stocks' all the while. We could have met any time—'

'I thought you were a tea broker in London,' Clarrie said, steering him away from such talk.

'I was for a while. I went back out to India after Bertie's wedding. But circumstances brought me back again, and the opportunity to buy the café. I intend to open several more.'

Clarrie felt a sharp stab of envy that he could so casually talk about owning a string of tea rooms. She would be happy with just one of her own. It reminded her how the Robsons' success had always overshadowed the Belhavens'.

He held her tighter. 'If only I had a good business-woman to go into partnership with – someone who knew the tea trade well.'

Was he mocking her again? Or making her a proposition?

'Always thinking of business, even at a wedding,' Clarrie said drily. She thought of the elegant woman in the red hat she had seen him with. 'So there is no Mrs Wesley Robson yet?'

'No,' he admitted. To her surprise she saw his jaw line redden. 'We should have met sooner, Clarrie. If only I'd known you were here in Newcastle.' His gaze intensified. 'I've never seen you look more beautiful.'

'Don't,' she whispered.

'It's true. I hate to think of you married to someone nearly three times your age.'

Clarrie said in agitation, 'How dare you say that on my wedding day? It would have made no difference when we met. Do you think I would ever have considered marrying a Robson?'

Wesley gripped her close as they spun. 'But you did,' he said urgently. 'You came to the Oxford to see me. I know you felt something—'

She cut him short. 'I was a young girl then – I went out of despair. But I wouldn't have made that mistake again.'

'I don't believe you,' Wesley said. 'If I'd found you before Herbert proposed, I think you would have been quite willing.'

Maddened by his arrogance, she hissed, 'You're wrong. I had seen you long before two days ago. In the gardens at Summerhill after Bertie's wedding. If I'd been so willing, I would have spoken up then, instead of pretending to be Dolly.'

His eyes widened in disbelief. 'That maid? It was you?'

'Yes, it was me. I could have let you know then who I was but I didn't want to.' She steeled herself to be cruel. 'I don't love you and never have. So please leave me alone. I'm Herbert's wife and you shouldn't be saying such things.'

He frowned, his jaw clenching in sudden anger. 'I was never your father's enemy, nor yours. But you've made yourself quite clear. You're the most stubborn and blunt of all the Belhavens. Forgive me for speaking my feelings. I can see now how wrong I was. Marriage between us would have been a disaster.'

Abruptly he brought her to a stop and led her back to Herbert. With a curt bow he left them. Clarrie collapsed into a chair, shaking and dizzy.

'My dear, you don't look at all well.' Herbert was worried. 'Has the dancing been too much for you? You seem upset.'

'I feel a little sick,' she panted. 'It's the heat.'

'Do you wish to leave?'

'No,' Clarrie said, trying to calm the turmoil she felt. 'I'll just sit out the dancing for a bit.'

Herbert ordered a glass of water and she drank

thirstily. She watched the dancing and merriment through a fog of pain, her head pounding. Wesley had ruined the celebrations with his sudden appearance and treacherous words of love and marriage to him. Why tell her now when she was married to Herbert? Or had it been part of his cruel teasing to say such things knowing that she was safely married to another? She could not fathom his reasons, or whether he had been sincere.

But even if he had, it made no difference. She would never have married the man who had had Ramsha dragged back to his death on the Oxford tea estates and thought more of profit than the welfare of his workers; who attempted to put good men like Daniel Milner out of business. If Wesley could be so ruthless in his professional life, how could he possibly be trustworthy as a husband?

Clarrie attempted to push such thoughts from her mind and enjoy the remains of her wedding tea. Despite her dizziness, she danced with Johnny and once more with Will. Then the band stopped and it was time to make their way back to Summerhill. They had decided not to go away after the wedding, as travelling could be hazardous in January. Herbert had promised her he would take her to the Lake District in early summer.

Friends came to say goodbye.

'Dancin' with all the bonniest-looking lads in the room,' Lexy crowed, 'and you not wed five minutes. I take me hat off to yer, Clarrie hinny.'

'Good luck, lass,' Ina said, looking tearful. 'We're that proud of you. I'll hear from our Sally how you get on.'

'Don't forget us now you're one of the posh folk,' Maggie teased.

She kissed them all and promised she wouldn't.

Outside it was dark. The snow had stopped falling and was beginning to freeze underfoot. It was bitterly cold. Back at the house, awkwardness gripped all four. Olive stoked up the sitting-room fire and said she would prepare a light supper.

'Let me help,' Clarrie said.

'Not on your wedding night,' Olive reproved her. 'You put your feet up. You look all done in.'

Herbert fussed over his new wife, leading her to an armchair by the fire and fetching a rug for her knees.

Will suggested they play cards, but Herbert declined.

'I've a small matter to attend to before tomorrow. Will you be all right, my dear?'

Clarrie looked at him in dismay, but nodded. She would rather he went upstairs to work than pace around disapprovingly while they played games.

Will glanced between them. 'Why don't you stay and read a book, Papa?'

Herbert shot him a look of irritation. 'It won't take long. I'll come back down for a bite of supper.'

But Herbert did not reappear. Clarrie struggled through and lost a game of backgammon with Will, then watched him beat Olive at cards. Olive served up some pea soup.

'Shall I take a bowl up to Mr Stock?' she asked.

Clarrie hesitated, then nodded.

'Only Papa could think of doing paperwork on his wedding day,' Will said impatiently. 'I'm sorry for you, Clarrie.'

'Don't be.' Clarrie summoned a smile. 'Your father's just being conscientious. It's his way.'

Soon afterwards, Clarrie retired upstairs. She knocked on the study door. Herbert was writing at his desk, utterly absorbed.

'I – I'm going to bed,' Clarrie said.

His head jerked up and he pulled off his spectacles. 'I'm so sorry. I lost all track of time.'

'Don't worry,' she said hastily, 'I was too tired for cards anyway. Will and Olive are playing music together.'

Herbert came over and rested his hands on her shoulders, his face creased in concern. 'You must rest, my dearest. I fear you're sickening for something.'

'It's just a cold,' Clarrie said.

'Still, we must take the greatest care with your health.' He cleared his throat. 'I can sleep in my own room tonight, if you like. So you can have a good night's sleep.'

'There's no need for that,' she blurted out, and then blushed. She wanted to get the awkwardness of their first night together over and done with. They must consummate the marriage, else she would not properly be Mrs Stock. In her mind, it was one of the main measures of her transformation from being merely his housekeeper. She must be his wife and lover; in time she wanted to bear children.

'I think it would be for the best if I did,' he said firmly, 'just for tonight.' He brushed her forehead with his lips. 'Goodnight, my dear.'

'Goodnight,' Clarrie murmured, swallowing down disappointment at the chasteness of his kiss. He made her feel like his daughter, not his new bride.

Alone in the large bedroom, Clarrie struggled out of her wedding dress and flung it over a chair. She pulled on the nightgown that Olive had specially embroidered with green butterflies. Earlier, her sister had drawn the curtains, lit the fire and taken the chill off the room. Still, Clarrie shivered violently as she sat on the edge of the bed, hugging her breasts.

From below, she could hear soft lilting music from the violins. She felt like rushing downstairs to join Will and Olive in the warmth of the sitting room and wrap herself in their companionship. She stood up and went to the window, lifting the curtain to peer into the dark night. Her wedding day. Out there were the people who had gathered to celebrate it. Now they were scattered and the day was over.

She sighed and climbed into the empty bed, curling up tight between the chilly sheets. Her head swam and her body ached. More than anything she craved the comfort of warm arms round her. She had never felt so alone. If only Herbert would come. Perhaps he would change his mind? Clarrie attempted to stay awake in the hope that he would. She listened for the sound of his footsteps, but none came.

The events of the day turned over and over in her mind: the intimate service, the snowstorm, the tea dance, Wesley's startling appearance. She shook at the memory of his grip on her hand and the small of her back, the way he had looked at her with undisguised wanting. He was a man who knew how to kiss with passion. Sudden longing for him gnawed inside her. Clarrie buried her burning face in the icy pillow and smothered a cry. She despised herself for the lust she felt towards Wesley; it was base and destructive. How could she lie there waiting for her husband with her marriage not even a day old, and be thinking such thoughts about Wesley? She was despicable.

In her shame, she sought to blame him. It was Wesley who had disrupted her wedding party, forcing her to dance and mischievously stirring up her feelings again. It was just another attempt to try to exert control over her, even when she was married to another. He was the source of all her troubles – had been since the day fate had thrown them together at the swami's clearing in the Khassia hills.

The only thing that was certain in her feverish mind was that she must keep Wesley at arm's length in future. She must do all she could to stay away from him.

As the night wore on and Herbert did not come, Clarrie wrestled with her tortured thoughts. When finally she fell asleep, she dreamed she was back at Belgooree, lying on a divan with a hot breeze blowing over her. A man was calling her name over and over, but she could not see who it was.

She awoke startled, her pillow soaked with tears.

'Herbert, is that you?' she gasped.

But the soft glow from the dying fire showed her that the space next to her was empty.

CHAPTER 23

1910

The first weeks of marriage were difficult ones of adjustment for them all. Clarrie struggled not to assume her usual role of rushing around as housekeeper, keeping her eye on everything from ordering groceries to cleaning the grates. Herbert, who had employed a Mrs Henderson as cook, chided her for doing too much.

'Go out more, my dear,' he urged. 'Go shopping or take tea with your friends.'

Clarrie bit back the remark that all her friends were working hard making a living. She did not belong in the leisured class and none of Louisa's former circle thought her worthy of their company. Neither the neighbours nor the well-to-do from church thought to invite her to their houses.

In turn, Clarrie berated Olive for doing menial tasks.

'You don't need to polish the stairs any more – leave it to Sally. You'll ruin your musician's fingers.'

But Olive said she felt bad letting Ina's daughter do everything.

'You have to. You're family now.' Clarrie was firm.

'Then what will I do?' Olive asked.

'Anything you want,' Clarrie exclaimed with impatience. 'Haven't you longed for the time when you didn't need to skivvy any more?'

'Aye,' Olive admitted with a sigh. 'But it's boring without Will here. There's not enough to do.'

Clarrie silently agreed but could not say so.

After that, Clarrie cleared out Verity's old dressing room and turned it into a studio for Olive to paint in. To her delight, Olive soon rediscovered her former passion for art. But her sister was happier down in the kitchen chatting to Sally and Mrs Henderson than sitting upstairs during the lengthening evenings keeping Clarrie company while Herbert worked.

In frustration, Clarrie saw her life with Herbert little changed from what it was before. She was Mrs Stock in name only. He was kind and affectionate in a distracted sort of way, and appeared to enjoy her company at mealtimes. But they went nowhere socially except to church, and he was happiest retreating to his study after a long day at the office. He was wedded to his work.

All this she had known before marrying him. But she had not expected him to avoid the intimacy of the marital bed. At first, Herbert had used her bout of illness as an excuse to sleep apart. Her heavy cold had turned to bronchitis and had lingered on into February. Yet even when she was fully recovered, he kept away. She was baffled and hurt by his rejection, but did not know how to raise the subject without causing them both red-faced embarrassment.

As spring came, and the evenings lengthened, Clarrie wondered if she should force the issue, go to his room and climb into his bed. But he stayed up working late into the night and was often so testy in the morning that she did not want to risk provoking a rebuke. She wondered about confiding in Olive, but what could her sister do? Perhaps her sham marriage was already the subject of gossip below stairs. It must be obvious to Sally, who lit their fires in the morning and made their beds, that she and Herbert slept apart.

While Olive spent her days sketching and painting, Clarrie's thoughts turned more and more to her ambition of running her own tea house. She shared her plans with her friend Rachel. Whenever Rachel was off duty they would try out different cafés and make notes on menus, prices and standards of service. Clarrie watched with envy as the Robsons opened up another Empire Tea Rooms in Ridley Place and a third on Jesmond Road. They were stylishly furnished with carved chairs and elaborate wallpaper, brass statues of Eros and stained glass lampshades. The waitresses were dressed in expensive tea gowns like hostesses and had runners to fetch and carry for them. The baking was fresh, the linen spotless and the blends of tea first class. And they were popular. When visiting the two new branches, Clarrie and Rachel had to wait in line for a table.

Clarrie left these tea rooms with both relief at not running into Wesley and sharp envy at his success. She would do just as well, she vowed, but she would not choose to pander to the affluent, bored women of the middle classes. Her aim would be to open up a tea house among the beer shops and public houses of the working-class west end. She walked the streets of Elswick and Benwell looking for vacant premises. Here, businesses frequently changed hands; a general dealer would close one week and a furniture shop open the next. Cobblers, bakers, drapers, butchers and toyshops came and went like the seasons. Few became rich supplying the working classes along Scotswood Road, but Clarrie was sure that with a lot of hard work she could make such a business pay.

Frustratingly, every time she tried to raise the matter with Herbert, he brushed her off. He was too busy. It would be a huge undertaking. Yes, she could gather information. They would talk it through at a later date.

Will, returning for the Easter holidays, distracted her from her search and filled the quiet house with noise and laughter. It was Will who fulfilled Clarrie's ambition to find the Belhavens' old farm in north Northumberland. With Olive, they took the train upcountry to Wooler and hired a horse and trap from the station. From an old map found in Herbert's library, they worked out that the farm lay halfway between Wooler and the coast. Dodding-ham, when they found it, was a clutch of sturdy farm buildings by a river, surrounded by lush fields and ringed by the rolling foothills of the Cheviots.

Clarrie was gripped by a sharp pang of familiarity, of belonging. It was just as her father had described it. Walking to the top of a steep-sided, heather-clad hill, they could see the blue-grey North Sea spreading out to the east.

'Father never lost his love of the sea,' Clarrie mused, 'even though he'd been away from it over half his life.'

Olive slipped a hand into hers and they stood in silence, letting the memories wash over them. Jock and his shells from Bamburgh beach. His tale of local heroine Grace Darling saving shipwrecked pass-engers from the rocks of the Farne Islands. In the distance they could see the ancient fortress of Bamburgh Castle guarding the coast and the treacherous islands beyond.

As they dropped down out of the wind and shared a picnic, the sisters regaled Will with reminiscences about their father and his many tales.

'I like the sound of Jock,' Will said with a wistful

smile. 'I can't remember my father telling me a single story. Mama was different. She loved stories. I could never hear them often enough.' He stopped, his fair face reddening. 'Sorry.'

Clarrie put out a hand quickly and squeezed his. 'Don't be. You must never feel you can't speak of your mother to me. I like to hear you talk of her. Your father never mentions her and that's much harder to bear. It's as if I'm not really part—' Abruptly, she stopped. She had been about to say, not really part of the family, despite the ring on her finger.

There was an awkward silence after her remark, both Will and Olive glancing away. Clarrie berated herself for having let slip her criticism. What ever her difficulties with Herbert, she had no right to air them with his son.

She led the way back down to the farm and they called at the farmhouse out of curiosity. The present tenants were called Hudson. Mrs Hudson, a broad-faced woman in a faded cotton bonnet, invited them in for a drink of milk. She cried out with astonishment when she heard they were Belhavens.

'Aye, I remember your father in his scarlet uniform – I was a child when he left. Me father was the blacksmith – used to mend Belhavens' machinery. They had a business selling ploughs, didn't they?'

Clarrie coloured. 'Yes, until they were bought out by the Robsons.'

'Oh, the Robsons,' the woman said with

reverence, 'they knew how to turn a penny into a pound. First ploughs, then boilers – always canny with their money. Still hold the tenancies to a couple of farms round here.' She sucked in her breath. 'But there's not a Belhaven left.'

Clarrie felt resentment quicken. 'No, the Robsons saw to that.'

Mrs Hudson gave her a quizzical look. 'Robsons were just better at making and selling things than others. Me father always said that. That's why your father went in the army – knew he'd make a better soldier than farmer or businessman. By, he looked a bonny sight in his uniform. Turned all the lasses' heads!'

Clarrie felt uncomfortable at the woman's blunt words. It was not the story her father had constantly told, that the money-grabbing Robsons had swindled the Belhavens out of their livelihood. But there was no one left now from those days who would be able to tell her the truth. Mrs Hudson was only passing on the gossip from her childhood.

As they took their leave, the farmer's wife was still marvelling over meeting them.

'Eeh, fancy meeting old Jock's bairns! I can see the likeness in the both of you.'

Clarrie shot her a look, but the woman was sincere. She felt a flood of warmth towards her, that she could see a glimpse of Jock in her and not just in red-headed Olive.

It was late by the time they returned to

Newcastle, but they talked about their trip animatedly over supper, telling Herbert in great detail about the farm and the meeting with Mrs Hudson.

'I'm so glad it was a successful day,' Herbert beamed. 'I can see how the fresh air has done you good. Perhaps Will can organise another outing before he goes back to school?'

'Of course,' Will agreed at once.

Clarrie had expected to return feeling content at having at last found the place where the Belhavens had belonged, but it only left her more restless. She had had a taste of real country air again, of open skies and rugged hills. She had not experienced anything as remote or wild since leaving Belgooree. Now the knowledge that such places existed beyond the smoky bustling city made her crave more.

So when Will came back with an invitation from Johnny for them both to go riding, Clarrie jumped at the chance. Olive, who was wary of horses, declined. Clarrie was given a sleek grey mare called Mayflower. Nervous at first after such a long time out of the saddle, she soon felt her confidence return and relished the ride. They rode upriver, beyond the sprawling munitions sheds, until the housing petered out into orchard, scrubland and old cottages that had once housed workers at a former drift mine. At Wylam they rode into a cloudburst and sheltered at an inn where they were served a platter of ham, cheese and thick hunks of bread.

'Where did you learn to ride so well?' Johnny asked in admiration.

'In India.' Clarrie smiled wistfully. 'I had a pony called Prince. Rode him every day.'

'You can ride Mayflower whenever you want,' Johnny said generously, 'even if I'm away at school. I'll let Papa know.'

Clarrie felt a rush of warmth towards Will's friend. 'That's very kind. I'd like to very much.'

After enjoying Will's companionship, Clarrie and Olive missed him twice as much after he left. The months until his next return seemed to stretch ahead interminably. To stem her restlessness, Clarrie reminded Herbert of his promise to take her to the Lake District.

'I'm afraid I've far too much work to attend to at the moment,' he said. 'Perhaps in a month or two.'

But he always found some excuse to put off their delayed honeymoon. By midsummer Clarrie knew she would go mad if she had nothing to occupy her beyond the concerns of the household. She confronted her husband one evening in his study.

'I want to discuss my plans for a tea house and I won't be put off any longer,' she said, coming straight to the point. 'Remember how you promised you would help me?'

Herbert glanced up. 'I'm not sure I ever promised, my dear. It was said half in jest. I didn't think you were really serious about wanting one.'

Clarrie stemmed her annoyance. 'Oh, but I am.

You know how I've been planning it – how Rachel and I have been observing the competition.'

'And I'm glad that's given you an interest.' He smiled. 'But going into business is quite a different thing. There's no necessity for you to work, my dear.' He was already looking down at his files again.

How pompous he sounded. She knew now how Will must feel being dismissed with that slight air of irritation. She marched forward and leaned across the desk, placing her hands over his papers.

'Yes there is. I need to work.' She held his look. 'I want to run a tea house here in Newcastle. I know I'm capable.'

He sighed and sat back. For a long moment he studied her as if assessing her seriousness. He tried a different tack. 'I am not a man of endless means. If you're thinking about something like the Empire Tea Rooms on Blackett Street, I can't begin to afford anything of the kind.'

Clarrie felt her insides twist at mention of the Empire. She had not been back since their wedding day; it was for ever tainted with the encounter with Wesley.

'No, I don't want a grand city centre place where only the middle classes go. I want to open one in Elswick.'

'Elswick?' He frowned, removing his spectacles. Now she really had his attention.

'Yes,' she said with enthusiasm, 'somewhere where

lasses can meet, get out the house for a bit. And lads can come in at dinnertime and have a warm meal instead of beer to fill their empty bellies.'

'More like a soup kitchen, you mean?' Herbert asked.

'No, not charity.' Clarrie was adamant. 'This will be as grand as any Empire Tea Rooms – a bit of luxury but at prices workers and their families can afford. We'll do it up nicely and serve up good quality dinners and teas.'

Herbert studied her. 'You really have been thinking about this, haven't you?'

'Ever since I worked at the Cherry Tree and saw what passed for entertainment – drunken fights and wives like Maggie given a hiding for doing nothing – I've dreamed of this. Please, Herbert, help me make it come true.'

'I think it's an admirable idea,' he said with a condescending smile, 'but I'm not convinced it'll be a good investment. And you have no experience. It would be far too risky.'

Clarrie banged her hand on the desk in frustration, making him start. 'Don't be such a coward! You were quite prepared to take a gamble on Daniel Milner when everything seemed against him, and you're constantly helping other businessmen find their feet. Why not me? Is it because I'm just a mere woman who shouldn't be meddling in men's affairs?' she blazed.

He looked aghast at her outburst. 'You're being

hysterical, my dear. We'll forget what you just called me and leave it at that. Now I have work to do.'

But he could no longer dismiss her from his presence when her words displeased him.

'I'm not your housekeeper any longer, Herbert. I'm your wife. This is something we could do together. At least do me the courtesy of considering my request.'

She stepped back, anger choking her. She could see from his mulish look that he was unconvinced. He did not treat her as his partner in marriage, so why should he see her as a partner in commerce? At that moment, she was tempted to run to Wesley and beg him for a loan. But she could just imagine how he would mock her for being an impulsive Belhaven, rushing into a business with her heart not her head. It would be worse than Herbert's patronising dismissal.

Clarrie turned from her husband in bitter disappointment and walked to the door.

'Wait.' Herbert spoke at last. 'I can see how much this means to you. I'm prepared to look into it further.'

Clarrie whipped round. 'You will?'

After a long moment he sighed and nodded. 'I'll ask my agent to look out for properties, if you like.'

'I've got two possible ones in mind,' Clarrie said quickly. 'We could view them together.'

'Perhaps,' Herbert said, raising a cautious hand. 'But I'd have to consider it very carefully – it would mean selling some rental property in New Benwell to fund the venture.'

Clarrie felt chastened. In her single-minded pursuit of her dream she had not thought finding the capital would be a problem for a prosperous solicitor. Perhaps Herbert was not as well off as she imagined. Fleetingly, she wondered how much Bertie was pulling out of their legal practice to fund Verity's lavish lifestyle.

'Thank you, Herbert,' she said.

They regarded each other awkwardly. It was their first argument and Herbert was unused to being challenged.

'Is that all, my dear?' he asked a little tensely.

'Yes.'

He put his spectacles back on and straightened the papers she had disturbed. It was the signal that she was dismissed. Clarrie left with a small flicker of triumph.

CHAPTER 24

1911

Herbert's initial scepticism vanished in the face of Clarrie's enthusiasm and drive. Each time he raised a cautious objection she was ready with a solution.

'I worry about the size of the premises,' Herbert warned, when Clarrie set her heart on a cavernous former draper's in Tyne Street with an upstairs flat.

'We'll turn the back room into a meeting room and get extra income,' she said brightly. 'And we can rent out the flat.'

'The cost of decoration will be substantial.'

'Olive will help paint it – keep the costs down.'

'And what about staff?' Herbert fretted. 'How can you be assured of their reliability?'

'I'll hand-pick them. Interview them at home and talk to their parents.'

With a combination of charm and persistence,

Clarrie persuaded Herbert to purchase the premises on Tyne Street and began refitting them. She consulted him on everything from joiners and plumbers to furniture and menus, determined that he feel it was as much his venture as hers. It was Clarrie's idea to call the tea house after her husband.

'Herbert's Tea Rooms,' she declared. 'You're the patron, so you should get the credit.' Herbert was ridiculously pleased and enfolded her in a rare hug.

'Named after me, eh? What an honour!'

Olive was swept into the project too, painting the walls with exotic murals of birds of paradise and luxuriant foliage. Clarrie observed her sister's happy absorption with pleasure, proud of Olive's fair beauty and talents. In addition, she commissioned three large paintings of local scenes, two to hang in the meeting room and one over the counter. They were done in bright bold colours quite unlike the traditional sombre oil paintings that hung in the city's gallery. They alarmed Herbert but Clarrie said they were perfect.

'People don't want reminding of the dreariness on their doorstep. They want to escape from all that for half an hour.'

Olive was kept busy for the six months that it took Clarrie to set up the café. As the building was taking shape she went in search of suppliers. Cherry Terrace was two streets away. She steeled herself to face her cousins again. It was nearly four years since she had delivered them her final pay packet, and over the past two she had seldom even glimpsed them at church.

The pub had not seen a lick of paint since she had last visited and Jared looked ill-kempt and weary.

'I've heard about the refreshment rooms,' he nodded. 'You're wasting yer money – no call for a posh tea house round here, lass.'

'We'll see.' Clarrie smiled. 'I was wondering if Mrs Belhaven would like to make pies for us?'

Jared looked embarrassed. 'She's not making 'em any longer.' He hesitated, then said, 'She stops upstairs these days. Can't get down easy. Doctor says it's dropsy.'

'I'm sorry,' Clarrie said. 'Can I go and see her?'

'Best not. She never took to you, lass. You'd just get a mouthful.'

From his dejected look, Clarrie guessed that Jared got his share of verbal abuse too. She touched his arm. 'You call in and have a cup of tea when I'm open, won't you?'

He grunted. 'Maybe's I will. Good luck with it, lass – you'll need it.'

For the tea, she chose the Tyneside Tea Company as the supplier. Both she and Herbert went to visit Daniel Milner at his warehouse in Scotswood. He now employed eight salesmen with rounds as far afield as North Shields to the east, Wylam to the west and the pit villages of north Durham across the river. Clarrie knew from Olive that Jack Brewis still called with their delivery every fortnight, but she had long got into the habit of avoiding him after their falling out. Now that she was no longer housekeeper there was no reason for her to come across him at all.

So when Daniel showed them proudly round his premises, Clarrie was startled to find Jack in the tasting room, slurping samples of tea and spitting into a bucket. He had thickened out and his moustache had grown more bushy.

'You remember Jack?' Daniel said. 'He's learning to be a master blender.'

Jack reddened at sight of them. He shook Herbert's hand and nodded awkwardly at Clarrie. She had been right about him; he had ambition and was making his way up the company fast.

'Hello, Jack. I thought you were still delivering round the west end?'

'Just a few of me regulars,' he answered. 'I like to keep me hand in at the selling too.'

'That's right.' Daniel was approving. 'Got to keep your finger on all aspects of the business. That's the way I've taught him.' He told Jack why the Stocks were there.

'Aye,' Jack nodded, 'I've heard. You would think it was Alexandra Palace opening, the way folk are talking.'

Clarrie laughed. 'Well, that'll save on the advertising.' Before they left, she said, 'I hope you and Mr Milner will come to the grand opening?'

'Be pleased to,' he said. The smile he gave her reminded Clarrie why she had found him so attractive when they had first met five years ago. If the unfortunate encounter with Wesley in the Summerhill garden had never happened, she might well have been married to Jack by now.

Clarrie suppressed such thoughts. There was no point in rueing what might have been. All that mattered now was getting the tea house up and running. All her energies were channelled into that one aim. She shook Jack calmly by the hand and left on her husband's arm.

By New Year of 1911, Clarrie had interviewed and appointed her first three waitresses: Dinah, a tall girl from Scotswood; neat, dark-haired Edna; and the irrepressible Lexy. Herbert was dubious about the choice of Lexy.

'She's more suited to the laundry,' he said primly.

'She's lively,' Clarrie said defensively. 'Just the sort to cheer up customers on a dull day. Put her in a uniform and give her a bit of training in how to serve at table, she'll be grand.'

Clarrie took on Ina to wash up in the kitchen and Grace, another of her daughters, to act as runner for the waitresses. She had wanted to give Maggie a job too, but her husband had vetoed it. 'I'll not have you working for that half-breed barmaid and her fancy tea room. She'll be out of business by Christmas.' Despite Lexy and Ina's encouragement, Maggie did not have the courage to defy him.

Finally, Clarrie tracked down Dolly. When Dolly saw how Clarrie held no grudge about her ill-tempered departure from Summerhill, she needed little persuasion to leave her dull position in a school kitchen to work in the glamorous tea house. Clarrie spent a great deal of time with Olive designing the uniforms. The waitresses would wear dark green skirts, green and white striped blouses with neck brooches, and large frilly white aprons and mobcaps. Grace would wear a green pinafore dress. For herself, Clarrie would wear a smart tea gown with an apron to show that although she was in charge, she was prepared to work alongside her staff.

By February, they were ready to open. Long before then, they were getting enquiries about booking the meeting room from local societies. It prompted Clarrie to furnish the back room with a couple of desks with pens and blotting paper. It would be a reading room with newspapers when not being used for meetings. Under Olive's painting of the waterfall in Jesmond Dene, she put a bookcase of second-hand volumes from Herbert's library.

'They're just sitting on the shelves unread,' she pointed out when her husband protested. 'People can borrow them and bring them back.'

The week before opening, Clarrie gave her staff training in setting tables, taking orders and serving out teas. On Saturday the eleventh, at half past nine in the morning, they opened for business.

They did not stop all day. Shoppers along Scotswood Road came in to break their walk back uphill; children came to gawp and snatch eagerly at the free sweets that the waitresses gave them off silver trays. At one o'clock they ran out of Dolly's pies and Clarrie had to send out for more. At three, Olive stood at the far end of the tea room and played waltzes and popular tunes. A group of women from the co-op on Adelaide Terrace broke into song and would not let her stop.

Clarrie did not sit down from the early morning until after eight in the evening when they finally closed. Herbert came to collect her and found her and Lexy slumped in chairs with their feet up, giddy with fatigue and the success of the day.

'Can you persuade my wife not to overdo it, Lexy?' he chided, with an affectionate hand on Clarrie's head.

'Easier to teach a dog to walk on its hind legs, Mr Stock,' Lexy snorted. 'She never listens to my advice any road.'

Clarrie laughed and took Herbert's hand. 'I've never enjoyed a day's work as much in my whole life.'

'Well, tomorrow's a day of rest,' said Herbert, 'and you *will* rest, my dearest.'

The following week was quieter, but they did a steady trade in cooked dinners with some of the foremen from Armstrong's works, and the afternoon teas grew in popularity with women of all ages. Retired men came in to browse the newspapers in the morning and make a cup of tea last an hour. Lexy complained.

'Leave them be.' Clarrie smiled. 'They may not be spending much but they'll come back regular as clockwork once they're in the habit. Then it's up to you to charm them into having a bite to eat here instead of calling into the pub on their way home.'

The meeting room was soon in constant use. Apart from those who came to read, it was patronised by a temperance group, a spiritualist church, a branch of the boilermakers' union, an antiquarian society and a sketching group. Some nights, Clarrie stayed open till ten to meet the demand.

As March ended, two suffrage campaigners from the local branch of the WSPU – Women's Social and Political Union – approached Clarrie. They were young and talkative and Clarrie recognised them as office workers from the Co-op depot who came in for tea on a Wednesday.

'We want to hire the whole café,' Florence, the fair-faced one, said.

'For the whole night,' said the dark-haired Nancy.

Clarrie gaped in astonishment. 'But we don't open at night.'

'This is a special occasion,' said Florence eagerly.

'Third of April.' Nancy smiled. 'Census night.'

To a baffled Clarrie they explained, 'It's a protest against the government census. They won't treat us as proper citizens and give us the vote, so we refuse to be counted as if we were.'

'A protest?' Clarrie looked doubtful. She admired these women for their tenacity, but the last thing she wanted was to draw adverse attention to the tea house. 'What if there's trouble?' she asked. 'I don't want broken windows or the police at my door.'

'No, no,' Florence assured her, 'there won't be. We're not breaking the criminal law.'

'We just want somewhere to throw a party,' Nancy said, grinning.

'Let me think about it,' Clarrie countered. 'I'll let you know in a day or two.'

Will was home for the Easter holidays with his rather solemn school friend Robert Spencer-Banks. It was their final break before the summer term and leaving school. There had been much discussion with Herbert about the prospect of university. He was keen for Will to try for Oxford to read law. Will wanted to go to Durham to read divinity and music.

Into the debate, Clarrie flung her dilemma about the suffrage protest. Robert was horrified.

'They're practically revolutionaries. Don't touch them with a barge pole,' he shuddered.

Will laughed. 'Christ was a revolutionary.'

'Don't be blasphemous,' Herbert reprimanded him.

Will would not be cowed. 'I think you should let them have their party. What's the harm in it?'

'The harm, my dear friend,' said Robert, 'is in encouraging these outlandish women in their pursuit of the impossible.'

Clarrie gave him a sharp look. 'Wanting the vote is wanting the impossible?'

'Absolutely.' Robert nodded vigorously.

'And why should that be?' Clarrie queried. 'You're not one of these *outlandish* men who believe women incapable of thoughts beyond the domestic, are you, dear Robert?'

He gave her a wary look, not quite sure if she was teasing him. When Will laughed, Robert shrugged and said nothing.

'What do you think, Herbert?' Clarrie asked.

He studied her. He was bound to err on the side of caution, she felt.

'Let them hire it.'

Clarrie stared at him in surprise. 'Really?'

'They have good grounds for being dissatisfied with the present government. I'm increasingly of the opinion that women's talents are being wasted by blinkered men such as Asquith.' He smiled at her. 'So why don't we let them have their protest?'

Clarrie took his hand and returned the smile. 'Thank you. That's what I hoped you would say.'

Not only did Clarrie allow the women to hold their all-night party at Herbert's Tea Rooms, but she also stayed up through the night helping. Dinah and Lexy gave their services too. The suffragists came in fancy dress and waxwork noses, lampooning figures in the government. They played charades and danced to a band made up of their own members. Clarrie, who laid on soup, sandwiches and endless pots of coffee and tea, was intrigued.

She had never come into contact with such women before. A few like Florence and Nancy were working class with clerical jobs, but the rest were mostly middle class and professional: teachers, secretaries, a couple of doctors and students at the university. Clarrie was struck by their camaraderie and sense of fun, quite at odds with their portrayal in the newspapers as mannish and humourless. These women joked and teased each other, debated, gossiped and reminisced. Their closeness and sense of purpose reminded her of the nuns at Shillong. Above all, they were infused with optimism.

'It's just a matter of time,' Florence told her. 'I trust in the good common sense of our people to right a wrong.'

'They just need a bit of prodding to see it,' Nancy added. 'Folk are frightened of change, but they are changing.'

'And we're not afraid of doing the prodding.' Florence flashed a smile.

Outside, during the night, some of the husbands and male friends of the women took it in turns to stand guard in case of trouble. But there was none. At six in the morning they trooped off home to go to bed or get ready for work.

While Clarrie sent Lexy and Dinah home for a few hours' sleep, she stayed on dozing in a chair until Ina, Edna and Grace arrived. They were full of curiosity about the night's events and it was the talk of many who came into the café that day. By closing time that evening, Clarrie was exhausted and ready for a quiet meal with Herbert.

As soon as she entered the house, Olive met her in a state of agitation.

'What's wrong?' Clarrie asked.

'Bertie's here. He's in a terrible temper. Shouting at Herbert.'

'What ever for?'

'Cos of you. It's in the evening papers,' Olive said tensely. 'Oh, Clarrie, why did you have to let those women use the café?'

'Why shouldn't I? It was in a good cause.'

'Bertie doesn't think so,' Olive fretted. 'You'd better go up and sort it out.'

Clarrie felt indignation quicken. Bertie had no right to come here berating his father. He and Verity had shunned them for the last year and a half and the café was nothing to do with him. Tired out though she was, she hitched up her skirt and took the stairs in twos.

She found them in the study, Herbert sitting defensively behind his desk, Bertie standing the other side, still shaking a newspaper in his face.

'Ah, here she is,' Bertie cried at sight of her, 'the little Bolshevik suffragette giving my family a bad name.'

'Please, Bertie,' Herbert said with a wary glance at his wife, 'you're being quite ridiculous.' He stood to greet her but Bertie was immediately on the attack, advancing on her with the newspaper.

'Have you seen this?' he thundered. ' "Solicitor's wife gives succour to law-breaking suffragettes"?' He thrust it at her.

Herbert looked worried but said, 'You know how they exaggerate to make a story.'

'They don't have to with this one,' Bertie snapped. 'Go on, read it. Read about how you were the only café owner in Newcastle stupid enough to let them make their protest. Not just that – it says you joined in with gusto – you and your common waitresses from the back streets of Elswick.'

Clarrie's anger lit. 'Don't you dare to criticise me or my staff in my own home.'

'Your home?' Bertie was indignant.

'Yes, mine. And I'm proud of what we did and I'd do it again tomorrow if they asked me to.'

Bertie turned to Herbert and threw up his arms. 'Papa, how can you stand by and let her make a fool of herself – of you? Your name has been sullied by this spectacle. These women have shamelessly used you to gain publicity.'

Herbert gave a fraught sigh and sat back down again. Clarrie waited for him to say that he agreed with their protest, but he said nothing.

'No one's name has been sullied,' she snapped, when it was clear Herbert wasn't going to back her up, 'and it's you who are making a fool of yourself.' She gave Bertie a challenging look. 'Your father was in complete agreement with my opening the café for the WSPU, and so was Will. If he hadn't been, I wouldn't have gone ahead.'

'I don't believe you,' Bertie barked.

'Tell him, Herbert,' Clarrie said. They both stared at Herbert. He looked strained and uncomfortable. Finally, he nodded. Clarrie let go a breath in relief.

'Oh, Papa!' Bertie cried in annoyance. 'How has this woman clouded your judgement so? I never thought you'd be so weak.'

'Don't speak to your father like that,' Clarrie retorted. 'The matter has nothing to do with you. Your rudeness to me I can put up with – I'm used to it – but you will not come here bullying my husband about something that does not concern you.'

'Doesn't concern me?' Bertie exclaimed. 'It most certainly does. The Stocks' law firm has been plastered all over the evening newspapers and for all the wrong reasons.'

'Well, maybe you'll gain a few suffragist clients from it all.'

'I'll not be mocked by someone who used to count our bed linen,' he said in disdain.

'Then leave,' Clarrie challenged him, holding the door open.

Bertie glanced at his father, expecting him to intervene and press him to stay.

Herbert frowned. 'I think it best if you go. Tempers are running too high.'

Bertie smothered a gasp of disbelief. With a furious look at Clarrie he stormed from the room, puce-faced. Clarrie resisted the impulse to follow him out and see to his leaving as she would have done as housekeeper. They listened in silence to Bertie's stamping tread descending the stairs and crossing the hall. The front door slammed shut, setting the chandelier in the hall tinkling.

For a long moment, Clarrie and Herbert regarded each other.

'Herbert, I'm sorry,' Clarrie began. He limped towards her, holding up a hand to silence her apology.

'Don't be,' he said. 'Bertie had no right to speak to you like that.'

'I don't care for myself,' Clarrie insisted, 'but it upsets me to hear him raise his voice to you. It didn't occur to me that they would use my connection to your law firm.'

Herbert laid his hands on her shoulders. 'And would it have made any difference to your decision if it had?'

Clarrie gave a rueful smile. 'No, I don't suppose so.'

He smiled at her. 'I didn't think so. And I love you all the more for it. You are such a courageous young woman. I wish I had half your spirit.'

'It's nothing compared to those suffrage women,' Clarrie said. 'Some of the stories they had to tell of getting beaten and arrested would make your blood run cold. Keeping a café open all night doesn't even compare.'

'Still, you stuck your neck out where others didn't,' Herbert said. 'If the newspaper is to be believed, all the big establishments in town, like the Empires, refused to have anything to do with the census protest.'

Clarrie gave him a startled look. 'The Robsons refused them?'

Herbert nodded. 'Wesley Robson is quoted as saying he'd have nothing to do with politics. In his opinion it has no place in business.'

Clarrie snorted. 'That's so typical of the man – sounding all high-minded but really just frightened of a handful of women harming his business.'

Herbert studied her. 'You don't like Wesley Robson very much, do you?'

Clarrie felt herself redden. 'No.'

'Why is that?' he asked, curious.

Clarrie forced herself to speak of the past. 'He upset my father very badly at a time when his business was in the balance. Father went downhill very quickly after that.' She felt her eyes sting with sudden tears. 'And there were other things. Wesley was an over-zealous recruiter for the Robsons' tea estates. The son of my nurse ran away from their employment – he was very sick – and I'm pretty sure Wesley was responsible for rounding him up and taking him back. He died.' Clarrie glanced away. 'That is why I dislike him so,' she whispered.

Herbert pulled her into his hold. 'My poor Clarrie. I had no idea.'

She slipped her arms round his waist and held on to him, enjoying the rare intimacy. She felt utterly spent and wanted to be cradled in his arms for ever. But it did not last long. Herbert pulled away.

'You look tired, my dear. Let us go and eat, so you can get an early night. I insist that you go in later tomorrow. Olive could open up for you just this once.'

'Herbert.' Clarrie grabbed his hand as he turned to go, emboldened by his support for her and the tenderness he had just shown. 'Why won't you – why don't you . . .'

'What, my dear?' He smiled, puzzled by her sudden bashfulness.

'Come to my bed at night?' she blurted out.

She saw the blood flood from his neck into his jaw and cheeks. He glanced away quickly.

'Do we have to talk of this now?' he murmured.

'When else?' Clarrie asked. 'I'm your wife, Herbert. I care for you and know you do for me and yet you avoid the marriage bed. Is it because you still think of it as Louisa's? Is that it?'

Herbert's jaw clenched.

'It is, isn't it?' Clarrie cried in dismay. 'You can't get her out of your thoughts. I'm not Louisa, so you can't bear to be intimate with me. I'm not good enough for you, is that it?'

'No!' Herbert forced out the denial between gritted teeth.

'Then why?' Clarrie demanded. 'Look at me,

Herbert, and tell me why you married me if you didn't want to sleep in my bed?'

He fixed her with troubled eyes, his expression harrowed. 'I do want to,' he answered, his voice shaky, 'but I dare not.'

Clarrie was baffled. 'What do you mean, dare not?'

'I'm terrified of losing you,' he confessed.

'How could you lose me? I don't wish to be married to anyone else.'

'I'm frightened that if I . . .' he struggled to explain, 'that if you became with child – it might kill you.'

She stared at him in disbelief.

'I blame myself for Louisa's death,' he whispered, 'and I couldn't bear the thought that you might die too – through my own selfish desires.'

He stood shaking at his confession. Clarrie was appalled.

'But it wasn't your fault,' she said, putting her hands to his burning cheeks. 'Louisa was weakened by melancholy – she didn't want to live after she lost the baby. It would be different with us. I'm half her age and fit and healthy. I'm not going to die in childbirth.'

'You don't know that,' Herbert said in agitation, gripping her hands. 'It's such a risky business. And I refuse to take that risk – not with you.' He lowered her hands and pressed them between his. 'You are so dear to me, Clarrie. I will do nothing that might harm you.'

'But there is risk in everything we do,' Clarrie argued. 'Crossing tramlines, slipping on wet steps, being trampled by a bolting horse. You can't go through life being scared of something that's never likely to happen.'

'You're young and don't see the need for caution,' Herbert countered, 'but I do. I have already lost one beloved wife and I know I couldn't go through such grief again. That is why, God forgive me, I have never consummated our union. Please say you understand.'

She looked into his tortured face. His fear was plain to see. But where did that leave their marriage? It would continue to be a pretence and perhaps become a topic of ridicule if the truth of their separation leaked out. She did not know if she could bear the loneliness of such a platonic relationship. But what choice did she have? She gulped down her bitter disappointment.

'I understand,' she answered. Turning from him quickly, so he would not see how sad he had made her, she led the way downstairs.

CHAPTER 25

Contrary to Bertie's predictions, the census affair harmed neither the Stocks' legal business nor Clarrie's café. That autumn, when the hoped-for reform bill was talked out of Parliament, sparking a militant campaign of window-breaking, Herbert was asked to represent two of the WSPU in court. They were fined and chose to go to prison instead, but Clarrie was grateful that her husband had stood up for them, especially in face of Bertie's anger with him for taking on the cases at all.

As for the tea room, Clarrie had a rush of interest from other political groups in hiring her meeting room. Lexy and her youngest sister, Edith, who had taken her place at the laundry, lived rent free in the flat above in return for opening up early and closing late. Herbert's Tea Rooms became well known as an informal debating house for radical branches of the Independent Labour Party, trades councils and women's groups. Clarrie revelled in the mix of people who came and went, weary shoppers and the elderly rubbing shoulders with artists and union leaders.

She did not always agree with some of the politics discussed around her tea tables, but it gladdened her to see both men and women eschewing the pub for the café and viewing it as a safe haven. When the school holidays came, she would lay on cut-price teas for families and give out free apples, bananas and sweets to children on their birthdays. Herbert's became renowned for its wholesome food at modest prices, its cheerful, hard-working staff and the attractive, ivory-skinned Mrs Stock who inspired their loyalty as well as the growing affection of the west end's working-class inhabitants.

The radical reputation of the café spread and the avant-garde and bohemian of Newcastle came out of curiosity and stayed. They liked its colourful décor and proletarian chic. Olive got a couple of commissions for her vibrant paintings with their startling mix of oriental birds and northern scenes. Nobody had seen anything like them before. Clarrie was glad that Olive was making a go of her art and keeping occupied, for she no longer had time to do things with her sister, or even her friend Rachel. The café consumed her every waking hour.

One busy winter afternoon, when the windows

were misted up with the warmth inside and rain drummed on the pavement outside, a tall man entered shaking the wet from his umbrella. Clarrie went to take it from him to put in the stand and flinched in shock.

'Good afternoon, Mrs Stock.' Wesley smiled stiffly, removing his hat. Rain glistened on his handsome face and dripped from his dark sideburns.

'What are you doing here?' she gasped.

He looked nonplussed for a moment. Then his green eyes took on their usual appraising look. 'I've come to drink tea. That is what you're advertising outside.'

'Of course,' she said, recovering hastily. 'Let me show you to a table, Mr Robson. There's room at the back.'

She threaded her way between the crowded tables. The atmosphere was fuggy with tobacco smoke, damp wool and cooked food. The scrape of cutlery and clatter of cups punctuated the chatter and laughter. Clarrie led Wesley to a small table tucked behind a potted aspidistra on an old stand that Olive had painted yellow. It was Florence and Nancy's favourite spot, out of the draught from the main door where they could discuss business undisturbed. If they came in it would not be until this evening. Clarrie smoothed the linen tablecloth and pulled out a seat for him.

'I'll send Lexy to take your order, Mr Robson,' she said without making eye contact.

Back behind the counter, Lexy raised her eyebrows.

'Yes, it's Wesley Robson,' Clarrie confirmed, 'come to spy on us, no doubt.' She nodded at Lexy. 'Go and take his order – and find out what he's after.'

Clarrie was kept busy with the flow of customers seeking refuge from the downpour outside that was turning to sleet. People squeezed together two on a seat and she pulled up her sleeves to help with the demand for food and hot drinks. An hour later it occurred to her that she had not seen Wesley leave.

'He's still there,' Lexy confirmed, 'and on his third pot of tea. Taking notes, bold as brass. Says he wants a word with you before he goes.'

Clarrie's heart began to race. She had no desire to speak to him but was curious as to what he was up to.

'Probably wondering where some of his posh customers have gone to.' Lexy winked. 'He'll hate this place doing so well.'

Clarrie laughed. 'We're hardly a threat to the Robsons' tea houses.' But she was secretly pleased that Herbert's was so well known that even Wesley had to sit up and take an interest. In less than a year she had achieved what she had set out to do: prove that a high-quality tea room could thrive in working-class Elswick.

Half an hour later, the rain abruptly stopped and the café began to clear.

'He's asking for you,' Lexy said, nodding to the back of the room.

Clarrie took a deep breath to still her nervousness, pushed stray tendrils of hair into place and went to deal with Wesley.

'Is everything to your liking, Mr Robson?' she asked, smoothing clammy hands against her dress. She was twenty-five, married and a successful businesswoman at last, yet he made her feel like a gauche girl with his mocking look.

'Very much, Mrs Stock. May I congratulate you on the quality of your tea? I must admit to being surprised by how quickly you've made your mark in the café business.'

Clarrie gave him a dry smile. 'Didn't think a Belhaven could make a success of anything?'

A smile flickered across his lips. 'So you are still a Belhaven at heart? I'm glad to hear it.'

Clarrie coloured. 'I was being flippant, of course. I am proud to be Mrs Herbert Stock, as you can see from the name of this place.'

'Indeed.' Wesley eyed her.

'Is there anything else you would like before you leave?' Clarrie said pointedly. 'Or have you seen enough to report back to your business partners?'

Wesley gave a short laugh. 'You think I've been spying on you?'

'Haven't you?'

He murmured, 'No more than you did when you were planning your tea room. I believe you visited my new Empire branches with that pretty friend of yours, Mrs Garven, isn't that her name?'

Clarrie's eyes widened in surprise. 'I never saw you.'

'No,' he said with a smile of triumph, 'but there's not much I don't see or get to hear about.' He saw her discomfort and added quickly, 'Please, have you a moment to sit down with me? There is something I would like to ask.'

Reluctantly, Clarrie pulled out the chair opposite and sat upright on its edge, her hands clasped in her lap to stop them shaking.

'I've heard a lot about this place,' Wesley said, dropping his voice to a low rumble, 'and I'm very impressed by what you've done. It's an interesting social experiment.'

'Not an experiment,' Clarrie replied, 'but a necessity. I saw such a need here when Olive and I first came.' She was doubtful about how much she should tell him, but decided it no longer mattered now she was Herbert's wife and had standing in the community. 'We lived in a pub two streets away from here and had to serve beer and spirits to men until they fell over blind drunk. We tried to avoid getting hit as they punched each other senseless on a Friday night. It was very frightening. A far cry from the genteel society of Shillong.'

Wesley frowned. 'Go on.'

'I know from bitter experience how liquor can ruin lives, poison people's souls as well as their bodies. Worse than what it did to the men was what the women had to put up with. Lasses like Lexy would come in to warm up, escape the drudgery of the washhouse for twenty minutes and numb it all with a couple of whiskies or a glass of stout. They were seen as the lowest of the low – my cousins despised them and my friend Maggie was regularly beaten by her drunken husband for being a drinker. It was no way to live. Women like them deserve better than that.' Clarrie nodded towards the counter. 'Look at Lexy now. She never touches a drop – she's kept far too busy for one thing.' Clarrie smiled briefly. 'But she doesn't need it – she's got her self-respect instead. Nobody would dare come in here and call her names – they'd be out that door quicker than you can say King George.'

She held Wesley's gaze. 'You might think from all the fuss over suffragists and the like that this place is a hotbed of revolution. Well, if it is, then that's by the by – cos it's really for lasses like Lexy and Ina. A little bit of paradise. Some of us are lucky enough to glimpse it in our lifetime. Belgooree was mine. Why shouldn't they have a little bit on their doorstep too?'

Wesley looked at her in such a strange way that Clarrie wondered if she had been foolish to say such things. Why had she? He might twist her words about revolution and paradise to denounce her as a political troublemaker and damage her business.

He leaned across the table, his look intense. 'Why

don't you expand your idea – these Utopian cafés – to other working-class areas? You've proved the business model works.'

Clarrie felt a stab of annoyance. 'It's not a business model – it's about real flesh and blood people in this particular community. It works because we know them and they know us. I don't know about other areas.'

'But you make a profit, don't you?' Wesley said eagerly. 'And it's hugely popular. What ever your reasons for beginning the venture, it's proving highly successful. You should be capitalising on that success – spreading out to other areas. Or don't you want the poor in other quarters to benefit from a bit of your paradise?'

Clarrie could not decide if he was really a convert to the idea or planning to exploit it in some way. 'I do not have the funds or the will to expand – all my time and energy is taken up here. I've put myself into it, heart and soul. This is where I want to stay.'

He gave a look of impatience. 'I could finance an expansion.'

'You?' Clarrie gasped.

'Yes,' he said, eyes alight. 'Come into business with me, Clarrie!'

Her heart jolted at the unexpected offer. 'No,' she said at once, 'certainly not.'

'Why not?' he demanded.

She was momentarily lost for words. Had she not

at one time thought of that very solution when Herbert had kept putting her off?

'We're incompatible,' she managed.

'I'm quite aware of your dislike for me on a personal level, Mrs Stock,' he said drily. 'I'm merely offering a commercial arrangement.'

Clarrie blushed. 'I understand that. But our ideas about business are quite opposite – I'm content with keeping things small-scale just as long as the business pays its way. The people matter more than profit.'

'That's just being naïve,' Wesley retorted. 'The more profit you make the better you can pay your staff.'

'Your staff are no better paid than mine despite your profits,' Clarrie retaliated. 'But no doubt the pockets of your relations and shareholders are heavy with dividends.'

Wesley flushed. She had rattled him. 'The Robson tea rooms are more likely to weather a slump in trade because of such prudent financial backing. Yours won't. And when the next one comes, where will that leave your precious staff?'

Clarrie was scathing. 'I'm touched that you've come all this way to show your concern about whether I stay in business or not.'

'I'm offering you a chance to ally yourself with the Empire Tea Rooms,' Wesley said impatiently. 'Between us we could have cafés all over the north-east. You could become a wealthy woman in your own right, no longer dependent on your husband's largesse.'

'But dependent on yours? It might sound tempting to some, but I have no intention of being at the beck and call of the Robson shareholders. Here, I can run things as I like and rent my meeting room to whoever I please.'

'That wouldn't change,' Wesley insisted. 'The shareholders don't care about that sort of thing.'

'Then why was I the only proprietor who would hire out my café to the WSPU on census night?' Clarrie challenged. 'You didn't dare.'

Wesley threw up his hands in incomprehension. 'Why are you so stubbornly against me?' he cried.

'Because I don't trust you,' Clarrie said, holding his look.

His face was taut with frustration. 'Why not?'

'I know how you Robsons do business,' Clarrie said. 'I've seen it in India and I've seen it here. You're not happy until everyone is either working for you or squeezed out of business.'

'That's ridiculous,' Wesley retorted. 'I don't want to see you out of business – I want to help you grow bigger.'

'Do you?' Clarrie asked. 'Or do you just want to grab a bit of my success? I don't believe for one minute that your family would agree to your funding a "social experiment" unless they thought there was something in it for them. I think you Robsons are jealous at my doing well. You see something flourish and the next thing you have to control it.'

Wesley's eyes narrowed. 'By God, you're as infuriating as your father to do business with,' he accused. 'He could never see the bigger picture either. Stay small if that's what you want, but without my backing you won't last more than two or three years at the most.'

'Is that a threat?' Clarrie asked indignantly.

'No it is not,' Wesley said angrily, 'it's economics.'

'Then I'll take my chance,' Clarrie declared. 'I'm used to weathering storms. I thank you for your offer, but I will never take Robson money.'

They glared at each other. Wesley sat back, his jaw tense. Clarrie got up to go. He stood and caught her arm as she moved away.

'I can see through your proud Belhaven act, Clarrie. You sneer at my offer, but you were not too proud to marry an old man for his money so you could set yourself up in this place.'

Clarrie gave him a blazing look. 'I did nothing of the sort. I married Herbert for—'

'For love?' Wesley said derisively. He gave her a knowing look. 'That's not what I've heard.'

Clarrie went hot with indignation, pulling away from his hold. 'I don't know what you mean.'

'I'm not judging you,' Wesley said, 'but others do.'

'You shouldn't listen to idle gossip.'

'I'm not talking about title-tattle below stairs.' He blocked her way. 'You are wrong to think I'm the enemy. There are some who do wish to see you fail, but I'm not one of them.'

Abruptly, he seized his coat and hat and strode through the tea room, hardly breaking his stride to lift his umbrella from the stand. Clarrie watched him tip his hat to an astonished Lexy as he thrust a ten-shilling note into her hand and then left.

Ten minutes later her heart was still hammering from the encounter as she helped clear tables.

'That was generous of Mr Robson, wasn't it?' Lexy said, eyeing Clarrie. 'What did he want?'

'What he always wants,' Clarrie muttered, 'a piece of someone else's business.'

Lexy snorted. 'I hope you told him to gan jump in the river!'

Clarrie laughed. 'Yes, in so many words.'

'Quite right,' Lexy said. 'Lads can't stand it when lasses make a go of some'at all by their selves.'

Clarrie swung an arm round her friend. 'Thanks, Lexy.'

'What for?'

'Making me feel better about turning my back on Robson's money.'

'Well, it wouldn't be right, would it? Not after what you said about him being all high and mighty with your poor da,' Lexy said with disapproval. 'Money's not everything, is it?'

CHAPTER 26

1912

A year after opening, Clarrie threw a birthday party for Herbert's Tea Rooms. Even though the weather was still wintry, with flurries of icy rain to mar the pale sunshine, they set up extra tables in the street and decorated the outside with balloons and paper flowers. They served piping hot ham and lentil soup, steak and kidney pies and curried fish and rice. For desserts there were steamed puddings and custard, and cakes and biscuits iced in the café colours of green and orange.

Scores of people were fed that day and there was an article about it in the *Newcastle Chronicle* with a photo of Clarrie and her waitresses standing outside the tea room. Daniel Milner was also interviewed for his part in supplying the high-grade tea.

' "One of Newcastle's most popular tea rooms

celebrates its first birthday," ' Herbert read out with pride over supper the following evening. ' "Tea merchant Mr Daniel Milner said, 'Mrs Stock is very particular about her tea. She likes to sample the blends before buying. She's a very valued customer.' " Then it goes on to say, "Mrs Stock, the wife of esteemed solicitor Mr Herbert Stock, is an Anglo-Indian by birth and grew up on a tea garden in Assam." ' Herbert glanced at Clarrie over the newspaper and smiled. ' "Mrs Stock said, 'Tea is our national drink more than anything else. Everyone enjoys it. At Herbert's we serve the best quality we can at a price everyone can afford.' " '

'Stop,' Clarrie cried, pressing hands to her blushing cheeks. 'Did I really say that? I sound like a commercial traveller.'

Herbert chuckled. 'I'm very proud of you, my dear.'

They were sitting either side of the study fire, having eaten a late supper on the card table.

'Where's Olive?' Clarrie asked. 'I meant to tell her how popular her paper flowers were. Is she still upstairs painting?'

Herbert folded the newspaper and set it aside. 'I don't think she's back yet.'

'Back from where?'

'Wasn't she going to a concert?' Herbert asked uncertainly.

Clarrie yawned. She could not remember the last time she had been to a concert or a film. Well over a year at least. Her only night off in the week was Sunday when she wanted nothing more than to go to bed early and sleep. But she was glad Olive was getting out and about. It was a long time since her sister had complained of being bored and without a role as the sister-in-law of Herbert Stock.

'She'll have gone with Rachel, I imagine,' Clarrie said. 'It makes me feel less guilty at not seeing her.'

Herbert frowned. 'You don't need to drive yourself so hard, my dear. Why don't you take a day off during the week so you can do something more frivolous?'

Clarrie gave a wry smile. 'As you do, you mean?'

'I'm not very good at being frivolous, I admit,' Herbert said ruefully.

They sat for a while longer as the fire died down, Herbert reading and Clarrie dozing. Eventually, they heard the front door open and close. Clarrie stood up.

'That'll be Olive coming in,' she said.

Herbert looked up with expression of surprise. 'Has she been out this evening?'

Clarrie glanced at him sharply. 'It was you who said she had, remember?'

'Did I?' His face clouded.

'You thought she was at a concert,' Clarrie reminded him.

'Ah, a concert.' Herbert nodded, still looking unsure. Clarrie approached him and stroked his brow.

'You're tired. It's you who should be spending less time at work, not me,' she chided him.

He took her hand and squeezed it, his look affectionate. 'What would be the point of that if you weren't here with me? It would be very dull indeed.'

When Will came back from Durham for the Easter holidays, he caused a stir by helping out in Herbert's Tea Room. He was full of ideas about University Settlements where privileged students lived and worked alongside the poor in the slum areas of big cities. Some of his friends were choosing to do so in East London and Johnny had stayed to help at one in Edinburgh rather than come home for the holidays.

The news brought a censorious Bertie to their door. 'It's bad enough having that woman using our name and mixing with all the riff-raff of Tyneside,' he told his younger brother, 'but you should know better. It's common and demeaning.'

'For who?' Will asked in surprise.

'For all of us!' Bertie blustered.

'Not for me,' said Will. 'In fact it's tremendous fun.'

'Well, it's awkward for me and Verity,' Bertie snapped. 'We have a standing in society. How do you think it looks when I'm entertaining influential business clients and they ask me if I'm anything to do with the Bolshevik café in Elswick? They don't like it one bit. And as for Verity's family, they shudder every time it's mentioned.'

'Have they seen it for themselves?' Will asked mildly.

'Of course not,' Bertie shouted. 'Don't be so impertinent!'

'Then they can hardly judge, can they?' Will smiled.

'Listen, Will,' Bertie commanded, 'I'm asking you to stop making a fool of yourself and steer clear of that place. I see it as a matter of family loyalty. You should be studying in any case, not slumming it down there with the hoi-polloi.'

To Clarrie's delight, Will ignored his brother's lecturing and continued to help her in the café and play his violin for customers on wet afternoons. Dark-eyed, giggling Edna was particularly smitten with Will's good looks and friendly easy manner. She flirted with him and he teased her in return.

'That would really give Mr Bertie a seizure,' Lexy joked, 'Mr Will running off with our Edna.'

When Will had to return to Durham for the summer term, Edna moped for days and no amount of ribald teasing from the regulars lifted her spirits. Clarrie felt a pang of envy at the girl's transparent adoration of Will. What must it be like to be so simply and completely in love, she wondered.

Returning home late one evening, Clarrie found Herbert looking distractedly out of the sitting-room window. It was odd because he hardly ever used the room, preferring to keep to his study at all times. Clarrie knew that Olive sewed in there by the light of the large windows, because she left her sewing basket on the window seat. Otherwise it was largely unused.

'Herbert, is everything all right?' Clarrie asked, greeting him with a kiss on the cheek.

'Yes.' He smiled, seeming relieved to see her. 'Quite all right.'

'Then why are you standing in here in the half-dark?' Clarrie asked in amusement. 'Are you hiding from someone?'

'Hiding?' He frowned. 'No. I had something to tell you . . .' His voice tailed off.

Clarrie felt a flutter of alarm. He was becoming increasingly absent-minded.

'Was it important?' she asked.

'Yes, I rather think it was. Stupid of me,' he said, growing agitated.

She took him by the arm and steered him to the door. 'Not to worry. It'll come back to you if it's that important. Let's find some supper. Is Olive about?'

'Olive,' he repeated. 'That's it!' he cried. 'I remember now.'

Clarrie smiled. 'What was it? Olive's gone to the pictures again?'

'No, no, much more than that,' he said in excitement. 'That young man came to see me about Olive.'

'What young man?' Clarrie asked.

Herbert's face twisted in annoyance as he searched about for the name. 'Oh, you know who he is! Cheerful – ruddy-faced – tea.'

'Jack Brewis?' Clarrie guessed.

'Brewis, that's it.' He beamed. 'Brewis.'

Clarrie waited for him to say more, but Herbert just stood smiling.

'What did he want?' Clarrie prompted. 'You said he came about Olive.'

'Olive? Yes, yes, that's right. He came out of courtesy – to ask if I had any objection. He wants to marry Olive.'

Clarrie gawped at him, dumbfounded. '*Marry* my sister? When did he – how – I had no idea—' Her insides knotted. 'What did you say to him?'

'Said it was entirely up to Olive,' Herbert replied, patting her hand, 'but that he had our blessing if that's what they wanted. We'd help with the wedding costs, of course.'

Clarrie felt sick with shock. How had she not known about this? Olive had never even mentioned she was courting. And Jack, of all people!

Herbert looked at her anxiously. 'You don't seem pleased. Did I say something wrong? It is a good thing, isn't it? Brewis seems a personable young man and Daniel – Daniel?'

'Milner,' Clarrie prompted.

'Daniel Milner speaks most highly of him as an employee,' Herbert finished.

'Yes, of course,' Clarrie said, feeling breathless. 'It's wonderful news.'

All of a sudden, a sob rose up in her throat, and to her shame she burst into tears.

Olive was defensive when Clarrie tackled her later that night in her bedroom.

'You've never asked me if I was courting. You've always been too busy with the tea room to care what I was doing.'

'That's not fair,' Clarrie protested. 'I've always cared. I just assumed you were going about with Rachel – not gallivanting around town with Jack.'

'What does it matter?' Olive said impatiently.

'Because I would like to have known,' Clarrie chided her. 'My own sister and Jack Brewis. Am I the last person to be told?'

'Maybe I never said anything cos I knew you'd be like this.'

'Like what?'

'Disapproving.'

'I'm not,' Clarrie said. 'I'm just surprised.'

'Surprised that Jack could fall for poor little Olive, the timid, less pretty sister?'

'No, of course not,' Clarrie said, springing towards her. Olive fended off her attempts to cuddle her.

'I'm not a child any longer,' she gulped, 'and I don't need your permission to marry. I'm sorry for your sake that it had to be Jack, but that's the way it is. Why do you think he's carried on delivering tea here instead of letting one of the boys do it? We've known each other long enough now to be sure we love each other. I just want you to be happy for me.'

Clarrie felt chastened. 'I am, and I'm sorry. It's

selfish of me to expect you to stay here with me for ever. I just thought you were happy here.' She spread her arms in a helpless gesture. 'I did all this for both of us. Remember how I promised to always take care of you?'

Olive's look hardened. 'I don't want you to take care of me any longer – I'm tired of you thinking I need your protection. It may make you feel better, but it doesn't me.'

Clarrie looked at her, aghast. 'You think I've done all this just to make me feel self-righteous?'

'Yes!' Olive cried. 'Sometimes I feel like one of your charity cases.'

'You're my sister and I love you—'

'Yes, I'm your sister, but you have no idea what I want from life. You never spend five minutes with me any longer to find out – otherwise you would have known I'm in love with Jack. I hate living here like some useless orphaned relation beholden to the Stocks, painting pretty pictures for my successful married sister and expected to be for ever grateful.'

Clarrie felt winded by her accusations. How long had her sister bottled up such resentment? She lashed out in her hurt.

'You're right, I don't know you. I had no idea you hated living with me and Herbert or that you were so ungrateful for the sacrifices I've made to take care of you,' she said angrily.

'That's not what I'm saying,' Olive shouted tearfully.

'Then what?'

'You don't need me – you've got your precious tea room and that's all you really want. Well, Jack needs me. I'm going to run my own home and be his wife and hope one day to be the mother of his bairns.'

'What about your painting? Your music?' Clarrie cried. 'After all this, you're going to settle for being the wife of a tea delivery man?'

Olive looked so angry Clarrie thought she would strike her. 'Yes,' she hissed, 'I am! And it'll be a proper marriage, not one of convenience like yours. That's what really frightens you, Clarrie, isn't it? Being left alone with a man you don't love!'

Clarrie stormed from the room, before Olive could see how much her words had wounded her. She locked herself in her bedroom and buried her face in a pillow to muffle her racking sobs. How she had wanted to slap Olive's haughty ungrateful face!

But as the night darkened and the house fell deadly quiet, Clarrie was tortured by the truth of much of Olive's attack. They had grown apart without her realising. She had been too wrapped up in the café to notice. It had not occurred to her to ask about Jack or question why he still came to Summerhill even though he was now Milner's master tea blender. She had no right to belittle Olive's choice of Jack as a husband and was ashamed of her hypocrisy. There was a time when she would have gladly married Jack.

Perhaps the truth was she had not wanted Olive to grow up so that she would always have an excuse to take care of her? She had always loved her sister with the intensity of a mother and with Olive around she could justify her sacrifice in marrying Herbert. Despite her remorse at her words, Clarrie was seized again with anger at Olive for throwing all she had done for her back in her face. Let her go to Jack Brewis if she wanted and discover just how hard it would be in the world without her. No one would love or care for her the way she had. No one!

CHAPTER 27

After their row, Olive hardly spoke two words to Clarrie. The wedding was set for the end of August. In return for one of Olive's paintings, Daniel Milner gave Jack and his fiancée the deposit on a terraced house in Lemington so as to be near the Scotswood depot. It was Rachel's help not Clarrie's that Olive enlisted in helping choose the material for her wedding dress and linen for her new home. Herbert seemed not to notice Olive's coolness, but Will did.

'She's flexing her wings,' he told Clarrie. 'Don't take it too much to heart. You've done a good job. The Olive I remember as a boy wouldn't have had the temerity to thumb her nose at anyone, least of all you,' he teased.

She was grateful for his kindness and his help in the café over the summer. It was Will who persuaded

Olive to accept Clarrie's offer of holding the wedding reception at Herbert's Tea Rooms. Will knew it was Clarrie's attempt to mend the rift between them.

Olive and Jack were married in the Methodist chapel on Elswick Road, in front of a small group of family and friends, and then walked down to the tea room in the hazy sunshine. Lexy and Edna had gone to great lengths to decorate the café with fresh flowers and ribbons, and the tables groaned with food.

Clarrie was tearful throughout the day, from the moment she saw Olive in her lacy dress to the time the married couple left the café. Olive looked flushed and happy on Jack's arm, and he so adoring of his new wife that Clarrie felt ashamed of her jealousy and doubts about the marriage.

She pushed her way to Olive's side and hugged her tight. 'I'm sorry for the things I said,' she whispered. 'I do love you, you know – more than anyone. Come back and see us whenever you can.'

Olive's slim face crumpled at the fond words and she clung to Clarrie. 'Yes, I will, I promise.'

A touch from Jack on Olive's shoulder made her pull away.

'Time to be off, lass,' he said, with a wary glance at Clarrie. 'Ta for all you've done for us – the tea and that. We're both very grateful.'

Clarrie nodded, still holding on to Olive's hand. 'You will take good care of my sister, won't you?'

He regarded her with solemn hazel eyes. 'Aye, I

will. She means the world to me.' He slipped an arm possessively round Olive's waist, and Clarrie noticed a tender smile pass between them. She let go of Olive's hand.

As everyone gathered in the doorway to wave them away in one of Milner's vans, Clarrie felt the first real stab of loss. In a few turbulent weeks, she had gone from chief carer and confidante to a bystander in Olive's life, waving her off to a new life with Jack. Perhaps Olive would be more suited as Jack's wife than she would ever have been. Olive craved her own home and cosy domesticity, and had done ever since being wrenched from Belgooree. She would create a comfortable nest for Jack and in return he would give her security. But would it be enough for her artistic temperament? Remembering the smile she had seen her give him, Clarrie rather thought it would.

It was still only mid-afternoon and the café, at Herbert's insistence, would be closed for the rest of the day. Clarrie wondered how she would get through the long hours before bed.

'Change out of those clothes,' Will instructed when they returned to Summerhill. He laughed at Clarrie's startled look. 'Johnny's back for a few days, and we've arranged to go riding. I'm to meet him at the stables at four and I'm sure he'd be delighted if you came along too.'

'That would be grand,' Clarrie gasped and kissed him on the cheek. 'You wonderful lad!'

An hour later, they were saddled up and riding north-west out of the city with Will's old friend. It was an age since Clarrie had ridden and she relished the familiar feel of horse and rider moving as one. At times she rode ahead alone, at others dropped back to join in the men's conversation. They stopped at a farm trough so the horses could drink and sat against a warm stone wall, watching the sunset bleed into the sky like an angry wound.

Will and Johnny resumed their discussion of politics. Johnny was full of admiration for Keir Hardie, the fiery Scots leader of the Independent Labour Party, whom he had heard speak at the Edinburgh Settlement.

'I'm thinking of joining,' he said eagerly.

'The ILP?' Will asked, looking shocked.

'Yes, why not?'

'They're Socialists. Your father would blow a fuse,' Will exclaimed.

'He's always encouraged debate in our house, so he can hardly complain,' Johnny replied. 'Besides, I'll tell him what you're always saying, that Christ was a Socialist. He's a minister's son – he'll have to approve.'

'Yes, but I just say that to annoy my father and brother.'

'What do you think, Clarrie?' Johnny asked unexpectedly.

Clarrie tore her gaze from the sunset. 'About the ILP or you joining it?'

'Both.'

The young men watched her keenly, as if her opinion mattered to them. Two years ago, she would not have known what they were talking about, but she had gleaned much about current politics from the groups who used her café.

'I think Hardie is a good man, and the working class need a champion like him. Women too. He was one of the first men to speak up for women getting the vote. Now that seems as far off as ever,' she sighed.

'Clarrie,' Will cried in mock horror, 'are you a closet Socialist just like Bertie feared? Pass the smelling salts.'

'Don't faint,' she said wryly. 'I'm a café-owning member of the bourgeoisie, remember?'

'I'm serious, you two,' Johnny said impatiently.

Clarrie put a hand on his arm. 'I'm sorry, I was trying to be too. If you believe wholeheartedly in something then you should pursue it, no matter what your father or anyone else thinks. Only you can decide. Why don't you come to the café before you go back to Edinburgh and listen to some of the debates we hold?'

'Yes, I'd like that,' Johnny agreed eagerly.

As the sun dipped, they remounted and set off home. Clarrie felt deeply reluctant. When would she have the chance to do this again?

'Make the most of this, Clarrie,' Will warned, as if reading her thoughts.

'Why?' Clarrie asked, startled.

'Once Johnny's in the ILP,' Will grinned, 'he'll have to sell off these bourgeois horses and give his money to the party.'

Johnny snorted with laughter. 'Only your horse, Will. Clarrie and I will need ours for the revolution.'

It was dark by the time they got back to Summerhill. Will changed and went out again, leaving Clarrie feeling bereft. He would be staying the night at Johnny's house. Their stimulating company had kept at bay the emptiness that had gripped her at Olive's departure. Now it returned like stomach cramps. She went in search of Herbert.

Uncharacteristically, he was not in his study working or reading. Passing his bedroom she saw light shining under the door. It had been a tiring day and he had gone to bed early. Clarrie had hoped for his company and a chance to sit up late talking over the high points of the day, even if it meant having to keep reminding him of the names of the wedding guests.

Against her better judgement, she went up to the next floor and looked inside Olive's bedroom. But it was empty of her belongings and Sally had already stripped the bed. There was nothing of comfort here. Then, in the glow from the streetlight, she glimpsed a crumpled dress discarded over the back of a chair. Picking it up, Clarrie recognised it as an old dress that Olive had made when they had first come to Summerhill. It had been her Sunday best, then after a few years of wear demoted to a work dress. More recently, Olive had used it to paint in. Clarrie lifted it and pressed it against her face. It still smelled of her sister's scent and a whiff of turpentine.

'Oh, Olive,' she cried aloud, 'I miss you!'

She was assaulted afresh by the loss of her past life; of her parents, of Belgooree and the Khassia hills, of the closeness she had shared with her sister. Clutching the dress like a talisman, she returned downstairs to her own bedroom. It was ghostly quiet and empty too. She realised how little she had personalised the room. She slept in it and dressed in it, but it was a room still in mourning for its previous owner.

Mechanically, she undressed, pulled on her nightgown and lay down. She fingered Olive's frock, wondering what Jack and Olive's new house was like. Her sister had not taken her to see it, but perhaps she would call on Olive in a week or so when she had had time to settle in. She could take her something for the house: a set of fancy fire-irons for the parlour or a plant urn with a colourful glaze. She would take an hour off from the café in the afternoon and visit when Jack was not likely to be there. Jack and Olive.

Abruptly, Clarrie pushed the faded dress away. She did not like to think of what they might be doing now. It made her insides clench and loneliness overwhelm her. Restlessly, she got up and paced to the window. The gardens in the square were bathed in ethereal moonlight, the dark leaves of the trees rippling like the sea. It was seldom the sky was clear enough of smoke or clouds for such bright moonlight.

It stirred something in her. Then she was reminded of that other wedding night – Bertie and Verity's – when she had come across Wesley in the garden. How foolish she had been to pretend to be Dolly. It would have been better had she told him at once who she was instead of letting him come close and flirt. Then there would have been no misunderstanding by the prying servant whose gossip had turned Jack against her.

Unwelcome desire for Wesley gnawed inside. She must not think of him! She was married to Herbert, a man of whom she was genuinely fond, even if she did not love him wholeheartedly. Clarrie turned away from the mesmerising movement of the trees. She would go to Herbert. She was sick and tired of this lukewarm marriage. She would make herself love him and if he really loved her as he claimed, he would tell her so physically and not just in words.

Crossing the bedroom in her bare feet, Clarrie hurried into the corridor. There was no one to see her, and if either Sally or Mrs Henderson happened to be on the stairs and heard her knocking on her husband's door, she did not care.

'Herbert?' she called softly. 'May I come in?'

There was no reply but the light was still on. She

knocked again and thought she heard a faint noise, perhaps a snore. He was already asleep. Clarrie's courage began to fail her. She backed away and then stopped, annoyed at her own timidity. She was his wife and had every right to go to him. Trying the door, she found it unlocked.

The large table lamp bathed the spartan room in yellow light. Clarrie had hardly stepped in here since she had been housekeeper, but its dark mahogany furniture and fringed brown curtains were unchanged. The old marble washstand supported a pile of books. She glanced at the bed with its severe black metal frame. Herbert lay facing away from the door with his left arm out of the covers and flung backwards in an awkward position. Tiptoeing forward, she could hear his breathing. He was asleep after all. At least he had not been deliberately ignoring her calls.

She stood over the bed, wondering whether to pull back the bedclothes and slip in beside him or retreat. Suddenly, he let out a strange animal grunt. Clarrie jumped. But he did not move or turn over. He was making noises in his sleep. Clarrie sighed. What foolishness had made her come? Even if he had been awake, Herbert did not desire her. He would be deeply embarrassed if he woke and found her standing there in her gauzy nightdress fingering his sheets. She felt hot shame at her longing for intimacy. Quietly, she padded out of the room and returned to her own.

'Miss, oh, miss, come quickly!' Sally's shouts woke Clarrie from a deep sleep. The bedroom through the muslin curtains was bathed in the pink light of dawn. Befuddled, Clarrie sat up.

'What is it?'

'It's the master,' Sally gabbled, 'he's in a queer state. I went with hot water for his shave. He's not making any sense. Haway, miss, please!'

Clarrie struggled out of bed, still groggy but alarmed by the girl's panic. She threw on a dressing gown and followed Sally.

Herbert lay just as she had left him, turned towards the far wall, his arm at an angle. Rushing round to the other side of the bed, Clarrie froze. Herbert was staring right at her, eyes wide open.

CHAPTER 28

'Herbert?' Clarrie gasped.

Her husband continued to stare at her without saying anything, his mouth slack. She leaned closer. He was still breathing. She touched him but he did not flinch.

'Herbert, what's wrong?' Clarrie demanded, shaking him gently.

All at once, he gave a strange groan like the one she had heard him make in the night. She put a hand to his face.

'Speak to me, Herbert! What is it?'

He looked at her with puzzled eyes as if not sure who she was. He grunted, his face empty of expression. She lifted his arm and it dropped back down lifeless. In fear, Clarrie gripped his hand and brought it to her cheek.

'Can you not speak?' she cried. When he did not reply, Clarrie turned to Sally. 'He needs a doctor. I'll go and ring. Stay with him.' She bolted from the room and half fell, half ran down the stairs in her haste to reach the telephone in the cloakroom off the hall.

With shaking hands, Clarrie gripped the receiver as she waited for the doctor to answer. When he finally did, she described Herbert's condition as calmly as she could and got the doctor's agreement to come at once. She rang off, close to tears.

How long had he been lying like that? An hour or two? The whole night? She knew the answer to her own anxious questioning. Herbert must have been already incapacitated when she had come seeking him. He had tried to communicate but she had gone away, swallowing down her lust, thinking him asleep. If only she had got into his bed, she would have known there was something wrong. What if he were to die because of the delay? She would never forgive herself.

But, dressed and waiting for the doctor, holding Herbert's stiff hand, a bitter little voice inside reminded her that if he had been a proper husband to her and shared her bed she could have acted sooner.

The doctor diagnosed a stroke. Herbert was paralysed down one side and had lost the power of speech. It was too soon to know if he would recover any of his faculties. He would need constant nursing, either in hospital or at home.

'I want to keep him here,' Clarrie said instinctively, 'I'm sure that's what he'll want.'

The doctor left to make arrangements.

Clarrie was stunned. She telephoned Johnny's parents and told Will, who came racing round to be with her. Later, they sent word to Bertie at the office. He castigated Clarrie for not alerting him at once.

'We knew you would be busy,' Clarrie said lamely, not wanting to admit she could not have faced his censoriousness any earlier.

'And how was it you let him lie there all night before doing anything?' he demanded.

'I didn't know,' Clarrie said, consumed with guilt, ushering him quickly out of the bedroom. Will followed and closed the door.

'How could you not?'

'I – I thought he was asleep,' she said, trying to keep her voice down.

She did not like the way Bertie scrutinised her, his eyes full of disdain. It was none of his business if they had separate bedrooms.

'You weren't with him, were you?' he accused her. 'Where were you? Out with one of your Bolshevik yobs?'

'Leave her alone!' Will rounded on his brother. 'Clarrie's not to blame for this. And you are in no position to preach at anyone. When was the last time you visited Papa at home? You've shown how little you care for him.'

'Well, I'm here now,' Bertie shot back, 'and I'm going to keep an eye on him – see that he gets proper nursing care.' He gave Clarrie a hard look. 'The way my mother should have.'

Clarrie was winded by the implication. Will sprang at his brother and grabbed his jacket.

'How dare you bring Mama into this? Clarrie couldn't have been more caring!'

He shoved Bertie backwards against the banisters.

'Will, stop!' Clarrie intervened, pulling him away. 'None of this helps your father.'

The two brothers glared at each other, Bertie smoothing down his jacket in indignation. Will let out a big sigh.

'You're right, I'm sorry. What do you want us to do?'

Clarrie felt fear take hold. She was still too shocked to know what to do. What if Herbert were never to recover? How could she cope without him? What about his clients? What about the café if she had to nurse him full time? She tried to stem her rising panic and think clearly. The brothers watched her.

'We need to sit down together – all of us,' Clarrie began falteringly. 'Verity too if she wants to help. Then we can discuss how best to cope with this terrible situation.' She gave Bertie a warning look. 'What I don't want is for anyone to go shouting their heads off and upsetting my husband. He might not be able to speak but I'm sure he hears and understands us. A family row is not going to help his recovery.'

Will's look was contrite. He nodded in agreement. They looked at Bertie.

'Very well,' he snapped. 'But I have a business to run. We will talk about this later. Keep me informed about what the doctor says.'

The following days were a blur of doctor's visits and people calling round in concern: clients, neighbours, their church minister and elder, and friends from the tea room. The Landsdownes sent a basket of fruit and Verity came without the twins.

'It would be too upsetting for the children to see him in such a state,' she told Clarrie, hardly able to hide her own distaste at Herbert's rigid features and drooling mouth.

Clarrie swallowed a bitter retort that she should have brought them to see their grandfather long ago.

'Perhaps in a few weeks when he's improved,' Clarrie suggested. 'I'm sure seeing Vernon and Josephine would lift his spirits no end.'

Verity hurried away with a vague promise to bring them soon.

Two nurses were employed on a rota system to help with lifting, bathing, changing and feeding Herbert. Clarrie took sole responsibility at night, setting up a camp bed in her husband's room so that she would hear him if he needed her. Strangely, she was comforted by their proximity. Rather than lying alone in her own room fretting, she could fall asleep listening to his breathing and the soft tick of his bedside clock. When she could not sleep, she would sit beside him stroking his face or his useless arm. He looked achingly vulnerable. So seldom had she been able to touch him physically in the past that she was filled with a new tenderness towards him at such simple contact. She realised how much she wanted him to live and get better.

She spent her days going to and fro between the café and the house, checking on Herbert every couple of hours, taking it in turns with Will to be with him. Sometimes she would read to him, but was never sure if he understood the words. She would hold his good hand and sometimes he would press hers back, yet his eyes showed no sign of recognition.

Bertie took his father's work in hand, sorting through the mound of files in his study and contacting his clients.

'You mustn't worry about the business side,' Will assured Clarrie, 'Bertie's seeing to all that. That's one thing he's good at – sorting out finances.'

'But Herbert can't sign for anything,' Clarrie worried.

'He doesn't need to – Bertie has powers from the courts to do it on his behalf.'

With so much to do, Clarrie was relieved that she did not have to concern herself with Herbert's legal caseload. When he recovered, she would not allow him to go back to such a demanding schedule. He had driven himself far too hard, unable to let go proper control to his son, as he should have. They would both work fewer hours and spend more time together, she determined. All she wanted now was the chance for them to be better companions.

Word of Herbert's stroke reached Olive via Daniel Milner and Jack. She called round while Clarrie was at the café, but Will persuaded her to stay until her sister returned. They hugged briefly.

'It's terrible to see him this way,' Olive said tearfully. 'He seemed so well on our wedding day – so kind and cheery.'

'Yes,' Clarrie agreed, 'it was a happy day.'

'I can't stop thinking,' Olive trembled, 'that it might have been too much for him. If we hadn't—'

'Stop it,' Clarrie chided, taking her sister's hands. 'You mustn't think like that. It had nothing to do with the wedding. Herbert's been pushing himself too hard for ages.'

They went down to the kitchen where Mrs Henderson made a fuss of Olive. The sisters shared a pot of tea in Clarrie's old sitting room where they both felt more at home with each other. At Clarrie's prompting, Olive talked eagerly of married life.

'It's only been a few days but I feel so at home in our new house – and Jack's that proud of it. He makes such a fuss of me too, bringing back little treats every day. I tell him not to, that he should be saving his money and putting it by, but he won't listen.' She smiled.

Clarrie looked at her sister's blushing cheeks and smiled too. 'Enjoy the treats, why shouldn't you?'

'That's what Jack says,' Olive answered. 'And I suppose I should, cos you never know what's round the corner.' Abruptly she stopped, a look of consternation on her face. 'Sorry, Clarrie, I didn't mean to upset you.'

'You haven't,' Clarrie said, tensing.

After that, their conversation faltered. Clarrie tried too hard to put Olive at her ease, not wanting her to go, but to no avail.

'I must be getting home,' she said, rising hastily, 'and get the tea on for Jack.'

She promised to come again soon, but Clarrie could see the relief on her sister's face as she left, like that of an animal escaping a trap. She knew that Olive was thankful not to be still living at Summerhill, dealing with an invalid Herbert.

After a month, Will had to return to Durham. He was reluctant to leave, for there was no sign of improvement in his father's condition, but Clarrie was adamant.

'Of course you must go back. Your studies come first.'

Will gave a rueful smile. 'That sounds like something my father would say.'

'Good,' Clarrie said, 'then all the more reason for going.'

She hid from him just how much she relied on him for support and company. Will left, promising to return when he could before the Christmas holidays.

Clarrie drove herself all the harder after Will's departure, snatching a few hours' sleep between running the café and watching over Herbert. She helped with his daily therapy of exercises and massage, to keep his good limbs from wasting and encourage movement in the paralysed half.

As the weeks progressed, there were small improvements: some control over his facial muscles returned so that he could chew soft foods and he began to get movement in his left leg. By November they had him up on his feet, aided by two nurses, and walking unsteadily to the door and back.

One winter's evening, Clarrie carried in a tray of food to feed him and placed it on the table beside Herbert's bed. He was propped up against pillows watching her with his usual vacant expression.

'Soon.'

Her head jerked round at the sound. She stared at him, wondering if it was just a noise or an attempt at a word.

'Soon,' Herbert repeated and pointed with his good hand to the tray.

Clarrie scrutinised it. Then it dawned on her. There was no spoon for the mashed food. 'Spoon?' she queried. She seized his hand. 'You were trying to say spoon!'

Herbert's mouth pulled into a grimace. She kissed his hand. 'You clever man. You said spoon. Say something else.' She pointed at the bowl of food.

'Mince,' Herbert said slowly, 'and 'tatoes.'

'Mince and potatoes!' Clarrie shrieked. She pointed to herself. 'Who am I?' she asked, holding her breath in anticipation.

He gazed at her for a long time, his expression baffled and half-frowning. Perhaps it was too much to ask all at once.

'Never mind,' she said, banishing her disappointment, 'just wait till I tell Will.'

She rushed off for a spoon and to break the news to Mrs Henderson and Sally of Herbert's first coherent words.

'He's not daft in the head like Bertie thinks,' she said, wiping away a tear of relief. 'He's not!'

Back upstairs, Clarrie watched and encouraged her husband as he ate his food with painful slowness. But for once, her watchfulness appeared to irritate him.

'Book,' he grunted.

Clarrie laughed. He wanted her to read. All those months of reading to him and not knowing if he took any of it in had not been futile. She sat and read to him while he finished his meal. It was stone cold and half of it over his pyjamas by the time he gave up, but Clarrie sensed the triumph in his panting.

As she lifted the tray, he touched her with feeble fingers. Their eyes met. There was a new glimmer in his, a recognition, she was sure of it. He struggled to speak. Clarrie leaned closer. He said it again, more forcefully.

'Cl – Clarrie.'

Clarrie gasped. 'Yes, I'm Clarrie. You do know me!' His look was fixed on her, beseeching her. 'What else, Herbert – what else do you remember?'

'I – 'ove – you.'

Clarrie's heart jolted. Tears sprang to her eyes: tears of joy and relief and tenderness. She bent down and kissed his forehead.

'I love you too,' she said hoarsely.

He gave a loud grunt. A trickle of tears spilled out of one eye and ran down his gaunt cheek.

'Oh, Herbert,' she whispered in wonderment, 'you've come back to me.'

CHAPTER 29

At Christmas, Clarrie was determined to gather the family around Herbert. It would be her first Christmas without Olive, who was entertaining Jack's mother and brother, so the distraction was welcome. Will was eager to help and to their surprise Bertie and Verity agreed to come and bring the children. Vernon was a spoilt four year old with a temper who threw tantrums if he did not get his way. But Josephine was chubby and mild-natured and ran around her grandfather's chair trying to play hide-and-seek.

'Chase me, Grandpa!' she cried and squealed when Will came after her pretending to be a grizzly bear.

Clarrie knew that Herbert delighted in having his grandchildren there. He made a huge effort to try to speak to them clearly.

'He's dribbling!' Vernon screeched in disgust. 'I don't like it.'

'I think he's hungry,' Josephine diagnosed and, clambering on to Herbert's lap, began to feed him chocolate. Soon it was melting and they were both a sight to behold.

'Oh, Josey!' Verity scolded. 'You're ruining your dress. Get down at once.'

Her daughter ignored her and Verity turned puce with annoyance. 'Do something, Bertie!'

Quickly, Clarrie plucked the little girl from Herbert's knee. 'Come on, we'll go and wipe you down with magic water.'

'What's magic water?' Josephine cried, taken by surprise.

'You'll see.'

Down in the kitchen, Clarrie filled a bowl full of very soapy water and distracted the girl by blowing bubbles while she cleaned up her face and hands and sponged her dress. Josephine giggled at the wayward globes floating away and bursting on the shelves of pans and crockery. Clarrie had sent the staff home early so they could enjoy the day with their own families, and it was a relief from the strained atmosphere upstairs to escape to the quiet of the kitchen.

'Clarrie,' Josephine piped up. 'Are you my grandmama?'

'No,' Clarrie smiled, 'but I am married to your grandpapa.'

'So you are my relation?' the girl persisted.

'I suppose I am.'

'Daddy says you're not.' She frowned, swinging her legs. 'He says you're one of the servants.'

Clarrie's insides knotted. 'I used to be, but not now.'

'Is that why we're allowed down in the kitchen?' Josephine asked. 'I'm never allowed in the kitchen at home.'

Playfully, Clarrie tapped Josephine's nose. 'Well in this house, you can go anywhere you like.'

Josephine's face lit up. 'Can we play hide-and-seek down here without getting into trouble?'

'Just for a few minutes,' Clarrie agreed.

They both hid twice and then heard Bertie shouting for them. He came into the kitchen to find Clarrie on her hands and knees under the table with Josephine jumping gleefully beside her.

'Found you!' she screamed.

Clarrie scrabbled to her feet, uncomfortable at Bertie's look. She remembered how he had once pinned her to that very table and forced a kiss on her.

'Come here at once, Josey,' he barked. 'You shouldn't be down here.'

'We can go anywhere,' she said stubbornly. 'Clarrie says.'

'And I say you can't,' Bertie snapped. 'Come along.'

Clarrie quickly took the girl's hand. 'Let's see if Uncle Will can give you a piggy-back ride,' she coaxed.

Swiftly, she led Josephine upstairs. At the top, Bertie hissed at her, 'Don't you ever take her down to the servants' quarters again. It's quite inappropriate.'

Clarrie was thankful when, soon after, Verity declared it was time for them to leave. Unexpectedly, Josephine threw her plump arms round Clarrie's neck and gave her a slobbery kiss in goodbye.

'Can you come and live with us, Clarrie?'

Clarrie smiled. 'I have to stay here and look after Grandpapa Stock.'

'Uncle Will can do that,' she said.

'He needs me too,' Clarrie said, kissing her soft cheek and gently disengaging. 'But I hope you'll come back soon and visit us.' She shot a look at Verity.

'In the New Year, perhaps,' Verity said vaguely.

Clarrie and Will waved them away. 'She's a bonny one,' Clarrie sighed as they retreated into the warmth, 'and so affectionate. She reminds me of you, Will, when you were young.'

'Yes,' Herbert agreed, looking at Clarrie with glimmering eyes, 'like Will. Vernon – awk'ard – like – Bertie.'

They all laughed. Later, after they had got Herbert into bed, Clarrie sat up talking to Will. He told her about his surprise at the Christmas card Edna had made for him with a cutting of mistletoe inside. What did she mean by it?

Clarrie smiled. 'She's in love with you. You must know it!'

Will laughed with embarrassment and shook his head. 'I thought she was kind to everyone.'

They talked about future plans. 'I can't think too far ahead,' Clarrie sighed. 'I just want your father to get better.'

Will looked thoughtful. 'You seemed to hit it off with Josey. Perhaps you'll see more of her now Verity's making an effort to see Papa.'

'I hope so. But I wish we could have our own child,' Clarrie blurted out, and then coloured. 'Sorry. I shouldn't have said that.'

But Will did not appear embarrassed. 'Perhaps you still will.'

'No,' Clarrie said quietly, 'your father never wanted that – not after what happened to your mother. He's too frightened of losing anyone else. So I'm not destined to be a mother.'

Will took her hand. 'Dear Clarrie, you have been a marvellous mother to me.'

Tears sprang to her eyes at his kindness. 'Thank you,' she whispered, with a trembling smile. 'And I could never have had a better son than you.'

By the spring of 1913, Herbert's condition had improved enough for Clarrie to take him out in a Bath chair to the park and for him to walk a few paces with two sticks. His face lost its greyness and his speech improved, but he often fumbled in exasperation for the right word. His memory for recent events deteriorated further, so that when Clarrie talked about a visit from his grandchildren, Herbert grew cross that he had not been there to see them.

'You were, Herbert,' Clarrie reminded him. 'Josey was showing you her new skipping rope, remember? She got it tangled round your feet and you said she was like a cowboy lassoing an old horse.'

'Ah, yes,' Herbert said, 'so she did.'

But she could tell from his expression that he had no recollection of his granddaughter's visit, and it saddened her. There was a special bond growing between the two. Josephine delighted in the attention of this man who allowed her to clamber over him and said silly words that made her laugh and did not tell her to keep quiet or go away because he was busy. Herbert, although he forgot quickly, delighted in her inquisitive questions and giggling and the way she showed no fear or distaste of him as the squeamish Vernon did.

Clarrie knew that Verity only brought the children at Bertie's request. The reminder of his father's mortality seemed to have shaken him badly and Clarrie wondered whether he felt guilty about neglecting Herbert. What ever the reason, she was just glad that Verity brought them at all.

Vernon was fascinated by mechanical toys, so Clarrie bought a boxful to keep him occupied while his sister played with Herbert and her. Verity quickly grew bored; she was used to leaving the twins with their nanny. After a couple of duty visits, Clarrie suggested, 'Why don't you go into town for an hour or two? I can look after the children and Mrs Henderson can give them their lunch.'

After that, the children came every Tuesday morning, Clarrie arranging for Lexy to be in charge at the tea room until the afternoon. With the onset of summer and warmer days, Clarrie took the twins to the park too and they both enjoyed pushing Herbert in his chair, Vernon making motor car noises.

It was on one such occasion, in mid-July when Will was newly returned from university and accompanying them on a picnic, that they ran into Wesley. Vernon and Will were chasing a runaway hoop and Josey was perched on Herbert's knee, flicking her skipping rope and shrieking like a charioteer.

Wesley, walking towards them arm in arm with an elegant young woman, caught the hoop.

'Mr Robson,' Will greeted him, 'good day to you!' The men shook hands.

'Give me back my hoop,' Vernon said crossly.

'Don't be so rude,' Clarrie chided him, catching up. Wesley rolled the hoop to the boy, tipped his hat to her and took Herbert's good hand.

'I'm glad to see you out and about, Mr Stock,' he said. 'I see you are being well looked after.'

'Very,' said Herbert. 'My wife – is a – marvel.'

Clarrie glanced awkwardly at Wesley.

'Indeed,' he murmured, giving her a brief sardonic look.

'These are – my . . .' Herbert searched for the word.

'Grandchildren,' Clarrie prompted. 'Josephine and Vernon.'

'How do you do?' Josephine said, sticking out a hand as Will had done. 'I'm not Josephine, I'm Boadicea. Clarrie says I'm a brave leader and this is my chariot. Grandpa is my horse.'

Wesley's eyes widened in astonishment. He smiled and shook her hand. 'I've always wanted to meet Boadicea. I admire strong women.'

'You can be one of my warriors if you like,' the girl said, looking pleased.

'Thank you.' Wesley bowed.

'Are you his wife?' Josephine asked the well-dressed woman, startling everyone.

Wesley's companion laughed. 'Not quite yet,' she replied.

Wesley hastily introduced her. 'This is Miss Henrietta Lister-Brown, my fiancée.'

Clarrie's insides clenched. She realised where she had seen the woman before.

'You were at my brother's wedding,' Will declared, 'wearing a very striking red hat.'

'I was.' The woman laughed in delight. 'What a memory you have.'

Will grinned. 'You stood out from the crowd, Miss Lister-Brown.'

'What charmers you northerners are,' she smiled.

They exchanged pleasantries. She was from London, related to the Landsdownes by marriage, and loved to visit the north. She and Wesley planned to marry the following year.

'Hurry up, Uncle Will,' Vernon whined, 'I want to play.'

'Quiet, you little scamp,' Will gave an exaggerated frown, 'or Boadicea will whip you for your rudeness.'

'Yes, I will,' Josephine piped up, shaking her skipping rope with eagerness.

'Come, dearest,' Henrietta said, squeezing Wesley's arm, 'let these nice people get on with their outing.'

Wesley tipped his hat to them again as they said their goodbyes. He glanced briefly at Clarrie, his look almost triumphant. He was enjoying showing off his beautiful fiancée. Her heart beat erratically in her breast. She forced a smile.

'Congratulations on your engagement, Mr Robson,' she murmured, looking away. She could not bear to see his handsome face.

A moment later they were gone and she and Will were pushing Herbert forward towards the bandstand. Clarrie forced herself to enjoy their picnic but her stomach felt leaden and her appetite had deserted her. She hated to think the news that Wesley was soon to be married could upset her so. How ridiculous to be jealous of that aristocratic woman. She was just the sort of well-connected bride who would suit an ambitious Robson. Good luck to them! She determined to banish all thought of them from her mind.

She drove herself at work and filled every waking minute with running the tea room or tending to Herbert. On Tuesday mornings she entertained the twins, so the only day she had a spare moment was Sunday. After church and lunch, she would often settle to paperwork. But when Will was at home over the summer holidays, he arranged for them to go riding with Johnny on Sunday afternoons. Sometimes they rode up the Tyne valley or crossed the river into the undulating Durham hills.

These few hours of freedom were among the happiest she could remember since India. To be out riding with her young companions in the breezy sunshine through woods and across open moor was pure joy. When she laughed and joked with them, the cares of the week shrank back. Gone were the burdens of management and the worries over Herbert's health. She felt young and invigorated once more.

In September, Will went away to Edinburgh with Johnny to help at the University Settlement before returning to his studies in Durham. Clarrie felt their absence keenly and Sunday afternoons were all the duller by comparison.

'Why don't – you – call on – Olive?' Herbert suggested one blustery Sunday. 'Too – windy for – park.'

They both knew how Clarrie would struggle to push him in the chair on such a day without Will to help. Her heart leaped at the suggestion – it was not the first time Herbert had made it – yet she was hesitant. Olive had not called to see them since Easter and at the time Clarrie had been distracted by a telephone call from the café about a failed delivery of flour. Dolly was in a temper and threatening to walk out of the kitchen.

'I can see you're busy,' Olive had said hastily. 'You go and sort it out – I'll come back another time.'

Her sister had left before Clarrie had been able to ask her about anything more than whether she and Jack were well. Olive had not been back to Summerhill since and Clarrie had the impression that her sister found it uncomfortable being there. It reminded her of her lowly status as housemaid and her dependence on her older sister, a past that she seemed bent on erasing from her memory. She had been into the café twice, but on Tuesday mornings when Clarrie had not been there. Will had visited Olive the previous month, but he had been reticent about it, save to say that Olive was well and happy and urge Clarrie to go and see her.

'So what is she doing all day?' Clarrie had questioned, eager for details.

Will had shrugged. 'Taking care of her home and Jack.'

'Not exactly a full-time job,' Clarrie had retorted. Will had seemed on the point of saying something more, but instead had given a rueful smile and said, 'Why don't you go and see for yourself? They've been married for over a year and you've been to see them once.'

'When do I have the time?' Clarrie had protested.

But it was the nearest Will had ever come to a reproof and the criticism had hurt. She was avoiding Olive as much as her sister was avoiding her. That one visit before Christmas, clutching a poinsettia, had been fruitless. Olive and Jack had been out and Clarrie had left the plant with a neighbour.

So now, when Herbert urged her once more to visit, Clarrie summoned up the courage to go. She cut some roses from the garden, wrapped them in brown paper and cycled upriver to Lemington on Will's old bicycle. As she drew nearer to the neat terraced row with its large front windows denoting foreman status, Clarrie was half hoping that they would be out.

A bleary-looking Jack, his fair hair standing up in clumps, answered her knocking. For a moment he stared in confusion, not recognising her under the large hat tied on with a scarlet scarf.

'Clarrie?' he queried.

'Hello, Jack.' She smiled, holding out the bunch of roses. 'These are for Olive.'

He took them with a wary glance. 'She never said you were coming.'

'I only decided half an hour ago. Herbert suggested . . .'

'She's having a lie-down.' Jack looked unsure what to do.

Clarrie felt foolish. She had obviously interrupted their afternoon nap. 'Sorry, I shouldn't have come without warning. I can come back another time.'

'No, don't be daft,' Jack said, recovering from the surprise. 'She'll be pleased to see you. Haway in, lass.'

Leaving the bicycle propped against the front railings, Clarrie followed him into a tiny green-painted hallway with a parlour to the right and steep stairs to the left. The banisters and door frames were painted white, giving the illusion of light. A waft of sandalwood made her insides twist. Belgooree. Straight ahead, a door was open to the kitchen. Jack led her in.

'Have a seat,' he instructed, plonking the flowers on a scrubbed pine table by the window, 'and I'll fetch wor lass.'

She heard him mount the stairs as she looked around in curiosity. The whitewashed walls were decorated in a leaf pattern that looped round the room like garlands, some green, some in autumnal orange and yellow. Small birds painted in turquoise, gold and scarlet flitted among the leaves. The furniture was plain: a table and four chairs, a dresser and a linen chest. But they were painted primrose yellow, bringing a brightness to the room that was almost dazzling. Two narrow armchairs, upholstered in blue and yellow flowers, sat either side of the range and fireplace. A blind of white slatted wood hung at the open window, tapping gently in the breeze. The plates displayed on the dresser were blue and white willow pattern – like their mother's at Belgooree.

A lump came to Clarrie's throat and she quickly looked away. She crossed to the kitchen window and peered out at the scrubbed back yard with its whitewashed walls and tubs of flowers – a rhododendron in a large barrel, azaleas, nasturtiums and pansies growing out of painted and varnished tea chests. The riot of colour assaulted the senses. She thought how reserved and muted were the dark red roses she had brought, which were already wilting on the table.

Eventually, Clarrie heard footsteps approaching and turned to see Jack entering with Olive behind him. Her sister was red-cheeked and bright-eyed, her red-gold hair tumbling loose about her shoulders.

'This place is beautiful!' Clarrie exclaimed. 'It's like a little bit of—' She stopped, the words dying on her lips as Jack stepped aside and Olive moved into the room. She stared at her sister. Her heart knocked in her chest.

'Olive,' she gasped, 'you're expecting?'

Her sister, large-bellied, swayed forward with her hands supporting her back as if she might overbalance. She nodded, her look almost defiant.

'Aye,' Jack said with a proud grin, 'she's a month off her confinement.'

Clarrie's throat constricted. 'That's grand,' she croaked. 'I didn't know.'

Olive and Jack exchanged quick looks. 'Did Will not tell you?' Olive asked.

Clarrie shook her head. She held out her hands, unable to speak. Olive hesitated, then went to her sister. Clarrie enfolded her in her arms. It was an awkward hug over Olive's distended belly. Clarrie felt a movement, like a gentle nudge, and stood back, wide-eyed.

'Was that the baby?' she asked in astonishment.

'Aye, it was.' Olive smiled, placing protective hands over her bump.

Jack ushered his wife to a fireside chair and placed a cushion at her back.

'Sit down, Clarrie,' he insisted, 'and I'll brew the tea while you lasses have a bit chat.'

With Jack fussing around between them, making a pot of tea, Clarrie felt at a loss as to what to say. Why had no one told her? When was Olive going to tell her? Imagine if she had heard through gossip at the café! Will should have said something. But as she swallowed down her hurt bewilderment, she guessed why it had been kept from her. They knew it would cause her pain as well as joy, for it would reinforce her own childlessness.

Clarrie quelled her rising resentment. This was her beloved sister who was about to have her first baby. She would be an aunt. It was a cause for rejoicing, no matter what her own marriage lacked.

Sipping on the tea Jack made, she made an effort to chat about the café and riding with Will, and about outings with Herbert and the twins.

Gradually, Olive relaxed her guard and was able to talk about her excitement at the forthcoming arrival.

'If it's a lass, we'll call her Jane, after Mam,' Olive said, 'and George after Jack's dad if it's a lad.'

Clarrie leaned over and squeezed Olive's hand. 'That's grand.' She smiled. 'Whichever it is, I want to be the first to be told.'

As she was leaving, a thought struck her. 'I was wondering — have you thought about who you'd like with you when your time comes? Cos if you want—'

'That's all arranged,' Jack said firmly. 'Me mam's ganin' to help out. She's seen to dozens of births.'

Olive avoided her sister's look. She was blushing furiously. Clarrie hesitated about kissing her goodbye, and then Jack put an arm about his wife's waist as if warning her off. She took hold of the bicycle.

'Ta for the flowers, Clarrie,' Olive said stiffly.

Clarrie nodded and began wheeling the bike away. At the end of the street she looked back to wave, but Olive and Jack's front door was already closed and they were gone. She felt utterly excluded by them. She swallowed down a sob of unhappiness. Why was Olive behaving like this? As she cycled away in humiliation, Clarrie blamed Jack for coming between them. He must have discouraged Olive from keeping in touch.

Back home, Clarrie wished that Will were there for her to talk to about the situation and her hurt at being excluded from the pending birth. She felt awkward telling Herbert. She waited until the nurse had helped with his bathing, got him into bed and left for the night.

He was propped up on pillows, his skin sallow against the white linen.

'I don't think they were ever going to tell me,' Clarrie said unhappily. 'Imagine having a niece or nephew and not being told? Will knew but he probably didn't think it was his place to tell me. How did I ever let us grow this far apart? It was like talking to a half-stranger.'

Herbert raised a shaky hand and took a breath before speaking.

'S-sorry,' he stuttered.

Clarrie regarded him. 'It's not your fault we fell out. You've always been more than kind to my sister. It's me she was angry with for some reason.'

Herbert shook his head. 'Not – that.' His eyes looked sad and regretful.

'Sorry for what, then?'

'For – being – selfish,' he forced out the words. 'Not giving – you – a child.'

Clarrie felt her chest constrict. It was too late for an apology, she thought with resentment. He tried to grope for her hand.

'You – are s-so – g-good with – twins,' he panted. 'I should – have – been b-braver. Can – you – f-forgive me?'

Clarrie struggled with her emotions. How they had wasted their time together! She blamed him for their lack of intimacy, yet she had been happy to channel her energies into the café. Perhaps, deep down, she had been relieved that he had never attempted to make love to her. He was so much older and she had never desired him physically. But he was a good man and she was sure would have made a kind father to her children, perhaps wiser and more tolerant than with his first family.

Clarrie reached out and took his searching hand. 'I understand why you did so. I remember how much you grieved over Louisa – and the daughter you never had.'

He gazed at her, his look guilt-ridden. Shaking, he raised her wrist and pressed it to his half-paralysed lips. She rose and kissed his forehead, then settled him down for the night.

Later, she came back, having changed into her nightdress, ready to lie down in the camp bed she had slept in for the past year. As she moved around the half-lit room, she realised that Herbert was awake and watching her. She approached, peering at him uncertainly. He was crying out of one eye, silently. On impulse, Clarrie drew back the bedcovers and climbed in beside him, on the side where he had sensation. Tentatively, she touched his face, rubbing away his tears with her thumb.

'Do you want me to stay with you tonight?' she whispered. 'Here in your bed?'

He gulped and grunted, 'Yes – very – much.'

Gently, she laid her head on his shoulder and put an arm across his chest. She felt him let out a sigh. Neither of them spoke, each just enjoying the warmth of touching and the unexpectedness of the moment. Clarrie fell asleep in contentment. She awoke once in the night and wondered where she was, startled by the feel of Herbert's body next to hers and the gentle rasp of his breathing. Then she slept again until the nurse knocked on the door at seven in the morning. Clarrie kissed Herbert as she rose to let her in.

After that, she had the camp bed packed away and slept beside her husband every night. There was no lovemaking, but it was comfort of a kind and a new tenderness grew between them.

CHAPTER 30

One Thursday evening in late October, there was a message waiting for Clarrie when she came back from work. Olive had given birth. She and Jack had a son called George. Clarrie resisted the temptation to rush round there and then to see them. She would wait until her sister was ready to receive visitors. But after a week with no word, she could wait no longer. Getting Lexy to mind the café, she went round to Lemington on a Friday morning with a box of fairy cakes and a large teddy bear she had bought at Fenwick's.

Jack's mother answered the door. She was a little in awe of Clarrie and said in a fluster, 'Wor Olive's in bed with the bairn – she's not seeing visitors yet.'

'I'm her sister,' Clarrie said firmly, 'and it's high time I saw both her and my nephew, don't you think? I shan't stay long or tire her, but I do want to see her.'

She followed Mrs Brewis up the steep stairs and into a darkened bedroom. The green curtains were drawn and it was stuffy from a lit fire and a stale, sour bodily smell. A wood-framed bed dominated the room and lying curled to one side in a loose gown was Olive. There was neither sight nor sound of the baby.

'Olive, are you awake, hinny?' her mother-in-law whispered. 'Mrs Stock's come to see you.'

'Clarrie?' Olive murmured, but did not move.

'Yes, how are you?' Clarrie asked, moving round the bed. 'I won't stop long but I had to see you. I've brought you something.' Reaching her sister, she heard a small snuffling noise. With a jolt, she realised that the baby was tucked inside Olive's gown feeding on her breast. He was tightly swaddled with just his head and a tuft of pale hair visible. Her sister's hair was damp and straggly about her face, yet her expression was one of dreamy contentment.

The intimate scene overwhelmed Clarrie. She felt on the verge of tears.

'He's so bonny,' she exclaimed, 'from what I can see of him.'

'Mrs Stock,' Jack's mother said nervously, 'perhaps you should leave them be for now. Our Olive's tired out with the feedin'. It takes a bit of gettin' used to.'

Clarrie stepped back.

'Stay,' Olive said. 'He's getting sleepy again – I think he's nearly finished.'

'Would you like the curtains pulled back and the window open?' Clarrie asked. 'It's that stuffy in here.'

'No,' Mrs Brewis said at once. 'Can't have them catching a chill. Best leave things as they are.'

'Mam,' Olive said, 'can you fetch me a cup of water? Maybe's Clarrie would like a cup of tea an' all.'

Clarrie nodded in thanks and the woman bustled off downstairs. 'You call her Mam?' Clarrie queried. For some reason it upset her.

Olive replied, 'Jack likes me to.'

The baby's sucking stopped and his grip slackened. Olive drew away and sat up, pulling her gown over her full breast. She picked up her son and laid him against her shoulder, rubbing gently at his swaddled back. Clarrie sat on the edge of the bed and handed over the toy bear.

'It's twice his size at the moment,' she said. 'Hope it won't frighten him.'

'It's canny,' Olive said. 'Bet it cost you a fortune.'

'He's my first nephew and worth every penny,' Clarrie answered. 'You both seem grand.'

'We are.' Olive smiled. 'Jack's mam does everything for me. I just lie here like a queen eating and sleeping and feeding George. And he's such a canny baby – hardly makes a squeak. Think I'll have half a dozen.'

Clarrie's insides twisted with envy. She got up restlessly and reached to draw back a curtain. 'I don't care what Mrs Brewis says, I want to have a proper look at my nephew.'

Bright autumnal light fell across the bed, illuminating Olive's flushed face. She looked tired yet beautiful, her expression softened and eyes shining with happiness.

'Would you like to hold him?' she asked.

'May I?'

Olive held out her bundle. Cautiously, Clarrie took him and laid him carefully in the crook of her arm. She went back to the window to get a better look. His pale-lashed eyes were closed, his cheeks rosy from feeding and his tiny mouth glistening with milk. He looked sated and peaceful. Gently she stroked his head, marvelling at the softness of his downy fair hair.

'What a handsome lad you are,' she crooned. 'You'll break all the lasses' hearts, eh?' He gave a little juddering sigh and his lips pursed into a sucking shape, then he was still again. Clarrie laughed softly. 'Auntie Clarrie thinks you're the bonniest lad she's ever seen.' She felt a flood of emotion towards him, enjoying the warmth and weight of him in her arms.

Mrs Brewis returned with water for Olive and one of Clarrie's cakes on a plate. 'Your tea's waiting for you downstairs, Mrs Stock,' she said, crossing the room to yank the curtain back into place. 'Let me take the bairn from you.'

Clarrie kissed George and reluctantly handed him over. 'Is there anything you want?' she asked her sister.

'She's got owt she needs.' Mrs Brewis smiled proudly. 'Me and our Jack see to that.'

Clarrie swallowed her irritation at the woman's proprietorial attitude and went to kiss Olive goodbye. 'I'll call again soon,' she promised.

Her sister lay back sleepily. 'Ta for the bear, Clarrie.'

Encouraged by Olive's more relaxed manner towards her, Clarrie determined she would not let weeks and months go by without seeing her, as they had this past year. Downstairs, she took one sip of Mrs Brewis's stewed tea and poured the rest down the sink. It must have been sitting in the pot since breakfast. Clarrie left, George's milky smell still on her hands.

The next time she visited, both Jack and his mother were at the house and Clarrie was made to feel she was intruding. They did not let her up to the bedroom, insisting that Olive and the baby were resting. Yet, as she left, Clarrie could hear George mewling upstairs.

She was baffled as to why Olive and the Brewises tried to keep her at arm's length. The following week was George's christening at the church where Olive and Jack had been married. Clarrie consoled herself that at least she and Herbert were invited.

There was a simple tea put on at the house in Lemington afterwards. Clarrie had offered cakes and biscuits from the café, but the Brewises had insisted on doing it all themselves. With difficulty, they hauled Herbert through the door and sat him on the largest chair in the pink and white parlour. Clarrie made sure she got to hold her nephew. His wrinkled face had filled out and he felt twice as heavy as before. She rocked him tenderly, but he grew fretful from all the handling and Jack's mother quickly prised him from her grasp.

'He wants his feed,' she insisted, quickly dispatching Olive upstairs.

The motor taxi they had hired to take Herbert home arrived, and Clarrie had to leave before seeing her sister or nephew again.

Despite her resolve to see as much of Olive and George as possible, it was Christmas before she did so. She was so busy with the tea room and caring for Herbert that she did not have a spare moment, except on Sundays when she knew Jack and his mother would be there. Two days before Christmas Clarrie called with presents, to find Olive out.

'She's down the shops,' Mrs Brewis told her. 'I'm minding the bairn for her. It's his nap, else I'd invite you in.'

Clarrie handed over the presents and left in frustration. Somehow she could not summon the energy to tackle their wariness towards her or breach the stifling protectiveness with which they enclosed Olive and George. It would be far easier for her sister to visit the café, Clarrie thought with a swell of resentment. Let Olive come to her.

1914 came, Clarrie turned twenty-eight and her

busy life continued as before, except that Tuesday mornings with the twins came to an end as the children started full-time schooling. She missed them greatly and the only way she could numb the loss was to absorb herself in her work.

The café was doing so well that they purchased the terraced house beside it and knocked through to create extra meeting rooms. Clarrie had to get Bertie's co-operation as he was handling his father's affairs, but the café was proving so successful that his earlier opposition had long since melted away. Indeed, he offered to make some investments on her behalf. After consultation with Herbert, Clarrie agreed. Dislike him though she did, she trusted Bertie's expertise. Judging by his and Verity's lavish lifestyle of house parties at Rokeham Towers, private schooling for the twins and holidays in the south of France, he was good at both making and spending money.

When Clarrie went to discuss business with him at his office, Bertie treated her with the deference due to a client in front of his secretary, and not with the disdain he showed her at other times. Clarrie was faintly amused by his eagerness to be associated with the proprietor of Herbert's Tea Rooms now that the café was well established and prosperous.

It was from Bertie that Clarrie heard the news that the Robsons were selling their chain of Empire Tea Rooms.

'Made a fortune on them,' he said enviously. 'Touch of Midas, that family. Buying up land in East Africa with the proceeds.'

'Africa?' Clarrie cried in astonishment. 'Why?'

'To grow more tea. Land's cheap and conditions are similar to Ceylon, so I'm told. Thinking of investing there myself.' He pushed out his plump chin with an air of importance.

'And Wesley Robson?' Clarrie could not resist asking. 'Has he gone to Africa?'

Bertie gave her a sly look. 'Why do women always ask about Wesley?'

Clarrie flushed. 'I'm just curious to know what my rival is up to.'

'Quite so,' Bertie said, lolling back in his large leather chair. 'As far as I know, he's gone back to London and Mincing Lane. He's engaged to be married, did you know? Attractive woman – family made their money in jute – related to the Landsdownes. No doubt he's gone south for her sake. He'll be inheriting another fortune when he marries into the Lister-Browns.'

Clarrie did not want to hear any more about Wesley's charmed existence and made the pressing demands of the café an excuse to leave.

By Easter, Will was full of plans for what to do after he left university. He and Johnny were going to do a tour of the Continent until the autumn, and then he was going to take up a place on a teacher-training course in Newcastle. Clarrie was thrilled at the thought of his living at Summerhill once more while he trained, and Herbert put up no objection. He appeared to have forgotten that he had once harboured the strong opinion that Will should become a lawyer. Bertie had not.

'Teaching?' he cried in disdain. 'It's for those without enough brains for business or the law. I want you to come into the family firm with me. That's what Papa always intended.'

'Not now,' Will answered. 'He's happy for me to—'

'Papa's practically gaga.' Bertie was contemptuous. 'He hardly remembers what he's had for breakfast. You could say you wanted to be a dustman and he'd give you his blessing.'

'Nevertheless, that's what I mean to do.' Will was adamant. 'I'd make a useless lawyer. Legal documents are double-dutch to me. Give me a musical score any time.'

'Well then, at least put your musical talents to better use,' Bertie said, getting nowhere with his stubborn brother. 'Go professional.'

'I'm not good enough.' Will was frank. 'But I know I'd enjoy teaching others. I've done a bit already at the Edinburgh Settlement.'

'Oh, that place!' Bertie snorted. 'Full of Bolsheviks and religious lunatics. If you end up working for the likes of them, I'll disown you.'

Afterwards, Clarrie congratulated Will on standing up to his brother, knowing that if she had spoken in his defence Bertie would have somehow blamed it all on her.

'He's not nearly as tough as he likes to make out,' she said in amusement. 'All he cares about is keeping up appearances and being upsides with the Landsdownes.'

'Yes.' Will laughed. 'He's terrified of Verity giving him a ticking off about his embarrassing family.'

With Will in support, Clarrie summoned the courage to call on her sister once more. They took chocolates and flowers and chose to visit just after they knew Jack would have gone to work. They caught Olive in a housecoat, hair undone, washing up at the scullery sink. There was no Mrs Brewis senior to fend them off.

'Goodness me!' Olive cried, quite unnerved by their sudden appearance.

Unabashed, Will kissed her on the cheek and marched into the house. 'Where's young George? We've come to ply him with chocolate.'

'You mustn't do that!' Olive gasped, coiling her hair quickly into a loose bun. 'He's not properly weaned.'

Will laughed. 'Poor Georgie, he'll just have to watch us scoff the lot instead.'

Striding into the kitchen, Will spotted the baby kicking on a blanket on the floor and swooped to pick him up. George flung out his arms in alarm, his blue eyes bulging. A moment later he let out a wail.

'Careful!' both sisters cried at the same time.

Will ignored them, twirling George above his head and jiggling him up and down until his screams of alarm turned into screeches of delight. Will turned and almost threw the baby into Clarrie's arms. Clarrie grasped her nephew, rubbing her nose against his.

'Hello, bonny lad! Haven't you grown?' She settled him into her arms and George put up a plump exploring hand, stuffing fingers into her mouth.

Olive watched tensely.

'Relax,' Will said, throwing an affectionate arm about her. 'Clarrie's not going to eat him. She's just had breakfast.'

Olive rolled her eyes. 'You should have said you were coming. I'm not even dressed properly.'

'And give you the chance to be out,' Will said, stealing the words from Clarrie's lips.

Olive blushed and shrugged him off. 'Can I get you a cuppa?' She busied herself around the pretty kitchen without waiting for an answer. Clarrie noticed the changes: a clothes rack suspended overhead with nappies drying, a child's bowl and two-handled cup displayed on the dresser, and a pram wedged between the back door and the pantry.

While Will kept Olive occupied with questions and conversation, Clarrie sat with George in her lap, cuddling and making silly noises to entertain him.

'Brow-berry,' she smiled, pointing at his smooth brow. She worked her way down his face. 'Nosenebby, chin-cherry, kerry-erry-erry!' she laughed, tickling him under his chin. George giggled in delight, his mouth opening in a gummy grin. Clarrie repeated the game until the baby grew suddenly bored, noticed his mother and squealed for her attention.

Olive came over swiftly and claimed him from Clarrie's arms. Clarrie watched in envy as the boy settled easily on Olive's hip, her sister giving him frequent absent-minded kisses on his fluffy blond hair. Will did most of the talking, but Olive told them proudly how Jack was now a qualified tea blender.

'He helps Mr Milner decide which teas to bid for an' all,' she told them.

'I'm glad he's doing so well,' Clarrie said.

Olive gave her a sceptical look. 'You never had as much faith in Jack as I did.'

Will shot Clarrie a look of surprise, but she let the jibe go. 'You were right,' she said, getting up. 'Would you like to come to us for tea on Easter Sunday? It would just be us two and Herbert at home – Bertie and the family are away in France.'

'Go on, Olive,' Will encouraged. 'Papa would be greatly cheered to see your Georgie.'

'We don't call him Georgie,' she said in irritation. 'And I'm sorry, we've got Mam and Thomas and his lady friend coming round.' When Will looked disappointed, she said in a lighter vein, 'Jack's hopeful that his brother might finally get round to proposing. We've dropped enough hints. Poor Annie will be past childbearing age if he doesn't hurry up.'

Clarrie saw Olive redden and look away, clutching George to her almost fiercely. There it was again, that unspoken gulf between them, the mother and the childless one. It saddened her that her sister did not want her near either her or the boy, as if she somehow threatened their cosy world with Jack. She wondered briefly why her sister should distrust her so, for she had no desire to take anything from her.

'Take care,' she said as they left, hoping for a last cuddle with George. But Olive held on to him, his plump legs hooked around her waist as if he were part of her.

As she walked back to town with Will, Clarrie became tearful.

'Why is she so cold to me these days? What have I done?'

Will was thoughtful. 'Was there ever an understanding between you and Jack?' he asked.

Clarrie said impatiently, 'Not really. We courted for a short while, but barely saw each other. When he broke it off, Olive took his side and said it was my fault. But that was years ago.'

'Perhaps she's still jealous,' Will suggested.

'Jealous of me?' Clarrie asked in bewilderment. 'How can she be?'

'Because,' Will said, 'Jack cared for you first and maybe she worries that he still does.'

Clarrie cried, 'That's nonsense! They couldn't be

happier – and they've got George – she has no right to be jealous of anyone.'

Will stopped and took her hands, his look affectionate. 'Dear Clarrie, you have no idea just how easy people find it to love you, do you? You draw them to you like the sun.'

Abruptly, Clarrie laughed, though tears glistened on her dark lashes. 'Will Stock, you are the best tonic anyone could ever ask for. What a wonderful teacher you will be. No child will stay grumpy or down-hearted in your class.'

Linking arms, they walked back to Summerhill, Clarrie's mood lightening. She would stay away from Olive until her sister needed her.

CHAPTER 31

Clarrie refused to believe the gloomy predictions of a conflict with Germany. There was some discussion about it at the café, but the main preoccupations among the politically aware were the fight for paid holidays, union representation and the progress towards women's suffrage.

Regulars such as Florence and Nancy, who had seen many of their friends imprisoned over the issue, were in buoyant mood.

'Just wait till the election campaign this autumn,' Florence said eagerly. 'If the Liberals don't promise us emancipation, they'll be voted out in droves.'

'Aye,' agreed Nancy, 'they'll be hoyed into the wilderness with a gnashing of teeth!'

Will sat his finals and graduated. Clarrie threw a family dinner party for him when he came home in mid-June, inviting Johnny too. Bertie and Verity brought champagne, knowing that there would be no wine at dinner, and talked endlessly about their last French trip. They had letters of introduction for Will and Johnny.

'The Guillards have a wonderful château outside Nice,' Verity said. 'You simply must stay there.'

'And there's our good friend Count de Buffois in Paris,' Bertie boasted, 'whom you can stay with on your way south. He keeps an excellent cellar. We met him on the Riviera last year.'

'Aren't you concerned about the talk of war between France and Germany?' Clarrie felt compelled to ask. They were making plans as if there was no tension on the Continent at all. 'I hear things at the tea room.'

'Really, Clarrie,' Bertie was dismissive, 'that's a lot of hot air. I think our French friends are more reliable informants than your café gossips, don't you?'

She sat back listening to the young men's excited discussion of their grand tour of Europe – France, Italy, Austria, Germany – and said no more.

At the end of June, Will and Johnny departed for France. Clarrie went to see them off at Newcastle's central station with Lexy and Edna. Clarrie tried to remember what she had felt like arriving there with Olive nine years previously: nervous, awestruck, cold.

'What a sight we must have looked in our home-made dresses and sola topis,' she laughed as she recounted the occasion, 'like something out of a Kipling novel. Then Cousin Jared loaded us on to the rolley for all to see.'

'Folk must've thought the circus had come to town,' Lexy teased.

'Two birds of paradise, more likely,' Will said gallantly.

They laughed and embraced, and then the women were waving them away in the echoing, steam-filled hall.

Two days after their departure, the newspapers reported an assassination in central Europe. Clarrie had been working late at the café and did not get round to reading Herbert the newspaper until the following evening. A Serbian student had shot Archduke Ferdinand, the heir to the Austro-Hungarian Empire. Clarrie skimmed the report, wondering vaguely if Will and Johnny had intended visiting Sarajevo. But in the following days and weeks, the newspapers began to fill with anxious articles on flag burning in Austria and her deteriorating relations with Serbia's patron Russia, and their respective allies Germany and France. Would Britain be dragged in too?

There was no appetite, as far as Clarrie could gauge, for war with their neighbour across the German Sea. It seemed impossible. Their royal families were related and there were strong trade links between Tyneside and the German ports. On occasion, sailors off their merchant ships had found their way into the café and flirted with the waitresses. Will had once spoken to some in halting German.

August came with news of the worsening situation on the Continent; Austria had declared war on Serbia. Clarrie's prime concern was for Will and his friend. A postcard had come from Paris and a second from Switzerland. They were already detouring from their original plan so she had no idea where they might be. Switzerland sounded safe.

Opposition to war was vocal, especially locally, from trades unions to religious leaders. Clarrie wheeled Herbert to the park on the first Sunday in August to watch a peace rally. It was warm and sunny and the flower beds were a blaze of red, pink, yellow and blue. Women were dressed in colourful outfits and hats, and the air was filled with the noisy play of children. War seemed as remote a possibility as a comet landing in their midst.

That night, sitting up in bed next to Herbert, Clarrie fretted, 'It can't happen. We wouldn't be so mad as to go to war, surely?'

Herbert said, 'At – least – Will is – safe.'

Clarrie shot him a look. 'Well I hope so, but we've no way of knowing.'

He looked unconcerned. 'Durham – perfectly – safe.'

Clarrie's insides tensed. She put a hand on his. 'Herbert, he's not at Durham any more. He graduated, remember? Will is travelling abroad with Johnny.'

Her husband's face clouded in confusion. 'Abroad? Is he?'

'Yes,' she said gently, 'we've had postcards.' She reached over and picked up the latest one, which she kept as a bookmark, and showed it to Herbert.

He sighed, half in frustration and half in resignation. 'S-sorry. Should remember.'

She leaned across and kissed his rigid cheek. 'Don't worry about it. I'm sure no harm will come to our Will.'

Two days later, in the middle of serving lunches at the café, Clarrie heard that war with Germany and her ally Austria had been declared. Edna and Grace ran screaming into the street in a panic, staring up the street as if they expected to see German soldiers marching along Scotswood Road. Clarrie quickly brought them back in, sat them in the kitchen and calmed them down with cups of hot sweet tea.

'They're never going to come here,' she assured them. 'It'll all get sorted out soon. You're quite safe. If there's any fighting to be done, it'll be hundreds of miles away on the Continent.'

But over the next week there were wild rumours of German spies round every corner and Prussian baby-eating monsters on the march through Belgium. The newspapers turned suddenly bellicose, angry crowds attacked German butchers' shops and recruitment posters went up on advertising hoardings. By the end of the month, the town began to swell with migrants coming for jobs at the munitions factories along the river and the parks resounded to the bark and stamping of army recruiters and their volunteers.

In the café, Clarrie heard more divided opinion, many of the union men openly scornful of the jingoism and rush to the colours. Burton, who had once been a regular at the Cherry Tree, declared, 'It's the bosses' war, not ours. Let the toffs stick bayonets in each other if they want; the working man's not so daft.'

But the working man in west Newcastle, Clarrie observed, was put to work doubly hard in the factories and mines to help with the war effort, while clerks and engineers banded together with workmates to form local companies of volunteers, eager to join the British Expeditionary Force helping defend France's eastern border.

Clarrie kept the tea room open later to cater for the longer shifts, and opened at dawn to serve breakfasts and dissuade workers from fortifying themselves at the pub before the hooters blew. Yet it all seemed unreal, the mood of the recruiting parades and the waving, excited crowds too cheerful for war, as if the men were embarking on a charabanc trip to the seaside.

She wondered what it might mean for India and was glad to think that Kamal was long since retired from army service. She did not even know if he was still alive, for he had never answered any of her letters. But above all, Clarrie wanted news of Will and Johnny. Post from abroad was now erratic since the one noticeable effect of the war was the attack on shipping. They had heard nothing for a month. Perhaps a mailbag containing a letter from Will had been sunk on some torpedoed merchant ship? But she kept her worries to herself. There was little point in distressing Herbert with them. He was far happier in his state of forgetfulness.

On a misty September morning, as Clarrie was helping Lexy with breakfasts, a bearded man in a large-brimmed hat and scruffy tweeds came into Herbert's Tea Rooms. He stood looking about him, then removed his hat and gave her a tired smile.

Clarrie banged down a tray of bacon and eggs. 'Will?' she gasped. His smile broadened. 'Will!' she shrieked and flew at him with her arms outstretched.

They hugged tightly and Lexy and Edna gathered round in excitement, showering him with questions.

'Where've you been?'

'How did you get back?'

'We thought you'd been hoyed in a German gaol.'

Ina hobbled out of the kitchen to hear and Dolly burst into tears. 'You little devil! You were always running off and getting into scrapes; nothing's changed.'

Over a fried breakfast and a large pot of tea, Will told them how, in mid-August, he and Johnny had been arrested in the Austrian mountains where they had been staying at a monastery, unaware that war had broken out. After being held for a week, they were taken to the Italian border and expelled. But resting in a border town they had been robbed of their passports and money, and they had had to work their passage home on boats via Spain. They had been three weeks at sea, unable to get word home and praying not to be attacked in the English Channel.

Clarrie took Will to Summerhill. 'Don't be surprised if your father asks you why you're back from Durham. He thinks you're still a student. His memory's worse than ever.'

'Well, as long as he doesn't tell me off for not doing my prep,' Will joked, squeezing her arm. 'I'll just be glad to see the old boy.'

Herbert, sitting in his favourite spot by the study window, appeared baffled by Will's appearance and did not seem to recognise his son. But once Will had bathed and shaved off his beard, Herbert's attitude changed.

'My – boy!' he croaked, attempting to raise a shaking hand. 'You – come – back.' When Will held his father's veined, trembling hands in his, Herbert let out a strangled sound and tears oozed on to his immobile face.

Clarrie's heart squeezed to see the light of recognition in Herbert's eyes and the tender way Will talked to him about his travels, playing down the danger in which he and Johnny had been. But her hope that Will would now begin his teaching course and remain safely in Newcastle was soon dashed. He was restless and could not settle, especially after Johnny returned to Edinburgh to continue his degree in medicine.

When a letter came from his old school friend, Spencer-Banks, telling him that he was joining up, Will followed suit.

'But what about your teaching?' Clarrie protested. 'At least get qualified first.'

'How can I sit around teaching music when there are children all over Europe whose very lives are threatened by this war?'

She knew that when Will got that stubborn glint in his dreamy blue eyes, nothing would shake his resolve. She swallowed her fear for him.

'Better pretend to your father that you've gone back to university,' she said in resignation. 'I don't think I could stand him asking after you every five minutes.'

Will signed up at a recruiting station south of the river so that he could train with Spencer-Banks in the Durham Light Infantry. For the first few weeks, they were stationed in the county and he got home once a month, including Christmas. Clarrie, determining to make it a happy one for Will, organised a Boxing Day party and invited Johnny and his family as well as Olive and hers.

Please come, she begged her sister by letter. *Will might not get back home again for months, even years.*

To her delight, Olive and Jack turned up, bringing

George who now staggered around on unsteady legs and grabbed on to passing skirts or trouser legs. When Clarrie produced the box of mechanical toys, six-year-old Vernon snatched them to himself.

'They're mine! He'll break them,' he protested.

'You can show George how they work,' Clarrie suggested, firmly extracting the box. 'He's much too small to manage himself. He needs a big boy to help.'

Will came to her aid, ending up on the floor making train noises, with a giggling George tumbling about his legs and Vernon riding him like a horse. Josephine, despite Verity's carping that she would spoil her dress, joined in too. Clarrie noticed how Olive and Jack visibly relaxed at the sight of their son playing happily with the twins. It was the first time she had seen them out together in company since George's christening and it struck her what a fine couple they looked. Her sister's beauty had deepened with age; she was fuller-faced, and her hair was swept up into a lustrous reddish crown. Jack, his hair now tamed with oil and his looks less boyish, had the confident, energetic air of a businessman. He reminded her of a young Daniel Milner.

For the first time, Clarrie was convinced that Olive had been right to marry Jack. Perhaps her sister's reasons had been mixed and it had partly been to escape Summerhill and her, but that hardly mattered now. Olive and Jack were suited, and she could see from their quiet fussing over George how much they adored their son.

As they left, Clarrie gave her sister a tentative hug. 'Thanks for coming. Will really hoped you would.'

'I know how much you'll miss him, Clarrie,' Olive said, suddenly tearful. 'He's a grand lad.'

'Come on, lass,' Jack said, carrying a sleeping George on his shoulder. 'Will knows how to look after himself. Don't go getting upset. Not in your condition.'

Olive pulled away with a sharp glance at her husband. Clarrie caught her hand.

'Are you expecting again?' she murmured. 'You don't have to be embarrassed on my account, please.'

Olive nodded. 'March,' she whispered.

Clarrie squeezed her hand. 'That's grand.' She smiled. 'No wonder you're looking like a flower in bloom.'

Olive gave her a grateful look, then Jack was steering her out of the door and into the December twilight. Will came up and stood by Clarrie, waving, his other hand resting on Clarrie's shoulder.

'Tomorrow,' he said to her cheerfully, 'we're going riding. I've arranged it with Lexy. You're barred from the tea room all day. We muster at the stables at ten o'clock.'

She turned to him and smiled. 'Two months in the army and you're as bossy as Field Marshal French.'

He grinned. 'You have to be with a Belhaven. They're notorious for disobeying orders.'

Linking arms, they returned to the warmth of the sitting-room fire and a dozing Herbert.

CHAPTER 32

1915

In February, Will's regiment embarked for Egypt and Olive gave birth prematurely to a daughter called Jane. The baby was born tiny and wizened, with a shock of dark hair.

'Just like you and our mam,' Olive whispered tearfully to Clarrie, whom she had unexpectedly sent for. 'I want you to see her – just in case . . .'

Jane was swiftly baptised at the house, and Jack's mother moved in to help with George while Olive nurtured her delicate baby. Clarrie's concern for her niece was compounded with worry over Will's safety.

They heard nothing for weeks, nervously following reports in the press of action in the Mediterranean. By late April, news was spreading of fierce fighting in the Dardanelles and of heavy losses among British and Allied troops against the Turkish army, dug in above the beaches of Gallipoli.

Clarrie got out Herbert's old atlas. These were places she had never heard of, despite having travelled through the Suez Canal on their return from India. Daily she prayed for news that Will was alive and safe from injury. She daydreamed about his being injured just enough to bring him home, but not enough to threaten his life. How much was just enough? An eye? Half a leg? She tortured herself with grim and fruitless speculation. Worse was the regular scanning of casualty lists. The dread of bad news lay on her stomach like a stone weight.

Finally, a heavily censored letter arrived from Will. He was alive and well and back in Egypt. That day at the café, Clarrie gave out free cake in celebration. There was no word as to where he was going next, but as the trench warfare in Flanders grew ever more ferocious and bloody, she hoped he would remain out east.

The casualty numbers mounted grimly as the summer campaigns raged. Demand for volunteers in the forces was insatiable and there was growing talk of conscription. Men were pressed into registering their fitness for combat. On a rare visit to Olive, Clarrie found her in a terrible state. She had lost weight and her eyes looked bruised with fatigue. Mrs Brewis had taken George out to the shops.

'She won't take the baby,' Olive said resentfully, rocking a fretful Jane in her arms, 'says she's too much trouble.'

'She's looking bigger,' Clarrie encouraged her, 'so you shouldn't worry.'

'But I do worry,' Olive cried. 'How can I not? The baby's got me worn out and what does Jack do? He's gone to attest.' She gulped in air and raised her voice over the baby's grizzling. 'I told him not to – said he wasn't to volunteer. He's needed at the company – he's Mr Milner's main man – specially after three of the lads joined up. And how could I possibly manage with George and Jane on me own? It doesn't bear thinking about!'

'Attesting is just registration,' Clarrie pointed out. 'It doesn't mean he'll ever have to join up. Married men with children will be the last on the list – specially lads like Jack who are keeping a business going.'

Clarrie kept to herself the recent difficulties she was experiencing in obtaining tea from Milner's. Bonded stocks were running out and shipping tea from India and Ceylon was a hazardous job. There was plenty of tea still being grown, picked and packed, but much of it was being stockpiled at the ports waiting for someone to ship it. On top of that, there was a huge demand for tea in the forces and much of the supply was being diverted as rations.

Jane's wailing grew more querulous. 'And the bairn never stops crying!' Olive said in agitation.

'Here, give her to me,' Clarrie ordered, taking the red-faced, squawking bundle from her sister. Jane was rigid and hot. Clarrie loosened the blanket that wrapped her and walked about the untidy kitchen, gently rocking and pacifying the baby with soft words.

Olive watched, her expression miserable. 'I can't get anything done. Look what a mess this place is in.'

'I thought Mrs Brewis was helping out,' Clarrie said.

Olive sighed. 'She's only interested in George – spoils him rotten. To be honest I wish she would move back home – it's just someone else to cook and wash for. But that's not going to happen – Thomas and her have rented out her room to a munitions worker.'

Jane had fallen quiet at last. Clarrie brushed her tear-stained face with a kiss.

'Why don't you strap her on to you while you work?' she suggested. 'The way Ama and the Khassia women used to. She likes movement and being held close.'

Olive pulled a face. 'And have Jack's mam calling me a peasant or a coolie?'

'What does it matter what she calls you? You'd be getting jobs done and rocking the bairn at the same time.' She came close to her sister and said quietly, 'I remember Mother doing that with you.'

Olive's eyes widened. 'Did she?'

Clarrie nodded. 'Strapped you to her back when we walked down to the village or watered the flowers on the veranda. Even shopping in the bazaar at Shillong. No doubt the memsahibs called her names too, but she didn't care.' Clarrie gave a tender smile as another memory resurfaced.

'What?' asked Olive. 'Tell me more.'

'I remember her saying she liked to feel you close – feel your heartbeat – then she knew you were all right,' Clarrie said. 'I'd ask her, "Is baby's heart working?" and she'd say, "Yes, it's working very well, thank you." '

Olive's tired eyes welled with tears. Gently, Clarrie placed Jane back in her sister's arms. 'Do the same for your lass,' she urged, 'and you might worry about her less.'

She left, promising to call when she could. But after a year of war, the demands of the café were growing. Prices were rising and two of her staff left: Dinah to have a baby to the sweetheart she had hastily married before he volunteered for the Navy, and Grace who was tempted away by better wages in a shell-making factory. At home, it was getting increasingly difficult to find nurses for Herbert as more were needed to staff army hospitals, and Sally upped and left to marry a riveter who had come to the yards from Scotland. Marriage seemed to be in the air. Clarrie's housekeeper friend, Rachel, swiftly married a sergeant with the Tyneside Irish and to Clarrie's regret moved away to South Shields.

One cold, damp November evening, Clarrie returned to find the house in darkness. She was later than she had intended as the tea room had been full of migrant workers reluctant to leave its warmth for the overcrowded, temporary huts built to house them near the docks. She knew Mrs Henderson would have gone home at six, but hoped the young agency nurse would have waited for her return.

Turning on lights as she entered, Clarrie called out that she was home. She kept her coat on against the chill of the unused downstairs rooms and took to the stairs. The bedroom was deserted and the bed cold. Herbert had not been put to bed by the nurse, and yet the blackout blinds had been drawn down. She hurried along to the study.

'Herbert?' she called out.

The remains of a fire and a residual warmth told of recent occupation. Clarrie's heart lurched. A blanket that was used to tuck round Herbert's knees lay discarded on the floor. Where on earth could he be? He could not have gone anywhere without someone's help. In panic, Clarrie flew from room to room, searching.

The door to her own neglected bedroom was ajar and light gleamed at the window from the open curtains. She crossed quickly to draw them before putting on a light, and tripped. She grabbed on to the bed rail to stop herself falling. Herbert's stick lay at her feet. Her heart lurched sickeningly. Not caring about the blackout, she turned on the light. Slumped on the floor between the bed and the window was Herbert.

'My God!' she gasped, rushing to his side. He was lying on his back staring at the ceiling. A faint pulse beat in the hollow of his neck.

'Herbert, can you move?' she cried. 'Can you hear me?'

He did not respond. Only his eyes flickered towards her.

'I'll get help,' she said, forcing down the fear in her throat. 'Just hold on. Don't die on me, Herbert,' she hissed, 'please don't die!'

By the time she had rung for an ambulance, alerted Bertie and returned upstairs, Herbert's eyes were closed and his breathing so shallow she had to lean close to feel it on her cheek and convince herself he was still alive. She stroked his head and whispered encouragement.

It seemed an age before the ambulance came, ringing its bell and alerting the neighbours that something was amiss at No. 12. She went with Herbert, not waiting for Bertie. He found her at the hospital pacing in a waiting room. Clarrie rushed to hug him but he fended her off in embarrassment and demanded to know what had happened.

'He's had another seizure – a bad one,' she gulped. 'The doctor's not sure he'll . . .'

Bertie wanted the exact details. He was horrified to hear his father had been left alone.

'There should've been a nurse,' Clarrie said, holding back tears. 'And I don't know how he got from his study to the bedroom. He must've dragged himself there. What do you think he was trying to do?'

'We might never know,' he said accusingly. 'You should have been with him, not at the tea room.'

'I'm sorry,' she said wretchedly.

Eventually a doctor came. 'Mr Stock's condition is stable but poorly. There's nothing to be done tonight. Go home and get some rest.'

Bertie left without a word and Clarrie returned through the echoing fog to the empty house. It was the longest night of her life. She stoked up the fire in Herbert's study and sat in his chair under the discarded blanket, waiting and dozing.

A startled Mrs Henderson appeared at seven.

'When I left, Mr Stock was sitting in his chair by the fire, I swear to it,' she said in a fluster. 'That young nurse was called away at six too – some emergency. I didn't think you'd be far behind. Oh, Mrs Stock, I feel terrible.'

'Not as terrible as I do,' Clarrie answered. 'It wasn't your fault. Tell me how he seemed when you left him.'

Mrs Henderson shook her head. 'Same as ever – no trouble – just dozing and staring at the fire.' Then her expression changed. 'He did say some'at strange – maybe's I misheard.'

'What?'

'Asked me about you.'

'Me?' Clarrie queried.

'Aye, "See if Mrs Stock needs anything," he said. And he called me Mrs Pearson, an' all. But he often gets his words mixed up, doesn't he?'

Clarrie's heart thumped. 'Mrs Pearson was the cook here before I came,' she said. 'Perhaps he was thinking of the old Mrs Stock too.' Her lips trembled as she added, 'That must be why he went to her room – he wanted Louisa.'

For the next week, Herbert's condition neither worsened nor improved. He lay still as an effigy under the white sheet and hospital blanket, his face grey and lifeless. He was fed through a tube. On the rare occasions his eyes opened, his look was vacant. Clarrie came at visiting hour and sat holding his hand, but he showed no sign of recognition or even of knowing that she was there. Verity came once but said it was too distressing; Bertie came every other day for a few minutes to berate her for her neglect of his father. A message was sent to Will, now in Alexandria, to prepare for the worst.

Yet Herbert clung on. A month later, at Christmas, there were minor improvements that Clarrie seized on with hope: he could partially swallow again and his eyes looked more alert, though he could not speak. Will wrote her a long encouraging letter. She had confided her belief that Herbert had been searching for Louisa, his mind having regressed into the past.

He might just as well have been looking for you, Clarrie, Will wrote. *You have been his greatest comfort and love these past six years. Don't let Bertie tell you otherwise. My father would never have lived this long without your loving care.*

As 1916 dawned, a conscription bill was hurried through Parliament, and to Clarrie's distress she found the house at Summerhill being requisitioned by the nearby barracks as an overflow for new recruits.

'You hardly need all that space,' Bertie was unsympathetic, 'and it looks unlikely Papa will ever be fit enough to live there again.'

'It's Will's home too,' Clarrie retorted, stung by his callousness.

'Will won't need a home till the war's over,' Bertie said, 'and he can come to us when he gets leave.'

'And what about me?' Clarrie demanded.

His look was unconcerned. 'There's the flat above the café – it's roomy enough and very handy for work.'

Furious, Clarrie went to confront the officer in charge of requisition, suspicious that Bertie had tipped them off about the empty house.

'We were led to believe you were living there on your own,' the officer said, embarrassed, 'and that you had other property you could go to.'

'It is my husband's home – he must have some-where to return to,' she insisted. 'I'm willing to share the house, but not with billeted soldiers.'

In the end, it was agreed that administrative staff would use the downstairs rooms and two female clerks lodge on the second floor. Clarrie's frustra-tions and worries were thrown into sharp focus that summer, when news spread of the offensive on the Somme in France. Hailed as a massive assault on German lines, the appalling death toll spoke of carnage. Whole regiments had been decimated or wiped out in a matter of hours.

Clarrie sat in the café with others, hunched over

newspapers trying to glean information, unable to take in the scale of death and injury. Dolly's cousin was killed, one of Jack's tea boys was missing and Ina's youngest daughter was a widow at twenty. In the midst of trying to console her staff and reassure Olive that Jack might not be conscripted, Clarrie received a telegram.

She tore it open with trembling fingers and nearly fainted at the message. Will was back in England. He had a week's leave. He arrived on an overcrowded train, looking thin and sallow-faced, but with a smile that lifted Clarrie's troubled heart.

She wanted to take him to the café for something to eat, but he asked to go home. On the way Clarrie explained that they were now sharing the house with army personnel but his own room was secure. He went straight to bed and slept until evening. Clarrie decided that Bertie could wait a day before being informed of his brother's arrival. After bathing, Will shared her simple supper of ham and potatoes, while she told him everything that had happened in his absence. But when she tried to ask about Gallipoli the previous year, or his time in Egypt, Will shrugged off her questions.

'Eighty per cent of army life is dull as ditchwater,' he said.

'And the other twenty per cent?' Clarrie asked.

He hesitated. 'That's the bit one tries to forget,' he answered.

The next day, Clarrie arranged to meet him at the

hospital after she had been to work and he had been to visit Bertie and Verity. She found him already on the side ward to which Herbert had been moved, sitting at his father's side. When he looked up at her, he could not hide his shock at Herbert's fragile appearance.

'Talk to him,' Clarrie encouraged him gently. 'He gets comfort from the sound of voices even if he doesn't understand.'

Will tried, but his usual eloquence deserted him. Clarrie squeezed his shoulder. They sat in silence until suddenly Will began to sing 'The Cliffs of Old Tynemouth', softly at first and almost under his breath, then louder. It was a traditional air he had learned as a boy in school and sung a hundred times in snatches around the house.

'Oh, the cliffs of old Tynemouth they're wild
and they're sweet,
And dear are the waters that roll at their
feet . . .'

As his melodious tenor voice swelled around them, Clarrie remembered times when Will and Olive had sung it together in the nursery. Her eyes prickled and her throat watered.

'Other lands may be fairer but naught can be
seen
Like the shore where our first love and boyhood
have been . . .'

She noticed how Herbert's eyes fixed on Will as if in concentration, a part of him trying to remember through the fog of confusion.

'. . . 'Tis the joy of my fancy, the home of my heart.'

When the song came to an end, Clarrie urged him to sing another. But Will shook his head, overcome with emotion at the effort.

So Clarrie sang one that she had heard often in the tea room, 'Red Sails in the Sunset'. Lexy and Edna were always singing it. Will joined in. After that, they sang snatches of all the popular songs they could remember.

Eventually the matron put her head round the door and told them visiting time was over.

'I'd pay to hear you two sing,' she joked.

When Clarrie bent to kiss Herbert goodbye, she was sure he knew who she was.

'Isn't it good having Will back?' she murmured. 'You'll see him tomorrow too.'

Turning in the doorway, Clarrie saw that Herbert still watched her. She blew him a kiss and left with a lighter heart than for months.

A ringing telephone woke Clarrie from a deep sleep. Struggling out of bed, she ran down to the cloakroom in her nightdress. It was the hospital. Herbert had died in his sleep, just before dawn.

CHAPTER 33

Will's leave was extended so that he could attend his father's funeral. Clarrie was thankful to have him there to support her and to prevent Bertie from dictating how everything should be done. Bertie wanted a lavish affair at the cathedral, but Clarrie insisted it should be at the John Knox where Herbert had worshipped most of his life. Privately, to Will, she declared that Bertie was only trying to impress his in-laws. She gave way on the funeral wake. It was to be held at Tankerville Terrace as she could not entertain at the partially requisitioned Summerhill.

'I can hardly bear the thought of a party anyway,' she told Will.

Clarrie went through the motions of funeral and mourning, her feelings numbed by the shock of

Herbert's going. Deep down she had known he would never recover from the second seizure and yet she had got used to going to the hospital and seeing him week after week, lulled by the routine of visiting and spurred on by hope.

She was touched and humbled by the scores of people who turned up to offer their condolences: friends, clients, church members and regulars from the café who had held him in high regard. Her staff came to support her, as did Olive and Jack, and Johnny travelled overnight from Edinburgh to be there too. Herbert's Tea Rooms were closed and shuttered for a week as a mark of respect.

As soon as the funeral was over, Bertie summoned Clarrie to the office to sort out Herbert's affairs. 'There is much to discuss,' he told her over the telephone. But she refused to waste Will's precious last days of leave on dreary legal matters and Will was not the least bit interested either.

'Leave Bertie to it,' he said drily. 'He loves nothing better than sorting out a juicy probate.'

Both Clarrie and Will rued the fact that Johnny's horses had long since been requisitioned. Instead of riding they went on long walks, out into the countryside where the corn was ripe and women labourers were already harvesting crops.

'Perhaps I should be volunteering too,' Clarrie agonised on their final meander. 'I really don't know what to do. For so long my first consideration has been Herbert. Without him I feel like a plant without roots.'

'What you do at the café is important too,' Will encouraged her. 'You're providing sustenance for scores of people, and it will only get worse — rationing's bound to come in sooner or later. Keep the café going, Clarrie; it cheers people up and by God they need it. And think of Lexy and Edna and Ina and Dolly – they still depend on you.'

'Yes, you're right,' she sighed, 'and I would hate to close it. It'll give me something to keep me going when you're gone.'

Will linked her arm as they walked on. 'That's my Clarrie.'

'And maybe this'll be the last year of fighting and everyone will come to their senses before we have to ration anything.'

But Will gave a bleak little laugh. 'There's no end in sight to this ghastly war. We'll starve each other to death before either side surrenders.'

It was an emotional parting, the day Will had to report to his regiment.

'Don't come to the station,' he advised her. 'It'll be chaos as usual and we won't know what to say.'

'What else could I possibly be doing?' Clarrie asked, stomach knotting.

'Go to the tea room,' he urged, 'and keep busy. It will comfort me to think of you there. Let me wave you off as if it's a normal day. Please, Clarrie.'

She swallowed her disappointment that she would

not be with him until the last possible moment. 'If that's what you want, then of course I will.'

The clerks were already busy below when Clarrie took her leave of Will in Herbert's study. He had not yet changed into his uniform and looked boyish in his flannel trousers and open shirt. She took hold of his large hands with her small neat ones.

'I'm glad you were here when your father died,' she said. 'I don't think it was pure chance – I think Herbert was hanging on for you. I've never seen him as peaceful as when you sang to him. Thank you for that.'

Tears brimmed in Will's eyes. 'I hate to leave you all alone,' he said, his voice cracking.

'I'm not alone,' she assured him. 'I have my family at the café.'

'I wish things weren't so uncertain. I want to picture you writing to me at Papa's desk and holding family tea parties in the drawing room – not a house full of army secretaries,' he said, his fair face full of concern.

She gripped his hands. 'What ever happens, you will always have a home wherever I am,' she promised. 'Just come back safe and sound, that's all I ask.'

They hugged and he held on to her tightly, as he used to as a boy when he was missing his mother. She stroked his hair and willed herself not to break down in front of him. 'God protect you,' she murmured.

'And you,' he echoed.

When she pulled away, his face was damp with tears. They stood for a moment longer, smiling sadly at each other. There was so much to say and yet nothing more to be said, at such a moment.

Clarrie left quickly, and did not let go a sob until she was out of the house. It felt as if a great weight pressed on her chest and would not let her breathe. She gulped for air and wiped at escaping tears. At the corner of the square, she turned and looked back at the house. She gasped in shock. For a split second, she saw Herbert's tall figure standing at his study window, the way he used to look years ago. But of course it was Will gazing out for a last glimpse of her. He raised a hand in farewell. She waved back and blew him a kiss. Then she turned her back and hurried on, the image of him waving and smiling staying with her all the way to the tea room.

It was a difficult day, her first back at the café since Herbert's death, but she got through it by keeping busy while trying not to dwell on Will's departure: Will leaving the house in his uniform, Will at the station, Will on a crowded train crossing the Tyne and rattling southwards.

Rather than return to an empty house, Clarrie accepted Lexy's invitation to have a late supper in the flat upstairs. Lexy's youngest sister Edith had recently taken a job in Sunderland and Lexy, who had never lived alone before, was unnerved by the quiet.

'Spent all me life wishing me sisters would emigrate to Timbuctoo,' she joked, 'but now I find I'm talking to meself for company.'

They shared a pot of tea, halved a boiled egg and talked of the mundane: recipes that would use less sugar, a possible local supply of honey as a sugar substitute, Edna's latest infatuation with a Belgian refugee working at the docks, Ina's arthritis.

Lexy took a sip of tea and pulled a face. 'This stuff is getting worse,' she complained. 'Smells like tar and doesn't taste much better.'

Clarrie snorted. 'You're becoming quite a tea snob in your old age.'

'Taught by the master,' Lexy retorted.

Clarrie sighed. 'You're right though. The last lot we got from Milner's was coarse as anything – bits of twig in it the size of nails. But it's not their fault – it's the best they can buy for the money. It's the planters getting greedy and taking fourth and fifth pickings off a bush. They don't care about quality when the government have guaranteed them pre-war prices.'

Lexy belted out a laugh. 'Clarrie, you're wasted in a teashop. I divvn't follow the half of it, but if it was up to me, you'd be running the Board o' Trade.'

They never mentioned Will once, until Clarrie was on the point of leaving. Lexy squeezed her arm. 'He'll be canny, divvn't you worry about the lad. He's got himself out of plenty scrapes before.'

That night, Clarrie climbed into Herbert's bed,

grateful for the sound of movement above where the secretaries were billeted. They kept to themselves, wary of the widow below, whose house they were appropriating. She hugged the pillow that still smelled of Herbert. The dull weight that she had carried around all day rose up inside and caught in her throat. The grief she had held in check since Herbert's death suddenly engulfed her, triggered by Will's going. She wept, huge racking sobs, for the loss of her affectionate, diffident husband who had shown such courage through his long illness. And she wept for Will because she could do nothing to protect him; kind, loyal, loving Will, who lit up her life as if he were her own son.

A week later, Clarrie returned to the house early feeling overtired, to find two men in Herbert's study sorting through books. When she challenged them they said they were valuers from an auction house.

'I have no intention of selling my husband's books,' Clarrie protested.

The senior man said with an embarrassed look, 'You'll have to speak to Mr Stock about it.'

'But he's dead,' Clarrie cried in confusion.

The man's expression turned pitying. 'Mr Bertram Stock. He has appointed us to deal with his father's effects.'

Fuzzy-headed though she felt, Clarrie went straight round to Bertie's office and demanded to see him at once.

'What is the meaning of this? I've said nothing about selling Herbert's books. I want to keep them for Will – he's had no chance to choose anything.' Clarrie railed for several minutes, infuriated by Bertie's insouciance. He picked at his nails with a letter opener, hardly glancing up. Finally he held up his hand.

'When you've quite finished your hysterical outburst, perhaps you'd care to sit down?' He flicked his hand at the seat opposite his huge red-leather-covered desk without getting up.

Clarrie sat rigid with indignation. He surveyed her.

'I've been trying to get you to talk about legal matters since my father passed away,' he said as if it were her fault.

'I'm not ready,' Clarrie replied. 'I don't wish to rush into anything. It's too soon. You have no right to try to sell off Herbert's things.'

'I have every right,' he said with a satisfied look. 'All Papa's possessions belong to me – the books, the furniture, the house.'

Clarrie gawped at him in incomprehension. 'That's not possible.'

'Perfectly possible,' he said. 'I've been managing his affairs for years, remember.'

'The business, yes,' Clarrie said, 'but not his personal things.'

'Everything,' Bertie said, with a malicious smile. 'I made sure of that when he signed over power of attorney.'

Clarrie was stunned. 'You tricked him,' she cried. 'You've tricked me!'

'No,' Bertie said, leaning across the desk with eyes narrowed. 'All my father's things are mine by right. Do you think I'd let you keep what belonged to him and my dear mother? You, the housekeeper?'

Clarrie rose out of her seat, glaring. 'I don't care about any of it for myself—'

'Good,' he interrupted, 'then you won't mind the army taking over the rest of the house. I've renegotiated the requisitioning of the entire building. When they're done with it, I intend to sell. It will always be tainted in my eyes by you – your vulgar Anglo-Indian taste and your attempts to usurp my mama.'

Clarrie flinched at his vitriol. 'Why do you hate me so much? I made your father happy.'

'I don't hate you,' Bertie said with a contempt-uous look. 'I don't feel anything towards you.'

'And what about Will?' she demanded. 'It's his home and his inheritance too.'

'My brother will be adequately provided for; I shall see to that,' Bertie said brusquely.

Clarrie's heart raced uncomfortably. 'What about the investments you made on my behalf?'

He looked suddenly awkward. 'Ah yes, those.' He cleared his throat. 'They were sound investments at the time, but with the war – they've lost their value. You can only hope they will pick up afterwards.'

Clarrie's head throbbed as she tried to take in

what he was saying. Dread suddenly clawed at her insides. 'Herbert's Tea Rooms,' she gasped, 'at least they must be mine?'

Bertie could hardly keep the smile of triumph from his face. 'I'm afraid not,' he answered.

Clarrie swayed forward, gripping the desk in disbelief. 'You vindictive bastard!' she cried.

Bertie sat back in his chair with a flicker of alarm.

'Still your father's daughter,' he sneered, 'with the language of the barrack room.'

She swallowed down bile. 'So you'd throw me out on the street, would you? Is that what Verity wants? Is that the thanks I get for being kind to your children?'

Bertie reverted to his brusque tone. 'I'm intending no such thing. I want to make you a proposition. You continue to manage the tea room and I will pay you a reasonable salary and allow you to live rent free in the upstairs flat.'

Clarrie looked at him dumbfounded. With one breath he insulted and humiliated her and with the next expected her to be grateful when he offered her what was rightfully hers.

'You have a nerve!'

'The choice is yours – manage it or I'll sell up.'

Clarrie saw bitterly that she had no choice. All the time she had been slaving to build up her business he had been plotting to steal it. She clenched her teeth to stop herself retching. She managed to hiss, 'Lexy lives upstairs, remember?'

'Then she will have to leave,' he said indifferently.

'If you try to evict her, I'll see you have a riot on your hands,' Clarrie cried.

Again uncertainty crossed his face. 'Well, I'm sure you can come to some accommodation with that woman if you must. How you run the café will be your concern, as long as it makes me a profit.'

'Profit?' Clarrie spat out the word. 'In this climate it'll be a miracle to keep it going.'

'Then produce me a miracle,' he said.

Clarrie rushed blindly from the office, head pounding. She was gripped by fear. How had Herbert produced such a selfish, cruel son? He would spin in his grave if he knew what Bertie had done. If only Will were there to fight on her behalf, she agonised. But Will was far away, moving up to the Front, and could do nothing to help even if he knew. As so often before, Clarrie was going to have to fight her own battles.

Out in the September air, dizzy with panic, Clarrie staggered forward and vomited into the gutter.

CHAPTER 34

1917

Clarrie said nothing of her troubles in the chatty letters she wrote to Will. She had moved into the flat above the café because it was more convenient for work, she explained. She and Lexy would be company for each other. In fact, Clarrie quickly realised that Lexy's cheerful banter and brusquely caring manner were just the tonic she needed in the aftermath of Herbert's death and being evicted from Summerhill by Bertie. She found that she hardly missed the old house.

Her main worry was keeping the café going. She had kept from almost everyone, even Olive and Jack, her new precarious situation, not wanting it known that Herbert had left her so vulnerable. Only her old trusted friends Lexy and Ina knew.

By early summer, the price of flour, sugar and tea

had risen to new heights. Clarrie was increasingly relying on tinned foods to supplement their meals and meaty drinks in place of cocoa and coffee. Daniel Milner's business was under strain as, with soaring prices, customers deserted, his vans and horses were requisitioned and his workforce was decimated by conscription. He had gone to tribunal at the end of 1916 to have Jack exempted from war service, arguing successfully that his business would collapse without him. On a rare visit just before Christmas, Clarrie had found Olive nearly sick with relief.

'Now I can sleep easy at night knowing Jack's safe from the call-up. I don't care if it's selfish. I'm not like you, Clarrie. I'd never cope on me own.'

Clarrie kept her own troubles to herself, saddened at the gulf between them. These days, she and Olive had so little in common that they did not know what to say to each other. She saw the relief in her sister's eyes when she got up to leave. There had been no invitation to share Christmas with Olive and her family, Olive telling her hastily that they would be spending it at Jack's mother's. Clarrie masked her hurt and decided to keep away. It was Lexy who, along with her sisters, made Clarrie's first Christmas without Herbert or Will bearable by inviting Ina and her family round. They pooled their food and small gifts and ended up with a sing-song, Ina's youngest playing the mouth organ. It was a long way from the genteel drawing room and party games of Summerhill or Tankerville Terrace, but it lifted Clarrie's spirits more surely than any tonic.

As business worsened, Clarrie and Lexy closed the extra meeting rooms in the next-door annexe and rented them out to lodgers from the munitions works. That spring, Cousin Lily died and Jared closed the Cherry Tree, his heart no longer in it. Business had been dwindling since the government had restricted drinking hours and liquor was harder to come by. He appeared at the tea room one day for his dinner. Clarrie welcomed him in. Sheepishly, he handed her over a cloth-wrapped parcel.

'Found this at the bottom of Lily's wardrobe,' he said. 'I'm that sorry – hope it still works.'

Unwrapping it, Clarrie found Olive's old violin, the one that had belonged to her father.

'She never sold it after all?' Clarrie exclaimed. 'Fancy keeping it all this time! Why on earth did she do that?'

Jared shrugged. 'She was jealous of you lasses – wanted a bit of what you had. I reckon you ganin' off to the Stocks was the last straw. She was worse after you went. But I swear I didn't know about the fiddle.'

'Don't worry. It's all too far in the past to get angry over. Worse things happen at sea, as Father would have said.'

'Talking of which,' Jared sighed, 'the Navy have called up Harrison. They must be scraping the bottom of the barrel.'

Clarrie thought the violin might rekindle some of the lost affection between her and Olive, but her sister showed little interest in the rediscovered instrument. She had stopped playing long ago. She was preoccupied with worry that the Tyneside Tea Company might go out of business and Jack be unemployed or, worse still, conscripted. His mother was finding the boisterous George too tiring and spending more time with Thomas and Annie's baby son, while Jane was proving as delicate as Olive had been and prone to asthma attacks.

'Bring them to the café and we'll keep George entertained,' Clarrie offered, but Olive never did.

After Jared's appearance with the missing fiddle, he came two or three times a week, often just to sit and queue to read the newspaper, make a cup of Bovril last an hour and chat to other customers. There was much excitement amongst the ILP about the bloodless revolution in Russia and the ceasefire on the Eastern Front. They speculated all summer about its bringing the wider war to an end, but fighting in France appeared as relentless as the summer before.

Clarrie went about her work as cheerfully as she could, but underneath she felt an ever-present tension at the thought of Will on the Western Front. When a much longed for letter or postcard arrived, she would experience a heady sense of relief. But it was always short-lived. He had been safe at the time of writing, but what now? she would fret.

Guess what? he wrote one time. *Last week I was sent with a message to HQ and who should I meet but someone who knew you in India! Colonel Harry Wilson. He's a real veteran, one of the few regular soldiers from before the war that you don't often come across. He was only a subaltern when you knew him, but he said you had kindly entertained him at Belgooree. It was strange how the subject came up. He said he had a good friend from my part of the world, Wesley Robson. He was bowled over when I told him I knew him too! Col Wilson says Wesley has been conscripted, so perhaps he'll be joining us out here shortly. The Colonel said to pass on warm regards to you and your sister. He particularly said to ask after Olive and was she still painting? Isn't it a small world?*

The letter left Clarrie shaking, as if the past had reached out and touched her with ghostly fingers. Harry Wilson! She thought of Olive's girlish crush on the red-headed soldier and the time they had gone to watch him fish while her sister painted. That day Wesley had argued irreconcilably with her father and the row had exacerbated Jock's destructive addiction to liquor and opium. How strangely their lives were intertwined. The war had tossed them all about like jacks in the air, carelessly displacing them. Now even the charmed Wesley had been plucked from his comfortable life and sent into the fray. She wondered if Henrietta – his wife now? – lay awake fretting about him in some London mansion.

Clarrie debated whether to call on Olive and show her the letter. It might make her sister laugh at the memory, or it might make her cross for being reminded of Belgooree. Olive refused to talk about their old life in front of Jack and the Brewises as if she was ashamed that they had once led an existence so alien and eccentric. But before Clarrie could make up her mind, Jack appeared at the tea room asking to see her.

He hovered in the doorway, looking awkward.

'Is it Olive?' Clarrie asked in panic. 'Are the children all right?'

'Aye, they're canny,' Jack said hastily. His look was restless, uncomfortable.

'Come to the back,' Clarrie said, leading him to an empty table and calling to Edna to bring tea.

'There's no need,' he said, 'I'll not be stopping.'

'I need,' Clarrie said, with a brief smile. 'You can watch me drink if you like.'

They sat down opposite each other in embarrassed silence. The tea arrived. Jack took a sip and cleared his throat.

'Olive doesn't know I'm here. She'd go light if she did. But I'm worried about her – how she'll manage.'

'Manage what?' Clarrie asked, putting down her cup.

'I've had me call-up papers again.'

'But you're exempted!'

Jack shook his head. 'New rules. There's nowt Mr

Milner can do about it. This time I have to gan.' He met her look for the first time. 'I'm not afraid – I'd have gone the first time if Mr Milner hadn't put his oar in. But our Olive, she's ganin' to pieces over the thought of me leaving.'

Clarrie's insides knotted. 'Oh, Jack, I'm so sorry. And poor Olive. When will you go?'

'Have to report to barracks tomorra.'

'So soon?' she gasped.

'There's a need,' he said tensely. 'But I'm not bothered for meself. It's Olive and the bairns. Will you look out for them?'

'Course I will,' she said at once. She saw him struggling to say more.

'We've not been good to you,' he said. 'I let you and Olive grow apart.'

'That wasn't your doing,' Clarrie said gently.

'Aye, some of it was.' He looked round, then hunched his shoulders and lowered his voice. 'When I realised you didn't care for me – not enough to wed – me pride was hurt. I thought one way to get back at you was courting your sister.'

Clarrie flushed. 'You shouldn't be saying this.'

'Let me finish,' he said. 'It might've started as a game, but in time it changed. I grew to care for Olive more and more. The day we wed was the happiest in me life.' He held her gaze. 'I love your sister more than anyone in this world.'

'I'm glad,' Clarrie gulped. 'And I've never doubted it.'

'But she does,' Jack said, his fair face creased with anxiety. 'Even after all this time – with two bairns of our own – she can't believe that I could love her more than you. So I've been harder on you than I should've, just to prove to Olive that I love her best. And that's why she doesn't like you coming round when I'm there. She's jealous of you, Clarrie.'

'No!' Clarrie exclaimed.

'It's true. I used to be too,' he confessed.

'But why?' Clarrie was bewildered.

'You were always falling on yer feet – working for the Stocks, then marrying Mr Herbert and living in the big posh house, running yer own business. Seemed like you could do anything you put yer mind to.'

'Everything I've done has been from hard graft.'

'Aye, maybe's.' Jack shrugged. 'What I do know is that we're all in the same boat now – all hanging on to our businesses by the fingernails. Doesn't seem to matter if you're a posh Stock or a working-class Brewis.'

Clarrie was tempted to tell him how much more precarious was her position than his. At least, thanks to Milner's generosity, he and Olive owned the roof over their heads. But she could see he was overwrought with worry about his family. What was there to be gained by burdening him with more?

He went on. 'Mr Milner's promised to keep me job open for when the war's over and Olive will have me army pay. It's not the money so much. But she needs someone to be strong for her and the bairns – and Mam's that busy with Thomas and Annie's little lad.'

Clarrie reached out and put a hand on his arm. 'Stop worrying. I'll keep an eye on them. They're my own flesh and blood, remember?'

Briefly he touched her hand with his own. 'Ta, Clarrie. And I'm sorry for any bad feeling between us.' He stood up quickly and fixed on his hat. 'There's one other thing, in case you don't know. Bertie Stock is no longer Mr Milner's solicitor – hasn't been for some time.'

'No, I didn't know,' Clarrie answered, eyes widening. 'Why is that?'

Jack hesitated. 'Company can't afford his fees, for one thing.'

'And?' Clarrie probed.

Jack looked awkward. 'Mr Milner never got on with him like he did with Mr Herbert. Never trusted him.'

'Why was that?'

'You hear things.' Jack shrugged. 'And he advised the company badly – made investments on our behalf that came to nowt. Mr Milner told him he could be rash with his own money but not with other people's.'

Clarrie let out a groan. 'He did the same with me.'

Jack gave her a look of surprise. 'Well, Mr Milner could recommend another solicitor. You don't have to stick with Bertie Stock just out of loyalty.'

'I wish it were that simple,' Clarrie said quietly.

He looked perplexed. 'Isn't it?'

Clarrie shook her head. Now was not the time to unburden herself of how she had nothing left to invest, her only possession of worth was a set of emerald jewellery that Herbert had once given her, and it was Bertie who owned the café and paid her wage.

'Well, from what I hear,' Jack said, 'you must be one of the few clients he's got left.'

Clarrie's insides clenched. She might not care about Bertie's business, but she cared that the café remained solvent. Still, he was married to a Landsdowne and no doubt his in-laws would bail him out if necessary.

'Thank you for the warning,' she said.

With a nod and a flicker of his old dimpled smile, he stepped away. 'Take care of yersel', Clarrie.'

'And you too, Jack.' She watched him hurry from the café.

Clarrie waited until the following week before going round to see Olive, so that her sister would not be suspicious about the timing. It was young George who answered the door. Clarrie heard Jane crying fretfully in the background. Following the source of the noise, she found her niece sitting in her own mess on the hearth mat, the kitchen untidy and the fire out.

Picking up Jane and trying to calm her, she looked around in alarm.

'Where's Mammy?' she asked the small boy.

'In bed,' George said. 'Mammy's sick of her life. Jane's stinky, isn't she, Aunt Clarrie?'

'Just a bit,' Clarrie agreed, pulling a face and holding her nose. George copied her and giggled.

'You help me find her some clean clothes,' Clarrie instructed, rummaging through a basketful of unironed clothing, most of it Jack's. She cleaned up the baby at the sink and dressed her in a pair of George's britches. The boy produced a piece of dry crust from the bread bin and handed it to his sister. Jane grabbed it and chewed hard, her whimpering stopping abruptly.

Clarrie smiled. 'Good lad. Now let's see to your mammy.'

Olive was lying under the covers with the curtains drawn. Clarrie could hear her wheezing, laboured breathing. Quickly she went to her sister, clutching Jane in one arm. 'How long have you been like this?'

'J-Jack,' Olive panted, 'g-gone.'

'I know,' Clarrie said, smoothing back Olive's damp hair. 'Let me help you sit up. George, go and get Mammy a cup of water. Do you think you can manage?'

The boy nodded and darted away. Placing the baby on the bed and giving her a reassuring smile, Clarrie hauled Olive into a sitting position and began rubbing her back. Her sister was shaking violently; she coughed and choked, trying feebly to push her away.

'Slowly. Deep breaths. Don't worry,' Clarrie murmured.

'W–want Jack!' Olive gasped. 'N–not y–you.'

'Well it's me you've got,' Clarrie said more brusquely, alarmed by her sister's capitulation to her fears. 'And the world hasn't come to an end so stop acting as if it has. Jack's not dead; he's been called up. By the time George comes back with that water I want you to have calmed yourself, do you hear? You're frightening him and you're frightening me.'

Olive was so startled by Clarrie's sudden bluntness that she did as she was told. Her breathing calmed and the trembling lessened. Jane began to crawl over her mother and grab her hair. Olive protested but Clarrie tickled the girl and made her shriek with delight. George returned and held up a cup sloshing with water to his mother. His grin was so like his father's that Clarrie's heart squeezed in pity.

'Clever lad,' she praised him. 'Just what Mammy needs.' She encouraged Olive to drink.

'Is Mammy not sick any more?' he asked hopefully.

Clarrie saw tears welling in her sister's dark-ringed eyes. 'No, she's not sick, pet. She's sad about Dadda not being here. But we'll cheer her up, won't we?'

George clambered on to the bed and put his arms round his mother's neck.

'Don't be sad, Mammy.' He gave her a noisy kiss.

Olive sat rigid. Clarrie held her breath, fearing her sister would push the boy away. Then Olive let go a deep sob and her arm went round her small son in a desperate hug. Her face was tense with pain as her look met Clarrie's.

'Oh, Clarrie, how will I manage?' she whispered.

Clarrie put a hand out and squeezed her shoulder. 'One day at a time, that's how.'

CHAPTER 35

1918

With constant reassurance and support from Clarrie, Olive rallied and did her best to keep her house and family going in Jack's absence. Clarrie, mindful of her sister's fragile mental state, spent alternate nights at the Lemington house, helping with the children and calming Olive when panic overwhelmed her.

Rationing came in and Jack's wages seemed to shrink as the year wore on. Olive spent long hours queuing for food, leaving the children at the tea house in Clarrie's care. The bright and friendly children were a constant source of amusement to the staff and Clarrie was grateful for their easy acceptance of their disrupted life. She adored them.

Their lively chatter was a distraction from the unrelenting worry of dwindling supplies, higher prices and bad news on the war front. That spring brought a new German offensive in Flanders. The country was jaded from months of deprivation, hunger and long hours at gruelling work in mines and factories. But it was the grief of so many lost that caused despair and tempers to fray. Everyone knew someone killed in battle or lost at sea. And they carried around the dread of the stark War Office telegram telling them of further loss.

Olive would physically shake every time the postman paused in the street outside her door, torn between wanting a letter from Jack and fear that the delivery would bring the worst possible news. Yet both Jack and Will appeared to be surviving trench life with a stoic cheerfulness at odds with the mood at home.

The tea room had always been a hotbed of debate, even with government restrictions on meetings and dissent, but now people openly began to criticise the conduct of the war, from the Prime Minister's refusal to let American President Wilson broker a peace to the army generals' squandering of so many lives. There were strikes over factory conditions and riots over bread prices. All of it was openly discussed around the tea tables at Herbert's, despite the paucity of the menu and the weakness of the tea.

'What's it all been for?' men would ask.

'I hear they're striking in Germany too.'

'Starving, I heard.'

Others muttered with wary glances over their

shoulders, 'Maybe there really will be revolution like in Russia.'

For Clarrie such concerns came secondary to keeping the café open and her staff employed. Bertie, who had paid her a good wage at the beginning and left her to her own devices, had been badgering her for months to make economies. In the light of what Jack had told her, Clarrie suspected he was trying to squeeze money from the café to cover shortfalls elsewhere. But he and Verity had always been wantonly extravagant and no doubt resented the reduced lifestyle that war had brought even to the rich.

He never came near the tea room. Business was conducted by brief, hectoring letters with hints of 'unfortunate consequences' if she did not cut costs. Since January, wages had been paid late, but Clarrie had taken comfort in the thought that Bertie needed the tea room too much to let it go under.

Then in April Bertie stopped paying her altogether. Alarmed, she went to his office. It was the first time she had been back since her humiliation after Herbert's death. She had had no social contact with either Bertie or Verity; they had cut her off like a cancerous limb. When Verity's father had died the previous year, she had written a letter of condolence but received no reply. Apart from missing seeing the twins, their snubbing of her suited Clarrie. She had no appetite for a confrontation with Bertie or being the butt of Verity's waspish remarks. But this was an emergency.

Clarrie hammered on the peeling office door several times before it dawned on her that it was locked. She peered in the window and saw with shock that the secretary's room was empty of furniture and its floor bare. She stood back, wondering for a moment if she had gone to the wrong building, but she recognised the dolphin-shaped door knocker that Herbert had chosen, now tarnished green with neglect.

Unease gripped her. There was nothing for it but to go to Jesmond and confront Bertie at home. Saving the tram fare, she walked across the town moor to the elegant suburb. But even this part of town looked jaded from war, its streets empty of traffic and paint peeling from doors and window frames.

To Clarrie's dismay, she found the house in Tankerville Terrace shuttered and silent. When she knocked at a neighbour's door, a maid was happy to gossip.

'Haven't been here since Christmas. Said they can't get the staff to keep it running, but between me, you and the gatepost,' she said, arching her brows, 'I heard they were having difficulties.'

'Difficulties?' Clarrie queried.

The woman nodded. 'Financial. Mr Raine – that's our butler – he's friendly with their one – or was until they shut up the house. Anyway, Mr Raine says they'd lost money cos of the war and they couldn't afford to keep all them staff – not when folk can get better wages elsewhere.'

'But what of Mr Stock's clients?'

She shrugged. 'I wouldn't know about that.'

'So where have they gone?' Clarrie asked anxiously.

'Up country some place. Let me think of the name. Something Towers.' She frowned.

'Rokeham Towers?' Clarrie said.

'That's it!' the maid cried. Clarrie gave a groan of disbelief. The woman surveyed her with a pitying nod. 'Yes, I'm sorry to be the one to tell you, but you'll not get a job with the Stocks. You were after a job, weren't you?' She suddenly looked unsure, as if she had said too much.

Clarrie looked down at her worn shoes and patched coat. Over the past two years she had shared out her good clothes with her staff. She could hardly blame the woman for mistaking her for an out-of-work servant rather than the manager of a tea room.

She nodded. 'Thank you for your help.'

'Any time,' the maid said cheerily and watched her walk away up the street.

That evening, Clarrie sat down and wrote to Bertie, asking for payment of wages, and sent the letter care of Rokeham Towers. Three days later, she received a curt reply informing her that Bertie could no longer afford to pay her or the staff and that he was putting the tea room up for sale.

'He can't do that!' she fulminated to Lexy.

'Just watch him,' Lexy grunted. She was unusually subdued. 'I'm surprised we've lasted this long. No one in their right mind is ganin' to buy a tea house just now.'

Somehow, Lexy got hold of some home-distilled liquor and later Clarrie found her drunk and tearful in the back lane. Olive, who had come to collect the children, helped get her upstairs and into bed without fuss.

'What's this all about?' Olive demanded. 'Why's Lexy ganin' on about Bertie selling off the tea room when it's yours?' Clarrie's stricken look made her gasp, 'It is yours, isn't it?'

After a long moment, Clarrie shook her head. 'Sit down, Olive. It's time I told you.' Briefly, she spoke of Bertie's treachery, and how he had taken everything from her except her personal possessions.

'But the tea room?' Olive said in bewilderment. 'It means everything to you. He has no right.'

She looked white-faced with anxiety and Clarrie feared she would crumple into one of her trembling states of fear. 'I'm sorry I had to tell you,' she said.

Olive stood up. 'No, it's me who's sorry. You shouldn't have had to face this alone. If I had been half the sister to you that you've been to me . . .'

'You've had your own problems,' Clarrie murmured.

'Don't try to make excuses for me,' Olive said, shaking her head. 'All my life you've been protecting me and looking out for me and I've never been grateful enough.' Her look was harrowed. 'At times I hated you for it – couldn't wait to get away from you and Summerhill — wanted to prove to myself that I could run me own life without you.'

Clarrie flinched at her bluntness but said nothing. Too often she had spoken soothing words to pacify her sister's outbursts instead of simply listening.

Olive stood gripping her own arms. 'I've been so wrapped up in my own worries, it never occurred to me that you might need *me*.'

They stood holding each other's look. Softly, Clarrie said, 'I couldn't have stepped off that boat from India or got through that terrible year with Cousin Lily without you. I wouldn't have tried so hard to build a new life with the Stocks if you hadn't been with me.' Tentatively, she held out her arms. 'You were the one person I cared enough for to make myself carry on. Without you, Olive, I would have given up years ago.'

Olive let out a sob and rushed into her arms, clinging on fiercely. 'I'm so sorry,' she wept. 'I love you, Clarrie.'

Clarrie let her own tears come as she hugged her sister in relief. Their past differences and jealousies, and the hurt that had been inflicted, dissolved as they clung and cried together. Just when she seemed to be losing everything and her security was collapsing like quicksand, her sister had come back to her. It felt like sunshine breaking through storm clouds.

It was Olive who pulled away first. She fixed Clarrie with a determined eye.

'That man,' she said angrily. 'He's not going to do this to you! I'm not going to let him!'

Clarrie was heartened by Olive's fighting talk but she knew that her sister was powerless against a vindictive Bertie.

The following weeks were some of the most tense of Clarrie's life as she struggled to galvanise her staff and keep the tea room going without Bertie's money. When word got out that the café was likely to close, people came with donations of food and offers of free help. Clarrie was touched by the concern and loyalty of her customers. Daniel Milner did his best to give her credit even though his own business was teetering on the edge of failure. In order to have something to offer to his customers, he was reduced to selling tinned fish and powdered egg, and doing most of the delivering himself. Clarrie did not like to take advantage of his generosity in case there was no business for Jack to return to after the war, if it ever ended and Jack was spared.

So, despite the kindness of others, she still had to subsidise the café herself by pawning the jewellery that Herbert had bought her. By May, all she had left was her wedding ring and the pink stone that the swami had given her on her departure from India. She was determined not to sell either. But by June, with no sign of a sale and no wages, she was forced to do so.

Steeling herself to enter a pawnbroker's in town, Clarrie was almost choked with resentment and fury that Bertie had reduced her to this. She did not believe his protestations that he could not afford to pay her when he must have access to wealth through his wife. No doubt what Verity spent in an afternoon's shopping would keep the tea room going for a further month. That morning, wrenching the ring from her finger and unfastening the chain that she had had made for the swami's stone, she had almost been physically sick.

As she handed them over and took the pawnbroker's money, Clarrie rubbed her fingers one last time over the smooth pink stone and thought of the swami content to live in a hut of leaves with one cooking pot and a bedroll. The thought of the wise, dignified man with the compassionate eyes and toothless smile brought her calm. Like him she would trust that she would be given the means to survive day by day, and not worry beyond the moment.

Later that day, a letter arrived from Will with a generous cheque enclosed. Clarrie could hardly believe it.

Why did you never tell me you were in such straitened circumstances? he scolded. *You know I would gladly have helped – intend now to help as much as I can. I have a sum of money from Papa's estate and Bertie continues to pay me an allowance the way Papa did, but what use is it to me out here? You must use it to keep the tea room going, I insist on it. I'm furious with my brother for the way he has treated you and have written to tell him so. When I return we shall have it all sorted out. In the meantime I am putting things in motion to buy the tea room from him so your livelihood and home are secured. A friend of mine is shortly to get leave and I have entrusted him with making the arrangements on my behalf so matters can be resolved more swiftly. Dearest Clarrie, I can't believe that you have kept this burden to yourself for so long. Promise me you will never keep secrets from me again!*

Clarrie sat down and wept in relief. Lexy and Ina found her in the storeroom and thought she had received bad news until she managed to splutter the truth.

'You don't know what a relief it is that Will knows,' she said, crying and laughing at the same time.

'Who told him?' Ina asked.

Lexy and Clarrie exchanged looks. Lexy grinned.

'Can only be one person,' she said. 'Mrs Olive branch.'

That evening, returning to Lemington, Clarrie found Olive bathing the children in a tub in front of the fire. George was splashing and soaking the rug and Jane was copying him with noisy squeals of delight.

'I've heard from Will,' Clarrie said.

Olive looked up, startled. 'Have you?'

Clarrie knelt down beside the tub. 'Your

mammy's a tell-tale,' she said, flicking water at her nephew and niece. 'A lovely, interfering tell-tale!' She turned and threw her arms round Olive. 'Will's going to buy the tea room and it's all thanks to you.'

'Buy it?' Olive shrieked in surprise. 'That's more than I dared hope for.'

'It's true!' Clarrie laughed, fumbling for the letter in her skirt pocket.

Olive snatched it and read, letting out another scream of delight.

'See,' she said with an I-told-you-so look, 'me and Will are right. You shouldn't be too proud to share your burdens.'

'Oh, pride is it?' Clarrie gave her a wry look.

'Aye, pride,' Olive pouted. 'You're too proud by half.'

Clarrie laughed and flicked water at her sister. Olive gasped in indignation. 'Watch the letter!' She thrust it behind her and then splashed Clarrie back. The children gawped in astonished delight. Clarrie splashed again. They giggled. Suddenly they were all screaming and laughing and hurling water at each other.

After they were thoroughly soaked, the sisters lifted the children out and wrapped them in towels by the fire. Olive read them a story while Clarrie got on with making the tea. Looking out of the window at the dazzling pink flowers of the rhododendron in one of Olive's painted tubs, Clarrie's heart swelled with joy. Listening to Olive's animated voice and the children's lively questions, she was filled with a new optimism. Perhaps the swami's blessing still reached her without the pink stone.

The next morning she left early for the tea room, re-energised by the thought of Will's cheque in the bank and the plans she had. They would redecorate, giving Jared and some of the older men a job to do, plant more potatoes in the café allotment for the autumn and start a Christmas savings scheme. And she would redeem the swami's stone and her wedding ring.

It was mid-afternoon when Olive tore into the café, her hair loose, babbling incoherently. She collapsed into Clarrie's arms, shrieking, a telegram crumpled to a ball in her fist.

'Missing!' she sobbed. 'My Jack's missing!'

CHAPTER 36

Olive's new-found courage dissolved under the cruel uncertainty of what had happened to Jack. Eventually she received sketchy details from his commanding officer. He had gone missing on a night patrol that had turned into a skirmish. No one had returned. She was left in a turmoil of questioning. Was he dead or had he been captured? Was he badly injured or being badly treated?

Clarrie watched her sister torment herself with doubts and fears, helpless to lessen her suffering. No words would reassure her and no one, not even her loving children, seemed able to comfort her. Thin already, she barely ate. She could not sleep though she hardly had the energy to climb the stairs.

Once again, Clarrie shouldered the burden of caring for Olive and her family. The children became moody and difficult, prone to bouts of tears or over-boisterous play. Clarrie's heart ached for them as they tried to cope with their silent, withdrawn mother and their tired and sometimes irritable aunt.

Lexy and Ina were the biggest help, keeping the children entertained during the long weeks of George's school holidays and teasing Clarrie when she fretted too much.

Fortunately, the transfer of the café went through swiftly and without any problems. Bertie as usual did it all from a distance. She received notice by letter of the sale to the new owners, a company called Stable Trading. Clarrie smiled at Will's oblique humour. It was both a reference to their love of riding and an assurance that the business was back on an even keel. She wrote him an effusive letter of thanks, promising to work doubly hard to make good his investment.

In the middle of August, as news was filtering back of a huge counter-offensive by the Allies, Olive got word that Jack was alive.

'He's a prisoner of war,' she said tensely, showing Clarrie a letter from the Red Cross.

'Thank God!' Clarrie cried, going to embrace her.

Olive sat rigid, hands clenched in her lap. 'Thank Him for nothing,' she said bitterly. 'I know my Jack's not coming back.'

Then, as autumn arrived, the first stirrings of optimism that the war might be waning began to spread. Reports of mutiny among the German navy and peace demonstrations appeared in the news-papers. They echoed moves at home to force the pace of peace that had been gathering momentum all year but had got little coverage in the press. Clarrie had signed a Women's Peace Petition months ago, organised locally by her old friend Florence from the Co-op. Now it appeared their counterparts on the Continent were doing the same. The Allies had made gains in the latest bloody attrition at the Front and there were rumours of starvation and unrest across central Europe.

By late October the rumours had turned into a clamour. For the first time Clarrie allowed herself to hope that the war might be nearing an end.

'Likely we'll have Jack and Will back by Christmas,' she chivvied Olive, 'so you'd better practise smiling again or your face might crack at the shock.'

To her delight this produced a glimmer of a smile on Olive's gaunt grey face. But even Clarrie hardly dared believe her own words. Yet, by early November, everyone was talking about the possibility of an armistice.

It came suddenly on the eleventh. The news spread with an eruption of noise: church bells clanged and hooters blew along the riverside. People downed tools and rushed into the streets to hug and shout and dance with excitement. By the evening fireworks were showering the night sky and bonfires were set ablaze in celebration.

Clarrie and her staff served free hot drinks and

she persuaded Olive to take George and Jane out to watch the spectacle. They went to bed exhausted, leaving the lamp burning and the blackout blinds open in happy defiance. They had survived.

Three days later, when the town was still heady with the notion of peace, a message boy ran into the tea room with a telegram. Clarrie felt her knees buckle as he panted out her name.

'Please no, not now!' she gasped.

People turned to stare, their faces a mix of pity and relief that it was not for them. Lexy went to her at once and bundled her into the kitchen. 'Give it here,' she ordered. 'It's worse not knowing.'

She tore it open. Her eyes widened, then abruptly she belted out a laugh. ' "Get champers on ice we are coming home love Will." '

'What?' Clarrie gasped.

'Aye, it's from Will, not the army,' Lexy cackled.

Clarrie felt dizzy with relief. 'Iced tea if he's lucky,' she spluttered, and laughed. Then suddenly she was crying.

'Haway,' Lexy said, giving her a cuddle. 'You have a good cry. It's about time.'

In the following weeks, the first rash of euphoria soon faded. Life was just as difficult materially as before with rationing and restrictions. The population was weakened and undernourished and a particularly severe viral disease was spreading with frightening speed. Edna's mother took to her bed on a Tuesday and was dead by Sunday. George's school closed two weeks early for Christmas because staff numbers were decimated by the Spanish flu.

George caught a cold and Jane's wheezing cough returned as it did every winter. Olive was beset by a new fear that her children would die and refused to let them out of the house. She wrapped them in layers of clothing and confined them to bed, despite their protests that they were bored and wanted to play outside.

Both Olive and Clarrie waited impatiently for news of Jack's and Will's return, but the aftermath of war appeared chaotic. Men were coming back haphazardly and news from the Continent was of seething numbers of refugees, overcrowded ports and railway stations, and countless soldiers trying to make their way home.

The Sunday before Christmas, as Clarrie was bossing Olive into helping her string up some home-made streamers, she heard the latch on the back gate lift. Glancing out of the window she saw a man in a cheap, ill-fitting suit and a large hat stepping into the yard. He stopped as if unsure he was in the right place. For a moment he stood staring around him. Then he took off his hat and scratched his shaven head.

'Olive,' Clarrie said hoarsely. 'Olive!'

Her sister looked up.

'Go to the door,' Clarrie urged, 'go to the door now – you've got a special visitor.'

She saw the look change on Olive's face, her eyes lighting in half-fearful expectation. Clarrie nodded and smiled, her throat suddenly filling with tears. Olive stumbled towards the door and heaved at the latch with newly skinny hands. Clarrie watched at the window as her sister ran into the yard. Olive would have fallen over if Jack had not reached out and caught her. His unshaven face showed bewilderment, then quickly recognition. His wife had changed more than he had in the eighteen months of separation.

'Olive?' he croaked.

'Jack,' she sobbed, touching his face in disbelief.

As their arms went about each other, Clarrie turned away with a shameful stab of envy. Yet she was thankful at Jack's safe return, for her sister could not have endured much more. Olive was worn out both physically and mentally. Jack was the only one who could restore her to life. Blinking back tears, Clarrie hurried upstairs to prepare George and Jane for their father's return.

The next day, Clarrie moved back permanently to the flat above the café, although both Jack and Olive asked her to stay. But she saw how much they wanted to be left alone together. She trusted Jack to look after her sister now.

'I can't thank you enough for helping my Olive out with the bairns,' Jack said. 'I know how difficult it's been.' His look was contrite. 'She's told me everything about the tea room and what Bertie

Stock did to you. I'm that sorry, Clarrie. If we can ever help you out in return, you just have to ask.'

Clarrie left, promising to return and visit on Christmas Day. Lexy, Dolly and Ina were overjoyed to hear of Jack's safe return. But Clarrie could not hide her anxiety that there had been no word from Will about when he would be demobbed. It was well over a month since he had sent the telegram.

'Probably gone to Paris for a knees-up,' Lexy joked.

'Bet he'll just walk in the tea room whistling any day now,' Ina said.

'Aye,' Dolly agreed, 'he'll turn up like a bad penny, don't you worry. Start scrounging for food and asking when it's teatime.'

They talked and laughed about Will until Clarrie felt reassured. She just had to be more patient.

Two days before Christmas, she was helping Jared lift parsnips in the café allotment when Lexy and Ina appeared. Their breath billowed in the sharp air as they approached. Clarrie did not see their strained expressions until they were close.

Her heart jerked. 'What is it?'

They came either side of her. Ina was clutching the local newspaper. It trembled in her hands. Clarrie saw her gulping as if she were trying to speak but could not.

Lexy said, 'It doesn't make sense!' She sounded bewildered and angry.

'Tell me,' Clarrie whispered.

'There's to be a memorial service,' Lexy said. 'But they must have got it wrong.'

Ina held out the folded newspaper and pointed to a short announcement. Dread clawing at her insides, Clarrie took it and read.

A memorial service will be held for Capt. William Henry Stock in the side chapel of St Nicholas's Cathedral on Friday 27 December at 2 p.m. Capt. Stock, the younger son of the late Mr Herbert Stock, solicitor, died tragically of septicaemia on 9 December and is buried near Albert, Northern France. Mr and Mrs Bertram Stock request the attendance of family and close friends only.

The words danced in front of Clarrie's eyes. Will dead? Impossible! He had survived the war. How could he possibly have succumbed to blood poisoning after it was all over? It was not right. She would not believe it!

'No,' she gasped, shaking her head, 'no, no, no!'

She read it again. But it could only be about Will. *Her* Will. There was no other. He had been dead for two weeks and she had not known. No one had told her. How long ago had Bertie and Verity been given the terrible news? Her heart pounded so hard she could barely breathe. Her legs were suddenly too weak to support her. Lexy and Ina grabbed her arms and held her up. Jared quickly upturned a pail and guided her to sit down.

'They should have told me,' Clarrie gasped, 'not let me find out like this!' She shook the newspaper. 'How could they let me find out like *this*?'

'They're a pair of wicked selfish devils!' Lexy cried.

'Poor Mr Will,' Ina said tearfully, 'such a kind, canny lad.'

The hugeness of what had happened crashed over Clarrie like a tidal wave. She buckled forward, gripping her stomach to try to contain the pain. But she could not; it spewed out of her in a high-pitched wail.

'Oh, Will,' she sobbed, 'my darling, darling boy!'

In the bitter dank air, Clarrie rocked to and fro in distress as her friends tried to comfort her with loving arms.

CHAPTER 37

Clarrie could not wait until the memorial service to confront Bertie and discover what had happened to Will. She could neither eat nor sleep. She could not contemplate celebrating Christmas. The decorations and excitement on children's faces, the brass bands playing Christmas hymns in the street, all made her want to weep. They brought back poignant memories of a young, affectionate Will showing her his nativity scene the very first Christmas she had spent in England. She yearned for something of Will's – something tangible – that she could hold on to and remember him by.

Lexy wanted to go with her to find Bertie, but Clarrie insisted she stayed to run the café. It was Olive who volunteered Jack to support her sister in the ordeal.

'I'll not have you facing that man on your own,' a tearful Olive said. 'Jack'll take no nonsense.'

But they found the house at Tankerville still shuttered. When Clarrie enquired at the neighbouring house, there was no sign of the gossiping maid and no one knew when the Stocks were returning.

'They must still be living on the Rokeham estate,' Clarrie concluded. She wanted to go there at once, walk all the way if necessary, but she hesitated to say so. Jack's ordeal in prison had left him less robust than he had been and he tired easily. She could not jeopardise his health further when he needed to regain his strength to take up his old job at the tea company.

'We could always try Summerhill,' Jack suggested. 'Someone there might know.'

Clarrie nodded in resignation, then had an idea. Before they left Jesmond she would seek out Johnny Watson. The last she knew from Will was that his friend had qualified as a doctor and was working in an army hospital in Edinburgh. But perhaps he was home for Christmas. When Johnny came to the door, she could hardly believe her luck.

'Oh, Johnny!' she cried.

At once he gripped her hands in his and said, 'I know, I heard. It's awful, awful.'

He guided them inside and, in the quiet of his parents' drawing room, asked Clarrie what she knew. She shook her head.

'Only what I read in the newspaper,' she said with a bleak look.

'Bertie Stock never bothered to tell Clarrie in person,' Jack explained, growing breathless with indignation. 'He's never tret her like proper family. It's a disgrace.'

Johnny looked stricken. 'Tell me what I can do to help, Clarrie.'

Clarrie gave him a grateful look but shook her head. 'Just be there at the service with me.'

She left, her heart a little less sore for having seen Will's old friend. It made her feel closer to her lost stepson. But of Christmas and Boxing Day she remembered little. Numbness settled over her like a smothering blanket, distancing her from the world. She was aware of Lexy and Ina being with her – a distraught Dolly had been dispatched home to her family – but she did not take in what they said. Jared made her pea soup. Olive and Jack brought the children round as a distraction. Only George and Jane managed to reach through her defensive cocoon.

'Why are you sad, Aunt Clarrie?' Jane asked, eyeing her with curiosity.

'Cos Uncle Will's gone to heaven,' George answered for her. 'Here you are. We made this for you.'

The boy handed Clarrie a picture, the figures cleverly made out of pressed flowers and scrap pieces of cloth. It showed a tall woman on a tiny horse riding through trees.

'That's you, Aunt Clarrie,' George told her. 'I know you don't have a horse, but Mammy says you like them.'

'I want a horse too,' Jane said. 'I want to be like you.'

Overwhelmed, Clarrie hugged them both and gave Olive a grateful look.

'Aunt Clarrie, you're crying again,' Jane exclaimed. 'Don't you like it?'

'I love it,' Clarrie croaked, tears spilling down her cheeks. 'Thank you.'

At the memorial service, Clarrie was well supported. As well as Olive and Jack, there were Lexy, Ina, Dolly, Edna and Jared from the café, and Johnny and his parents. Rachel in South Shields had read about it and come to pay her respects too. The old friends hugged with emotion. They all sat together in the packed side chapel while Bertie, Verity and her brother Clive sat on the opposite side and barely nodded a greeting. Among the dozens of mourners were men in uniform from Will's regiment.

It occurred to her that Wesley might make an appearance. Will had mentioned him in some of his earlier letters but not since the spring. Most likely he had been deployed elsewhere and was now safely back in London with his wife.

Clarrie knelt down and closed her eyes, trying to summon Will's youthful grinning face to mind, but it would not come. The service began. The lump of grief in her throat was so stifling that she could not manage to sing the first hymn. Prayers followed, the sombre words ringing around the echoing stone chamber. Then they sat for the eulogy. Clarrie tensed as a uniformed man walked forward from the back of the chapel.

He turned and faced them. Her heart jolted at the sight of Wesley. His hair was closely cropped and face leaner than before, but his eyes had lost none of their vitality. They shone with emotion, almost fiercely, as he surveyed them all. Clarrie's pulse drummed as he began to speak.

'Before the war I hardly knew Will Stock. To me he was Bertie's younger brother – bashful, musical, not a sportsman, friendly but perhaps a bit too gentle for his own good. Very much in his older brother's shadow. Will did not strike me as tough enough to succeed in life. He had no ambition to go into the family firm and seemed content to settle for being a school-master.' Wesley gave a rueful smile. 'I have to admit that my heart sank a little when I discovered we would be fellow officers in the same company. I imagined that I – the older more worldly-wise man – would be the leader and protector. How wrong I was.'

He went on to tell them of Will's courage, his kindness to frightened comrades, his irrepressible good spirits and humour.

'Will was hardly ever quiet.' Wesley smiled wryly. 'If he wasn't chatting about cricket or horses or music, he was whistling tunes and singing songs. He didn't let the fact that he had no musical instrument with him hold him back. He could do impressions of a whole brass band or orchestra and raise the spirits of the most downhearted. Not once did I ever hear him complain or criticise others. I was the one who lost my temper with the men and got depressed at the conditions. It was I who railed against our lot. Will was the one who listened and sympathised, then encouraged and chivvied me out of my brown study.'

He paused, and Clarrie saw his jaw clench. 'He was wise beyond his years,' he continued. 'He showed far more common sense and sensitivity to others than many of us older men. Yet he had a childlike quality, an optimism and belief in the goodness of others that was humbling. When anyone asked him how he could remain so cheerful amid the hell of war, Will always said, "I think of home and the people I love. There lies the real world, not this madness here. They are my anchor." '

Wesley looked round the congregation, his gaze briefly meeting Clarrie's. 'Will was sustained by thoughts of his beloved Newcastle and the northern hills that he loved to ride over. But most of all he was kept going by the knowledge that he was dearly loved by so many – by his family and friends.' He hesitated, his eyes glimmering in the dim light. 'Will was a man of greatness. He would have made an excellent teacher of music. The world is a lesser – and a duller – place without him. I count myself privileged to have known him, to have served beside him and to have received his generous friendship.'

He bowed his head. Clarrie felt a sob rise up from deep inside that nearly choked her. Tears streamed silently down her face. She was amazed by Wesley's tribute, so frank and yet so tender. He had captured the spirit of his friend and by doing so had conjured up the Will she had known.

As he came by, she gave him a grateful look. He glanced at her, frowning, then gave a brief nod and strode on.

After that, Clarrie felt lifted by the music. How Will would have enjoyed it! At the end of the service they emerged into icy rain. Clarrie, seeing that Bertie and Verity were making straight for a taxi-cab without any attempt to speak to her, rushed after them.

'Bertie, please,' she cried, grabbing at his coat sleeve. 'I need to talk to you.'

He shook her off. 'I have nothing to say.'

'Why did you not tell me about Will?' she demanded.

'I have no obligation towards you,' he said with contempt.

'Hurry up, Bertie,' Verity said impatiently, 'you're letting in the rain.'

Clarrie held on to the door. 'Will's things,' she said. 'I know they will have been returned to you. Can I have something to remember him by? A keepsake – anything – his pen or a book of poetry—'

'Will's possessions will be passed on to my son Vernon – his nephew and blood relation,' he said coldly. 'Now please leave us in peace to grieve for my brother.'

He yanked the door closed and the cab moved off into the traffic. Clarrie stood shaking and staring after it in pained disbelief. Lexy and Johnny hurried up. Johnny held his umbrella over her, putting a protective arm round her shoulders.

'Forget about them,' Lexy said. 'Haway, you're wet through. Let's get you home.' She invited Johnny and his parents back to the café for refreshments. As they moved towards the tram stand, Clarrie saw Wesley break off from the huddle of uniformed men sharing a smoke together and approach her.

Rain streamed down his face into his upturned collar. He eyed her cautiously under dark furrowed brows. 'I'm so sorry about Will.'

Clarrie nodded. 'Thank you for what you said about him. It was a great comfort.'

'I was pleased to do it,' Wesley murmured. He hesitated. 'How are you?'

She wanted to say that the pain of Will's dying was like having her insides gored, that she could not imagine how she would get through the days ahead without him. That she was utterly worn out and war-weary.

'I'm getting by,' she said. 'I have good friends.'

'So I see.' He glanced at Johnny sheltering her under his umbrella. Clarrie introduced them.

'Would you like to come back to the tea room?' she asked, suddenly not wanting him to go. There were so many questions she wanted to ask about Will that he might be able to answer.

He gave a regretful smile. 'I'm afraid I can't. I have a train to catch in half an hour.'

'Back to London?'

'Yes. I shall be back on the trading floor at Mincing Lane tomorrow. It hardly seems possible that life will take up just as before.'

Clarrie's insides twisted. 'It can never be as before,' she said quietly.

'No, I suppose not.'

They held each other's look.

'Were you with Will – at the end?' Clarrie forced herself to ask.

His expression clouded. He shook his head. 'I was on a few days' leave – resting behind the lines. He died in the field hospital.'

'How did it happen – the blood poisoning?'

He gave her a sharp look. 'Don't you know?'

Clarrie shook her head. 'I've been told nothing,' she said bitterly. She saw the pity in his eyes and wished she had not spoken.

'Will cut his leg on some barbed wire. He didn't tell anyone. He wasn't the type to make a fuss. It went septic. They were going to have to amputate, but he died before they could.'

Clarrie groaned, feeling suddenly faint. Johnny gripped her round the waist to steady her.

'Come on, Clarrie, you need to sit down,' he said. 'I'll pay for a cab.'

Swiftly, Wesley nodded and exchanged polite goodbyes. He returned to his comrades. Clarrie, supported by Johnny and Lexy, allowed her friends to lead her away.

CHAPTER 38

1919

Herbert's Tea Rooms were Clarrie's lifeline in the months that followed. She did not allow herself to think beyond each week, planning her days around the needs of the café. Slowly, she began to pull it round from its precarious wartime position. Olive, who was rediscovering her love of painting, helped her redecorate with a more modern Egyptian design.

Through sheer hard work and stubborn determination to persevere, Milner's tea delivery business had also survived and with Jack's help was beginning to pick up again. They gave Clarrie generous credit terms and she was able to offer quality teas once more. To her relief, Stable Trading allowed her to continue running the business as she saw fit, despite Will's death. They kept her rent low and did not interfere, merely asking for accounting details at the month's end, which she sent to an address in North Shields. Somehow, Will appeared to have secured the company so that Bertie could not get his hands on it, for she was sure that if he had, the grasping man would have sold it from under her once more.

Rumours abounded about Bertie's financial difficulties. Lexy's sister Sarah, who had once worked for Verity, heard that the Tankerville house was up for sale. Summerhill had changed hands. Back in February, Jared had spotted in the newspaper that it had sold at auction. Gossip reached the tea house that Bertie had fallen out with Clive Landsdowne over some investments and that the Stocks were no longer welcome at Rokeham Towers. Dolly had heard that Bertie and Verity were back in town living in a small terraced house in South Gosforth with one maid-of-all-work. Clarrie could only imagine how ill-suited Verity would be to such reduced circumstances. Yet there were many a well-to-do who had lost a lot more, their pre-war stocks and shares worth only a fraction of their former value.

Clarrie was determined not to go under and would have worked herself to a standstill if Lexy had not forced her to take time off to sleep. By summer, they had reopened the downstairs annexe as meeting rooms and the tea room's reputation as a place of affordable glamour and radical talking shop was revived.

But it was the times when the café was closed that she found hardest to cope with, and many was the night she lay awake exhausted yet sleepless, grieving for Will and wondering what the future would bring. Olive and Jack were happily bringing up their children. Ina was talking of retiring and going to live with her son in Cullercoats. Jared, to everyone's surprise, had started courting Lexy – taking her to the pictures for the Wednesday matinee – and, to their greater surprise, Lexy was encouraging his attentions.

'He's kind to me,' Lexy told Clarrie. 'Give me a canny man over bonny looks any day.'

Clarrie was glad for them all, but it left her feeling restless and wondering if running the tea room was to be her lot in life for ever. And if so, would it always be enough? She was thirty-three, widowed, childless and living in a country that was not her spiritual home but which she had come to love.

Olive, alert to her sister's underlying sadness, tried to involve her in their family life and was constantly inviting her round. One Sunday when she joined them, Olive turned to Jack and said, 'Tell our Clarrie what Mr Milner wanted.'

Jack nodded. 'The boss was wondering if you could help him out with the horses.'

'Horses?' Clarrie queried.

'Aye, the ones that are past workin'. Three or four that were used by the government in the war are now too old to pull a load. Mr Milner hasn't the heart to send them to the knacker's yard, so he keeps them on a farm near Wylam.'

'Like a home for retired ponies,' Olive said.

Clarrie smiled. 'What a kind man he is. Does he take worn-out tea room managers as well?'

Jack grinned. 'He wondered if you would do him a favour and gan out there once in a while – give them a bit of a walk out.'

Clarrie felt her interest spark. 'Course I would.'

After that, she went once a week to the Wylam stables to help groom and exercise the horses. They were stocky but docile and Clarrie never took them far or rode them at more than a trot, but she grew to relish her Mondays there. Daniel Milner had come to an arrangement with the landowner to stable his old horses alongside half a dozen thoroughbreds.

'They've worked hard all their lives,' Milner told Clarrie cheerfully, 'so why shouldn't they enjoy a bit of God's fresh air now?'

One Monday morning in early September, when Clarrie was getting ready to go to Wylam, Edna came running up the stairs to the flat shouting for her.

'There's a lad downstairs asking for you,' she told her breathlessly.

Clarrie made an impatient noise, reluctant to be delayed.

'Well, he was askin' for Clarissa Belhaven. But we put two and two together.'

'Really?' Clarrie turned in surprise. No one had called her that for many a year. 'Who is he?'

Edna hesitated. 'Sounds foreign. Canny lookin',' she grinned. 'Looks a bit like you.'

'Me?' Clarrie snorted.

'Aye, Indian lookin'.' Edna pulled her towards the door. 'Haway, don't keep a good-looking lad waitin'.'

Intrigued, Clarrie hurried after the impatient Edna. Sitting at a table in the window sipping tea was a young Indian with a broad face and well-groomed dark hair, wearing a cheap blue serge suit. As soon as he saw her, he stood up to greet her with a wide smile. There was something oddly familiar about him, but Clarrie could not think what. She was sure she had never met him before.

He shook her hand with a polite bow. 'I am Arif Kapur from Bengal. Very pleased to meet you.'

'Mr Kapur.' Clarrie smiled. 'How can I help you?'

'I am coming with greetings from my great-uncle Kamal,' he explained.

Clarrie's heart thudded in shock. 'Kamal!' she exclaimed. 'You are Kamal's great-nephew?'

He nodded. 'He is telling me all about you. Since I was a boy, Uncle Kamal is always telling stories of Belhaven sahib and life in Assam.'

Clarrie held on to his hand as if to assure herself that he was not a dream. 'Tell me, is Kamal still alive?'

Arif gave an Indian nod of the head. 'Yes, alive. He is blind but his mind is sharp and he is still telling stories.'

Clarrie felt overwhelmed. Sudden tears stung her eyes and she pressed her hands to her mouth to stop herself crying out. Arif looked alarmed.

'I'm sorry to upset you.'

'No, no you haven't,' Clarrie was quick to reassure him. 'It's just such a shock after all this time. I had thought never to hear from Kamal again.'

She gestured for Arif to sit down and drew out the chair opposite. 'Did he ever get my letters? I wrote to him for the first couple of years. How is he? Is he happy? Has he ever been back to Assam? Does he hear from Ama and her family? Tell me all about yours. I want to hear everything!'

Arif laughed and tried to answer the questions that came tumbling out of Clarrie like a river in flood. Kamal was happy and well respected in his village for his wisdom and knowledge of the world beyond. He used to ride round the countryside on Prince until his sight went and the pony died. Arif did not think he had ever been back to Belgooree or heard anything of Ama. But Kamal had kept Clarrie's letters and when Arif had joined the Indian army and been posted to France, his great-uncle had urged him to seek out the Belhaven sisters should he get to England.

'Just ask in Newcastle, Uncle said. Miss Clarissa will be doing something with tea.' He grinned. 'It only took me two days to find you.'

Clarrie gave him a watery smile. 'And are you still in the army?'

Arif shook his head. 'I am going back to India to study science. Uncle Kamal is paying my fees. I want to work in the forestry service. He says I am loving trees because of his stories about Belgooree and Khassia hills.'

Clarrie's heart squeezed to hear him speak the familiar names. She felt a bittersweet longing for her old home and envy at the young man's impatience to get back to India. She recognised the homesickness in his eyes.

Her own eyes shone as she spoke. 'I wish I could go with you.'

Clarrie cancelled her trip to the stables and took Arif to see Olive. Her sister was equally taken aback but less shaken by his appearance. She reminisced as if Belgooree was some dim, far-off childhood place that she found hard to recall in any detail. It struck Clarrie forcefully how much Olive had taken to life on Tyneside. This was her home now and she had no hankering to travel or return to India.

Arif stayed for a few days, lodging in the annexe with Jared until it was time for him to leave. He had arranged to work his passage on a cargo boat to London and then on by steamship. Clarrie took him down to the quayside and saw him safely aboard with a letter for Kamal and some samples of tea from the Tyneside Tea Company.

'I know it's a bit like carrying coals to Newcastle, but I know how much your great-uncle likes his teas. Tell him these are my favourites and make him guess the blends before you tell him,' she teased. She shook his hand warmly. 'And give him my fondest regards.'

The days that followed were unsettling ones. Arif had reawoken her past and stirred her restless nature. She was distracted at work, and it was Lexy who told her bluntly, 'For pity's sake, lass! You've a face like a bucket of clarts. You're scaring off the customers. Tak' the day off and gan to the stables. Tell yer troubles to them horses.'

So, although it was Friday and the café was busy, Clarrie allowed Lexy to chase her out. Taking the train upriver to Wylam, she felt gradually better as the shipyards and factories gave way to woodland and the sun shimmered on the first yellowing leaves.

The stable boy greeted her in surprise. 'Didn't expect you the day,' he said nervously.

'Do you mind?' she asked.

'The landlord's visitin', that's all.'

'I won't get in the way,' Clarrie promised. 'I'll just take Florrie up the hill for an hour.'

She went into the gloom of the stables and made straight for Florrie's stall. The horse whinnied in recognition. Clarrie put her arms around her neck and buried her face in the warm flank. One of the most comforting smells in the world was that of warm horseflesh and hay. She thought of how Kamal had continued to ride her beloved Prince until the pony died, and began to weep.

A noise or movement made her suddenly aware

that she was not alone. Someone at the far end of the stables was checking over one of the thoroughbred mares. He was too tall for one of the stable hands. He stopped to watch her, and then came forward. Clarrie hurriedly wiped away her tears. Only when he was almost upon her did she realise who it was. She stared open-mouthed in disbelief. Wesley, dressed in riding breeches and jacket, stood looking down at her.

'Mr Robson!' she gasped. 'What are you doing here?'

'The same as you, I imagine.'

She continued to gaze at him in bewilderment. 'B-but here?' she stammered. 'I thought you were in London.'

'I've come north to see to business, tie up some loose ends,' he replied. 'Are you all right?'

She glanced away, stretching out a hand to pat Florrie.

'I'm sorry if my appearance upsets you,' he said. 'I thought you only came here on a Monday. I wouldn't have come if I'd known.'

Clarrie gave him a sharp look. 'How do you know so much about this place?'

Wesley gave a familiar sardonic smile. 'I own it.'

She gawped at him. Just then the stable lad appeared.

'Do you want me to saddle up Paladin, sir?'

'Yes, please, Tom.' Wesley eyed Clarrie. 'Would you care to ride with me, Mrs Stock?'

'With me on old Florrie?' Clarrie retorted. 'Thank you but no.'

'Take one of mine,' he offered. 'Tom tells me you're fond of Laurel.'

Clarrie flushed. 'I didn't know I was being spied on.'

'Don't be cross with him.' Wesley looked amused. 'I just like to know what goes on here.'

'Does Daniel Milner know you own these stables?' Clarrie asked.

'Of course,' Wesley said.

'I find that hard to believe.'

'Why? We've done business for years.'

'You and Mr Milner?' Clarrie cried. 'But you tried to ruin him — put him out of business when he was just getting started. He must be very forgiving.'

Wesley frowned. 'Who told you such a thing?'

'Mr Milner was Herbert's client. You can't deny it.' Clarrie was indignant. 'I heard how the other tea merchants were ganging up against the Tyneside Tea Company, pricing it out of the market. Don't pretend the Robsons weren't a part of it.'

Wesley's face tightened with annoyance, but his voice remained calm. 'I don't pretend. You were right — the Robsons were in on it. My uncle James was one of the main instigators.'

Clarrie felt sickened. Even though she had suspected his involvement all along, she had wanted him to prove her wrong.

'It was shameful,' she glared, stepping away.

'Yes, it was.' Wesley caught her by the arm. 'That's why I tipped off Milner that it was happening.'

She flinched. '*You* did?'

'Yes. My uncle tried to keep me in the dark, but I found out. I told Daniel and I put him in contact with a more trustworthy agent. After that his business thrived. The only thing I asked in return was that he never told my uncle or anyone else what I'd done.'

Clarrie gave him a look. 'Didn't want to spoil your own gilded nest?'

'Quite so.' Wesley's look turned mocking. 'I wasn't going to ruin my very good prospects if I could avoid it.'

Clarrie felt uncomfortable. 'You did the right thing,' she conceded. 'I'm sorry I accused you wrongly. But who could blame me? You are still a Robson, after all.'

Wesley gave an abrupt laugh. 'Ride with me, Clarrie! I promise we don't even have to speak if you don't want to. I know only too well your low opinion of me and it's far too late for me to try to change it, but the ride would give us both pleasure. Just this once, please?'

The urge to do so was too strong to resist. What harm could it do? She might never have the chance again to ride a thoroughbred – or to ride with Wesley. Clarrie nodded in assent.

Swiftly the horses were saddled and soon they were clattering out of the courtyard and into the country lanes. Wesley turned north, leading them uphill through the woods. Clarrie's heart beat faster as she was reminded of their long-ago ride through the forests around Belgooree. Looking back on that time, she could see how that young, impetuous, passionate Clarissa Belhaven had so easily fallen for the handsome Wesley Robson. For she could no longer deny that she had been in love with him. He had been infuriatingly brash and arrogant, yet charming and sensual too. She had been drawn to him against her better judgement.

As they emerged from the woods into open country, Wesley pulled up and waited for her. His strong features in profile made her stomach somersault. He still had the power to make her desire him. Yet this was the man who had been Robsons' most ruthless recruiter for their tea gardens, and the man who had gone after Belgooree and caused such grief to her father. She must never forget how Papa had warned her against him. Her longing for Wesley still felt like a betrayal of Jock.

The sun strengthened, and after riding a further mile they stopped by a stream and dismounted. Wesley laid out his jacket on the grass under a stone wall and invited Clarrie to sit down. Sheltered by the wall, they watched the horses drink and listened in silence to the birdsong. Clarrie had a sharp pang of remembrance.

'You're smiling,' Wesley commented. 'Tell me what you're thinking.'

'This reminds me of a special day before the war – with Will and Johnny – sitting by a farm wall. We used to go out riding together and put the world to rights.'

'Johnny is still a close friend?' Wesley asked.

Clarrie nodded. 'I feel close to Will when I'm with him.'

They lapsed into silence until Wesley broke it.

'Young Will,' he murmured. 'He talked about you a great deal.'

Clarrie gulped. 'Did he?'

'All the time.' Wesley gave a sad smile. 'The other men used to go on about their sweethearts, but he only spoke of you. They'd tease him by calling you the Wicked Stepmother. He adored you, you know.'

Clarrie's eyes prickled. 'He was the sweetest lad I ever met. Will loved everyone.'

'But you were special to him.'

'I miss him so much,' Clarrie whispered.

Wesley reached out and took her hand. He wrapped strong warm fingers round hers. 'I know. So do I.'

She met his look and saw the glint of emotion in his green eyes. 'Strange how fate threw you both together,' she said. 'Tell me what it was like.'

Still holding her hand, Wesley began to talk of his time in the trenches; not the harrowing moments of battle, but the mundane and the routine. He spoke of the moments when he and Will had joked and smoked together, and read each other's letters.

'You read my letters to him?' Clarrie was taken aback.

Wesley grinned. 'I'm afraid I did. I particularly looked forward to yours – you told him far more gossip than Bertie or any of his friends.'

Clarrie blushed and pulled her hand away. 'He had no right.'

'No, but it was good for morale,' Wesley teased.

Annoyed, Clarrie scrambled to her feet, trying to remember all the silly intimate things she had probably written to Will to amuse him. Wesley jumped up.

'Don't be cross,' he chided, catching her hand.

'I think we should go,' Clarrie said, avoiding his look. 'I shouldn't be here with you.'

'Why not?'

'You know why,' Clarrie said, thinking of Henrietta.

He pulled her round to face him. 'What is it, Clarrie? It's not just being with me that upsets you, is it? You were crying in the stables.'

She began to shake at the feel of his hands gripping hers. 'You wouldn't understand,' she whispered.

'Tell me anyway,' he insisted.

Clarrie swallowed. 'Last week I had a visitor from India – Kamal's great-nephew.'

'Kamal your khansama?' Wesley exclaimed.

'Yes. Do you remember him?'

'Of course I do. Kamal was the best khansama I ever met.'

Clarrie's eyes swam with tears. 'He's still alive. His great-nephew Arif came all this way to try and find me. It was like meeting a ghost from my past – he had Kamal's smile. Even before he turned up out of the blue, I'd been thinking more and more of Belgooree and how much I still miss it. Olive doesn't feel the same – it's just me.'

'India,' Wesley murmured, 'it gets under your skin. Everywhere else seems dull by comparison.'

'You feel it too?' Clarrie asked, meeting his gaze.

He nodded. 'It makes it hard to settle anywhere for very long. But I thought you were happy at the café? Will said how important it was to you.'

'I am,' Clarrie admitted. 'It's just been such a struggle these past years. But it's getting better again. I won't let it fail.'

He smiled. 'That's more like the fighting talk I expect from a Belhaven.'

'And what about you?' she said. 'You talked of tying up loose ends.'

'Yes. I've been offered the chance of running a new tea garden in East Africa. I sail from London next month.'

'East Africa!' Clarrie exclaimed, winded by the news. Her dismay surprised her. What did it matter where he went? But he read her look.

'Does that mean you still care for me just a little?' he challenged her.

Clarrie flushed. 'What makes you think I ever did?'

He pulled her closer, searching her face. 'You'd pretend to me even now when I'm going away for good? Clarissa, I know you! You felt it too – maybe not as strongly – but we both felt desire for each other. That time when we kissed at Belgooree – tell me you haven't forgotten! I never have.'

Clarrie's heart pounded at their closeness, at the feel of his breath on her face and the urgency of his look.

'I haven't forgotten,' she whispered.

'If you had not been such a stubborn Belhaven and I a Robson,' Wesley continued, 'we could have been man and wife. But your father made sure that would never happen. Only his prejudice against me and my family which he passed on to you like a poison has stood in the way of our being together, admit it!'

'No, that's not true,' Clarrie protested, trying to free herself from his hold. 'I saw you for what you were – arrogant and determined to get your own way no matter who got hurt. I'll never forgive you for the death of Ramsha.'

'Who's Ramsha?' he snapped.

'The favourite son of my nurse Ama,' Clarrie replied. 'He caught malaria working at the Oxford, but he escaped and Ama was hiding him. You knew all about it,' she said accusingly. 'You followed me that morning at Belgooree and found out we were hiding one of your runaways.'

Wesley stared at her, stunned. Clarrie felt sick

with anger. 'It's true, isn't it? You had him taken away—'

'Stop it!' He shook her. 'I wasn't interested in a runaway. I knew you were probably harbouring someone, but frankly I didn't care. It was you I was looking for.'

Clarrie was disbelieving. 'Then who was it arranged to have him dragged back to the Oxford if not you?' she demanded. 'You must have said something.'

He dropped his hold on her with an impatient cry. 'Good God, Clarissa! I wasn't the only recruiter at the Oxford and I was against employing hillsmen in the first place – they got homesick too easily and wouldn't take orders. I'm sorry about this Ramsha but I told no one about him.'

Clarrie's emotions were in turmoil. She did not know what to think.

'You don't believe me, do you?' He scowled. 'You really think I could have been that callous and calculating? If you thought so little of me then maybe our not marrying was a lucky escape.' Clarrie flinched at the contempt in his voice. His eyes blazed. 'Perhaps I was too full of myself back then, but I was young and newly out from England and eager to prove myself. But I never held a grudge against you Belhavens the way you did against us. I took people as I found them, including you and your father. I offered him my help, remember?'

'Your help?' Clarrie was scathing. 'You ridiculed

his managing of Belgooree and then tried to steal it from him by marrying me!'

'I was doing him a favour,' Wesley cried, 'and at personal cost to myself. My uncle James thought my suggestion of buying Belgooree was pure folly. And when I saw how ungrateful you were I thought he was right.'

'What did I have to be grateful for?' Clarrie said in fury. 'That you upset my father so much he locked himself in his room and drank himself to death?'

He seized her arm again. 'Have you been blaming me for that all these years?' he said in outraged disbelief. 'Your father was already a broken man and a drunk.'

'No he wasn't!' Clarrie threw him off.

'It was the talk among all the tea growers long before I came out,' Wesley said savagely. 'And do you know what else they said? They said it was because he had lost his beautiful Indian wife, but he had a pretty daughter Clarissa to run his household and that's the way he wanted it to stay. Nobody would have been good enough to be your suitor, as far as Jock was concerned. He wanted to keep you and Olive to himself even if it meant the tea garden going to rack and ruin.'

Furious, Clarrie slapped his face. 'How dare you!'

Wesley glared back, his face taut and a vein in his forehead throbbing. 'He did his job well, making you a slave to his selfish grief – making you feel guilty for having feelings for someone else other than him.'

'No,' Clarrie gasped.

'Yes,' he went on mercilessly. 'You've been running away from love ever since – real passionate love between a man and a woman. You've buried your true feelings, Clarissa, and hidden behind the excuse of always having someone to look after – your father or Olive or Herbert – even Will. You're too scared of loving any man with your whole heart. You think you don't deserve it.' He looked down on her with an expression of anger and pity. 'It's not me you really blame for your father's death and losing Belgooree, is it, Clarissa? It's yourself.'

The words were like a blow to the stomach. Clarrie clenched her teeth to keep back the sob in her throat. She would not let him see how much he had wounded her.

For a long moment they stood staring at each other in fury and misery. How cruel he was! Yet the truth of what he said made her feel faint. For years she had carried the guilt of her father's death like a stone weight. It had been too big a burden; so much easier to blame Wesley and the Robsons instead.

Clarrie could hardly bear to look at him for the shame he made her feel, yet part of her longed for him to take her in his arms and tell her that none of the old hurts and rivalries mattered any more. But with a fierce scowl, Wesley stepped past her and marched over to Paladin. Taking hold of the reins, he swung up into the saddle.

'Forgive me if I don't accompany you back,' he

said, his jaw clenched. 'I'm sure you'd rather see the back of me as quickly as possible. I'm sorry for the pain I've caused you all these years, Clarissa. But it's nothing to the heartache you have given me.'

He swung Paladin round and kicked him into a trot. Clarrie stared after him in fury and desolation. She felt achingly empty, yet battered by the rawness of his anger towards her. Had he really loved her all these years and not just seen her as a pawn in his business game or someone to trifle with when it amused him? She clutched her arms till they hurt. Let him go to Africa with Henrietta. He had no right to unearth such deep feelings at the point of leaving. No right! It was far too late.

Shaking and wretched, Clarrie forced herself to remount Laurel, but instead of returning to the stables she headed further west. It was late in the day and growing dark when she finally trailed back to Wylam. Tom came out to meet her.

'Mr Robson told me to wait till you got back,' he told her.

Her heart rose. 'Is he still here?'

'No, missus. He's gone and he'll not be back,' Tom said regretfully. 'He gans back to London day after the morra.'

CHAPTER 39

That night, exhausted and distressed, Clarrie
unburdened herself to Lexy.

'I can see the state you're in, lass,' Lexy said in
concern. 'Tell me what happened.'

Clarrie spoke of the encounter with Wesley that
had shaken her to the core, and of the past history
between Robsons and Belhavens that had been
made worse by her father's death.

'I blamed Wesley,' Clarrie admitted, 'but most
likely my father would've died anyway and the tea
garden would've failed. I was too willing to believe
the worst of him.'

'Perhaps you had every right to,' Lexy
retorted. 'You've never trusted him in business,
have you? And he's related to that stuck-up madam
Verity.'

Clarrie looked pained. 'But I've been too harsh. I've misjudged him on important things.'

'Such as?'

'I thought it was Wesley who had tried to drum Mr Milner out of business back in the early days. But it turns out he was the one who tipped Milner off and helped him over the bad patch.'

Lexy sighed. 'Well, that's as may be. But there's no point hankering after some'at you can't have. He's off to Africa with his missus, so you said. Best to put it all behind you.' Her friend patted her shoulder. 'You never know, you might find someone else to care for right under your nose, like me and Jared have,' she said. 'That canny doctor Johnny, for instance.'

Clarrie was beyond arguing. She allowed Lexy to make her tea and put her to bed.

'You lie in the morra,' Lexy advised.

Clarrie slept a long and dreamless sleep. She was woken by muffled voices, drifting into her consciousness as if she were submerged underwater. They tugged her up to the surface. She blinked and sat up. It was bright daylight and the voices on the stairs were becoming louder.

'You can't gan up there!' Lexy protested. 'She's not well.'

'I must see her, it's a matter of great importance,' a woman said, her voice rising querulously.

'Wait downstairs,' Lexy said, 'and I'll ask her.'

'No, no, I can't be seen in public,' the woman snapped. It sounded like Verity.

Clarrie struggled out of bed, her head groggy.

'Well you'll just have to,' Lexy was firm. 'You can have a cup of tea while you're waiting.'

'I don't want tea!'

The voices grew fainter again as Lexy steered the woman away. By the time her friend reappeared, Clarrie had pulled on her clothes and was pinning up her hair.

'It's Verity,' Lexy confirmed. 'Wouldn't tell me what it's about, but she's in a right state.'

Clarrie found Verity sitting tensely behind one of the potted plants trying not to be noticed. It struck her that it was the first time Bertie's wife had come anywhere near the tea room.

'I can't speak to you here,' Verity hissed. 'Surely you have somewhere more private?'

Clarrie led her into the annexe and showed her into an empty meeting room. They sat down at a table.

'How are the twins?' Clarrie asked.

'They're costing us a fortune,' Verity answered distractedly. 'But I haven't come here for a chit-chat, you must realise that.'

'I can't imagine what brings you here,' Clarrie said. 'Please tell me.'

Verity's hands squirmed in her lap. 'I'm sorry, I'm a bit on edge.'

'Let me call for some tea,' Clarrie suggested.

'Tea!' Verity sighed impatiently. 'That was always your answer to everything, wasn't it?'

Clarrie eyed her. 'If you haven't come for a chat or to taste how good my tea is, then what, Verity?'

'I wouldn't have come – except – I don't know who else to turn to,' she said anxiously, avoiding Clarrie's eyes. 'Things are a bit desperate.'

'Desperate?'

'I'm sure you've heard the rumours about our recent difficulties.'

'I've heard you're living in South Gosforth and that Bertie has been losing money,' Clarrie admitted.

'Losing money?' Verity cried. 'He's been hopeless with it! First his own and then mine. Clive won't lend him any more. We've had to sell Tankerville and Summerhill and still we have debts to clear. We're facing disaster!'

'He's spent all Herbert's inheritance?' Clarrie said, shocked.

Verity nodded. 'And much more.'

Clarrie thought how much she could have done with just a fraction of their income when the tea room was on the verge of closure. She kept her temper, but she spoke bluntly.

'It seems to me that Bertie will just have to stop relying on other people's money and go back to earning a living.'

Verity slid her a glance. 'If only it were that simple,' she croaked. 'I wish he had stuck to the law. But it seems he's invested clients' money unwisely – including my brother's – and now they've lost confidence in him.' Her voice dropped to a mumble.

'He might even be struck off and never allowed to practise again. I'm so frightened!' She covered her face with her gloved hands and began a dry sobbing.

Clarrie was at a loss. For the first time ever, she felt a stab of pity for Verity. What must it be like to live with the boastful Bertie, who had squandered his father's careful legacy and good name with his greedy gambling of other people's money? Yet both Bertie and Verity had been profligate spenders. It was the poor twins who would suffer the most.

'I'm sorry Bertie has been so foolish,' she said, 'but I don't see how I can help you.'

'You could lend us money.' Verity looked up, her expression pleading.

Clarrie's laugh was short. 'I have nothing to spare. Bertie took all that was mine a long time ago, remember.'

'Not all – you have the tea room,' Verity said. 'You can raise money with the banks.'

'Herbert's Tea Rooms are not mine,' Clarrie said in exasperation. 'Bertie took them from me and sold them. They belong to a company called Stable Trading – Will set it up so that I would always have a living. He made sure your husband couldn't get his hands on the café again.'

Verity gave her a strange look, half fearful, half triumphant. She scrabbled inside her handbag and produced a letter.

'No. It wasn't quite as you thought.' Verity held out the letter. 'This was amongst Will's box of possessions. We were wrong to keep it from you, but I thought you would have found out the truth by now.'

With a lurch of the heart, Clarrie saw that the handwriting was Will's and although it was addressed to her, it had already been opened. Fumbling, she took it out of the envelope. The writing was feeble, but it was unmistakably Will's. It had been written in the field hospital.

Dearest Clarrie,

I'm in hospital with a wretched leg injury, but you're not to worry as I'm sure everything will soon be fine and dandy. The bad news is it means I may be delayed in returning home, so I'm afraid you'll have to keep that champagne on ice a little longer.

All this time with my feet up has given me pause to think. I have a confession to make and it's easier to get it out in the open now, just in case. I haven't been entirely candid with you about the buying of the café or the nature of Stable Trading. It was set up with the help of a friend of mine — but not, I fear, of yours.

But listen, dear Clarrie. This man has been a good friend to me these past months — one of the best I've ever had. When I told him of your plight, it was he who arranged the funds to buy Herbert's Tea Rooms, as only he could lay his hands on that kind of money at such short notice. I did not have it. But he insisted you were not to be told, because of the bad feeling between you in the past. He feared you would be resentful and feel beholden to him. He made all the arrangements on his last spot of leave and he bought it in your name, so that you would have independence and a means of making your own living what ever happened.

He will be furious once he finds out I have told you, but I feel it is right you should know, if for no other reason than that you might revise your bad opinion of my loyal and trustworthy friend.

Clarrie, do you forgive me for misleading you? I do hope so. I know when we see each other again it will be such a joyous moment that you won't stay cross with me for long. How I wish you could be here playing Florence Nightingale for me now instead of the rather severe matron, who won't let me sing after lights out.

You will have guessed by now that the friend I refer to is Wesley Robson. I hope in time you can bury the bad feeling that was created by your father's tragic death. Often in life we wish we could have done things differently and I know Wesley regrets much of his callow behaviour when first in India. He has a high regard for you and, I believe, deep affection. Why else would he keep asking me to talk of you? It would be splendid for me when I return if you both could be friends.

Clarrie, how I long for that day! I can think of nothing else but coming home toot sweet to you and the family, to Newcastle and all my dear friends. Until then, I send you my fondest love,

Will.

Clutching the letter, Clarrie let out a soft moan.

Dear, beloved Will! It was like receiving a message from beyond the grave; her stepson's irrepressible presence conjured up by the affectionate words. But what words! All along, it had been Wesley not Will who had saved the café and her livelihood – saved her sanity. For if she had lost her home yet again at such a time, she might have given up completely. If only she had known this earlier, she would never have argued so violently with Wesley the day before or said such hurtful things.

'Well?' Verity said with a nervous smile.

'You knew about this?'

Verity blushed. 'Naturally, we had to go through all his things.'

Clarrie felt anger ignite after the shock of revelation. 'I pleaded with Bertie to give me something of Will's as a keepsake, yet you didn't even have the decency to give me the letter he wrote to me – his last letter!'

'I'm sorry, it was wrong of us, I see that now,' Verity gabbled, 'but I thought it was only a matter of time before you found out anyway. I can't believe Wesley Robson has been able to resist telling you of his grand gesture. Especially when he's been up here recently seeing to business before going abroad.'

Clarrie gave her a sharp look. 'Have you been asking him for money too?'

'Well he is a relation,' Verity said defensively. 'And we thought if he could bail you out when you're not even family, he could do the same for us.'

'But he didn't?'

Verity looked tearful. 'He was quite offensive – told Bertie to act like a man and get himself an honest job – as if he were some common labourer.'

Clarrie could just imagine Wesley's contemptuous look as he said it. 'Does Bertie know you're here?' she asked.

Verity nodded.

Clarrie could not hide her revulsion. 'Too cowardly to come himself, so he sends his wife to beg for him.'

Verity's look was pathetically pleading. 'Clarrie, for the sake of the twins, you must help Bertie out. Please!'

Clarrie swallowed down bile. This was the woman who had mocked and humiliated her at Summerhill, ostracised her for marrying Herbert and stood by while Bertie robbed her of her hard-earned business. Now she expected her to throw them a financial lifeline – was grovelling for her help. She felt revenge surge up inside. How good it felt to finally have power over the hateful pair.

Then Clarrie thought of Vernon and the bubbly Josephine. Herbert's grandchildren. They did not deserve to be punished for their parents' short-comings. Clarrie considered Verity's tear-stained face for a long moment.

'Very well,' she said at last. 'I will do this for you. Once the tea room is making a reasonable profit again, I will put some of it into a trust fund for the twins until they become of age.'

Verity's face brightened. 'Trust fund?'

'But on the understanding,' Clarrie cautioned, 'that neither you nor Bertie will be able to help yourselves to any of it.'

Verity frowned. 'What about Bertie and me?'

'Wesley was right in suggesting your husband look for a job,' Clarrie answered. 'If he's willing to work hard, I can find him employment around the café. That is my offer.'

Verity's face puckered in disgust. 'Work here? With these people?'

'You'll never find better,' Clarrie said, standing up. 'Go back and tell Bertie there's honest graft for him at Herbert's Tea Rooms. But I'll not lend him any more money – he's squandered enough of mine in the past.'

Furious, Verity got up. 'I feel dirty just coming here to this place and asking for your help. I don't care how badly we're in debt, I'll never let my husband lower himself to come and work in your common tea room.'

Clarrie did not wait for her to leave, but hurried to the door first. 'Then it's goodbye, Verity. You can see yourself out.'

Rushing upstairs to the flat, Clarrie grabbed her coat and hat. To an astonished Lexy, she shouted, 'I have to see someone urgently. I'll be back!'

She jumped on a tram that took her into the city

and then hurried down steep Dean Street to the quayside where the Robsons had their shipping and business offices. Taking the lift up to the third floor, Clarrie asked a clerk in the outer office for Wesley.

'Mr Wesley's not here any longer, ma'am,' he told her. 'Would you like to speak to someone else?'

'No thank you. Where will I find him?' Clarrie asked impatiently.

The clerk frowned. 'He's been staying at his cousin's house, but he's probably already left for London.'

'Today?' Clarrie gasped. 'But I thought he was here until tomorrow.'

'Changed his plans late yesterday,' said the clerk. 'He seemed keen to get away, if you ask me.'

'Do you have a telephone number for his cousin?' Clarrie asked desperately. The man nodded. 'Could you ring it for me and see if he's still there? Please.'

The clerk gave her a wary look but did as she asked. Her heart drummed as she watched and waited. All she wanted was this last chance to make her peace with Wesley and tell him how she had been wrong to stay so angry with him all these years.

The operator put the clerk through and he asked for Wesley.

'Oh, I see. Just a minute.' He looked over at Clarrie. 'He's left for the station. They could take a message and send it on.'

Clarrie's stomach clenched with disappointment. She shook her head.

'No message, thank you,' the clerk replied and rang off.

She thanked him for his help and rushed out, clattering down the stairs rather than waiting for the lift. Running along the busy quayside, dodging horse traffic, motor vans and porters rolling barrels, Clarrie headed for the steep climb to the station. Breathless, she paused halfway up.

'Clarrie!' a man cried. 'What you doing down here?'

Drawing up beside her was a tea van with Jack at the reins.

'I need to get to the station,' she panted.

'Lucky for you I've been picking up a delivery.' Jack grinned. 'Hop on, lass, and I'll give you a lift.'

As they trotted briskly through the streets to Central Station, Clarrie quickly told him of Verity's visit, the letter from Will and how she had misjudged Wesley for so long.

'I just want to set things right between us before he goes to Africa,' she explained.

Jack nodded. 'Our Olive always said you should've married him when you were out in India. But then I would never have met my lass, would I?' He pulled up by the stone portico and helped her down. 'Good luck. I hope you find him.'

A guard told her that the next train to London was in ten minutes from platform four and pointed her over the bridge. Buying a platform ticket, she ran as fast as she could. The train was already in the station, and porters were busy helping carry on luggage. She searched the throng of travellers for any sign of Wesley. With a lurch of alarm, it occurred to her for the first time that Henrietta might be with him. Had she not said once how much she enjoyed visiting the north? Clarrie stood hesitating, her courage almost failing. She was too late. She would only make a fool of herself on this crowded platform if she found him.

'Clarissa?' said a familiar voice.

She whipped around. There was only one person who still called her by that name. Wesley was leaning out of an open carriage door. She rushed towards him, but was overwhelmed by the sight of his handsome, frowning face. Her throat constricted with emotion. She could not speak. He climbed down.

'What is it? Has something terrible happened?'

She shook her head, her eyes smarting at his concern. He took her by the arm and steered her out of the way. Looking round, he nodded for them to go into the small waiting room. It was empty, and Wesley closed the door behind them.

'Tell me,' he said, standing close but not touching her.

She told him about Verity and the letter.

'So I know about Stable Trading,' she finished hoarsely. 'That it was you who saved the tea room.'

'I see.' Wesley looked stern.

'Why didn't you tell me?'

'Because I knew how proud you were,' he said. 'You would probably have thrown my money back in my face.'

Clarrie flushed. 'Perhaps I would have,' she admitted. 'But Will wanted me to know. He wanted to change my opinion of you – for us to be friends.'

Wesley gave her a sceptical look. 'So you're doing this for the sake of Will's memory?'

'Not just that,' Clarrie insisted. 'I wanted to say sorry.' When he said nothing, she went on. 'I'm sorry for misjudging you and blaming you for my family's troubles. My father was wrong about you, Wesley, so very wrong. You befriended Will and helped me without ever expecting anything in return. Those are not the actions of a ruthless and selfish man, but of a kind and generous one.' She held his look. 'I wanted to thank you and set the record straight before you left.'

'Oh, Clarissa!' He let out a long sigh, his face full of regret. 'Why have we spent so long at loggerheads? I forbade Will to tell you about Stable Trading because I didn't want you to feel in any way beholden to me. If you cared for me at all, I wanted it to be for who I was, not because of any financial obligation. That was where I went so wrong at the beginning – offering you marriage as if it was a business transaction to save Belgooree, instead of what it really was.'

'What was that?' Clarrie asked tensely.

'An offer of love,' he said, his eyes glittering.

Clarrie's heart twisted. She was engulfed by regret that they had left it too late. 'It wasn't just your fault,' she whispered. 'I was too stubborn to admit my feelings for you.'

His look intensified. 'So I was right – you did care for me?'

Clarrie nodded and looked away. 'Very much,' she murmured. Parting from him was so painful she wanted to end it quickly. 'You mustn't miss your train; it'll be leaving any minute.' She stepped past him so he would not see the tears brimming over her lashes. 'I wish you well in East Africa, Wesley,' she said as steadily as she could, 'both you and your wife.'

Wesley caught her arm. 'What did you say?' He scrutinised her face. 'You think I'm married?'

'Well, y-yes,' she faltered. 'To Miss Lister-Brown.'

He let out an impatient sigh and shook his head. 'I never married Henrietta. We were engaged for ages but I kept putting it off. I finally broke off the engagement when I returned from France.'

'I see,' Clarrie said, feeling bewildered.

'No, I don't think you do,' Wesley said. He leaned closer. 'I realised I could never marry her, because I was still in love with you.'

Clarrie's heart thudded in her chest.

'Seeing you at the memorial service brought back the strength of my feelings for you – seeing you with that young doctor made me so jealous.'

'Johnny?' Clarrie said in astonishment. 'He was just a friend of Will's.'

'So there is nothing between the two of you?' Wesley demanded.

'Nothing,' Clarrie said, going weak under his gaze.

Wesley grasped her by the arms. 'Clarissa, tell me truthfully – could you still love me? Knowing that there is no other standing in our way, could we start again as friends and maybe in time be more than that?'

Her heart leaped. 'Yes, of course.' She smiled. 'I still love you, Wesley.'

'Do you really?' he asked in disbelief.

'I always have,' she admitted. 'I've been fighting my feelings for you for years, wanting to hate you, but unable to. Yesterday, after you left, I realised how very much in love I still was. But I thought it was too late – I just assumed you'd got married. You don't know how happy I am to find out you are not!'

Heady with relief, Wesley pulled her into his arms. He bent towards her and kissed her hungrily. Clarrie slid her arms round his neck and kissed him back.

The door behind them opened.

'Train's about to leave, sir,' a porter called.

They broke apart. For a moment they held each other's look. Then Wesley drew a crown from his pocket and tossed it to the man.

'Take my bags off the train, please,' he ordered. 'I'm not going anywhere.'

As the astonished porter left, Clarrie laughed. 'What are you going to do?'

'That's up to you,' Wesley said. 'Come to Africa with me, or London, or I'll stay here, or we can go back to India. I don't care! Wherever I can make you happy.'

Clarrie's heart pounded. Perhaps they could finally go back to Belgoree? With Wesley anything seemed possible. As she looked into his vital, sensuous face, she realised that her yearning for her past home had been partly bound up with her yearning for him, suppressed though it was.

'It doesn't matter to me either,' Clarrie said passionately, 'as long as we're together. I never want us to be parted again, ever!'

Wesley let out a roar of delight. He clasped his hands round her face. 'Prove to me that I'm not dreaming,' he laughed.

Clarrie smiled tenderly. 'Kiss me then.'

With joy, they embraced with longing and passion, impatient to make up for the years of being apart. Tears of happiness fell on Clarrie's cheeks. Will's final wish – to see her and Wesley reunited – had been granted at last.

Now you can buy any of these other bestselling books by **Janet MacLeod Trotter** from your bookshop or *direct from her publisher*.

FREE P&P AND UK DELIVERY
(Overseas and Ireland £3.50 per book)

The Hungry Hills	£5.99
The Darkening Skies	£6.99
The Suffragette	£5.99
Never Stand Alone	£5.99
Chasing The Dream	£6.99
For Love And Glory	£6.99
The Jarrow Lass	£6.99
A Child of Jarrow	£6.99
Return to Jarrow	£6.99
A Crimson Dawn	£5.99
A Handful of Stars	£5.99

TO ORDER SIMPLY CALL THIS NUMBER

01235 400 414

or visit our website: www.headline.co.uk

Prices and availability subject to change without notice.